THE MAN WHO LOST
EVERYTHING

THE MAN
WHO LOST
EVERYTHING

by Paul Kuttner

BOLD FACE BOOKS

Sterling Publishing Co., Inc., New York

Second Printing, 1977

Copyright © 1976 by Paul Kuttner
A Bold Face Book
Published by
Sterling Publishing Company, Inc.
Two Park Avenue,
New York, New York 10016

Manufactured in the United States of America.

Library of Congress Catalog Card No.: 76-17142

ISBN: Trade   0-8069-0152-7
      Library   0-8069-0153-5

*Dedicated
to the memory of
Margarete and Paul, my parents, and Annemarie, my sister,
and also to
Stephen, my son.*

1 ═══════

It was the kind of weather expected only in Frankenstein movies or around the Manderleys of Gothic novels. Raindrops, plump as Malaga grapes, exploded on sidewalks, clattered down umbrellas, pelted windowpanes like gravel. Even Walter Cronkite saw fit to mention to Mr. and Ms. America that New York had gone through one of its heaviest October downpours ever, one of near-hurricane proportions, dumping almost three inches of rain on the city in the late afternoon.

A slashing gust of wind abruptly, without warning, whipped hats, newspapers, trash can lids, a debris of branches, Frisbees, down foliage-strewn Riverside Park. They bounced against trees and benches, skipped across sun-scorched patches of turf, creating new havoc in the sodden grass—a cacophony of chattering squirrels—and wherever windows stayed open along the Seventies and Eighties potted plants, pink seashells, plaster Liszt busts, Boehm porcelain and other knick-nacks toppled from their sills and shattered on the floor.

The bedroom window of Helga Lipsolm's apartment was barely ajar but even here the squall swelled the Chantilly-lace curtains ceiling-high before letting them recede in billows of slow-motion. Indifferent to the inclement weather, Helga's hot, sweaty body stirred in the dusk and her grasping hands wandered hungrily up the lean, naked thighs of the man lying beside her, then found, and savored the hardness of his member. The bed, dank with the perspiration of the two lovers, creaked with their every motion. But they did not hear, nor care. The shades were drawn, the room dim in the last twilight struggle that was the favorite refuge of illicit love.

Harry Bensonny flicked his tongue inside Helga's insatiable mouth and his full weight clamped down hard on the warm sticky crotch of the unappeasable woman until he felt the deliciously convulsive shudder of the orgasm travel down the entire length of her body. No sound, only the squishy contact of moist skin, and the swooshing of automobiles on the wet pavement outside. The cocoon of paradisiacal bliss had sealed them off from the cares and woes of the world. Love held them captive in the chains of lust. Nothing disturbed them . . . not the fresh deluge hurling itself tornadolike against the buildings' façades, not even the platform-shod clip-clop-clip-clop of footsteps passing directly beneath the iron-barred ground-floor window left slightly open to let the October air cool the damp jungle heat of their embrace.

Also indifferent to the torrential storm were a couple of giggling teenagers who happened to pass just then under Helga's window, swinging between them a briefcase-sized transistor radio from which a syndicated L.A.-based Wolfman Jack megaton-howled: "Oh man, this is it then! Come on, li'l chickadee, I wanna have you drop everything now out there, you cats and dudes and super-chicks in Burbank funland, and go naked into the moonlight with me tonight, yeah, naked, and—sugar—we'll have a ball and drop the fuzz and the narcs and do it tonight and every night and twice on Sundays and love it, yummy, love it, love it, with Elvis—just dig this wham of a socko platter—o' hol' me tight . . ." Then Presley took over the d.j.'s groovy double-trip hip chatter and the sound of megaphonic rock swirled on currents of air and wafted away under a bell-shaped umbrella in the distance.

"He's right, hon, hol' me tight . . . tighter . . . tighter . . ." Harry whispered as his hand stole down the woman's face, her throat, and came to rest on the full warm roundness of her breast.

His eyes devoured her every inch in the Toledo-blue dusk, taking rapturous delight in the sight of the female nude. He was giddy with excitation, feeling the hard erect nipple of her breast under his palm and absorbing the silky white fullness of her thighs, the black tousled hair where her legs met, and above it the rising crests of her incredibly white hips—the soft warm mold of a body so sensuous to his touch that her erotic form seemed to leap directly out of an Ingres painting.

"Touch me, oh God, touch me, Harry." Helga's words came hot and moist on his ear, and her whole being seemed to arch upward, toward him, with an intolerable desire, an irrational pain, to heave . . . and snap, snap in two, like a bow too tautly drawn, a bough too rich, too full of honeysuckle blossoms . . . and collapse on the sheets . . . spent. "Everywhere," she whispered. "Touch me everywhere . . . God, if only you had ten hands so I could feel your touch on me all at once."

"I love you . . . I love you." His tongue licked the seashell hardness of her ear's concha as their bodies clung together, insanely entwined, and again became one. "There's only you, my darling. Nobody else, only you, I swear."

"I know, my sweet." Again their lips met in a long thirsty deep kiss. "How I wish you could stay with me forever—for the rest of the night at least."

A couple of doors away, a refrigerator started humming feebly, the drenching rain outside that had plagued the city for the past three hours and snarled up traffic everywhere suddenly let up, and the deathly hush that followed made the lovers uncomfortably aware of the world beyond the realm of their warm-bedded ecstatic dreams.

"The rest of the night?" Suddenly Harry's drugged senses wrenched free of the sweaty skin throbbing beneath his cupped palm. "Oh, God, what time is it?" His bare feet swung around and touched the soft Rya-knotted rug as his hand reached for the watch on the night table. "Hell, almost half past seven!" He slipped the watch over his wrist. "We've never done it this late. I've got to go, Helga."

He turned on the light and the green shade of the Tiffany lamp bathed the bedroom in a pastoral glow, further enhanced by the print of Renoir's milkmaid over the bed. Without another word he rose and padded across the deep-pile Chenille carpet. He disappeared in the adjoining bathroom for a minute or two, and when he came back again —the carnal flesh treacherously coated with Palmolive and a few dabs of eau de cologne, his mouth rinsed—he noticed that Helga was sitting up in her bed and already wearing her diaphanous flesh-tinted robe. A fistful of soggy cleansing tissue huddled guiltily next to the glass-domed lamp.

As he emerged from the bathroom in his defenseless nakedness, her eyes critically assayed the body that only seconds earlier had been an aphrodisiacal almanac to her, the socket to her soul, had served and sated her, had dominated her every whim, her every desire. And if he, like all mortals, lacked the divine beauty of Michelangelo's "David" or Myron's "Discobolus" he was still the only excuse why Women's Lib might be wrong somewhere in their futile efforts to summon Helga's voice to their fold—rather than to a more appropriately named *Hu*man Lib she *would* have joined—and marshal her not inconsiderable literary clout indivisibly to their ranks.

Socks, underwear, pants, shirt, tie . . . the full office regalia of pretense metamorphosed the innocent flesh into the speciously cultured civilian ready to do battle, armed against those tribulations that a cruel city was ever-prepared to throw up at the slightest provocation against each and every of its scarred and scared residents, its brutalized psychos. At least in their nudity men assumed the cloak of honesty because the essence of undress revealed not only their defenselessness but stripped bare many of the sophistications and deceits that civilian muftis and military khakis imposed upon the mind and upon behavior, much like a decal impressing its spurious picture, its glittering image upon a snow-white sheet of paper. Could Herr One-Testicle Adolf really have rallied the Brownshirts at Nuremberg in the nude? Helga wondered, and she could not help but reflect on Bob Dylan's much celebrated lyric, concerning the fact that even the President of the United States finds himself naked at times.

Man definitely looked more preposterous and droll, unclothed, than woman; that much was certain to her, she who loved the man in her bedroom with a wild possessiveness. And she grinned inwardly, thinking, 'Here's looking at ya, kid' (playing Bogie to his Bergman)— yet *both* of them, undressed, in bed making love could also cause giggles to the unsuspecting. Vaguely, Helga suddenly recalled the eighth book of Homer's *Odyssey* when the bard Demodocus sang of the illicit alliance of Ares and Aphrodite, wife of the lame Hephaestus; of how the cuckolded Hephaestus forged the two lovers in unbreakable chains and then invited the gods to witness the act of love, causing them to roar with inextinguishable laughter.

But people in love could laugh at anything, except at the manifestation of love, the sex act, that by its very diversity willed itself into the evolutionary jet stream.

Silence, too, reigned supreme in Helga Lipsolm's bedroom on Riverside Drive. Except for the faint hiss of an atomizer spraying an erotically tangy perfume over her half-exposed cleavage, no sound was

10

heard. Harry Bensonny tied his shoelaces, then brushed back his dark unruly hair, watching her guardedly as she quietly returned the perfume to her night table. They looked at each other, not moving. A tired smile teased the corners of his lips as he became aware of the woman appraising him, of the full length of her slender body distinctly visible beneath the robe. The dark triangular forest of pubic hair glowed tantalizingly where the folds of the robe met. His hands toyed nervously with one of his cuff links which he was trying hard to push through the buttonholes.

"Come!" Her soft voice broke the uncertain stillness and she reached out for him as she rose from the bed. He took her hand and they walked into the living room.

"Wait!" Briskly and with great determination, she strode to the large French windows and drew the curtains. Only the light from the bedroom now stabbed a bright beacon into the dark cavern next door. "Better get yourself composed a bit first, darling."

She turned on the living room light and seated herself on the large L-shaped sofa, next to the white telephone resting on its wide arm. Her left leg jackknifed under her buttocks and a sliver of thigh gleamed between the open ends of the robe which almost immediately slid down, revealing still more of her firm satiny skin. "Sit down a minute before you go, Harry," and again her solicitously outstretched arm drew him to her, like a moth to the flame.

He leaned forward with the intent of merely brushing his lips over hers, ever so lightly, but her mouth was waiting for him, waiting eagerly, open and greedy, and he could feel her warm hungry tongue inside his mouth. His hand tightened on her neck as though trying to uproot her from where she had settled, and instead of drawing her up to him, he felt his resolve weaken and he bent further down, toward her, and lost his balance, almost tipping over the phone.

"Jesus! This perfume!" Already his free hand was slipping between the open folds of her robe and he knew that his determination to leave was quickly, hopelessly evaporating. He let himself down beside her, his hand revolving around her soft, warm breasts and slyly working its way down in fondling circular movements. "God, this scent of yours . . . it's driving me nuts! This perfume . . ." He kissed her hard. "Ruth never wears anything like it . . . and even if she did . . ."

His hand hovered in taunting anticipation above her pudenda and she sucked in her breath sharply. He was sure that she could not resist him now and would submit to his very touch as she had a few minutes earlier in bed. But her eyes were wide open and the hands that only seconds ago had mussed up his hair suddenly lost their hard passionate grip and dropped, almost lifeless, to her sides.

"Harry?"

He was still the helpless slave in the pincer of wanton lust, famished for every nook and cranny of her being. His tongue again tasted her sweat-salty throat, felt the kick of her pulse, and the words that she spoke vibrated titillatingly against his lips.

"Harry, when're you going to tell her about us? That you want a divorce?"

2 ═══════════

Only a micro-second and the vapor of lust shattered, vanished . . . opening up the great clear vista of life, of untouched reality in glaring harsh colors. His eyes staring into hers. Wide open. A millionth of a second and his brain's neurons had their synapses secrete the chemicals required for registering the self-destruct command of the love impulse. Messages of End of Love Play telegraphed information from the hypothalamus as ten billion dendrites sprang into action and transmitted the message electrically to him to withdraw his right hand from her moist vulva, as he grew dismally tense with a foreboding of the scene about to ensue.

"Tell her?" He cleared his throat. The words hadn't come out right.

"Yes." She tightened the knot of the belt of her robe and pulled the loose ends modestly over her thighs.

"Well." He wet his lips and ran his pocket comb through his hair to gain time to think of something to say. "Honey, why now? I mean, why bring this up this minute? And besides"—he glanced at his watch, and shook his wrist furiously. "Dammit, stopped again! Must have it fixed. Anyway," he shrugged, "you know I've got to go. It's late and we can't afford to let her get suspicious."

Helga sat up stiffly and again straightened her robe.

13

"Harry, please. When are you going to tell Ruth about us . . . and I'm *not* pushing you. But two years . . ."

For a few seconds he stared at her wordlessly, then moved away a few inches, not enough to hurt her feelings, but enough to get some distance from her, from his entanglement. Pretending he needed elbow room, he turned up and then smoothed down the collar of his jacket.

"Look, darling, I've . . . you know I already have. We have gone over this time and again. I did speak to her." He leaned forward and opened a shoelace, then tied a knot in it, taking his time before coming up to face her. "Not about us—I'm quite willing to admit it—I never brought you into the conversation; that would have been madness. It's just that I asked her for a divorce, told her that I didn't love her anymore, but she won't listen. She always comes back telling me it'll all work out. She simply won't grant me a divorce."

Helga's hands lay white and cold and clammy in her lap. "That bitch!" Her words were hardly audible as she pressed them out through clenched teeth. "Harry, may God forgive me, but I hate her so I could kill her." She gasped, blinked at the enormity of her statement, and even though shocked by her own verbalized confession was grateful to note that no emotion, no reaction registered in her lover's face. Her shoulders drooped with a deep penitent sigh. "I'm sorry, my sweet, I know it's a terrible thing to say but . . . seeing her between us like this and the way she obviously dislikes me, hates me, is . . ."

"Helga, I've told you a thousand times you're only imagining all of this. She doesn't hate you. She doesn't even suspect anything."

"No, not because of us. I'm just as sure as you she doesn't know about us, even though we *are* neighbors, but I can *feel* she hates me. Or people like me. Take . . ."

"What d'you mean people like you? You're attractive, but so is she."

"No, not looks, silly. Worse than that." She thought for a moment. "Take that block party we had a few months ago, for example. Now look, she knows about me, my religion, from my autobiography. Maybe you weren't around when she made those religious slurs."

"Aw, for crying out loud, Helga! That's ridiculous. I'm not married to a racist."

"Of course not. She's much too subtle for that, she and her stuck-up WASP-y New England upbringing. New York in the Sixties and Seventies must have taught her plenty about not coming out openly with anti-Semitic remarks."

"Cut it out now, Helga! I've been married to Ruth for twenty long years. I knew her as a teenager, and in all these years she has not insinuated once, hasn't given me, her husband, one inkling, she's anti-Semitic, and I think after living with a woman for twenty years—even if love's run its course—I should have a general idea about how she feels about people. I think, with your novelistic flair, you're just reading too much into her words, words incidentally that may apply to something entirely different from what you thought she had in mind. I think they call this meta-talk."

"Oh no, my dear man, I can't let her get off that easily. When she saw me at that party, standing there and talking to Mr. Franzell, you know, the fat asthmatic on the third floor, she came over to us, cut me completely dead, as if I didn't exist, and started complaining about the gasoline prices and the inflation, the way the middle class was being overtaxed, ripped off, and that it was all due to those Semites over there, and the oil crisis, and that they were the scourge of mankind, and that the best thing was to let them fight it out among themselves and just stay out of the Middle East altogether instead of listening to their lobbies over here and that she wished that all those vermin would go back where they came from and put . . . ."

"Now just a second! Take it easy, will ya? There's an explanation for all of this. God knows, I sometimes feel, when I'm angry, that *all* humans are the scourge of mankind. Just as Byron often felt that he detested all governments. So there! What's all this got to do with being anti-Semitic, anti-Jewish? Millions of Americans have turned isolationist as a result of the Vietnamese war. As I was saying you're reading things into it that simply aren't there. For all you know, she may just as well have referred to the Arabs, who also happen to be Semitic, and . . . ."

"Don't be so naive, Harry! We live in the second half of the 1970's. You and I and Ruth are all in our forties, and I think we've lived long enough in this hate-riddled city of ours to know that when people speak about Semites going back where they come from, they mean Jews. There are no Arabs living in this building. Besides, she would have said Arabs if she meant them."

"Or she would have said Jews, rather than Semites, if she meant Jews. Why the hell should she want you to go back to Europe? You're a writer, cause no trouble to the police, are a quiet clean neighbor of ours, so why in heaven's name should she want you out of the apartment when nobody knows for sure these days who will be their *next* next-door neighbor? It just doesn't make any sense, Helga."

"No, not to you, perhaps, but wouldn't you think that in the two-and-a-half years we have lived next door to each other Ruth could have returned my greetings just once? Just *once* mind you. And maybe you're right, Harry, about the Arabs and the Jews; they're both Semites. Possibly she doesn't discriminate against one of them after all, but against both of them."

"Bull! She was in a foul mood the day of the block party. It was blisteringly hot, sweltering. And with that faulty transformer servicing our neighborhood Con Ed had to impose voltage reductions most of that week. I remember it only too well, all the air conditioners flubbed, just went on the fritz, due to those local brownouts. She never could stand oppressive heat, especially humidity. Many times she's called this sultry weather equatorial and steamy. She comes from a part of Maine where they don't need air conditioners and that's why she always likes to go back there in the summer. Her old lady has a house on Monhegan Island, and that day in July—a real sizzler—she just couldn't take it anymore. Especially with this heart condition she has. And on top of it the streets stinking of garbage because of that sanitationmen's strike. Remember? So, she may have made a stupid remark, but I assure you she is not the sort of person to deliberately cast aspersions on people or hurt someone, malicious . . ."

"Oh, sure, go on, protect her! That's why she would thread her way through a crowd, head for Mr. Franzell and me and give a cock-and-bull story about the Semites. Especially when she knew about my childhood in Europe during the war. Everybody in the house knows about it, the hell I had to live through. Most of them read my book. So what a wonderfully convenient victim she found in me to vent her spleen on, to shoot off her big mouth at the Semites. That was just out and out cruel, Harry, premeditatedly so. And this to a woman who has never given trouble to anyone, who worships Bach, who . . . God, I don't even practice my faith any more, but she still had to put in this dig, to try it at least, make a beeline for me and rap with Mr. Franzell about the nasty old Semites."

"Okay, okay, okay, I got the message. She's strictly zilch and I never found out in twenty years of living with her."

"You're damned right you didn't."

"So what d'you want me to do? Confront her tonight with what is at best an apocryphal statement and then give her a belt in the mouth?"

"No. I don't want you to *hit* her. I want you to *leave* her."

"Leave her!" Outside an automobile screeched to a splashing halt on the wet pavement.

16

"Really comes as a shock to you, doesn't it, Harry? Leaving a woman you no longer pretend to love for a woman you do love."

"She's still my wife, you know. You can just imagine it, can't you? I tell her: Ruth, I'm leaving you, then pack my bag and move next door and shack up with you, hoping all the while she'll give me a divorce."

"Oh boy, go right ahead! I can see what goes through your mind: What will the neighbors think? Isn't that it?"

"Not only the neighbors, dear Helga, but there's just the small matter of an innocent wife being stranded. I'm not that callous. Neither to her, nor to you. But much worse, if my boss ever gets wind of this—and he's the world's greatest puritan when it comes to his staff, his 'family' he calls us—I'll be out right on my ass. Fired. He says as long as nobody knows what trouble you have with your wife, you can consider it a happy marriage. Difficulties at home to him mean bringing your worries with you to work. And with assistant editors a dime a dozen these days, and publishers laying off more every week, I don't stand a chance of landing another job. Or if I do, only at a fraction of what I make now."

"You know, that really is a laugh, your boss being such a puritan prig when he's the owner of a publishing house specializing in hard-core porno stuff."

"It's not hard-core porno stuff, Helga, and you know it. We have some raw, rather risqué material, I admit, something Philip Rahv calls redface literature, but it's no worse than what many of the big publishing companies are turning out, only *they* wrap it in artistic and sophisticated wit and maybe even get away with the National Book Award or any of the new prizes they hand out now. No, I simply can't afford to take the risk, Helga. When he heard of Debbie's affair . . . you remember, his private secretary . . . scoring with another man—all right, a married man I grant—and even though it didn't affect her work at the office, he fired her on the spot, gave her three months severance pay, and there's no reason . . ."

"We could always live on *my* money," Helga challenged him, sullenly.

"For crying out loud. That's childish! How long d'you think you could keep that up? You don't have that much left from your autobiography and . . ."

"Enough to keep us alive for two or three years at least. Time enough to give you a chance to find another job."

"But that makes no sense, Helga. What's the point of my risking

17

unemployment when millions are out of work and then sponging on you till we used up your royalties and then be completely broke, or close to it? With this inflation, the recession barely improving by the week, higher taxes. And don't think for a *moment* Ruth wouldn't ask for some nice chunk of alimony, which also would have to come out of your savings. Something incidentally I don't think you would relish very much . . . when all we've got to do, darling, is to sit tight till Ruth realizes it's just no dice, that she's simply *got* to come to her senses and make a settlement. It'll make it look better, coming from her. And I know sooner or later she will. She's not a bad person, far from it, regardless of what you may think of her." He placed a crooked finger under his mistress's chin and perked up her head. "Come on now. Things could be worse. We see each other almost every day; there isn't a day I haven't talked to you at least twice on the phone in the last couple of years; you've got your writing and I've got my job in which I'm reasonably happy. I'm perfectly aware of my shortcomings. I'm a run-of-the-mill guy, nothing outstanding, merely capable, and perhaps it's a sort of a dead-end job, but it does spell security, which means a hell of a lot for a breadwinner today who knows he's not the Maxwell Perkins he hoped he'd turn out to be ten, fifteen years ago, but only a . . . well, just a fan, like Exley, sitting in the stands with the multitudes. So there it is! I can't and won't be choosy. You've just *got* to take me the way I am."

A new silence, chilly and awkward, stretched between the lovers as they glared at each other, evaluating their lines of reasoning, the sheer weight of their exchange. At length Helga got up and moved to the other end of the kidney-shaped travertine table chaperoning the sofa and opened a ceramic cigarette box. Harry watched her warily, wondering what would come next, because suddenly she appeared nervous. The match trembled in her hand and she steadied it with her left to light the tip of her Kool. She inhaled deeply and as the smoke filtered out in an endless stream between her lips, they regarded each other again with unconcealed suspicion. He gnawed at his lower lip and tried desperately to think of something to say that would assuage her uneasy mind, and his. Again he glanced at his watch. Almost eight already.

"I've got to call her. Tell her I was delayed with an author."

Helga said nothing, merely watched him through the gauze of blue cigarette smoke. He picked up the white receiver, dialed his number and slouched back on the sofa. Closing his eyes for a few seconds, he let it ring four, five, half a dozen times. A tiny frown of concern placed two inverted commas on his forehead as if these were waiting for some dialogue on the phone to be filled in.

"Funny, not like her at all. She's never out at this time."

"Maybe she forgot to buy something and went to Daitch-Shopwell or the A & P," Helga suggested.

"No, not Ruth. You don't know her. She never goes out in the dark, not with all the muggings, and certainly not without me."

"Try again. Maybe you dialed the wrong number."

At once Harry replaced the receiver, picked it up again, waited for the tone, and dialed a second time. A few seconds later the first ring registered through the line. "She's regular as clockwork, so punctual and pedantic about everything, it really gets on my nerves sometimes," he said, still waiting for his wife's voice. "Bugs me so much that on occasion we've had arguments. Can't understand it. Almost eight o'cl. . ." A sense of alarm left the last word half-spoken. "Or do you think she's on to us?" The phone rang the third time, but Helga said nothing; she only shrugged and flicked a cigarette ash into a wine-red Merano-glass ashtray. He shook his head, more to reinforce his own feelings than to convince her. "Always knew that living next door involved too many risks." This remark caused her to raise an unmistakably contemptuous eyebrow but only for a second because his next move came so unexpectedly it caught her off guard. "Wait a moment!"

He put the receiver on the sofa's arm-rest and got up, moving quickly to the wall and stopping next to an ormolu desk piled foot-high with manuscripts. A chrome-framed Franz Kline print of a white background streaked by black brush strokes hung above it and Harry leaned forward now and pressed his ear against the wall under the picture. For a few seconds he listened intently, then beckoned Helga to join him at the wall and listen. "If you hold your ear to the wall, closely, you can just make out the phone ringing in my apartment."

Helga did not move from her spot and he gave no indication that he cared, or even noticed that she didn't comply with his request. Again he returned to the sofa, picked up the receiver and waited for another ring. "Just isn't like her." He replaced the receiver on the cradle and shook his head, puzzled and perturbed. "Nobody home."

"She could be having dinner with friends, you know."

"Not on your life. Besides, she'd have called me at the office."

Helga regarded him silently, apprehensively, but he did not

even look at her, instead frowned and stared into space, obviously trying to figure out where his wife might be at this hour.

"Harry, I'm afraid you're wrong."

This time he looked up, surprised. "You mean you knew all along she wasn't in?"

"No, I mean about waiting, you and me, till she agrees to the divorce."

He expelled a deep sigh of resignation, wondering why she would have to start all over again with this sore subject. "Why?" he asked with feigned patience and brushed a speck of paint-dust from his sleeve, which must have rubbed off while he was listening to his phone by the wall.

Helga stared at him long and hard and with a touch of annoyance that he seemed more concerned over the fate of his sleeve than their own. She took a long drag on her cigarette, then spoke: "Because I'm pregnant."

3 ———————

His hand stopped dead in mid-air and his head swiveled round to her. "What?"

She stubbed out the cigarette and faced him again. "Is that all you have to say?"

"Helga . . ." A thousand thoughts reeled through his mind, marriage, Ruth, a mistress, a lost job, friends snickering, money troubles, co-workers mumbling, 'That's the way the cookie crumbles.' Then, a wave of nausea overcame him.

"Well?"

"I . . . I just don't . . . Are you sure?"

The next second she was on the floor before him, kneeling, flinging her arms around his legs, desperately, like a vice, the pale face, the burning beautiful eyes pleading with him. "Darling, you've got to tell her. You must! There's simply no getting away from it now."

But as the words came bullet-quick out of her, his mind raced ahead, miles ahead, trying to think of a way to get out of this quandary. And as though sensing his growing rejection, she tightened her arms around his legs, desolately, and buried her face in his lap. But action, instantaneous clarification was needed. He pried her arms loose as if they were pincers blocking his blood, his thoughts, and grabbed her by the shoulders, holding her at arm's length. Her face shot up, wincing with pain, surprised at his brusqueness. "Helga, I asked you: Are you sure?" He waited a moment. "Why didn't you tell me before? We've been together for two hours and now you spring this . . ."

A twitch of hurt, physical and emotional, pinched her eyes close.

"Harry, you're hurting me."

He relaxed his grip immediately, sucked in a deep breath. But his voice still could not conceal the tension, the near-panic behind the words. "Sorry, I didn't mean to." Again he cleared his throat, as if to draw fortitude from this slight delay. "Helga, this is too serious to fool around with. How long have you known? You aren't putting me on, are you?"

She shook her head, her voice almost inaudible. "Two weeks I'm overdue. For a day or two I didn't pay too much attention although I was always on time. That's, of course, except in Auschwitz and Belsen. But I wanted to be absolutely certain and not worry you. Then last Monday I went to see my doctor, for a blood test. I got the answer last night. Positive."

He let go of her arms altogether now and just stared at the woman's drawn features. "Jesus!"

She continued searching his face for any clue other than the shock that visibly told on him now, yet when she perceived nothing but the gray terror of an ominous future, she suddenly felt a world, a whole lifetime slip by, collapse, and she seized his hands in hers.

"You'll hate me for it, won't you?"

He snatched his hands brutally out of hers. "For Chrissakes, Helga, this has nothing to do with hating. Or with loving. We're not married. And you knew about Ruth. Goddamn it, I trusted you. You always told me you took precautions. How in the name of hell could this have happened?"

She swallowed hard, crumbling before him, intimidated by his sudden flash of anger. "I tried to figure it out myself," she said in a whisper. "I can only think of that time, several weeks ago, when we had that power cut late in the evening, around ten p.m. Remember? And Ruth wanted you to go hunting in the house for some candles and you came to my door to ask if I had any, and then you made that dirty crack about candles, remember? Well, I gave you a candle and for five minutes we made love, right here on the sofa, and you said you had withdrawn before you . . ."

"Sure, sure, I remember," he cut in harshly. "You can spare me the details." He frowned and bunched his hands into white-knuckled fists. "I don't get it, Helga, I just don't get it. You've had affairs all your life. You never got pregnant in Auschwitz or Belsen, and now this! Heaven knows, you had plenty of experience, thirty years of it, to make sure this wouldn't happen."

Tears immediately welled in her eyes and she let them course down her cheeks unimpeded. Her lips trembled and she shook her head in disbelief. "Harry! Oh God, I never thought *you'd* hold that against me."

"What? Hold *what* against you?"

"That the Nazis forced me to become a *Feldhure*, that they used me in their concentration camp brothels."

For an instant he lowered his eyes. "Helga, I didn't say that. I . . . "

"But you meant it, that I had the experience. You said so yourself, and you damn well had this Auschwitz brothel business in mind." She stood up suddenly and clasped both her elbows so as not to let him see how hard she was shaking. "Harry, I never thought I'd see the day, at least where you are concerned, when I'd praise the name of Kate Millett or Gloria Steinem or Germaine Greer. I couldn't deny you. I knew you wanted me, I couldn't turn you down even then, even though I didn't wear the diaphragm. Your love, your wish to be close to me mattered more to me than that. Hell, why do I have to stand here and apologize? It isn't you who's pregnant, you who'll have to bear the stigma of illegitimacy if there was a conception."

He watched her helplessly, realizing that he had had no right to say what he had said and he wished he could unsay it again and lock her in his arms and ask her forgiveness, that those cruel words of his were only the first gut reaction of shock, nothing more. She let herself down again, on the sofa, noticeably away from him, wrapping the folds of her robe tightly around her legs and holding the top ends together so that they revealed nothing but her throat and face.

"First blaming me for the baby as if it were my fault alone," she spoke up, her voice already steadier. "And now this!" He was about to object but she cut him short. "Harry, I wasn't even thirteen! What could a twelve-year-old girl do when they pressured her into becoming a *Feldhure*, a field whore for the brave killers of the Third Reich? If I hadn't been attractive and well developed they'd have turned me into a cake of soap. And you probably would have had a more accommodating mistress."

"Helga, why in God's name do you . . ."

"What the hell d'you think it was that saved me from the gas cham-

23

bers?" she demanded in a high-pitched excited voice. "The fact that my father won the Iron Cross in the First World War?"

"Helga, for crying out loud, will you stop harping on the past!" Harry advanced one small step toward her, just far enough to reach out and touch her hand. She did not pull away this time. Her fingers were cold and felt small and bony against his skin. She let go of her robe and the folds fell back and once more exposed her cleavage. He held her hand firmly, warmly, protectively in his own and softened his voice. "Darling, why do you have to open up old wounds over and over? I read your book, like millions of others. But it's the future you should be concerned with." He raised her hand to his lips and kissed the cold white knuckles. "Like what you, what *we*, are going to do."

"Well, thank you at least for bringing yourself into this matter," she said sardonically and stood up, slipping her hand out of his grasp. "Only let's get this one thing straight, my dear man. Don't let me hear any claptrap about abortion now because I . . ."

"But, Helga, what are we going to do? I'm married to Ruth, not to you. You never had any scruples about abortion before, at least where other women were concerned."

"It's not a question of having scruples, of morality or sin," her voice was suddenly shrill. "But what I want for myself, Harry, what I need. And I *want* this child. Do you hear? I want it. I have lost everything in life I ever held dear. Everything. My family, my home, my youth. All the men in my life. And God knows I'm not even so sure about you. So you might just as well put the thought right out of your head that you can persuade me to give up my baby, to kill it, because I won't. I won't. I won't!"

He had never seen her like this, the Praxitelean beauty of her features as marble-cold and imperial as that of a Greek goddess. But she had already turned from him and was clutching her elbows again. Her voice was almost a whisper now as the words hissed through clenched teeth, "Besides, one life on my conscience is about all I can bear."

Harry strained his ears, not sure he had heard right. "What was that?" A frown of suspicion ruffled his brow. "That's not one of your little tricks I hope. Maybe I heard wrong, but did you say a *life* on your conscience?"

She whirled on him, eyes ablaze with anger. "Don't be so naive, Harry! As if you didn't know." She shook her head in disgust. "You always avoid unpleasant truths. What do you think happened in those concentration camps? To survive Treblinka, Birkenau, Bergen-Belsen, you lived like an animal, and became one. That's right, you're looking at a cannibal. Not the cultivated lady who wrote a best-seller and makes beautiful love between fresh-laundered sheets, but a beast, a groveling animal. Who knows, perhaps this pregnancy is supposed to be part of a penalty I must pay."

This time Harry had enough. He leaped to his feet and seized her by the arms. "Now pull yourself together, will you?" he shouted. "I know this news upset you. It came as a blow to me, too, and I know I made some pretty stupid remarks, but we're going to find a solution. We have to. Just let me sleep on it for a night. But we can't solve anything by being hysterical and you by blaming yourself for something that happened over thirty years ago."

"Not blame, Harry," she shouted back, "But guilt! I'm guilty! Convicted! Can't you understand this, you fool? Convicted . . . guilty!" Suddenly she grew limp and fell forward, burying her face in his shoulder. "I thought love, even having this baby, would make me forget, but I can't. Oh God, I can't!"

Harry could feel her slender body, the ribcage quivering ripple-hard under his hands as he gradually tightened his embrace.

"All right now, all right. For God's sake, calm down, sweetheart, please!" He began stroking her hair tenderly, no longer conscious of the sensuous perfume but only of the woman's body and the woman herself crying softly against him. "Will you stop punishing yourself, Helga! Please! The war's been over more than three decades. You can't go through the rest of your life blaming yourself for something Hitler set in motion. And I said I won't leave you. I will *not* desert you. Just give me this one night to make plans for the future. Is that too much?"

Helga lifted her face then and looked at him silently through tormented eyes. She brushed her cheek against his and whispered into his ear with an intensity that was meant to impart to him the magnitude of her message. "But that's why I *must* tell you. Don't you understand? To be certain, more certain than ever, specially now, that *nothing* will tear us apart."

"Tell me?" He drew his head back to look at her, puzzled. "You mean about the war?"

She nodded. He didn't want to hear any of this but knew there was no getting away from it now.

"All right." He heaved a heavy sigh. "If it's that important, okay . . . Good Lord!" He wagged his head in disbelief. "Full of news tonight, aren't you? But let's make it short! Please! I really *must* get going."

"I will. Still, there must be no secrets between us, my love. Because without trust, there can be no understanding, no lasting bond."

With the back of her hand, Helga wiped under her eyes where the tears were still wet on her skin. "And you promise not to breathe a word of it to anyone?" she whispered anxiously. "Ever! Not even to me in a moment of anger."

He sat down again on the sofa and tucked a leg underneath him, pulling her down with him. "I promise." He forced a faint smile and closed his arms around her, hugging her tightly. "Besides, arrest and conviction for crimes committed in the war expired after 25 years, unless you're on the war criminals list. So I don't think you have anything to worry about the statute of limitations from me. Or the cops." He gave her a teasing wink.

She only sniffled, trying to rearrange and sort out her thoughts, and showed absolutely no indication of having been put at ease by his last remark.

"Harry, near the end of my autobiography, do you remember where the Nazis seized Fritzi?"

"Fritzi? Oh, your little brother." He nodded. "Sure, the day before Belsen was liberated."

She stared hard at him and did not even seem to breathe.

"Well?"

She lowered her eyes. "It's all a lie, Harry, not a word of it is true. They didn't shoot him." She stopped all of a sudden—it seemed as if she were hanging onto her breath—then took the plunge. "Harry, it was me who killed Fritzi. I killed him."

Harry's arms dropped from her and she looked up. He felt sick and wanted to be away suddenly, far away, anywhere, but not here. He spoke rapidly. "Look, Helga, all this is so distant, far back in the past, it doesn't matter today. You can't judge Belsen in terms of . . . ."

She flung her arms around his neck as the words tumbled out. "Don't let go, Harry! Hold me! Tightly. I must be sure of your love. Now more than ever. Please!" She pressed her eyes shut, the tears again trembling on her long lashes, then cruising down unchecked along the ridge of her nose, forming black smudgy streaks of the remnants of her mascara—a face behind bars. And his arms slowly crept around her once more, unsure, but comforting.

"Well?"

Her eyes opened, large and round and haunted.

"There's no one in the whole wide world who knows." She sniffled. "Only you now. One fact, Harry, one fact in that last chapter *was* true," she said, visibly racked as she began to unearth her rotting grave of memories. "That the war was as good as over. And they knew it, the guards, when they went out on that last shooting spree, killing like crazed animals. You could already hear the guns of the Allies. But nothing could stop the SS. Wherever they saw corpses crawling, with an ounce of breath left in them, they put the muzzle of their guns to the skulls of the inmates and blew their gray matter into the German landscape." For an instant she shut her eyes, and when she opened them again they were wet. "All the girls in the camp-brothel got it—most of them in bed, right after the last SS man had squirted his stuff into them. One of the guards even took out his SS dagger and slit open a girl's vagina and womb, then cut her throat. The lucky ones ended up with three bullets in their Jewish bellies."

Harry gripped her tightly and buried his face in her hair. All he could do was whisper her name.

"Of all the whores only I managed to escape, Harry," she said, her eyes wild with the vision of death and decay. "With Fritzi. I found him in a bunk, half-conscious, where a homosexual was trying to masturbate him. I pushed the homo out of the bunk and carried Fritzi out of the shed. I don't think he weighed more than 35 pounds, a bundle of skin and bones. All his flesh had melted away, his head was gargantuan, tipping from side to side on top of his scrawny neck, his body wasted, the little darling. And thank God I was strong enough to carry his weight, even though I was only fourteen—Fritzi was eight— because the guards for the most part fed the whores pretty well so we could go on looking nice and full-bodied for them when they wanted us. By that time it was dark outside and I found my way across the latrine square to a place I was certain nobody would use that day—the guards' laundry room. To hide out till we were liberated. You just wouldn't expect any of those bastards to wash their shirts with the Tommies halfway around the corner, would you?" She drew her head back so that their eyes met again; hers reflected a hell of anguish and misery, being burned out, red from crying. "Harry, can you imagine what it means to be wedged between two boiling-hot water tanks for close to twenty hours, me dying of thirst, Fritzi half-dead with typhus, his body racked with dysentery and TB?"

Harry avoided her eyes; his tongue nervously moistened his lips.

"Look at me, Harry! Listen! Because it was after twenty hours that this horrible nightmare really started. That's when Willi entered the scene." Harry faced her again, reluctantly. "Will it shock you to hear that Willi was one of my regular customers? A guard I knew way back in Auschwitz when I was twelve, who was transferred to Belsen when the Russians liberated the Polish extermination camps. Willi, a nice guy. The pride of The Third Reich. Alive somewhere in Argentina today by the grace of God . . . and the Odessa. A 280-pound sex maniac, whose demands always ended with my having to give him a good blow job. Down the hatch!"

"For God's sake, Helga!" Harry squeezed his eyes shut. "Why don't you try and forget?"

"Because I can't!" she shrieked. "I can't, Harry. And I never want you to forget . . . what sort of woman it is that brings your child into this world!" Her breath was flying. "Only the night before his fat lips had slobbered all over me, his tongue licking my young cunt, but this was today! Will you listen, Harry!" she screamed. "And look at me! This was the day of reckoning as far as Willi and I were concerned." Then she got hold of herself almost at once—she had to—and tried to keep her voice down. "God knows what he wanted to do in the laundry room, probably change into civvies and get ready for the escape, but as soon as he shut the door he must have heard Fritzi, his wheezing, his gasping for air, behind the boiler. I closed my hand over Fritzi's mouth to stifle the sound of his breathing, but even half-dead as he was he had enough strength to raise his tiny matchstick arms and try to pry my hand from his mouth. The will of survival! And he succeeded. I was weak from crouching there without food and drink for twenty hours. I didn't even dare go to the faucet over the wash basin for fear someone might come in and discover us. I knew that if Willi caught sight of us now, it meant death, instant death, for both of us. He was one of the most vicious of them. He'd do anything to meet his minimum quota of twelve Jews a day. And there were days when he literally competed with the women guards, especially Ilse Koch, who often lectured the SS about the brutalities practiced at Buchenwald." Suddenly she paused and in no time two teardrops balanced precariously on her long lashes. "Harry, tell me, why was it at that particular moment that Fritzi had to start coughing? In the twenty hours we squatted there he hardly ever made a sound." And in a tormented whisper: "And what devil possessed me, then?" Outside a dog was barking, then absolute stillness.

28

"Almost without realizing it, Harry, without realizing, I pushed him from me. God help me, I pushed this little ragged bundle of my brother from me, so hard he landed at the butcher's feet. He was all I had left in the world and I loved him, so help me God, I loved him so, like . . . God! Harry, I loved him like my own life. And I handed him over to this brute. Gratuitously. I kept well out of sight, pressing against the wall, almost *into* the wall, between the hot-water tanks, not daring to breathe. I couldn't see what was happening. All I did was pray that Willi wouldn't bother to look for any more Jews where I was hiding. Only my prayer was cut short. Because I heard his footsteps and then the scraping of some steel pipe being picked up from the concrete floor and the next instant . . ." Helga let herself fall forward, against Harry, and she buried her face in his armpit, rent by sobs. Harry could not move, merely sat there, transfixed, listening against his will to the dreadful tale.

"Oh God, Harry, let me die! Let me die! I can't get that sound out of my mind. That dull bony crack as the pipe came down on Fritzi's head, hard, seven, eight, nine times, a dozen blows, and Willi, his 280 pounds, panting with the effort of making each swing a perfect hit. The little head cracked open, like wood, every time, the splintering of the skull, like dry fire wood. And finally . . . the mush of brain . . . God!"

Harry felt each tremor under his hands as it rippled and shuddered through the frame of her body and he held her closely against him.

"I stayed where I was," she continued in a hoarse voice. "I don't think I moved an inch in the next few hours. I hardly breathed all through the night. Willi left after he smashed Fritzi's skull, his farewell gift to Hitler, and he didn't even bother to close the door. He must have escaped from the camp shortly afterwards because he wasn't among the guards they captured. And all through the night the SS and the British battled each other outside the camp while the women guards continued mopping up more of the inmates. And for eight endless hours, while they were fighting and murdering, Fritzi's blood came toward me in a ceaseless trickle, like a serpent in the dark, red and sticky, till I was soaking wet, soaked in the warm sticky pool of my brother's blood. Squatting . . . squatting in the lifestream . . . the salty blood of my little brother, who had only coughed and . . ."

"Don't talk, darling," Harry broke in quietly. "Not another word." He stroked her hair, gently. She felt as frail as a bird in his arms.

They remained like this for a long, long time, hardly moving. Finally,

Helga stirred. She pulled her head back and stared at him through red-rimmed eyes.

"Why do you think I drink so much, Harry, or take all those barbiturates, my chlorate hydrate? To blot out what the Nazis did to my family?" She shook her head vehemently. "To drown my conscience, Harry, to drowse my guilt, to forget that awful cracking sound of the skull, to beat it out of my head. To forget *I* was the one who killed my brother. Oh Jesus, I . . ."

She sobbed heartrendingly now, and he could think of nothing to say. He simply clasped her in his arms, stunned by the revelation.

At length he simply had to break the silence. "Darling, you keep alluding to the fact of guilt." Harry said softly, frantically trying to find the right words. "You were still a child . . . who wanted to live. D'you understand what I'm trying to say? You had your whole life ahead of you. The most natural instinct in the world, self-preservation, demanded that you save yourself. You knew it was only a matter of hours before you'd be freed." He groped for more words, to soothe her, *and* himself. "As I said the will to survive is man's strongest instinct, and for you it was a matter of life or death. Besides, who knows if Fritzi would ever have recovered from his typhus, his TB, his undernourishment. So many prisoners died within days of their liberation. You only did what any other mortal trying to save his life would have done under the circumstances. I know I would have. Probably even today, and I'm not fourteen but forty-four. And your act was not premeditated but an impulse, a sudden impulse, an unconscious overpowering urge to live. Moreover, I think you have punished yourself enough over the past three decades for what you did and by today's criteria we have no right to judge you. I don't believe for a moment there would have been a soul on earth to reproach you for what happened even if you had mentioned the truth in your book. And that's another thing. If you hadn't saved yourself in that one flash of a second," he drew back from her so she could see the slight glimmer of a forced smile playing around the corners of his lips, "I would have been deprived of you, of my happiness . . . and the world of a literary masterpiece."

But Helga only shook her head, almost in rebuke. "How can you bring that up, Harry—writing, after what I told you? Words, words, that's all it amounts to. What are words, theories, sentiments, compared to a human life? When you must be aware that everything I tried since then has been a wash-out. All my affairs . . . and now you, you my greatest love, one that may never belong to me either, chained to

30

that anti-Semitic bitch of a wife. And worst, worst, worst, damn you, I *have* killed!"

His hands closed like a vice around the top of her arms then and he shook her angrily. "Now you cut this out, Helga! You have *not*! A cold-blooded killer doesn't have a conscience. You've paid over and over for your impulse to survive. And it was Willi who killed Fritzi, not you. You're alive. That's why you pushed him. In order to live. Not to be dead. To be killed *with* Fritzi would have solved nothing, except to make Willi happier. But to live. Do you hear? And you have me!"

This time his words appeared to have pierced her iron-clad conscience, the steel-trap around her heart, and they had a calming effect on her. She scrutinized Harry's face for an unbelievably long time through her large wet eyes. Then she spoke, "Do I? Do I really have you?"

"You know you do, even if it doesn't amount to much."

She cupped his face lovingly in her delicate hands. "You are all I have, all I want, my darling. All the other men are shadows now . . . nothing compared to you . . ." But a soupçon of doubt once more crept into her voice. "And you will *not* give me up . . . because of Fritzi?"

"What do you think?" The tips of his fingers dabbed at her wet cheeks. "Looks like I'll really have to prove it to you, doesn't it?" A faint new smile broke through the pallor of his taut features. "Like talking to Ruth, for instance. Tonight. And not wait till tomorrow; but tell her tonight. About us. *And* the baby."

Her pale hazel eyes rested on him a long wondrous moment, drinking in the words over and over again, and the sincerity and goodness of his strong face.

"Then it's all right." Her arms came up around his neck. "Everything is all right," she whispered. "Everything."

"I told you it was," he said, a faintly brighter smile softening his countenance. "Will you never have faith in me?"

"I had to be sure, my love, sure that nothing would stand in our way. Because only with trust can we forge a bond. And I'll try to be everything you want a wife to be."

Here then came the clarion call to reality, to life, not to the past, but to action, one he might still regret—the matrimonial cold-feet syndrome —and his features clouded over. "Yeah, of course you will." A dubious frown wiped the smile away altogether. "If only we knew how Ruth was going to take all of this."

"You're not going to tell her about Fritzi," Helga exclaimed, startled.

"Of course not. I mean about us, your pregnancy. God, it would be so easy if I really hated her; if she were a nasty old bitch. But she *is* a decent person, and I still think you're overly sensitive over her stupid remark, although I can't blame you, darling. For feeling offended after what you've gone through. But not hating, not even disliking her makes it so tough for me. Loving you makes it hardest of all."

"If she is as decent as you make her out to be she would give you a divorce, hard as it may be for her. She'd be cruel not to grant one, especially if you tell her about the baby."

"No, cruel she's not." Harry pondered each word carefully. "I've known her too long for that, more than half of her life. And mine. Maybe that's what it is, that we *have* been together too long without really being aware of each other's presence. Almost taking each other for granted, like sticks of furniture. You're sorry momentarily if you notice that the furniture has been removed, that it's gone, but you don't feel any pain over its loss, especially when it's being replaced by something you love so much more." He seemed to look right through Helga now. "Funny, for years you share your life with a woman and suddenly you can't even remember why you married her. There's no excitement, no surprises, no anticipation about seeing her, as there is with you; just nothing. She's simply there. No more than that. A wall. A cook. I've heard of it happening so often to other marriages and I'm always surprised when it's somebody who's been married as long as I have. Just doesn't seem natural, does it? Yet it never occurred to me it could happen to me, to my marriage . . . the failure to control the uncontrollable. Till two years ago, when you stepped into the arena . . . the arena of my life."

Fright, the fright that marriage would turn out to be a statistic ending once more in a cul-de-sac of passivity, a cop-out of strangled feelings, sullenness and shadowy substance, impelled Helga to seek reassurance and reach out for the warmth of his hand. He anticipated her unspoken question and quickly cupped his right over hers.

"Now, now, you know as well as I that life is never quite the repeat performance we dread it to be. Things always work out differently. The totality of terror once drove you to save your own life and today the girl is a woman respected for her insight into the terror of existence. And if I thought that the same thing would happen to us, if anybody ever did in their married lives, we'd be like worms, groping around in the dark with which we are familiar. But we really aren't familiar with the future since we hardly understand the past. So, all we're left with is hope. Because we must hope. Hope is our greatest strength, Helga, and if I didn't think so I wouldn't bring you into the scene tonight and ask Ruth for a divorce, would I now?"

He pulled her up then and she raised his hands to her lips. "I suppose not," she whispered. The first glimmer of a timid smile ventured around her lovely mouth. "I'm so glad, so happy, my love, that Fritzi won't stand between us. Isn't that right? Isn't it, Harry?"

Harry could only nod at this because he felt he had said everything there was to say. Besides, the situation suddenly struck him as incongruous; her eyes, red and puffy from crying, yet smiling, her pale cheeks smeared with mascara, and to crown it all a luscious fall of chestnut hair glowing silkily in the soft lamplight. And his wife next door.

"And you promise to call me tomorrow as usual, won't you?" Her voice brought him back to reality. "From the drugstore?"

He shrugged and began moving in the direction of the front door, up the three steps to the elevated foyer. "Be no need to, really," he said. "Once she knows about us, why go on being secretive about it all? And in any case, we *will* have to start making plans." He had reached the front door and Helga was following him now. "Let's see if the coast is clear."

4 ⸺

He turned the handle of the entrance door very, very slowly, not as if leaving the apartment but, on the contrary, like an experienced burglar breaking into it. Two years of trying to make his silent getaway, without being noticed by another tenant in the building, had given Harry practical experience in manipulating the door soundlessly. A faint gust of cool air rushed through the crack of the slightly ajar door. The next second he gestured with a finger to his lips to Helga to be quiet. She stopped short of him and glanced over his shoulder through the opening in the door, just in time to see a pint-sized, solidly built young man with a wild mop of dark blond hair walk in a jaunty step through the hallway toward the elevator almost opposite Helga's apartment door. He was pressing the button of the elevator and leaning with his elbow against the wall, grinning at a buxom blonde a good head taller than he was, who had followed him. She was wearing a tight-fitting sleeveless sweater that protruded in the most strategic places and a red pleated mini-skirt that revealed a pair of bronzed legs a trifle too heavy to be really attractive. The blonde gave the young fellow, who couldn't have been more than thirty, a flirtatious wink and in return he quickly glanced around to make sure the coast was clear, sneakily wound his left arm around her waist, pulling her close with a rapacious brusqueness right out of Dick Tracy, placed the other hand over one of her breasts and suctioned his lips to her throat. The girl, who most likely left her teens only a year or so earlier, squealed with delight, squirmed in his firm grasp and slapped his assaulting hand teasingly.

"Stop it, you little ole wildcat! Whatever will people think?" She pushed him from her, with some effort, but obviously was enjoying his attentions. "You better cool it, Mickey. My God, talk of being horny! At least wait till I see all those iron-on patches you said you've got over your waterbed, you kook!"

But Mickey was not the least bit put off. He grabbed her hand and aimed a typical Groucho Marx leer at her. "Confucius he say: man must always pinch tomato before biting into it," punctuating his remark with a wolfish "Humph!" And like an indestructible heat-seeking Sidewinder missile, he zoomed in once more on her face, beginning to nibble her left earlobe. The same game was repeated, the blonde dealt him a playful pat, but at the same time giggled with excitement.

Helga was still peering over Harry's shoulder, watching the juvenile performance in the hall when Harry very quietly closed the door.

"Whew! That was a close one," he whispered, leaning against the door.

"Fellow from the top floor, isn't it?" Helga inquired in a low voice.

"Worse than that. He's the nephew of my boss. And our promotion director. Mickey Glumm. Just got promoted to it, too."

"Oh yeah? I didn't know you had anybody from your job living here."

"Yes. And he's a royal pain in the ass if you want my opinion. A big loudmouth, a phony. Like in the hallway. Worst of all, he butts into everybody's business. Yakety yakety yak—all day long. Regular Joe Blow with diarrhea of the mouth."

"Don't give the poor guy much of a chance, do you?"

Harry held his head for a second to the door. "Still there. Elevator must be held up again somewhere." He shrugged. "No, it's just that not a single day passes when he doesn't come down to my office to discuss one of his wild schemes."

"Wild schemes? What sort of . . ."

"Well, he thinks he's some sort of a modern-day Damon Runyon. You don't know the plots he does come up with. You wouldn't believe them. I don't think even old Glumm himself would buy them. What really burns me up, though, is that sometimes he comes down at night,

35

unannounced, when Ruth and I are having dinner and he buttonholes me with questions. About some dramatic plot he's cooked up. And wouldn't you know, Ruth actually likes him, his enthusiasm, his youthful zeal, as she likes to point out to me. Sort of a backhanded slap, a hint, I guess, for my not trying hard enough as her wonderful Mickey Glumm, *her* Sammy Glick, does. I just lack his aspirations, she claims. I keep telling her it's just hot air with Mickey, lots of noise with nothing behind it—not very different from the line he gave that broad out there—and that writing such trash as he comes up with orally isn't exactly much to aspire to."

"Why don't you simply tell him to leave you alone, at least in your home?"

Harry shook his head glumly. "Can't afford to. He's no fool, and quite bitchy, besides, even with all his flirtatious savoir faire in the hall. If he's insulted by somebody, or thinks he's been slighted, maybe as a result of his size, off he goes to the big boss, and uncle lowers the guillotine." For emphasis, Harry drew his index finger in a line across his throat. "Sorry, darling, but with so many magazine and book editors and writers out of work in this town, I can't afford to give him cause to complain about me. Especially now, with the baby. So I go on apple-polishing. Some rat race."

"Well, maybe he'll leave one day and then you'll have your peace again."

"Not very likely. At the office we think old Glumm wants to keep him on the front burner and groom him for Numero Uno, have him take over one day when the old buzzard kicks the bucket."

"You mean your boss has no children?"

"Him? What woman would fall in love with that s.o.b.? With those books, all he's out for is a fast buck. He wouldn't have touched your life story with a ten-foot pole. With him it's all blood, murder, rape, kidnapping, and Mickey just laps it up. That's why we're certain at the office old Glumm's putting all his cards on his nephew. And I figure that if I play *my* cards right, go along with him, that one day Mickey himself may kick me upstairs, make me editor-in-chief. Perhaps then I can change the direction of the firm's literary output. *And* get a decent salary." He released a deep sigh of resignation. "That's all so far away in the future and I think right now the least of our worries. As long as I can hang on in there." He planted a kiss on the tip of her nose. "Especially with what's waiting for me, for us, next door. Tonight. With Ruth."

They regarded each other silently, then stole their arms around each other.

"If you have any trouble, any difficulties tonight, and you want me to come over, let me know. I'm not going out."

"There'll be difficulties all right, sweetheart, but I think that's something I'll have to clear up myself. Alone. With Ruth."

"And if she should ask for a lot of money, for . . ."

"Money? What d'you mean?"

"Alimony. Being hurt, she may want to take you to the cleaners. So just keep in mind when you talk to her tonight that I still have quite a bit left from the TV sales of my book, and that I'm sure we can manage, even with an addition to the family."

"Oh." He frowned, feeling suddenly swamped, overwhelmed by the burden of new obstacles, the additional responsibilities confronting him at the outset of middle age when most men could think of relaxing in the tried footsteps of their past. "Yeah, I guess so. Somehow I can't help wishing it had reached this stage already, where we can discuss money, and then go on from there, with life. Well, we shall see." He pulled himself together. "Let's see if Mickey's gone."

Again he opened the door a couple of inches and glanced through the crack. The corridor was deserted. "Safe." He turned back to Helga and whispered, "I'll give you a ring tomorrow."

Helga leaned toward him and kissed his cheek. "Tchin-tchin." She watched him slip out into the hallway, unnoticed, and quickly, quietly shut the door behind him. Only now she became aware of how cold she was, her feet particularly, since she had not worn slippers and had been standing barefoot all this time in the foyer. Slowly, full of old familiar doubts, of troublesome apprehensions, she made her way back to the bedroom where only a short while earlier the two lovers had been lying together in bliss, wrapped in the amorous cocoon of apocalyptic abandon, of a narcissistic Elysium that did not require an understanding of the world without but only of the selfish nucleus of love itself.

Entering her bedroom, Helga found her slippers under the bed but somehow could not rediscover the same Laurentian ambience that had made love possible and life so remote.

5 ⸻

Suddenly she felt like a stranger in her own boudoir, like a third person intruding upon a century-old rhapsodic transport of two hardly remembered ghosts, and she retreated in a hurry to the foyer where she turned off the light, then walked back into the living room, pondering, assailed by new doubts. Outside the swish of tires could still be heard on the slick asphalt. Otherwise, not a sound. Except for her own heartbeat. She cupped a hand under her left breast and stood, motionlessly, by the couch, listening to the pounding of her heart and staring unseeing at the varicolored ornate Aubusson rug spreading wall to wall across the entire length of the living room.

What would this night bring, she wondered. Screams, threats, murder, recriminations? Would he give in to Ruth, buckle under to her feminine wiles, tears, cajolings? Could Helga afford to daydream of going to Bloomingdale's with Harry to pick out the furniture for the nursery, the bassinet, the baby carriage, the diapers—or would they only use Pampers?—and should she breastfeed the baby or use formula? She'd have to discuss this with Harry. But then again, did he really know much about the baby business? She remembered him telling her many months ago that Ruth became pregnant once, soon after their marriage, when they were in their twenties, but that she lost the baby and later had a hysterectomy and that she never allowed him to talk of children in her presence. And neither of them wanted to adopt one.

Somewhere in the house a door slammed and Helga started. She crossed the room, somewhat ruffled by her upsetting thoughts, and at the mahogany sideboard stopped to fix herself a screwdriver. Tonight she felt she had a right to pour more than the usual jigger of vodka into the orange juice. For all she knew this might be the most important night of her life since her first book came out, perhaps even since being liberated from Belsen. Belsen! No, this memory had to be wiped clean at all costs, at once, out of her mind. She could not afford to sink into a morass of self-pity at this juncture when things for once might turn out positively and her life at long last could mean untroubled skies, calm waters, a rock, a good decent man on whom she could lean for support and whom she could enjoy and engage in intellectual duels. Thirty-three years of life without a father figure, a family figure.

She paused at the Zenith radio and absently turned it on. The WINS news bulletin reported that there was a storm warning along the entire New England coast and that a hurricane was blowing only a few miles off Maine and growing in intensity. Well, that's tough for the Maineiacs, she thought, and switched the damn thing off, sipping from her tall drink and settling down on the sofa where Harry had sat. A beat-up old teddy bear lay face down in the opposite corner, at the foot of a mountain of Oriental pillows, and she got up to fetch it and again dropped into Harry's place, cradling the bear in her arms.

Poor silly boy, she smiled, recalling how fragile he looked, so defenseless, coming out of the bathroom, almost like Mellor, Lawrence's gamekeeper, his loins so pure, delicate, white. Jesus, how lonely men looked in their nakedness, so forlorn, yet so beautiful, all those that she once loved, the warm white flesh of their bodies burning against hers, especially Harry's. How she wished to have him now, forever, to mother and smother and protect, to incorporate him in what was contemptuously referred to as a nuclear family. Her arms instinctively pressed the teddy bear against her bosom. But that was it, to melt into and merge with his flesh. Like lust, she simply had to be dominated by and yet be master over his person, to seize, consume him with love. No, better not to think in terms so visceral, selfish, unedifying—let the egocentric dream be erased forthwith! Such furious possessiveness was not becoming a woman her age, a sophisticated figure to the world at large, outwardly at least. Do not tarnish the public image! The bronzed statue erected by the p.r. team could not be sullied even to her own self, the vision that others had created for her, of her.

Helga took a few more sips from the cool drink and imagined she could see herself half-grinning in the reflection of it. Such True Romance worries, such insignificant domestic triangles—what a to-do! Well, not even the *News* would deign to carry such mod bummers in its inside pages, and yet here she already was fantasizing about herself struggling valiantly against The Other Woman (who no doubt reserved as much right to hold onto *her* part of the Chauvinistic Man as Helga claimed for herself) as if the whole wide world had to hold its breath until her battlelines were drawn, when much to her regret she knew damn well that natural and historical forces alike would not bow to any one life or love. Meanwhile the Middle East still played havoc with nations' economies, thousands died of starvation in Africa and India, bushfire wars dotted the globe, and that phony Kohoutek went unheedingly on its merry eternal way, refusing even to acknowledge the presence of gangrenous Mother Earth, let alone its pompous, self-centered lovers.

Still, one had to come down to earth and face reality as long as mortality was ineluctably thrust upon its terrestrial beings. It was, after all, the only life lived by humans, and it was no good avoiding the battle, however trite, however high or low the wave length on which it was being fought. And it didn't help a bit fooling oneself over what seemed inevitable and sooner or later had to be met head-on as befitted all life-surging forces. A point Hobbes no doubt would have understood, and Candide relished.

Trivial or not, each of the four billion lives on earth participated in a soap opera of sorts, either on a magnificent Wagnerian scale fizzling out in Monty Python skulduggery, or in the back alley of a ghetto. Or again, in a gigantic network of inter-locking plots, deceits and entanglements. Like Harry and Ruth, probably at this very moment next door. That anti-Semitic bitch! With her snide remarks, at best an unpalatable deprecation out of Harry's earshot! Why in hell's name didn't she join Johanna Wolf, Gerda Daranowski, Christa Schröder, Gerda Christian and Gertrude Junge and, with them, form a club of ex-private secretaries of Hitler's? Never mind, regardless of how much Harry was going to defend Ruth, Helga was more than convinced that his wife would be only too happy to see her dead, or rather once she found out about them tonight that she could be expected to utter aloud the ineffable wish that Helga should never have gotten out of Belsen.

Christ, what Helga wouldn't have given to witness the scene of confrontation about to evolve, just to see how much backbone Harry really would show, how fortitudinous he would prove to be on facing Ruth with the fact that there was only one woman for him: Helga.

6 ═══════

Not surprisingly, those were
the very thoughts also crossing Harry's mind as he walked down the
hallway to his apartment. He was prepared to do battle, yet be kind at
the same time, because he did not intend to hurt Ruth. She had never
wilfully hurt him, if one can call the gradual drainage of love painless.
Nevertheless, his mind was set to be firm and force the issue once and
for all. The pregnancy made this imperative. And he was in love with
Helga. And not with Ruth any more. So there it was!

Idling down the hall, he tried to calm down, stop his heart from
thundering away like mad, but it was no use and finally, for better or
worse, he took the plunge. He inserted his key in the Yale safety lock,
ready for anything, once more cleared his throat, and opened the door.
Instead of the bright warm light flooding the apartment and meeting him
with its customary hospitality to his home, a totally unexpected pitch
blackness hit him full-face. He had totally forgotten about the phone
calls he made from Helga's place and the fact that Ruth obviously was
not at home when there was no reply. His hand reached instinctively
for the wall switch and he let the door slam shut behind him as the
brightly-lit foyer and, beyond it, the living room flashed into view.

"Ruth?"

Somehow there had been no need to call out her name because he knew she was not at home. More than this, even if he had not concluded from the phone calls he had made from Helga's apartment that Ruth was mysteriously absent, he could sense her lack of presence at a glance, as though she had left a note somewhere in the place that she was out and would be back late.

Feeling strangely uncomfortable, he called her name again, frowning, and moved, puzzled and with a sense of unease, into the living room. By this hour, normally, Harry was starved, ready to eat anything, and Ruth always had an appetizing meal waiting for him in the kitchen where they would settle down together and chitchat about what had happened to them during the day. Small talk, not a discussion, and expressing little real interest in what each had to impart to the other, it seemed to him. Ruth was largely familiar with the whims and moods of Harry's co-workers, and she didn't lead much of an interesting life either, having stopped working several years earlier when the doctor told her to rest as much during the day as possible because of a weak heart. It came as a blow to both of them, the initial symptoms of chest pains and fainting spells in her late twenties and then the verdict, when she was 34, that she must give up work. They suspected it was inherited because her father had died at a fairly early age of heart disease, leaving her mother to fend for herself and her young daughter Ruth up in Maine. Only after Ruth met and married Harry did her mother, Mrs. Kirk, finally retire to a 19th-century saltbox house on the island of Monhegan, and she was always happy to have the young couple spend their summer vacations with her off the coast of Maine.

After Mrs. Kirk learned of her daughter's state of health she made it known that for the summers at least she preferred Ruth spend the hot muggy dog days with her on the island where the Con Ed power cuts were nothing but a nightmare one read about in the newspaper. Con Ed had little clout on Monhegan where the only electricity was powered by private generators and the idea of air conditioning did not occur to anyone since Mother Nature took care of this with the summer temperature averaging in the low seventies. The cool breeze from the sea was refreshing and invigorating even during the worst of the heat waves that usually hit the East and there were a few years when Ruth took her mother up on the offer and spent entire summers with her on Monhegan while Harry worked in the broiling city. But when it came to his three weeks vacation, he lost no time in going up north to join his wife and mother-in-law, a crusty old lady whom he genuinely liked and secretly admired for her spunk, lack of pretentiousness, and her independence. So, he usually spent the last three weeks of summer with them in the old cottage. A couple of weeks after Labor Day, both would bid the sweet old lady a fond farewell and head back for the Big Apple.

However, during the last two years Ruth's health seemed to be improving a great deal, not sufficiently to go back to work, but enough for her to insist that she stay with Harry through the hot spell in the city until he took his vacation and they could both go up together to Monhegan. Even though she had regained her strength and her color, Harry tried to argue her out of this scheme since it was during these very two years that he had embarked on his dalliance with Helga and would have been more than grateful if Ruth had taken the entire summer off and went up north on her own. He could not afford to argue with her, however, nor press the point to the stage where firstly, she might get suspicious, and secondly, they might have a disagreement that would aggravate her precarious state of health and cause her to have a relapse. This he certainly did not wish on her nor want on his own conscience—à la Gaslight—for anything as selfish as what started out as an affair. Besides, he knew that even in her frail state Ruth was uncommonly strong-willed, a trait she had no doubt inherited from her mother, and that as a rule it proved fruitless to start arguing with her on important matters, especially once she had made up her mind.

After all, it was not Ruth who wanted to get out of the marriage. In her own way she still loved Harry she claimed over and over, and she felt deep in her heart that one day, as she put it, he would find his way back to her again and the marriage would be salvaged. They had lived peacefully side by side all of these years and gotten quite used to each other, she persisted, so there was no reason to break all this up now just because he felt a little bit bored, maybe even falling prey to the vagaries of a particularly pernicious case of the male menopause. Of course, Harry tried to make clear to his wife that it was not a matter of being bored so much as of a distance growing between them, a remote feeling that had reached the embarrassing point where they seemed to have became strangers just meeting over a meal several times a week at Horn and Hardart. But Ruth adamantly refused to accept this verdict and in all those twenty-odd months Harry did not have the heart to bring up the matter of his love for Helga and face her with it. The fear of Ruth suddenly being seized by a heart attack (or worse) induced him to decide against forcing the issue by asking for a divorce. Many a time he had tried to imagine how he would have to act in such an emergency and he could not bear the thought of her dying in his arms like the tubercular star at the fade-out of a romantic movie while he would have to bear the brunt of this heartlessness, the stigma of the "murder" on his conscience for the rest of his life.

But tonight was different. The hide-and-seek game could not go on. It was not fair to Helga, to himself, and certainly not to Ruth, who simply had to be told the truth. The matter of the baby now forced his hand and compelled him to tell the whole story, no matter what the consequences. Naturally he'd be most gentle and considerate, most cautious in revealing the whole sordid matter to her because it was farthest from his intent to cause her any harm. She was too decent a person and, what's more, totally innocent of anything that might have been conducive to the break-up of the love he felt for her once. None of this really was her fault. Hard as she tried to please him, to humor him when he felt depressed from the dead-end job he had to endure for want of a better opening anywhere in the city, or simply when he was in a rotten mood, it seemed to be no use. Things like this just happened and he felt there was no one in particular to blame.. Their lives no longer converged, but ran, like trains, on two parallel tracks. Fate somehow played the deuce again with this ephemeral thing called love, and there were no two ways about it. Ruth, for all he knew, just drew the short end of the stick—that was all.

If only he could hate Ruth, he thought, slumping into an easy chair, the way Helga plainly made no bones about detesting her, the whole confrontation would so be much easier. But he could not hate her, not even dislike her. And whatever Helga imagined about Ruth being bigoted, or that she was patterned on Albee's Martha, set to the strains of Die Götterdämmerung, was absolute nonsense, a ghastly misunderstanding at best. Admittedly, she was no Little Eva in the Mood Indigo vein, although sometimes she did tend to display a bit of an arrogant streak—in her own fashion, since she could hardly afford to exhibit her temper and go into a tantrum with her weakened heart. Obviously, the remark she had made in front of Helga and Mr. Franzell, the asthmatic guy from the third floor, during the block party on Independence Day was indefensible, but at the same time nothing more than an example of the feminine bitchiness that he had come to expect from virtually every woman and homosexual he ever came in contact with (not that the straights behaved any better, just differently). Sexist, fascist, chauvinist, Women's Lib undoubtedly would label this evaluation of his, but it still held true in reference to a personal attitude that chance encounters had conditioned in him during forty-four years of living.

Well, it was futile to speculate on this issue when so many more important matters were at stake now. Helga's and his future, the baby's.

If only Ruth were around to ease him of what had burdened his heart for almost two long weary years. Now, tonight, this very minute, he'd have the courage, the heart, to tell her. Everything. But she wasn't home.

He couldn't understand it. Where could she be? This had never happened in all the years of their marriage. That she would not be home at night without calling him first at the office, or at least leaving a note that she *had* to go out (which, as he pointed out to Helga, she had not done in years because she felt almost paranoid about leaving the house in the dark alone, fearing she might be mugged), was inconceivable.

Harry eased himself out of the armchair, looked around the living room one more time for anything she might have left behind to indicate the reason for her absence, but there was nothing, so he headed for the kitchen. Through the rear window he heard the shrill rataplan arpeggio-Spanish of two men in the back yard exchanging what sounded to him like harsh words, then the slam of a door and silence, except for the almost inaudible hum of the refrigerator. He snapped on the light and the 150-watt bulb cast its glow on the white tiles and the bright gleaming Formica table where he and Ruth always had their dinner at night. A cockroach scurried along the edge of the sink and let itself drop on the floor before vanishing under the cabinet. Ruth always kept the apartment immaculate and positively loathed roaches, but despite the exterminator, the damned insects would make their habitual appearance, almost as if to thumb their noses at the city's residents and taunt them.

What perturbed Harry most of all was that everything indeed was so neat. Too neat. In fact, Ruth had made no preparations for dinner at all. For a moment Harry tried to trace back their conversation to the breakfast table that morning. Did she mention anything about going to see somebody tonight? What had they talked about while she was preparing his oatmeal and toast? Of course, there were the new stretches of glum silence between them, an interminable stomach-churning, painful muteness, like this morning, for the most part. But what else?

Harry unbuttoned the top of his shirt now and loosened his tie, sauntering to the refrigerator. And suddenly he recalled his insistence in the morning that he would not take a coat with him to work despite the weather forecast of a 90 per cent chance of rain during the day as the radio also mentioned it would go up into the seventies. (Strange how quarreling husbands and wives always tended to end up fighting over trifles, like stubborn children!) Anything else? He opened the door of the refrigerator and found only leftovers of the previous night's barbecued chicken. No message in here either, as Ruth had done once, ten, fifteen years ago. Just the usual: milk, eggs, jelly, butter, Oscar Mayer salami, some bananas and lettuce. What *was* happening? The freezer revealed only a pint container of Swift's vanilla ice cream and some Sara Lee pound cake on top of the ice-cube tray. He twisted the cold chicken drumstick from the plate on the bottom shelf of the refrigerator, leaving behind a residue of yellowish gelatinous fat, and closed the door.

Where in God's name could she be? Absently, and without much appetite, he began gnawing at the succulent chicken leg and slowly made his way to the bedroom. Turning on the light there, all he saw was the familiar neatness of the double bed, the blue satiny spread stretching across the spacious mattress. There wasn't even a speck of dust on the teakwood night tables that Ruth liked to polish every other day, and the Sheraton chest of drawers containing his belongings displayed nothing either, except for the spirelike ceramic reproduction of Dürer's "Praying Hands" which they had picked up at a shooting gallery in Mexico City one summer years ago when they did not visit her mother.

Harry stood in the doorway and zoomed his eyes around the room, much like a movie camera trying to acquaint the theater audience with the sticks of furniture of the romantic leads. He took it all in, absorbed every bit of what he had been familiar with for almost two decades, the things that formed the background to tears, joys and pain and in doing so assumed an importance in life almost as meaningful as that of one's limbs, except that Ruth liked to rearrange the furniture once in a while, much to his annoyance, and again he shook his head. No note on the two chairs either. Nor on her make-up table in the corner with the Louis xv bergère fronting it. Nor on the bed that had witnessed the wildest acts of lovemaking and then over the years saw the games people play gradually diminish in passion, intensity and regularity.

Ruth had never known any other man, only Harry, and entered their relationship a virgin. But over the years she became totally and uncompromisingly adjusted to each of his sexual whims, preferences, his attitudes and positions, and she learned in time how to respond in bed to the slightest nuance of his mood. Where sex was concerned, he could not have wished for a better partner; she grew increasingly enthusiastic, even ravenous in the erotic field, and if of late the frequency of their amatory activities had slowed down she obviously attributed it more to his fatigue, to pressures at the office, to the disillusionment and compromises with his high expectations and dying ambitions, or to his advancing years as he progressed into the forties, or again to the crushed spirit of his dreams unrealized as a Mod crusading H. L. Mencken or Maxwell Perkins, rather than to the real cause of which she was certainly unaware: Helga.

Never once had she, or anybody for that matter in the building, seen him emerge from Helga's apartment nor observed him enter it, so there was not a soul apart from the two adulterers themselves who could testify to their behind-the-scenes hanky-panky.

And after his clandestine assignations with Helga before dinner, Harry simply could no longer bring himself to repeat the sexual feat with his wife later that evening. Generally, he claimed that he was suffering from depression or headaches (which he dropped after a while as an excuse since he felt this really belonged to the feminine begging-off apologia), but tales of the vicious office caprices and dog-eat-dog Machiavellism provided as good an excuse as any to ward her off for the night. And yet, in the last eighteen months or so, quite frequently Ruth would snuggle up to him very early in the morning, a good half hour before the alarm clock was set to go off and rub her thighs sleepily over his until he became aware of the stirring in his groin, and helped along by nature's diurnal peak of sex hormones, a dozing subconscious and a full bladder felt his organ erect, almost against his will. This Priapean trick took her a good three weeks to develop to a seduction of the most consummate art, and as she did it with such deliberate refinement, such languorous tenderness, it seemed to him as good a way as any of being aroused after a full night's rest. Moreover, due to her hysterectomy she could afford to let him be as careless with his ejaculation as he wished to be, whenever he felt like it, so that on such awakenings he did not even have to conjure up the adulterous phantom of Helga. It certainly required little effort on his part to excite Ruth sexually as she had become so accustomed to his touch that the mere sensation of his hand on her breast or her labia would set her Paphian juices in motion.

Harry smiled. Helga knew nothing about this little trick of Ruth's.

He told her that sex hardly played any part in his life with Ruth any more and that due to Ruth's heart she did not seem to mind the absence of love play. This of course was a pretty awkward lie, besides being a desultory non sequitur, but Helga said she believed him and hardly ever broached the matter again. Most likely, she considered that it was wisest not to unearth the hatchet of jealousy at this stage of their relationship. Creating scenes was anathema to love.

Harry turned the light off in the bedroom and returned to the living room when he was struck by an odd sight. Perhaps not odd to the casual onlooker but strange nevertheless to Harry. He noticed that the drapes flanking the windows which overlooked the Drive were not drawn. This was the middle of October, and Ruth always turned on the light as soon as the sun began setting and it grew faintly dusky outside. Especially today, with the late afternoon thunder shower it had grown dark around six o'clock, and he knew from experience that under those conditions she would have turned on the lights any time between five and six and immediately drawn the curtains.

Although they lived on the ground floor, like Helga, the building's front lobby was elevated by a few stone steps and it was almost impossible to look into their apartments; all one could see from the street level were perhaps some paintings and sconces hanging on the walls, and the ceiling, so that a certain amount of privacy was guaranteed at all times of day and night, but in spite of this favorable location, Ruth always made it a rule to draw the curtains the minute the lights went on indoors. Now all of this meant that she must have left home before six, Harry concluded.

He moved pensively to the windows and looked out. Street lights reflected their butter-yellow puddles of light on the wet pavement and the vari-colored neon lights of New Jersey morsed their nervous mercantile codes across the black watery mirror of the Hudson to the residents of New York. At this moment a woman was passing under Harry's window, taking her huge Saint Bernard for a stroll; otherwise, he could not see anybody up or down the street. Riverside Drive was deserted. And Ruth was right—few people ventured out at this time of night unless they were prepared to take the risk of getting clobbered or mugged by the psychotic vultures preying on the foolhardy. Ruth certainly had no intention of taking such chances with her weakened heart and often chided Harry for still going out after dark to mail a letter which he wanted to be collected by the mailman early in the morning before leaving the house.

He was about to pull the cord of the drapes when once more he became conscious of the drumstick in his hand. Except for a few nibbles he had hardly touched it. The evening at Helga's, the revelations about birth and death, and then the surprise of finding Ruth absent, especially when he had to disclose Helga's pregnancy to her, completely robbed him of all appetite. He drew the curtains with his left hand which was not greasy from the chicken and slumped down on the Hitchcock rocking chair which Ruth's mother had sent them for Christmas the year before.

Rocking back and forth, he continued nibbling listlessly at the chicken meat and pondered the breakfast scene once more. But hard as he tried to recollect whether she had informed him of paying somebody a visit and not being home in the evening he could only conclude that she had made no such announcement. What's more, even if she had— and he knew she hadn't—there would have been some food for him in the icebox because she always insisted that he not splurge on restaurant meals and, besides, she was a good cook and enjoyed preparing dinner for him. Also, on the few occasions that she had happened to be out at night, she made it a habit to leave a message for him on the floor or some place where it would be visible from the front door. But this time there was no message. Nothing. No food even. Besides, she always left his mail, their mail, on the kitchen table so he could . . . Hell, the mail!

He jumped out of his seat, causing the chair to rock wildly, rushed back to the kitchen and after flicking the light on beheld that the table bore nothing but a Steuben glass bowl heaped with fresh fruit. He stared stupidly, uncomprehendingly, at the white Formica table, then turned the light out, the next second put it on again and headed for the garbage pail to throw the chicken bone into it. He washed and dried his hands and returned to the living room. If she left between five and six, he wondered, why in God's name didn't she give him a ring at the office? Between five and six would have been the latest she left because at that time the curtains would have been drawn by her and they weren't. Perhaps she left much earlier. And suddenly he recalled that during breakfast she *had* mentioned that next week she intended to visit her doctor for her annual Pap smear test and an examination of her breasts but that today she wanted to buy some yarns for a bargello stitchery which she had planned on sending to her mother. Yes, she even brought up the fact that Macy's or Gimbel's most likely would carry the colors Mrs. Kirk would want.

50

Macy's? Gimbel's? Should he call Macy's? Now? But this was ridiculous. First of all, they were closed at this late hour, and then even if anything should have happened to Ruth at either department store, or on the street, she always carried identification papers on her, in her purse, as well as an intricately engraved identification bracelet around her left wrist stating Harry's office and home phone numbers in case of an emergency, her blood group, and the fact that she had a heart condition. All of this was inscribed on a platinum heart.

No, that couldn't be it either. Such an accident could be ruled out altogether. He would have been notified long ago. But then something else occurred to Harry. Suppose she had not even looked at the mail and that letters could still be found outside in the mailbox. For some reason their house appeared to be the last on the mail deliverer's route and quite frequently letters wouldn't be delivered until two or three in the afternoon. A disgusting spectacle when postage went up every so often and you were waiting for an important letter, but what was the use of fighting City Hall?

Instinctively, his right hand reached into his pocket for his house and mail keys, and he made a dash for the front door. A few seconds later he stood facing the array of mailboxes in the deserted lobby and opened the Bensonny slot. A postcard lay diagonally inside against the rear of the box. He took it out and locked the mail slot again. The card merely proved to be an advertisement for a new radio and TV repair shop that had opened nearby on Broadway. Nothing else. His hand crushed the card into a ball and once more his mind started tracing what this particular discovery, this turn of events, could portend. For one, it meant that today Ruth did not look at the mail after it was delivered in mid-afternoon. This in turn could mean only that she had already left the house by two or at the latest by three o'clock, and never returned. Otherwise she would have emptied the mailbox. She loved waiting for the mail; it helped her to stretch the day, and as a rule she always answered her mail the same day if she received a letter from anybody. But today, there was only the advertisement, and even if she had left the house around one or two in the afternoon and missed the postman she would have been back hours ago from 34th Street. Nothing else seemed to be on the agenda for the day, that much Harry remembered most distinctly now. Equally important was the fact that the stores downtown closed at six on Fridays this month to spruce up for Christmas and that would have given her a headstart to get home by seven or seven-thirty at the very latest. And it was past nine already.

51

On his way back to his apartment he passed Helga's door and stopped momentarily. He listened but could not hear a sound inside. Perhaps she had retired for the night and in any case he did not want to run the risk of ringing her doorbell now and give her the news while, maybe, Ruth might suddenly make her appearance in the hall with some cock-and-bull story about why she was late and discover the two of them talking together. Although it should not have mattered too much if she did catch them together at this stage of the game, since he had made up his mind to tell her about Helga and himself anyway. His hand was already halfway to her doorbell when he withdrew it and beat a hasty retreat to his apartment, shutting the door quietly behind him. Most assuredly he did not want to give Helga the impression that he was unduly worried about Ruth and instigate a jealousy scene. Even though his love for Ruth was as good as dead he nevertheless felt her absence, and the empty apartment most pointedly. This came as quite a shock to him but he dismissed his feeling of unease as merely a sort of sympathetic expression for his wife in case anything untoward had happened to her.

He threw the TV advertisement into the wastepaper basket, loafed back into the kitchen and helped himself to a glass of milk. Back in the living room, he turned on the radio and heard that Dr. Kissinger had met earlier in the day with some Arab ambassador, again a bulletin about the storm brewing up over the Atlantic right off the coast of New England and Nova Scotia, and then Cousin Brucie Morrow came on with his verbal pitterpatter. He switched it off, annoyed, and in an almost mechanical manner reached for the TV knob. As the picture mushroomed into view, the dolled up coiffure of Zsa Zsa Gabor bobbed up from nowhere and beneath it the Revlonized face cackled with laughter as she told dah-link Merv Griffin about her latest romance. At once Harry turned off the set. No, to Harry romance had a different, a bitter connotation at this juncture, an intensely private one under any circumstances, and it certainly did not seem to be surrounded by so merry and bountiful peals of laughter. Funny how easy it appeared for others to laugh off a failed romance, even a botched marriage of long standing, while he had to struggle merely to find the right words, virtually ineffable words, moreover, that could not be subjected to journalistic pruning, to gag writers' honing up, and which he hoped to convey to Ruth about his love for Helga.

He paced up and down the dark-blue, wall-to-wall carpet of the living room and started rehearsing the line he would give her. A simple straightforward approach, nothing phony, just the truth, unadorned, not a brutalized statement that would destroy her and wipe out all the warmth with which they had genuinely, sincerely enveloped each other's lives, but an honest declaration.

"Ruthie, you can't be as sorry as I am," he heard himself launch into a dry run and it took some getting used to the strained effort of his voice breaking out into the open, into the funereal apartment. "God knows I have tried my best, but you must have noticed the change that's come over us, our relationship the last two years. No, believe me, I'm old enough to know it's not merely an affair: it's the real thing, Ruth. Hell, don't I know it sounds campy talking in clichés but what the devil d'you want me to do? It's not an overnight flirtation; it's been going on for two years, two whole years. Yes, you heard right, two long, lousy years . . . call it deceit, duplicity . . . now for God's sake, don't start crying, it's too late for tears. Ruthie, you knew as well as I there was no love between . . . well, that I no longer was in love with you. Goddamn it, I told you often enough. You can't blame me now for your not believing me and if it hadn't been Helga it . . . all right, Miss Lipsolm, if that's how you want her to be known in this apartment, but if it hadn't been her it would have been somebody else . . . sooner or later. Sue me, all right, sue me if you want to, it's your right. Call it adultery, what can I do? It's true. But with all the pressures of the office, of this city, the fragile thread of love was bound to snap some time. It's beyond all of our control. Ruthie, please let me finish! I never said it was your fault. Nor mine. It isn't anybody's fault. Things like this just happen. No, not only in novels and movies, in life too, among our friends, anywhere. Sure, we think it's unique if it happens to us, but it has happened a billion times before us and will happen a billion times long after we're gone and the world will go on just the same. Not that this is any excuse . . . or consolation, but . . . what can a person say when he has reached the end of love, Ruthie?"

Exhausted, he dropped into the chintz-covered easy chair next to the record player and the stack of albums both of them had accumulated over the years, and he placed the glass of milk on the top sleeve, an idyllic cover showing a nebulous nymph gamboling in the distance through a sun-dappled birch forest. In the album's jacket stuck the Bruno Walter recording of Beethoven's "Pastorale." Harry felt pooped, tired from the words tumbling from his sympathizing lips. Not because of the effort involved in producing the stream of logic behind this verbal soundtrack but, on the contrary, because he was possessed of the gnawing doubt, the suspicion that, primarily, logic had nothing to do with terminating a relationship, and secondly that it wouldn't quite work out this way anyway. Instead a scene verging on near-hysteria threatened to develop which he was absolutely terrified to follow through mentally to its harrowing end. What if Ruth should have a seizure? Tonight. The mere idea of it paralyzed him with dread. The fact that he would have to call an ambulance and then wait for this hooting beast to arrive and her words sentencing him in the meantime began to really get through to him, to unnerve him. Even a feigned heart seizure would diminish the importance of the message he meant to impart to her and perhaps cause him to waver and go back on his word to Helga. He certainly did not want his wife's death on his conscience, if this was the only way to find a clear path to the altar.

His eyes swerved frantically around the room, unseeing, his mind's crazed picture turning inward on how else to break the news to Ruth without upsetting her too much and perhaps even bring about some psychosomatic cardiac arrest. The matter of alimony also had to be considered although Ruth was not altogether without means and could always join her mother in Maine if worst came to worst, and Helga most decidedly could chip in financially or otherwise. On this he could count, thank God. But otherwise there was no way—*no way*—to save the marriage, not even if Brünnhilde herself came down from Valhalla to fix things up.

And then once more the cold moment of reality, of the present, broke through the doubts and the surfacing wishful-thinking-fantasies of the happy end. He glanced at his watch. Half past nine already and still no sign of her. A horrible thought crossed his mind then. What if . . . yes, what if the situation were reversed and it was Ruth who had played him for a sucker, two-timing him, been seeing somebody these last few months on the sly while he was out at work breaking his balls, and now it turned out to be *her* who had taken to the hills with some John and . . .

At exactly that moment the blood froze in Harry's veins.

7 ───────

He sat transfixed, refusing to trust his eyes. Straight ahead of him, across the full length of the living room, on the open roll-top desk, where he often worked late into the night to meet a deadline in editing a manuscript, or buckled down to write his letters and prepare income tax forms, stood the manual Smith-Corona that had served him faithfully for fully fourteen years. Now, in the typewriter's roller, bright as daylight, was a large sheet of paper. It projected at least three quarters of its legal-sized length, resting against the propped up V-support in the rear of the machine. Slowly, almost suspiciously, Harry stood up, muttered a surprised "I'll be damned!" and approached the desk. He leaned over, rested his elbows on the back-support of the imitation Hepplewhite chair that stood in front of the roll-top, and started reading the message in the typewriter.

Before he was two lines down the note he shot straight up and shouted "What!" He rubbed his eyes and shook his head violently as though trying to jerk free of some terrible nightmare and make a frenzied effort to wake up and erase forever what he had witnessed in his sleep.

Then he stared back at the machine, unwillingly, much like a frightened youngster who had good reason to be terrified of watching the movie, "Jaws," for which he shelled out good money, and slowly, reluctantly, he leaned forward again, over the back of the chair, and went through the entire message for the first time. His lower lip began to tremble as he kept reading and again he shook his head, but this time not in a shocked, but incredulous, manner. He stood up and regarded the sheet of paper from a slightly raised vantage point and then stooped back over the chair and started to peruse the note once again. This time his lips moved with every word, as if he were an old man who was unable to transmit the substance of the message to his mind unless his lips first pronounced each word in it separately.

When he had finished reading the note the second time, he grabbed the back of the chair, twisting his head in the direction of the bedroom, his eyes wild with terror, and shouted his wife's name. The next second he was in the bedroom, flicking on the light and then tearing open the wall closet. His hands scrambled through the dresses that hung from the center rod, then pulled down the three or four suitcases resting on the top shelf. He shook them frenziedly and found that they were empty. He piled them back on top, helter-skelter, and slammed the closet doors shut.

Next came the drawers in Ruth's night table. He pulled them open. Everything was in place, neat, clean, her pill-phials in a row. He snatched a couple of the medicinal tubes out of the drawer and pried them open. Although he had never paid much attention to the contents of these containers he noticed now that they were practically, though not quite, empty. He snapped the lids on again, replaced them and shut the drawer. His breath came in short gasps as he ran to the kitchen and flipped the light on. He stopped in the doorway, looking vacantly into empty space as if half-expecting to see Ruth sitting there, yet knowing full-well that she could not possibly be there since he had been in the kitchen several times since leaving Helga's apartment.

Helga! Like a madman, he stormed out of the kitchen, took the three steps into the foyer in one giant leap and a second later slammed the front door behind him. The hallway was deserted, but this time he did not care one way or the other as he hastened to her door to have her share the terror with him. He had already raised his hand and touched the buzzer when, to his amazement, his finger froze on the bell. He pulled it back sharply, as though he had received an electric shock and stared in stupefaction at her door. He could not explain why, but for some reason he would not rouse her from her privacy at this particular moment, the moment when he felt he really needed her most and she could prove to him for the first time that not only joys but grief and absolute terror could be shared, and in sharing these burdens somehow help him to reduce their impact—but there it was! An unknown force, an inexplicable something took possession of him and he felt himself drawn back to the safety of his own apartment. He walked down the corridor, as if in a trance, and let himself in.

8 ═══════════

Once more he stared at the empty living room and tried to decide what to do next. Virtually without being conscious of it, his legs literally led him back to the roll-top and the typewriter where in his impotence he could do nothing but read the horrendous message again. As before, he leaned over the back of the Hepplewhite and was grateful for the fact that so far at least he had not touched the piece of paper in his Smith-Corona.

As he straightened himself finally to the level of the two-masted hermaphrodite brig hanging in a glass bottle from the ceiling over his desk, he gazed at the sailing vessel and gnawed at his lower lip. He stood like this for about a minute, lost in deep thought, then made up his mind. He took a few resolute steps to the sofa and, sinking back into it, removed a private address book from the small mosaic-topped end table which also supported the telephone. He thumbed nervously through the book until he came to the page he was looking for. Picking up the receiver, he started dialing at once but his hand was so jittery that his index finger slipped out of the dial hole before it had reached the stop hook, and he had to begin dialing all over again. As luck would have it, he had to wait only two or three buzzes before the voice of Martin Mottello answered at the other end.

Harry sat up, rigid and tense. "Marty?"

"Yeah. Who is this?"

"It's me. Harry. Marty, I know it's pretty late, but do you mind coming down for a minute? Please!"

"You mean *now?*"

"Yeah, I'd appreciate it."

"Aw, c'mon, Harry. I'm already undressed. Can't it wait till tomorrow, or can't you tell me on the phone what it is?"

"No, I can't. I mean it. I must see you. It's a matter of life or death."

"Life or death! Come off it, Harry! You been drinking or something?"

"For God's sake. I wouldn't ask you to come down if it wasn't that important. I've simply got to speak to somebody, anybody."

"Well, go speak to Ruth. I'm sure all this can wait, till . . ."

No, it can*not* wait," Harry shouted into the receiver, exasperated "Please come down. It is a matter of life or death. I'm not kidding. You'll understand once you're here."

He heard Marty sigh at the other end. "Aw, all right, if it's that important. Let me just put something on. I'll be down in a few minutes. But you better make it worth my while."

Harry noted the click in the line and hung up himself. For a few seconds, he looked off into space and then felt his gaze slowly, irresistibly, drawn back across the furniture to the horrid letter sticking out of his Smith-Corona. With some effort he dragged himself out of what amounted to a self-hypnotic state and got up. He went into the bathroom and washed his face with cold water, then stared at the reflection in the mirror. He thought that perhaps the shock he had just received would somehow show in his physiognomy, as if the impact of it might stamp on his features the Spencer Tracy-like look of ruggedness, of deep fluted lines of worry that added a cinematic increment to the depth of his character, but he saw only the same smooth face of the Gothamite multitudes that the two women in his life had held in their hands and kissed with overwhelming tenderness.

He dabbed with his towel at the wet skin, noticing with some surprise that nothing seemed to be amiss in the bathroom either. Both his and Ruth's towels were still on the racks, their toothbrushes in their separate plastic cups, the sink gleaming enamel-bright, the faucet polished to a high gloss, everything ready for inspection, like a model apartment serving as a come-on for prospective tenants. It made so little sense suddenly. But then the only come-on in the works making sense would be Martin Mottello from the fourth floor.

Martin had been a friend of Harry's for a number of years, and Ruth was very fond of him, too. Whenever the Bensonnys gave a party, Martin was sure to be among the invited guests. By the same token, Martin always made it a point to invite the Bensonnys to his gatherings.

Harry and Martin had first met years ago in the basement of their building when both men were doing the wash in the house laundromat. They got talking and Harry learned that Marty had a great passion for writing and that he hated his job as assistant manager at a local supermarket and tried to find every available moment he could to utilize his free time in writing fiction. Naturally, Harry told him that he was an assistant editor at the Zwingler Publishing house, and before Harry knew it Martin pleaded with him to take a look at the manuscript he was in the process of editing and to give him his honest opinion about it.

In the course of the years, Harry had been asked many times by complete strangers at parties he attended with Ruth whether they couldn't possibly impose upon him and have him take a quick look at the short story or play or autobiography they had written and maybe publish it, because millions of people were just dying to read their kind of stuff. As gently as he could, Harry always gave these nudniks to understand in no uncertain terms that this was not the way a professional set about selling his material. They should first finish their work, polish it a dozen times, and then find an agent prepared to handle it for them.

But in Martin's case, he was cut short. The man began to blurt out his private woe, that his lovely wife Patti was sick and tired of him wasting all the evening hours sitting at his desk beating the typewriter instead of making love to her and that she was seriously considering leaving him. Or if that wasn't agreeable to Martin she might take a lover, because by the time he was finished with his nightly chores at the supermarket and then with fictionalizing his dreams on paper, he was so exhausted that he could merely fall into bed and be as good as dead to the world till the next noon. By the time he usually woke up, Patti was already a good three hours at work as a computer operator on Wall Street and when she came home at night Marty had found his way back to the supermarket to supervise purchases for the next day and assign work to the stockboys. And, while he was at work giving orders from his elevated glass booth in the rear of the store, most of his daydreams centered on making mad love to Patti for two or three hours a day and then tossing off a few Hemingwayesque short stories per night, with her squatting on the floor at his feet, looking up at him admiringly for being so clever, so unfailingly virile and resolute and full of perseverance.

The work of fiction he first mentioned to Harry in the basement laundry had taken him a good three years to write nights, and these years had begun to tell on him. And on Patti. She had threatened several times to leave him and once or twice even packed her suitcase to return to Mom, but each time Martin would forsake his beloved novel and make instead passionate, insensate love to his sex-starved Patti, which in turn would tie her to him for another month or so until the next showdown.

Martin was obsessed with his novel. He lived for it, and it undoubtedly proved a way of obliterating the humdrum job, the soul-killing ennui, the devastating boredom associated with his position at the supermarket. He even took his manuscript with him to the laundromat, as Harry noticed about a month after their initial encounter in the basement, and it was on this second occasion that Harry became uncomfortably aware of Martin's eyes so red and swollen that he could hardly make out the type on the sheets of paper he brought downstairs with him to edit.

The unavoidable finally *had* happened. Patti had left him. Only a couple of nights earlier. While the two men were waiting for the laundry to dry, Martin took Harry up to his apartment on the fourth floor and showed him Patti's farewell note. She simply could no longer compete with his mistress, the novel, and this proved to her that he loved the manuscript more than he loved her and therefore she was leaving him. She left no forwarding address and asked for no money. Not even her mother claimed to know where her daughter was.

Harry expressed his sympathy and somehow could not help letting his heart go out to Martin, only a few years younger than he, for his disarming honesty, his refreshing guilelessness and infectious frankness, and on the spur of the moment, against his better judgment, he promised to take a look at the manuscript. For a week or so Harry glanced at it, liked what he read, took it with him to the office and gave old Glumm a rather prejudiced rave report in his usual reader's evaluation. He even went so far as to mention that it was the only novel in the "slush pile" of unsolicited manuscripts that year which Harry could recommend without reservation, unhesitatingly, for publication. Glumm bought it mostly on the strength of this report, and although the old man insisted it be sexed up here and there and rewritten partly for a touch of more violence in other spots, Martin was so overjoyed that he readily agreed to every suggestion made to him by Zwingler Publishing. Exactly a year later, the Sunday *New York Times Book Review Magazine* dismissed the novel in three short paragraphs on page 28 as a combination of Irving Wallace, Harold Robbins and Mickey Spillane as Alfred E. Newman might have tapped it out on his Royal in one of his madder moments.

Martin Mottello was desolate, heartbroken, on the verge of throwing himself from his fourth-story window. All his efforts, his more than four years of labor, his terrible sacrifice of losing his beloved wife Patti, came to nothing because of the smart-alecky remarks of an insensitive reviewer, while other critics in the same issue of the magazine heaped sycophantic praise on a selection of Szechwan cookbooks, on an incomprehensibly obscure recent discovery of Wittgenstein's, and a new reprint of a long-forgotten Genet book as well as two new opuses covering the Punic wars and a page-long rave on Art Nouveau potato-printing.

Old Glumm proved his mettle. He was not the least bit upset or put out. For years he had gotten used to such drubbings by the press. Instead of disregarding the reviewer's supercilious slight, he in fact used the novice author's comparison to the three modern day high priests of rocking-chair literature and *Mad*'s hero in a racy, rather raunchy, ad in the *Times* and other biggies throughout the country, and within nine weeks Martin's book had risen to the number three slot on the nation's best-seller charts. One more success like this and Martin (whose spirits had risen relative to the rise in book sales) was convinced that Alfred Kazin and Jacques Barzun would devote their next blow-torch analyses to the literary output of Martin Mottello.

Buoyed by the extravagance of a lucky stroke, Martin immediately applied for a part-time job with his supermarket so that he could use his free time writing his second big opus. Glumm had signed him up for his next three books, and Martin was more than happy to oblige him. The irony of it all was that instead of working only in the mornings or evenings at the supermarket, Martin's hand was forced by the management who attempted to make him stay on as a full-time assistant manager. Unless, they smilingly challenged him, he was prepared to work at a very much reduced hourly salary as a stock clerk in the mornings till two p.m., or evenings from four or five till ten p.m. To their utter astonishment, Martin made a snap decision and agreed on the spot to work part-time as a clerk.

Of utmost importance to Martin was the fact that now he could utilize his working hours to think up the plot twists and character development of the *personnae dramatis* crowding his new novel, because the job at the supermarket demanded so little concentration that he could easily dwell on his literary efforts with impunity.

To his delight, a big paperback house soon picked up the option on the paper edition of his novel. Now Martin felt he really was in clover. He became increasingly "pally" with Harry to whom he felt he owed it all in the first place and confided to him that now, at long last, after the Police Department's Missing Persons Bureau had failed, he could afford to spend some money on a "P.I." who promised to find his runaway wife Patti. Harry warned Martin that a single financial success does not a writer make, but Martin was not inclined to listen to this unsolicited advice. Instead he invested almost his entire proceeds from the paperback sale, plus the not inconsiderable royalties of the hardcover success in the private detective agency. They asked twenty-five dollars an hour for their expenses in trying to locate "the little woman." Month after month passed but Patti's whereabouts remained a mystery, though Martin received a weekly report on leads and follow-ups which invariably turned up a blind alley. Harry and Ruth thought that these reports sounded phony, but they didn't have the heart to convey this to Martin, who was as crazy about Patti as ever and so stubborn he would not have listened to them, anyway.

Martin always emphasized in the strongest possible terms that even if he splurged his money on a detective agency he had the assurance that his second novel was bound to meet a more favorable critical reception in terms of media coverage since his first was now a bestseller. His name was something to reckon with, he decided. And he was not entirely mistaken. After publication of his second novel which his newly acquired agent and old Glumm did not want their staff to fool around with, figuring that now that the stone of fame was rolling his way it would not gather any derogatory moss, the papers and magazines indeed devoted more space to his book. Besides, the reviewers now were of a higher caliber than the third-stringers the editors had assigned to his first effort. Most important of all, this time Martin Mottello received truly good notices. Without exaggeration, Martin lived on Cloud Nine. The world lay at his feet. Years of frustration finally paid off in respect and praise. In fact, everything would have worked out all right with the first printing of 25,000 hard-back copies . . . except for one tiny flaw: this time the public did not respond. The plot lacked sufficient suspense. Set in the coal mines outside Pittsburgh, the book and its locale were symbolic of the darkness into which the United States had plunged. Apparently, the reading public had had their bellyfull of the harsh reality without having to read about it.

Martin was crushed. He could not believe the semi-annual royalty checks which came in with the mail from Glumm's New York office. He began to wonder whether it wouldn't have been wiser a year or two earlier to have stuck it out as assistant manager at the local supermarket after all rather than at the low-paying job of clerk. But for this roundabout Monday morning quarterback, the decision was too late. He confided to Harry that he should have listened to him with his advice about saving his royalties. At last, he canceled all future services with the private-eye agency which had still not located Patti.

With the financial flop of Number Two behind him, Martin went to work on novel Number Three, willing to sell his soul to the devil of *la dolce vita* by adding more than a generous dollop of sex and violence to it. He was stone broke and even Harry had to help him out with a loan at the beginning of the year. The second coal miners' novel, meanwhile, was remaindered, having sold only 7,000 copies during eighteen months after publication. The author was surprised and terribly hurt while browsing through Bookmasters and Marboro bookstores to find his Number Two $8.95 novel selling for a ridiculous $1.19, plus tax. Stacks of them groaned on the center tables while the "I'm-just-looking-around" crowds didn't even bother to thumb through them.

It took Martin's ego a good quarter of a year to get over this humiliating experience, although none of his friends and acquaintances ever made fun of him. More often than not they commiserated with him about the poor taste of John Q. Public. Oddly enough, all of these sympathizers were just that. To tell the truth, none of them were capable of wading through his Pittsburgh novel. In the supermarket he had become a hero, his rave notices pinned on a strategically placed bulletin board between the deep-freeze meat section and the dairy department. With Ruth and Harry he remained a loyal friend. Harry had seen enough writers go down after one or two initial successes and he hoped Martin would bounce back, and so gave him every bit of encouragement and advice he could.

But now the tables had turned: Harry needed the aid of his friend, maybe more so than Martin had ever needed Harry's.

9 ═══════════

The metallic buzz of the doorbell rocketed Harry out of the depths of retrospection. He rushed up the three steps to the foyer, and pulled the door open. Martin stood outside, clad in a pair of jeans, a striped polo shirt and sneakers.

"You better make this good, Harry," the wiry little man said, entering. "I just had these two characters in bed and . . ."

"You've got *what?*" Perplexed, Harry closed the door and followed him into the living room.

"A man and a chick. In my book. Made me horny just writing about it. And then you come on with . . . what the hell is this anyway?" He dropped into the easy chair next to the record player. "A matter of life or death? You look pretty healthy to me."

"Okay, wait till you hear what I have to tell you. Maybe you'll change your mind. You want a drink?"

"No. I just want to get out of here. Old Glumm wants the first chapter revised the end of next week and . . ."

"Yeah, I know," Harry dismissed his friend's objection impatiently. He rummaged in his pocket and fished out a flattened cigarette. Martin watched him curiously, noting that Harry had to steady the hand that held the match. Harry inhaled deeply and blew the smoke out in a long indigo-blue stream, then took at once a second nervous drag.

"Okay, Marty," he said finally, stationing himself akimbo in front of his friend. "What I have to tell you is strictly between you and me. Right?"

Martin raised an eyebrow. "Right!"

"Brace yourself for a shock." Harry took another puff and stared at his friend.

Far away, in the dark of the night, two cats were having a fight, their shrill feline mews screeching into the wind. Neither of the two men paid any attention to them.

"So?"

"Marty." Harry took a deep breath. "Ruthie's been kidnapped."

"Kidnapped!" Martin shot out of the armchair, toppling into the record player and holding onto the side of the chair to keep his balance. He gave Harry a searching look. "Hey, come on, man, what is this? You been drinking or something?"

"Damn it, no!" Harry snapped. He lowered his voice immediately. "Do you think I'd drag you out at this hour of the night for nothing? Okay, come with me!" He strode across the room to the roll-top desk and the letter sticking out of the typewriter. When he turned around he saw that Martin hadn't budged. "Come on! What're you waiting for? Read this!" Martin stirred, then walked over to Harry's side, slowly, apprehensively. "Read it, but don't touch it. I want the police to check on fingerprints later." Like Harry earlier, Martin now bent over the Hepplewhite chair and started reading the message. "No, read it out loud. Please! I want to be sure I'm not dreaming."

Martin glanced up at Harry, a deep frown kneading his brow. He cleared his throat. Then he read: "Your wife has been kidnapped." At this point he looked up and stared at Harry.

"For God's sake, read!" Harry insisted.

Once more Martin leaned forward, hunched directly over the letter. "Your wife has been kidnapped," he read with deliberation, as if trying to make the crystal-clear message intelligible to himself. "For $30,000 in cash she will be returned to you, alive and unharmed . . ." Again he looked at Harry but found him staring at the sheet of paper. ". . . and unharmed . . . provided you raise the money by Monday night in small, unmarked, non-sequentially numbered bills. If you inform the police or *anybody* your wife will be killed." Martin paused again, aware that *he* was included in the word 'anybody.' Then he went on:

"You may check what happened to the wife whose husband squealed to the cops last May." Stunned, Martin fastened his eyes on Harry but quickly leaned again over the message. "For further instructions be home alone Monday night after five."

Martin stood up straight. The two men gaped in disbelief at each other, speechless, for a full minute.

"You sure this isn't a prank, a hoax or something?" Martin asked at last, his eyes narrowing suspiciously. "I mean, maybe Ruth's trying to pull your leg or something?"

"And that she would cut each word from a newspaper and paste the whole damn thing up on this sheet? Marty, you know Ruth would never be party to such a . . . or that she herself . . . well, she just never enjoyed black humor to start with. Besides, this is one hell of a joke to play on a guy. Anyway, she hasn't been out at this time of night in years, at least not without me, and even if she were she'd leave *some* message."

Martin slouched back to the sofa and slumped down on it.

"Jesus double-Christ!" He shook his head. "No wonder you told me it was a matter of life or death." He cocked his head quizzically at Harry. "But what the hell are you going to do? How'll we get her back?"

Harry shrugged and took another draft on his Lucky Strike. "Damned if I know."

"I mean, are you going to call the police?"

"I don't know. Maybe. If they mean business, I could hardly afford to."

"No, I guess not." But an expression of misgiving, of anxiety registered in his face. "Wonder what they mean by the May kidnapping. Do you remember it?"

Harry shook his head. "There are so many people being kidnapped now it doesn't always reach the front page. Abducted children, grandsons of oil tycoons, liquor heirs, newspaper heiresses. I guess if I really wanted to find out I could go to the 42nd Street Library, hole up in a carrel and look up the *Times* Microfiche section for May. If I don't, I'll just have to take their word for it."

"Yeah, suppose you're right. May kidnapping, June, July, who cares, the bastards seem to have the run of the town anyway. But, Harry," Martin rubbed his chin pensively, "Monday at five p.m.—that's a hell of a short time to scare up thirty grand."

"I really don't get it, Marty." Harry moved to one of the little mosaic-topped end-tables and snuffed out his cigarette in an ashtray.

"Why me? Why Ruth? I mean, some rich guy who's got the dough on hand I could understand. Thirty thousand would be chicken-feed for him. Goddamnit, you know that three hundred thousand bucks isn't unusual, not even millions. But me, Marty! Me, just making ends meet? Why pick on a poor schmuck like me? And where in God's name am I going to find $30,000? Let alone by Monday afternoon?"

"I don't know. You sure, Harry, this isn't a hoax?"

"For God's sake, Marty, stop repeating yourself! I know as much about it as you do. Why should it be a hoax? There's no other message around and Ruth is definitely not home!"

For a few seconds Martin stared at the smoldering stub in the ashtray, then got up and began looking around the living room and foyer.

Harry watched his friend guardedly, as though expecting him to have something up his sleeve. "Okay, let's have it! What're you looking for?"

"Nothing. Just looking." Martin traced the tip of his right sneaker along the lip of the topmost step leading into the entrance hall. "There seems to be no sign of a struggle, like she had a fight or something."

"I know. Nothing." Harry shrugged. "I already checked. What's more, not a damn thing missing. See that . . . over there, by the typewriter?" He pointed to the roll-top desk. "See that green there? I asked her to get me a roll of stamps this morning before I left. Thirteen dollars worth of stamps. One ten and three singles. They're still there. Untouched. Heaven knows why they didn't even bother to take that."

Martin puffed out his cheeks and puckered his lips, ruminating. "Probably to show you they aren't interested in small change. But you got any idea when it may have happened?"

"How in hell's name could I? Use your brain! You *know* I only just got home."

"Look, Harry, I'm only trying to be helpful. All I . . ."

"All right, all right, I'm sorry, man. Well, you can imagine the state I'm in."

"Forget it." Martin dismissed the little flurry with a magnanimous wave and returned to the sofa. "What I meant was, did you call her today, speak to her around lunch time or so?"

Harry shook his head. "Nothing. Not since leaving this morning. Wait," he corrected himself at once. "I did call her, but that was around seven thirty tonight, from the office, and then around eight, I guess, to tell her that I'd be late for supper. But by that time she was gone. There was no answer."

"No kidding! At seven thirty?" Martin gave him a strange look, longer it seemed to Harry than warranted and with a twinge of suspicion. "And you just got home?"

"Well, maybe ten, fifteen minutes before calling you," he explained. "Took me that long to find this note. God knows I looked everywhere."

At this, Martin rose from the sofa and there was an edge in his voice when he spoke again, an edge of unconcealed unfriendliness. "Look, Harry, if you want me to be of any help to you, let's have the whole truth and own up, huh?"

Harry returned Martin's gaze, completely taken aback by his friend's sudden tone of voice, by his open hostility. "What the hell is that supposed to mean?" he mumbled. "The whole truth?"

"What it means," Martin replied, walking around the cocktail table and coming face to face with his friend, "is that you didn't come home ten or fifteen minutes ago. You entered this building a few minutes after six today—aaah—don't deny it! I'm home by two-thirty, maybe three at the latest, breaking my guts on this book for old Glumm. You know as well as I do that I've got a ringside window seat on the fourth floor. Every chick and dude coming down the Drive and entering the building I see. So don't gimme that bull about you coming home fifteen minutes ago. I saw you come in just after six. You were running in the rain. That was more than three hours ago. That's when I start my supper."

Harry was completely taken unawares. Never in his wildest dreams had he thought that someone other than Ruth might have observed him, or noted his comings and goings into the building. Perhaps he had not been so smart after all in concealing his affair with Helga. For once he had nothing to say, no alibi satisfactory to himself *or* Martin.

Martin responded with a haughty smile at his smashing surprise tactic. "You know," he said, "maybe if marriage had agreed with me more Patti would have looked after the cooking still and I'd never have noticed you coming in tonight. But it just happened that I got up from my writing to go to the kitchen and I saw you." The smile vanished from his face. "And you're not leveling with me."

Harry realized he was cornered. He turned away from Martin, toward the kitchen, not knowing where to go really, what to say, how to clear himself, without revealing anything. Behind him, he heard Martin continue: "You know, chum, as an occasionally successful writer, a

69

favorite of both the public and the critics, I may have been endowed with a trifle too much imagination to add one and one and come up with a rather ghastly solution."

Harry spun around, his eyes blazing with anger. "Meaning exactly what?"

"That you entered the building around six tonight." Martin suddenly was dead serious. "And, oh yes, I remember you telling me a couple of months ago how you wanted to split with Ruth because you felt there was nothing left between you—rather like the time Patti fell out of love with me and *she* disappeared—and after coming home at six tonight, you killed your wife and set up this . . ."

"Shut up! You and your cheap dime-novel conceits!"

". . . and you set up this phony ransom note in the typewriter, somehow managed to get her out of the building, unnoticed, and dumped her in the Hudson, then headed for home in the dark and gave me this red light S.O.S. to come down . . ."

Harry took three or four giant strides in the direction of Martin, who paused in mid-sentence, convinced he was going to be attacked. He stepped back, blanching. "Don't you lay a hand on me, you son of a bitch!" he cried in a voice high-pitched with alarm. "I'm not Ruth; I *can* take care of myself."

"For God's sake, will you shut up, you damn fool!" Harry shouted, stopping a couple of steps short of Martin who only had the cocktail table between himself and his potential slayer. "For crying out loud, don't let your imagination run away with you, you third-rate hack!" He saw the twinge of hurt in Martin's face at once, even at a tense moment like this, and immediately regretted having assaulted his intellectual sensibilities, wounding his vanity rather than his body, which he guessed Martin could defend as well as any man. It was stupid to hurt a friend. "Okay, Marty, let's cool it. I'm sorry I blew my stack," he added quickly, lowering his voice with some difficulty. "It's true I'm no longer in love with Ruth, but we never were enemies. And one thing I'm *not* capable of is murder." Suddenly Harry felt drained, his shoulders drooping with fatigue. "That may be a nice twist for your next novel but I can assure you . . ."

"Are you going to deny," Martin interrupted him coldly, as though he had not heard anything, "that you entered this building around six? And that you've had it?"

An unbridgeable chasm opened up between the two men in the living room, firmly cemented in mistrust. Harry moved aimlessly away from his friend and helped himself to another cigarette. When he turned to face Martin, he saw him still standing in the same spot, his eyes drilling acrimoniously into his.

"Sit down, please!" But Martin did not seem to hear. "Please!" Finally, Martin stiffly took a seat on the edge of the sofa. Harry approached him, coming to a stop in the middle of the room.

"Okay, you win," he said grimly. "I suppose sooner or later it had to come out anyway. But what I'm going to tell you now, Marty, I ask you to keep in the strictest confidence. Not a word to anyone!" However, Martin did not reply, remaining cooly noncommittal, waiting for the next bombshell to drop. "If you want to, you can check with her. But her alone. Later."

"Check what?" Martin asked distrustfully. "With whom?"

"With Helga. Helga Lipsolm. Next door."

"Lipsolm?" Martin tried to place the name, but only for a fraction of a second. "Oh, you mean the broad who wrote that book about Auschwitz and Belsen? About her experiences there?"

"Right." Harry nodded, aiming at as brief a confession as possible and getting it off his chest now that no other recourse seemed open to him. "Marty, Helga and I are in love . . . Let me finish. It's not just an affair. We're in love and have been for almost two years. We want to get married." He was relieved that he had gotten it out. "That's it."

Martin plummeted back, into the sofa's bank of cushions.

"My God! You've been screwing *that* broad?" he gasped. "So *both* of you planned to do away with Ruth!"

"For Chrissakes, will you forget for a moment that you're a mini-Mickey Spillane!" Harry shouted. He made a valiant attempt to simmer down. The issue was too important to be shattered by anger, especially when so much was at stake and he needed his friend's help. "Marty—the fact is, and it'll sound sort of melodramatic, but the fact is that tonight was supposed to be D-Day, the night I was going to confront Ruth with the whole truth and ask her for a divorce. And it took Helga till just about two hours ago to persuade me that I should force the issue tonight."

Martin whistled through his teeth. "Well, well, well," he said, skeptical, but willing to be convinced that Harry was telling the truth this time. Yet a scintilla of doubt intruded into his voice. "And you expected she'd be willing?"

Harry shrugged. "I don't know. Maybe. I have the feeling she won't release me. Not out of spite, but," he appeared to be groping for the right word, "perhaps pride, fear, the fact she'd be alone, something she'd never had to face, you name it. And she's no teenager, even though she *is* good looking."

Martin gave Harry a quizzical look. "Haven't you forgotten the most important element?"

"What's that?"

"She loves you."

"Yeah, I suppose you're right." Harry chewed at the hang nail on his thumb, deep in thought, whether regretting that his unloved wife was still in love with him or for another more selfish reason Martin could not tell. But in a moment Harry dragged himself out from under his dark cloud of despair. "Either way, Marty, if you want, you can check with Helga: the alibi." And then, as an afterthought: "Another thing: I really did call here at seven-thirty. No—it was just once. At eight o'clock, from next door, from *her* apartment, as I have so many times, claiming that I was with an author helping with a rewrite, or something like that. But this time there was no answer. That's the God-honest truth."

"Okay, okay, I'll take your word for it," Martin said. He was pondering on something else. Finally he came out with it. "And you're sure Ruth never suspected anything?"

"I don't see how she possibly could. Nobody ever saw me with Helga, or noticed me coming out of her apartment. We made sure of that."

"Don't forget that I saw you enter the building hours before you said you came home," objected Martin. "Maybe she did, too."

"No way! I'm sure of it. And even if she had, just once, she would have made a point of bringing it up when I got home. I mean if she saw me come down the Drive at six o'clock and not get home till eight she would have asked what had happened in those two hours, wouldn't she? But she never gave an inkling she guessed, was always happy to see me, greeting me with a smile and a kiss, every night, without fail, as if nothing had happened. And in her eyes nothing *had* happened. No, Marty, rule it out. In actual fact, you're the only one who knows about us."

In response, Martin rose from the sofa. It was his turn now to wander aimlessly around the large living room, glancing here and there, not uttering a word. He stopped near the window and poked his finger absentmindedly between the bars of the bird-cage that housed a couple of parakeets. The cage was suspended in mid-air from a man-high stainless steel frame to which the cage was hung from a parabolic hook.

"Hey, wait a second!" Harry exclaimed. He rushed over to the cage and inspected it with great care. "Look at this lettuce leaf!" He pointed to a green leaf stuck between the rods of the cage.

Martin stared at the leaf. "What about it?" he asked nonplussed.

"That's their dessert," Harry explained excitedly. "Ruthie always calls it their dessert. They love to nibble at it. You can see the inside half is almost all pecked away."

"So what?"

"I'll tell you what!" Harry looked at Martin and triumphantly struck a fist into his palm. "Ruthie gives them a leaf every afternoon, regularly, around three, never before. That means she must have been here still at three."

"Oh. Unless it's yesterday's leaf."

"No way! She always pulls the previous day's out the following morning. Just look at it. This leaf is still relatively crisp. Feel it. Yesterday's would have been limp and brownish by now."

"Well, that's something to go by." Martin became more interested. "So, we know she was here till about three. And here's something else. I have a hunch you should find out what happened to the woman who was kidnapped in May. It's just possible the police got hold of some clues that could come in handy today, this weekend."

"Maybe. I can go to the library tomorrow and find out."

"Tomorrow. Let's see. Tomorrow is Saturday. Is the microfilm section open on weekends?"

"I think it is. Not on Sundays though, that's when they're closed. But that reminds me. Tomorrow is Saturday. Now how the hell am I going to raise thirty G's by Monday night? You need weeks even to cash in a life insurance policy . . . Look, Marty, I know that kidnapping has become some sort of a modality. But hell! Everything is closed on Saturdays and Sundays. Why would these bastards pick a weekend for me to get hold of that kind of bread?"

"Search me. Could be to get everything organized for Monday. To give you two days clear thinking time and action on Monday."

"Clear thinking! You trying to be funny? I don't even know where to *start* thinking."

"Well, you can try and see if you have any back numbers."

"*Back numbers?* Of what?"

"Papers. Magazines. Dating back to May. So you can save yourself the trip to the library tomorrow."

"Aw, come on, Marty. This is October. Who the hell keeps papers stacked up for five months? Some crazy recluse? . . . No, hold it! You gave me an idea! Helga!"

"Miss Lipsolm?"

"Right." He snapped his fingers, pleased with himself. "You know, that last book she wrote, the second thing she published? She slaved over it for years but, like yours, it didn't catch on with the public even though it got good reviews."

"What's all this got to do with back numbers?"

"I'm coming to that. Her last work was a book of poetry. She had to get it out of her system, she maintained, and the critics called it a melancholic combination of Nelly Sachs and Sylvia Plath. For a hard-cover it did pretty well, selling about fourteen thousand copies, but, of course, she didn't make much money on it. So, this year she vowed to strike it rich and give the public what it wants, a philosophical novel about murder, about the foulest crimes on record, something to make your blood boil, especially with our dumb legal system manipulating the law so that it serves guilt more than the victims of guilt. Anyhow, for background material, she's been collecting magazines and papers this year describing the worst crimes in the country and the resulting trials which question the veracity of the victims, instead of penalizing or rehabilitating the criminals. There's a good chance she has some May issues left, maybe of the *Times* or the *News* or 'Time Magazine'."

"Dynamite! So what are you waiting for? Jesus! Go get them!" Martin glanced at his watch. "It's not even ten-thirty. I'm sure it isn't too late."

Harry needed no further prodding. He had already bounded up those three steps to the foyer. "Look Marty." He turned to his friend. "Wait here! I'll get the word quick, and then we can plan the next move."

"Okay!" But instead of waiting, he followed Harry into the foyer. "By the way, d'you mind if I bum a weed?"

Harry stopped at the front door and turned around. "Since when have you been smoking?" he asked, mildly amazed.

"Whenever I'm tense," Martin replied sheepishly, and grinned. "And I've got a good reason to be nervous right now."

Harry tossed him the crumpled pack of Luckies and let himself out of his apartment.

10 ─────

Harry rushed down the hallway and stopped in front of Helga's door. For a few seconds he held his ear to the peephole to determine if he could hear her moving about inside or playing records as she often did at night, but there was absolutely no sound. He rang the bell and again listened intently. With a surge of impatience and nervousness welling up inside him, he wished he had not given all his cigarettes to Martin; he was dying for a smoke.

To his annoyance, Helga did not answer the door. This time he rang four, five, six times, long stormy buzzes, which grated on his nerves, but again he waited in vain. Shit! he cursed himself, and for good measure, her, too. Hadn't she said that she would not go out and be available in case he needed her tonight when confronting Ruth? Then why didn't she open up? If she had gone out, he really was up the creek. Destiny! Screw it! Always insisting on wasting time and lives to ensure the continuity of Earth's organisms. Death, decomposition, fate, consuming young and old alike with the blithe indifference of the great white shark motivated by the murderous urge of its primitive brain . . .

Once more Harry thrust his finger on the button and left it there for fully two minutes, feeling both angered and irritated by the vacillations, the fickleness of women, and by the ugly steely buzz disturbing the quiet of the night. Finally, to his relief, he heard footsteps. A second later the chain was removed on the other side of the door and the safety latch turned. Then the door opened a crack.

Helga's drowsy pale face, her reddish-brown hair tumbling over one eye, came into view. "Who is it? What d'you want?"

"It's me, Helga. Harry. Open up, please! I've got to see you."

Without waiting, he leaned against the door and with his full weight pushed it open, upsetting Helga's balance and causing her to fall against the wall. He slipped in swiftly and closed and locked the door behind him. She was in her nightgown, leaning half-groggy with sleep against the wall beside the door, her eyes struggling to remain open. The beat-up old teddy bear was nestled in her arms.

Harry jumped down the three steps into the dark living room and immediately headed for the light switch. Her bedroom door was open, providing the sole source of illumination, cutting a bright swath of light across the Aubusson carpet.

The chandelier flashed its hard glare into his eyes as he turned around to face her. She was rubbing her temples with her free hand and seemed hardly aware of the identity of the intruder who had disturbed her deep sleep. The sight of her helplessness, her uselessness, when he needed her so badly, infuriated him.

"Helga, please try and wake up!" His voice was unmistakably urgent. "I need the papers, the ones you saved. Where do you keep them?"

Helga crossed the foyer unsteadily and gingerly moved down the three steps. "The papers?" she repeated, dully, squinting into the glare of the chandelier, not comprehending. She swayed into the sunken living room, more asleep than awake, holding onto the wall with one hand, for support.

"The newspapers, dammit!" he raised his voice. "Where are they?"

She bumped into a corner of the L-shaped white sofa, almost knocking the telephone off the armrest. Her eyelids were still drooping. "Newspapers?"

"For crying out loud, Helga!" He advanced on her and took her by the arms, shaking her without pity. She had to wake up. "Get hold of yourself, will you? The newspapers you need for background material for your new book."

She regarded him for what seemed like an eternity through half-shut eyes trying to find the labyrinthian way back out of her pill-induced sleep. "Oh!" she only said, then pointed with her teddy bear in the direction of the kitchen.

Even before she had a chance to utter another word, he had dashed away, out of her reach.

"Darling," she called after him in a near inaudible voice. "What's the matter? Did you speak to . . ."

But already she had tumbled half-conscious onto the sofa and bunched up, pulling up her knees under her chin. The powerful drugs had dragged her back into the safe swirling darkness of oblivion.

Meanwhile, Harry had turned on the light in the kitchen and was looking everywhere for the papers. He opened a couple of wall cabinets over the sink but only found dishes, cereal boxes and cans of vegetables on the shelves. The broom closet hid a Hoover and other cleaning paraphernalia. Then he walked around the corner where the window, and beyond that, the bottom part of the fire escape were located and there, on the floor, next to the cold radiators and half-hidden behind the drooping plumage of the green-striped red leaves of a potted Zebrina pendula on the window-sill he found them—a stack, a couple of feet high, of dozens of copies of *The New York Daily News* and *The New York Times*, weighted down by a folded Porthault towel and two or three empty Mason jars.

As far as he could make out, Helga had placed the latest issue on top. The bottom paper was an edition dating back to late January when she had first started saving the dailies. It took Harry less than half a minute to ferret out the May issues from the middle of the pile and he stacked the papers into two even heaps so he knew exactly where to replace those he had removed. He faced five issues of May papers and he riffled through them on the spot to find the article that might shed some light on the May kidnapping mentioned in the ransom letter. When he could not detect anything of a crime even remotely related to an abduction, he slammed the five papers angrily under his arm and strode with them back into the living room.

"Is that all of May you've got?" he demanded.

Helga who was fast asleep, stirred and in a stupor propped herself on one elbow. "May?"

"Yes, May. The month of May."

He slumped down on the sofa beside her, once more thumbing feverishly through the papers. To his dismay he noticed now that not only were there many pages missing but also that large chunks of paper had been cut out of those pages that were left between the front and back covers of each daily. To Harry these cuts did not look as though they were articles that had been excised for research purposes but oddly shaped cutouts in no way conforming to the layout of the columns of newsprint.

"Hey, what *is* this?" He was genuinely exasperated, and held up one of the peculiarly cut-up sheets for her to see. "What d'you *do* with these pages?"

The wrath of flak in his face, in his voice, could not be concealed any longer and Helga made another huge effort to draw herself up on the armrest of the sofa, and opened her eyes only with the greatest difficulty. The light blinded her and she squinted at the holes in the paper. "Oh, I cut out . . ." Her hand rubbed a temple as if to revive her thinking processes, but she did not seem able to haul herself out of her numbing semi-consciousness. She shut her eyes tightly and dug two knuckles into them. "God, those pills!"

Harry slapped the paper furiously on his knee. "Cut *what* out?" he shouted.

Her hand fell from her eyes and she stared at her lover, totally mystified. "Things . . . personal things . . . for myself."

"For Christ's sake!"

Again he turned page after page, becoming increasingly ill-tempered as he leafed through the different papers. He used his index finger this time to trace down the many columns of print until, at length, to his astonishment, his hand stopped in the middle of the front page of a *Times*. "Here we are!" He quickly folded the paper to a more manageable size and read aloud: "Kidnapped wife found murdered," then glanced to the bottom of the column, mumbling to himself, "Continued on page 67, column 4."

He opened the paper, turned to the last page of that section, swiftly went through the four other May issues, then turned back to Helga, who had once more rolled up on the sofa. "What did you do with the second part? Page 67. It's missing. Helga!"

But it was no use. This time she had fallen fast asleep. He was about to shake her awake again but changed his mind almost at once. He bent over her, and could hear her deep, regular breathing and he lacked the heart to rouse her for a third time. The teddy bear had fallen off the couch on the Aubusson rug and he picked it up and placed it next to her on a cushion.

He folded the paper with the kidnap article neatly three times and returned the other four dailies to the kitchen on top of one of the two stacks before turning off the light there. Although there seemed precious little need to tiptoe on the deep pile rug he did so nevertheless, fearful of rousing her, and finally came to a halt at the head of the sofa regarding her now with deep concern and anguish. In the two years he had been intimately involved with Helga he had never seen her so heavily drugged, although he had been told by her many times that she couldn't find sleep on her own since the day she left the horrible experience of Belsen behind. Only today had it become clear to Harry why she depended so extensively on artificial means to wipe out the memory of the extermination camp and needed to seek sanctuary in the haven of the unconscious. For a minute his own tension gave way to a wave of such indescribable tenderness, such heart-swelling compassion and pity that he leaned over her and stroked the mussed strands of hair off her forehead and kissed her pale cheeks.

Suddenly it occurred to him she might get cold on the sofa during the night—the heat was always shut off after ten p.m.—and yet he did not want to wake her by carrying her to her bed. Instead, he hastened into her bedroom to get a couple of blankets from her bed where she must have fallen asleep before being disturbed by him and then hurried back to the living room to cover her and place a cushion under her head. As he did so, her right hand blindly reached out and found the teddy bear in her sleep. She clutched it to her bosom, her lips moving and whispering, so it seemed to Harry, the name of her murdered little brother Fritzi.

He picked up the paper that had slipped from under his arm, stuffed it into his jacket and switched off the light in the living room. For an instant longer he deliberated whether to extinguish the light in her bedroom too but then decided against it in case she had to get up to go to the john during the night. At least she could orient herself in her drugged sleep by the light in her bedroom instead of bumping against the unfamiliar nocturnal furniture of the living room and ending up hurting herself.

Satisfied that everything was in order, Harry opened the front door and let himself out, shutting it slowly, carefully, with a quiet little click. As he turned to rush back to his apartment, his heart almost stopped.

11 ═══════

Mickey Glumm was standing by the elevator door, alone this time, with a sixpack of Schlitz. The little fellow stared at Harry in utter disbelief as he emerged from Helga Lipsolm's apartment. For two years Harry had taken extreme precautions, maximum care, to avoid being detected coming out of her place, and this one time when no romantic interlude had occurred in her apartment, he had thrown all caution to the wind, and he would have to run smack into Promotion Director Mickey Glumm, the Number One Blowhard of the world.

An icily friendly smile froze on Harry's face. "Hi there, Mick," he was the first one to find his voice. "How's tricks?"

Mickey burst into a toothy grin. "Why, you sly old dog you! Don't tell me you're shacking up with that dame from Krautland. Krautland, Krautland, *über alles*!" he sang in a mock version of the old German national anthem, ending it with the mischievous wagging of an admonishing finger. "What d'you know! Wolf in wolf's clothing, eh?"

Harry made a brave try at walking nonchalantly in the direction of his apartment. "No such luck, Mickey," he laughed it all off. "Just wishful thinking on your part *faute de mieux*. All I wanted was some

... you know ... some matches. Pilot light in our kitchen went out and we had none."

"Oh yeah? No kidding. Pilot light, huh?" Harry was just about to pass Mickey when the latter nudged him playfully with his elbow. "Pilot light, old buddy? Ruth know you no longer keep the home fires burning?"

"Sure she does. Don't worry. Everything is under control." Harry retreated crabwise from Mickey, winking at him and trying to read in his face whether he suspected any hanky-panky between him and Helga or really took his lie for all it was worth. "Sorry, Mickey, I better get back. She's waiting."

"Oh, really?" Mickey furrowed his brow and put his foot in the open elevator door. "Tell me, did she give you the circular I made up?"

Harry stopped in his tracks, galvanized, rooted to the ground. "Give me what?" He could feel the blood rush to his ears.

"The circular I made up. I meant to give it to you in the office today during lunchtime, but you were out and I wanted to leave early. You know, had an appointment upstairs with a fast blonde about my etchings," he heehawed with laughter. "And I didn't want to keep the broad waiting. So I gave Ruthie the dummy to show you when you got home, just a rough idea I had last week and probably needs some working over as far as the sales pitch is concerned till it's . . .."

"Mickey, are you sure you gave it to Ruth?"

"Sure I'm sure. Didn't she give it to you?"

"Approximately what time did you see her about it?"

"Oh, I should think around . . . Hey what is this? What difference does that make? All I want to know is if she gave it to you."

"Yes, it does make a difference to me," Harry barked back, hearing the echo of his shout flap back and forth in the hallway. He was truly agitated by Mickey's shilly-shallying attitude when his information could turn out to be so vital. "If it didn't make any difference, I wouldn't have asked you, would I?"

Nobody working for Glumm had ever dared address Mickey in this imperious manner, moreover give him an order; after all, he was the man most likely to succeed old Glumm himself and the staff knew it. Not unexpectedly, Harry regretted his burst of temper immediately and was about to apologize when to his amazement the little worm cringed, his face drained of all color. He blinked nervously and moistened his lips with his tongue.

"Around half-past two, I suppose. Three o'clock at the latest. But why, Harry? Hell, you aren't going to squeal to my uncle. You know how he feels about anybody leaving early. Even worse than giving a raise."

Harry smiled, relieved. His career was still safe. And at least he knew that at about two-thirty Ruth was still at home and actually had been seen by Mickey, and perhaps still half an hour later, having fed the parakeets around three.

" 'Course not," he reassured Mickey with a forced smile. "That's not why I asked. I wouldn't squeal on you if you were the last person in the world." At this point he didn't even know what exactly he was driving at with this unctuous subterfuge and was more than grateful he did not have to question Mickey in any greater detail about the timing of his visit with Ruth and thus further arouse his suspicions.

"I knew I could trust you. You're a regular pal, Harry," Mickey returned his smile, feeling alive and well again. "Well . . ."

"Oh, one more thing, Mickey," Harry hated himself for ingratiating himself with this little pipsqueak, but it had to be done. "Ruthie and I had an argument today about that mail arriving so late. I just couldn't believe it came that late. Could you tell me if you saw the letter carrier, since you got home so early?"

"The letter carrier? Oh, sure, I remember. In fact, I even had a blow-up with him. The clown didn't show up till around four this afternoon. All that these bastards are good for is taking Christmas bonuses and the rest of the year sitting on their asses in cafeterias sipping their Chock Full O'Nuts. I let him have it full and square . . ."

While Mickey went on with his he-man bluster, Harry made a fast mental estimate. At three o'clock Ruth fed the birds, but at four when the TV repair store advertisement postcard was placed in their mailbox she had already disappeared, or she would have emptied it. That much was established. The kidnappers had come between three and four, just before the downpour.

"Well, did she give it to you?"

"Give it to me? Oh, you mean that dummy? Yeah, yeah, she gave me some layout, but I haven't had a chance to look at it yet."

"Natch, still needs some jazzing up here and there. The coupon-part especially. Say, d'you mind if I drop in for a minute and toss the ole ball of wax around with you and see what we can run up the flagpole?"

Harry again retreated backwards, toward his door. "Not tonight, Mickey, if you don't mind. I'm bushed, really. All week that hassle at the office and with Bolltash, that new writer, during lunch today getting him to change his plot in the second half of the book. I'm sorry, Mick . . ."

"Okay, okay. How about over the weekend sometime? Tomorrow?"

Somebody upstairs banged on the elevator door, shouting, "What's holding up the elevator?"

"Hey, you better get going. We'll talk about it sometime."

"What's wrong with tomorrow?"

"Tomorrow? Well . . . okay . . . let me give you a ring, Mickey. Right?"

"Swell." He gave Harry one of his special pally winks. "Maybe I can get a free lunch outa you Monday, what d'you say?"

"You do that, buddy. I better run along now."

"Right on! Be seeing you."

Harry turned from the blabbermouth and dashed the last few steps to his front door; he had pushed his key already into the Yale lock when he heard Mickey's voice again.

"Hey, Harry, wait!"

Harry froze in mid-motion turning the key. Mickey was still standing in the elevator door, grinning from ear to ear. "Heard the latest joke?"

"Mickey, I . . ."

"Only takes a minute. Broad upstairs told me. How . . ."

"I wouldn't keep her waiting."

"What do they call the TV comedy in Saudi Arabia where this guy lives with this chick and his in-laws, the Sheik of Omar?"

Harry ingested a deep breath, resigning himself to the inane dribble; anything to get it over with as quickly as possible. "I give up."

"Oil in the Family." Mickey doubled up with gales of laughter that echoed back and forth between the walls, and slapped his thigh. "Got it? Like Archie Bun . . ."

"Great, Mickey. Take it easy now."

"You bet. Take care."

12

Without another word Harry let himself into his apartment and quickly closed the door behind him. Martin was sitting on the sofa, toying with the stub of the cigarette he had bummed from Harry.

"Just my luck, bumping into Mickey," Harry announced, loping down the three steps into the living room. "But at least it gave me a chance to discover when Ruthie vanished."

"Mickey?" Martin shot him a questioning glance.

"Yeah, you know, our promotion director. Guy on the top floor—Glumm—you've seen him. He gave me some corny story about a broad of his. But I found out that Ruth was abducted between three and four in the afternoon. Because she left the mail in the box and this mail wasn't delivered till four, according to Mickey. Since she can always hear the slots being opened by the postman she's out in a jiffy picking ours up. But not today. So it must have happened between three, when she fed the birds, and four."

"I see." Martin obviously tried to make sense of this and digest it in his imaginative tract. "And what about the papers? You find anything in them?"

"Oh yeah, here, I gave it a fast once-over, that's all." He pulled the

Times out of his jacket. "The husband's name and address. And a picture of him on the front page crying over his wife's body. Same picture they had on the *Daily News* cover. I recall it now."

"Let me have a look at it."

Harry handed him the *Times*. "Inside pages, at least the continuation, are all missing."

Martin flew over the article with a discerning eye. "Well, at least it's a step in the right direction. Name and address of the woman's husband. Doesn't even live very far from here."

"As if that made any difference," Harry said, slumping exhaustedly on the sofa.

Martin looked up from the paper. "Why shouldn't it? Isn't that the point of the investigation? As long as we've got this far, Buster, we might as well follow up on it. Go all the way."

"Meaning what?"

"That there's nothing like obtaining first-hand information." Martin elucidated. "C'mon, slowpoke! Where's your phone book?"

"Phone book?" Harry repeated absently as though in a sudden trance, far away in his unreachable private thoughts, but finally he got up and went over to the roll-top desk where the Manhattan phone directory lay on the top shelf. "You really think we should call him up?" he asked half-heartedly over his shoulder. "I mean, at this time of night?"

"Why not? Get him to come over! Lay all your cards on the table! Worst thing he can say is no." Martin encouraged Harry to go through with his scheme. "And I got a hunch he won't."

Harry settled down next to the telephone and leafed through the directory's pages. "How d'you spell his name again?"

"Let me make sure." Martin glanced down the *Times* article until his eyes caught the man's name. "Ives. I-V-E-S. Donald. On 126th Street. Tell him you're in the same boat he was in last May. Guy's bound to understand and come to your help. At least it'd give you some idea where *he* went wrong."

Suddenly Harry's finger stopped in the center column of the page he had opened. "Here he is. 701 West 126th Street. Must be near Broadway. That the one?"

"Check. Try to make an appointment for tonight if possible. Then we can go on from there."

Harry nodded and started dialing the number. He only had to wait two rings before Martin saw him slam the phone directory shut and tense up, speaking into the receiver. "Is this Mr. . . . What? I was

85

dialing Monument 2-9998. Mr. Donald Ives . . . Oh . . . no, hold on a second, while I get a pencil." He reached for a notebook and pencil peeking out from under the phone and then poised the pencil when he spoke again to the operator. "I'm ready . . . yes . . . yes . . . Isn't that a downtown number? . . . I see. Thanks."

He replaced the receiver and turned to Martin. "The guy's no longer on 126th Street. He moved downtown. Joint is some dash-dash Residence. I think she said near the Bowery."

"Jesus!"

"Probably lost his head after what happened to his wife and took a trip downtown in more ways than one."

He dialed the number he had jotted down, then leaned back, rubbing his eyes. Suddenly, without warning, a giant wave of fatigue, of utter exhaustion swept over him. The last couple of hours, Helga's pregnancy, her confession about her brother Fritzi, the challenge of asking Ruth for a divorce, the news of the kidnapping, the monumental projects planned for the weekend, had sucked all the strength out of him. "Oh is this the . . . the . . ." He sat up, stiff and alert. "Could I speak to Mr. Ives please, Donald Ives? Yes, I'll hold on."

Harry cupped his left hand over the receiver. "Switchboard sounds kind of Harlem-ish," he turned to Martin again. "Probably some seedy, flea-bitten dive." Then his entire attention was riveted to the mouthpiece of the receiver. "Yes? Is this Mr. Ives? Donald Ives? . . . Uh . . . Mr. Ives, you don't know me. My name is Bensonny, Harry Bensonny. No, not Benny as in Jack Benny. Bensonny. You don't know me but . . . look, I hate to impose on you at this time of night, Mr. Ives, but would it be possible for you to come over to my place? Tonight? You see . . . no, no, no, you misunderstand . . . you see, I . . . I'm sort of in the same predicament you were in . . . last May." Harry listened again intently, holding his left hand over the left ear as if trying to block out all extraneous sounds and concentrate on each and every word Mr. Ives was conveying to him. After half a minute of this, he placed the left hand over the mouthpiece and addressed Martin in a low voice. "The fellow's smashed, bombed out of his skull. Hardly make out a word he's saying." He turned back to the phone. "What was that? . . . Yes sir, that's right, a ransom note . . . No, I don't know if it resembles the one they left in your place. That's why I wanted you to come over, so you could take a look at it and we could . . . What? Okay. I'll speak slower." He curved the hollow of his palm and encircled the mouthpiece like a circular tube and spoke into it, slowly and distinctly. "Yes, that's right. She *is* kidnapped. Of course, I'll pay for the transportation. Yes, by all means take a taxi if you wish. Money's no object. No, you have the name—Bensonny. B-E-N-S-O-N-N-Y. Got it? The address is . . . What was that? Oh . . . No, I understand. If you can't make it tonight, tomorrow morning will do just fine. But before 12 o'clock noon, okay? Yes, I'm on Riverside Drive . . . Harry . . . Sure, if you prefer you can look it up in the phone book . . . Manhattan, that's correct. And don't worry about the money."

Harry stared at the mouthpiece. "Hung up," he said, and hung up himself. "Maybe just as well in his state not to come over tonight. Sure was high as a kite."

"Could have been his wife's murder that drove him to it," Martin ventured.

For a few seconds Harry's attention was diverted again to the photo on the front page of the *Times*. He studied it hard, then shook his head. "You know, Marty, whatever has been between Ruthie and me . . . this isn't how I want it to end." He tossed the paper into the far corner of the sofa.

"You're really going through with paying them off, aren't you?"

"Listen, buddy." Harry was a trifle piqued that Martin should even raise such a point. "I didn't ask Ives over for a game of Scrabble." Again he chewed at his underlip, gazing off into space. "If only he'd sober up by tomorrow."

"And the thirty thousand bucks?"

Mention of the financial aspect of the crime dragged Harry out of his momentary ruminations. "Still have to figure that one out," he said. He got up and again headed for the typewriter with the ransom demand. "Some dirty game of pool all right. Heaven knows how I'll do it. Certainly means scrimping and scrounging for it. Only I don't dig the amount: thirty grand! Still beats me why they should pick on *me*, Marty." He turned round to his friend. "Poor crummy jerk who just makes ends meet. Why me?"

Martin could only shrug. "I guess they don't want any publicity," he said. "If they tackled with one of the Rockefellers, they'd have half of New York's and Washington's police forces and the FBI on their tails, looking for them. But who the hell cares about you? A nobody. Since the Patty Hearst kidnapping, everything is dimestore stuff. You just can't compete with that Tania business, the tapes, the sex symbol going radical, bank robberies, love affairs, fingerprints all over the country, her copout in jail. If you're lucky, you'll make two paragraphs on page 86, next to the TV announcements. That's if the cops ever get hold of the Bensonny kidnapping bulletin. But to me, Harry, to be honest, that looks pretty risky. Just take a look at this picture in the *Times*!"

"What the devil do you think I did?" Harry raised his voice, but immediately took hold of himself. "Sorry, I didn't mean to . . . Look, Marty, I've got to figure out somehow if I can raise thirty thousand smackers. I've a little in stocks and bonds, which I can sell sometime on Monday. At least the stock I can. Not too much in the savings and checking accounts with Ruthie not working. Could withdraw that too." He paced slowly up and down the length of the living room as Martin watched and listened raptly. "Another thing I could do is sell the car. As a last resort." He stopped in front of Martin, and shrugged. "About wraps it up."

Martin shook his head and grinned. "Not quite, fella. Don't you remember? That cottage in the country that you're so fed up with?"

Instantly Harry's features brightened. He snapped his fingers. "You're right, Marty," he exclaimed triumphantly. "What would I do without you? How stupid of me to forget! Even kills two birds with one stone. As good an excuse as any to get rid of that old dacha. With all those property taxes. That *might* swing it. Of course! But I've *got* to step on it. Wait!" He bounded over to the roll-top desk and rummaged through some documents, then hastened back to the telephone and picked up the little address book. "Agent I know in Westchester, with a branch in Sullivan County, can handle this for me. And on the double, too." He had already found the page and was scanning it now. "Let's see. B—Bl—here we are."

"You trying to line *him* up for tomorrow as well?"

"Don't see why not," Harry said, dialing. "Girl-crazy son of a bitch if ever you saw one. Lives by himself, though." He spoke into the phone now, "Operator, will you give me Hillmount 4-2323 . . . Yes, New York . . . My number? Monument 1-2219 . . . Thanks."

"Better have a broad ready for him. As bait. Make it worth his while."

While listening to the dial tone at the other end, Harry stretched out on the couch and kept his eyes glued to the picture in the *Times*. "Poor bastard!"

Suddenly Martin seemed to enjoy himself hugely. He rubbed his hands. "Plot sure is thickening, chapter by chapter, ain't it?" he chuckled.

Like a whiplash, Harry snapped up, ramrod-straight, his face an iron-tense mask of wrath. "Knock it off, Marty! I didn't ask you down here to get background material for your next *Police Gazette* story."

The silly grin broadening across Martin's face vanished as swiftly as it had appeared. "Sorry about that. Don't know what got into me."

But Harry was not that easily placated and the look he gave Martin let him know how he felt about his gleeful remark. "Bad enough your using your break-up with Patti for a story in *Modern Romances*, but . . ."

"*True Magazine*, dear boy," Martin corrected him. "*Modern Romances* rejected the break-up part of the story—not romantic enough."

"Just don't bug me!" Harry turned back to the telephone, half-listening to the rings and half-remembering how after the smash success of his first novel, Martin had fleshed out his break-up with Patti, sexed it up here and there and embroidered it with a mythical third lover—a beautiful lesbian (his ego demanded that a man could never have broken his union with Patti)—and then got it accepted by *True Magazine*. It was something neither he nor Ruth appreciated very much, or even were willing to understand, unless it was to cash in on his personal misery à la Strindberg, but on second thought they couldn't blame him too much for doing everything in his power to exploit his reputation with as much productive output as quickly as possible to become reasonably well-known in all strata of America's literary circles.

"Come again?" The operator was addressing Harry now. "Oh, I see—no answer. You sure the line's all right? No, don't bother, operator. I'll try again later . . . Yeah, thanks for the area code."

"Not in?" Martin asked.

"Out with some woman, I suppose," Harry took a guess, returning the receiver to the phone's cradle. "But then he always comes in late." He rose from the sofa and massaged the nape of his neck with a measure of roughness. He was stiff and tired from the evening's experiences. "Haven't been up there in quite some time. Just as well to get rid of this property now. With all those damn taxes, it's just not worth it. The biggest drain on my savings, anyhow. And keeping that lot in good shape and . . ."

"So long as he's willing to pay you cash for equity—before Monday at five."

"That's why I'm counting on Ed. If anyone can do it, he's the one."

Like iron-shavings, Harry was drawn once again to the magnet of the ransom demand and he glared at it without even absorbing the meaning of the words any more. Martin watched from his chair, wondering how he would have reacted if he had been in Harry's shoes. There was little else he could do tonight to assist his chum. He got up, and, hunching his shoulders, stuffed both hands into his pockets and shuffled off in the direction of the foyer.

"By the way, Harry," he spoke in an off-hand manner, "when you went to get the newspaper, did you tell Miss Lipsolm about the kidnapping?"

"What?" Harry appeared startled. He straightened up, but still seemed riveted to the extortion note. "Oh, no, she fell asleep while I was looking for the story and I didn't have the heart to wake her again. She doesn't know anything about it."

"I see." Martin negotiated the three steps leading into the foyer. "You know, Harry, something strikes me as sort of odd, though."

At last Harry took his eyes off the note and confronted his friend. "What's that?" he inquired.

"Well," Martin said and turned to face Harry from the elevated level of the entrance hall. "You going all out for it. I mean putting everything on the block—selling the house—maybe you can even swing it by Monday without the bank's appraiser—and getting rid of your car, liquidating stocks and bonds, closing out savings and checking accounts. Phhht!—the whole works. Declaring bankruptcy. In other words, wiped out."

"What the hell d'you expect me to do? Desert her?" Harry's voice again slid up a couple of decibels. "She's my wife, isn't she?"

"Check! And under normal circumstances this is exactly the way I'd expect you to behave. Noble. Unselfish."

"Well?"

Martin headed toward the front door and then once more turned to Harry.

"Well, you did tell me you no longer love her," he explained. "That you want to get hitched to that dame next door. Also, that you feel Ruth isn't likely to release you. What I don't understand is why you're trying so damned hard when this thing," he pointed to the ransom note, "this scrap of paper should solve most of your problems and remove all obstacles . . . to your getting married to . . ."

Harry stood there by the roll-top desk, slack-jawed and bug-eyed, staring in utter amazement at the man from the fourth floor.

Martin opened the door and a draft of cool air blew into the

90

apartment. From somewhere in the building came the distant celebrating of merrymakers howling with laughter, over the sounds of Elton John's recording of *The Bitch Is Back*. "Sorry, kiddo," Martin was grinning at his pal, "but that's something even *Modern Romances* isn't likely to turn down. Nor Hitchcock, for that matter, if he ever got wind of it."

With this parting shot, Martin winked and made his exit, slamming the door shut behind him. Harry glowered at the closed door, blinking, stupefied, feeling the pulse throbbing in his throat.

13 ━━━━━━━

Deep in the darkest gorge of
his subconscious, Harry was vaguely aware of a growing sensation of
impending disaster, that today something important, something
terrible was about to happen to him. Lying face-down on the sofa in
the living room, in his rumpled pants and shirt, he only remembered
the night as a kaleidoscope of fear, nightmares, voices, doubts. In
between dreams he had flipped on his Panasonic transistor in the alien
dark of the living room to make contact with the real world of
bombastic, boisterous, bankrupt, forever alive New York. Outside on
Riverside Drive only an occasional automobile could be heard hissing
through puddles left behind by the late afternoon's flash floods, or a
patrol car wailing in the distance. Then came the familiar sound of static
on his transistor radio and the combative voice of the acerbic Long
John Nebel alternating with that of the pacifying Candy Jones on
WMCA arguing with a priest and a rabbi about the existence of God,
and following this—ungodly silence again.

Sneaking in between restless sleep, dark floating memories, swirling
Van Gogh-like headlights on the ceiling, and goddamn endless mind-
killing commercials, were incomplete erotic thoughts of Helga. He had
a mad, insensate craving for her, her milky-white body—part of his

male climacteric perhaps—so that this lust *could* possibly be ascribed to being the last flicker of physical love. Had he, indeed, ever really conquered a woman in his life, he wondered, or was it woman's nature to swallow men up inside *their* bodies? He no longer knew.

Lying on the couch, gazing up at the invisible ceiling now, his thoughts turned to the woman again to whom he had been married for twenty long years. Once during the night, around one-thirty when Long John started taking phone calls from listeners, he imagined he could see her through a wash of blood, flitting by in her transparent white nightgown carrying a glass of water, as she did every night before retiring so that if Harry woke during the night he could take a sip before turning over on his other side and falling asleep again. But, of course, it was just a figment of his imagination, a cloud of wishful thinking, and in the dark he began wondering if at this very moment she too was thinking of him. An instant later, he was dwelling on what might be happening to her this gloom-laden night, where she could possibly be, how frightened she was and how it might affect her heart. He dared not linger too long over such harrowing questions, fearing the destructive outcome of such speculations. Perhaps Ives would fill him in on all of this in the morning, provided he had sobered up sufficiently. But, no, on second thought, it might be wiser not to delve too deeply into the soft core of suffering.

The night continued to turn into a jigsaw puzzle, with pieces missing, an incomplete picture of fear and memories, the terror of the weekend ahead and stray odds and ends of a politely profuse Barry Farber on WOR and a midnight snatch first of Casper Citron, then of Barry Gray, tough and debonair over the air. Like voices from another world they intruded a thousand times upon the startled and fitful bits of sleep into which he lapsed. But each time he woke, bathed in a cold sweat, he shot straight up on the sofa, only to be ingested anew into the black stillness of the living room. Just like the night before the Regents exams. And again he flicked on the transistor, frantically turning the dial in a babel of voices burbling over the waves now à la Harry Hennessy, Herb Norman and Steve Flanders, hoping to drown out with them his memories, his fears, and forget . . . forget . . . erase the past, all personal history, just the way Castaneda's Don Juan advised . . .

14 ⸻

Through the misty curtain of slumber drilled the sharp metallic sound . . . a buzz . . . a circular saw . . . inside his head . . . another buzz . . . and another . . . Harry's sticky eyes slowly unglued themselves and focussed on the creamy white ceiling. Dappled coins of sunlight flecked the walls. Somewhere an automobile horn was honking impatiently, and somebody shouted, "Dope!" Another voice on the street responded with a belligerent, "Jerk!" Motors were set into full gear again, going their own separate ways. And then again the harsh buzz. The front door!

At once, Harry sat bolt upright. Everything swam inside his head. Saturday! Ives! All the horror of the last twelve hours and the imminent weekend ahead drowned him under a crashing surf, a black breaking roller. What time was it? He stood up, his legs unsteady, and swayed. A new wave of blackness overcame him, and as he squeezed his eyes shut, red droplets of rain poured down behind his eyeballs. Shakily he held onto the armrest of the sofa and rubbed his temples, his eyes. His shirt was clinging to his ribs. This time the stormy ringing of the bell lasted. And lasted. And hung in the air, like tolling churchbells. He glanced at his watch but couldn't make out the time. Groggy with sleep still, he staggered into the foyer and leaned his sweaty forehead heavily against the cool steel of the front door.

"All right, all right, all right," he muttered, but his voice was hoarse, his mouth rancid and pasty, and he cleared his throat and shook his head in an attempt to sort out his thoughts. With trembling hands he undid the chain and opened the door. The cool blast of air that met him from the hallway felt like a cold shower. And behind this shower he saw a man, perhaps in his late fifties. A red carnation stuck in the buttonhole of the lapel of a rumpled dark suit much too large for him, exposing a dirty white shirt without a tie. The man looked as if he had forgotten to shave for days.

Harry blinked at him. "Yeah?"

"Mr. Bensonny?" asked the little man.

"You must be . . ." Harry had forgotten the stranger's name although just a few seconds earlier he had literally given cursive shape to it in his mind.

"Ives. Donald Ives," the little man helped him out, glancing over Harry's shoulder into the dimly lit interior. "You called me last night and asked me to . . ."

"That's right. Come on in!" Harry moved aside to let Ives pass, and then shut the door. "You must excuse me, the appearance of the room. I've been up most of the night, and only fell asleep a few hours ago."

This apology did not quite jibe with the facts, but Harry wasn't thinking clearly. He ushered Ives into the living room.

"I understand, Mr. Bensonny," Ives said, stopping uncomfortably in the middle of the room, not knowing whether to sit down or wait for Harry's questions. "After all, I went through it myself. Not long ago."

"Look, Mr. Ives, why don't you sit down and let me get you some coffee." Harry went over to the window and drew the drapes apart. The harsh sunlight hit him full in the face, like a hot incandescence. "Ouch!"

"That's nice of you, sir, but don't bother. I already had my breakfast."

Harry turned and saw Ives sitting stiffly on the edge of the couch where he had thrown *The New York Times*. The little man was almost sitting on top of his murdered wife. "What time is it, anyway?"

Ives smiled an unctuously nicotine-toothy smile. "You said I should come before noon, so I took the liberty of getting here at eleven."

"Eleven, huh? Well, make yourself at home while I heat up some water."

"Go right ahead."

Harry was more sure of himself now, his steps steadier. He felt more awake, determined, as he disappeared into the kitchen. He was hardly out of sight, however, when Ives made a fast grab for something inside the breast pocket of his jacket. He came up with a pint flask of Four Roses and nervously unscrewed the top. In the kitchen, water was running into a kettle. Two, three, four greedy swallows scorched Ives' throat, but immediately on hearing the water stop running, he swept his sleeve over his lips to dry them and conceal any telltale evidence. He was just about to screw the bottle up tight when Harry emerged from the kitchen and stopped in the doorway. He hesitated a moment, then approached Ives warily. "Now see here, Mr. Ives, I can appreciate the terrible ordeal you must have gone through, but do you mind very much . . . I mean, wait till I . . . well, till I have all the pertinent information?"

Ives blinked uneasily at his host, his shaking hand still fussing with the flask top. "I . . . I'm sorry Mr. . . . Mr. . . . what was your first name again?"

"Harry."

"You call me Don, Harry, will you? After all, we seem to be in the same boat." He grinned sheepishly, raised the whiskey flask in a mock toast and replaced it inside his jacket. "Would you believe I virtually never touched a drop before Lilly copped it? But . . ."

"Lilly?"

"My wife." Suddenly, without warning, he leaned forward and dug both fists into his eyes. "I can't get over it . . . over her . . ."

Harry was stunned over this sudden display of emotionalism. He felt embarrassed, and not knowing quite what to do, placed a hand softly on the man's shoulder. "Christ, don't I know just how you must feel!"

Ives whipped up his head. "Do you?" he snapped. "Do you really? *Your* wife is still alive. Mine's gone. Dead and *beyond* recall."

"What makes you so sure, Mr. . . . Don?" Harry asked, removing his hand. "For all I know he may have killed Ruth an hour after leaving the ransom demand."

Ives shook his head. "Not this guy," he said grimly. "You don't know him. This son of a bitch is smart. He means business. Money business. By the way, where's the message you got?"

"Over there. In the typewriter," he said, watching Ives get up and walk unsteadily to the roll-top desk. "But don't touch it. You know, fingerprints."

In the kitchen the kettle began whistling. Harry rushed back, past

Ives, heading for the stove to turn off the gas and pour himself a cup of Decaf. When he returned with the cup to the living room Ives was just straightening up from the typewriter. "Money, money, money," he said disgustedly. "Oh, that reminds me—I spent six-seventy on the cab fare. Plus tips. You promised to . . ."

"Sure, sure, no sweat!" Harry got out his wallet and handed Ives a ten and a five. "Here. For the round trip."

"Thanks." Ives pocketed the bills and motioned with his head to the ransom letter. "Except for this warning about May, almost word for word the same as mine. Only that he asked me for five thousand more." He shook his head, like someone not even believing his own words. "And wouldn't you know it, I just managed to make it, too."

"Come on, let's sit down." As they took their seats, Harry turned to Ives. "You mean you had the full amount ready?"

"The whole loot—in small denominations, unmarked, non-sequential. Just as he asked. Twenty-four hours before the deadline."

"Then, what went wrong?"

Ives shrugged. "I could have sworn nothing. I still had my car, didn't have to sell that. Although I don't have it now. Got rid of it."

"Again, what went wrong?"

"Well, it could only have been that last day. I drove out real early-like, hardly a car on the road except for some incoming traffic. Went all the way out of town . . ."

"You realize, of course, he might have tailed you."

"Not a chance of it," Ives said. "There was no traffic I'm telling you. Not one car for miles and miles once I hit the highway, except for a few milk trucks, some rigs and trailers heading for the city. But there was no one following me, if that's what you mean. I can swear to that."

Harry leaned forward, resting his elbows on his knees. "Where were you heading?"

"An old pal of mine, Tom, a retired cop." Harry uttered a low whistle. "I told you there was no one following me. I didn't spot *any*body. Besides, how did the kidnapper know, even if I *was* shadowed, that I wasn't trying to raise more dough to meet his demand? I'd used the car all day before, to get hold of the money, and nothing happened."

"What did you see him for, anyway—the cop?"

"To find out if I did right. I mean by not contacting the police. But Tom couldn't tell me much more than I know now. He insisted I should call the cops in. He asked me if I minded if *he* volunteered all the information to the police and let them handle it from there, without *my* getting in touch with them. But I was too scared. I told him I had the money all ready and was prepared to go through with the deal as is. I was real confused, didn't want to upset the apple cart. But that was all, and then I left."

"And Tom didn't contact the police after all? Behind your back I mean?" Harry asked, watching with some concern as Ives took the bottle once more from his breast pocket and knocked down a few gulps.

"Nosiree." He wiped his lips with the back of his hand. "I found that out later. They had no idea about the whole mess. Anyway, I got home again, making sure all the while I wasn't being tailed. And I waited. A few hours later the phone rang. Five o'clock, same as in your note." He set the flask to his lips for the third time and took two big gurgling slugs.

"Do you really have to?" Harry made a half-hearted attempt with one hand to dissuade him from drinking, to prevent another debacle like the incoherent conversation on the phone the night before, but Ives pretended not to notice.

"There was a voice... Harry, that goddamn voice, so cool, so calm, no Southern, no Northern inflection, just like a radio newscaster. And the voice said: 'Mr. Ives, you can reconvert your cash into stocks and bonds. You saw the cops and you may pick up your wife on Hempstead Turnpike and Franklin Avenue.' And then he hung up."

Tears suddenly brimmed in the little man's eyes and he stared at his shabby shoes and dirty peppermint-striped lisle socks, shaking his head. Harry didn't know how to react. What could anybody say, or do, in a situation like this? What would Emily Post or Amy Vanderbilt have prescribed? To cover his own nervousness, Harry lit a cigarette and waited for Ives to calm down. But the disconsolate widower took another nip from the bottle, wiping his mouth, as usual.

"Go easy on it, fella, you better lay off the booze," Harry ventured gently, but this time did not move. "You're not doing yourself any good and me nei . . .'' He got no further.

Ives spun toward him with unexpected pantherlike ferociousness. "Goddamn, that's the second time! Why doncha mind your own cursed business?" he shouted. "And keep your dirty hands off me! You asked me for a favor—to come as a guest—so don't you treat me like I was some godforsaken bum . . . but with reshp . . . with respect!"

The words lay thick and ugly in the sun-dappled room. Harry stared back at him, unprepared for this new unprovoked outburst. It was all so weird, so incongruous: the bereaved drunkard with his galvanic rage and frustration, the ransom note, the portents of misfortune in the air, instead of the usual Saturday morning, Harry and Ruth having a late, leisurely brunch in their robes and talking about the activities they had planned for the weekend. How peaceful life could be, how well-ordered, calm, sunny, loving, rather than all messed up, bloody, dirty . . .

Harry sipped his coffee, looking apprehensively over the mug's brim at the thin beetle-red face of Donald Ives, at the spittle clinging like beads in the four-day growth of stubble. "Look, Mr. Ives," he said at last, forgetting that he was supposed to address the little fellow by his first name. "I didn't mean to offend you. I'm worried about my wife too. Terrified. All I . . ."

"Can't you see it, you fool?" Ives interrupted him thickly. "That it was *my* fault. *I* killed her."

"Why do you punish yourself like this? You didn't."

Ives' glazed eyes tried to focus on Harry. "If I hadn't gone to this cop, don't ya unnerstand, Lilly might still be alive."

"You can't blame yourself for that, Don," Harry reasoned, dissatisfied with the way the interview was going. Instead of trying to gain information, he was having to play Samaritan. "Listen, you're just through telling me that you were one hundred per cent certain nobody was shadowing you and couldn't possibly have known you had visited the cop . . . what was his name? Tom. And even if anybody had, that you might have been seeing him to get more money to meet the ransom. For all you know, he may have been a madman and never intended to return her alive."

"Then why bother phoning me?" Ives challenged Harry, and defiantly took another swig from the flask. This time he did not even bother to wipe the dribble of whiskey from his chin as it weaved its brownish stain through the gray stubble. The drink had ceased to fortify him. "He *must* have known about my visit, even why. I *had* gone to the police, a retired cop. An hour or two after I got home he gives me to understand in no uncertain terms that I double-crossed him. If he were a plain killer there would have been no need to check on my moves. He could have picked up the ransom without ever trying to get in touch with me." He banged a fist on his knees. "But he kept *his* end of the bargain," Ives cried out. "He was no longer interested in the money, even told me to reconvert the cash into stocks." He shook his head fiercely. "No, pal, it was *my* fault all right."

The words came out with difficulty. Even though the substance of his message was relatively clear, his tongue seemed leaden and gummed to the roof of his mouth. In the short time he had been in Harry's home he had downed more than half the bottle.

Harry glared at him, hard, no longer reprovingly, but attempting to extricate as much of a clue as he possibly could from his guest's blurred memories. "Look, Don," he said finally. "If no one knew about you and that cop . . . except for the cop . . . isn't there just a million-to-one chance that it was the cop . . . Tom, that it was Tom who engineered the kidnapping? As an old pal of yours he might have known your financial set-up. If he knew your wife, he could have wangled his way into your apartment without a struggle, and then got her on some carefully thought-up pretext into his car and out to the country where he lives. Or somewhere else."

Ives was sweating profusely now. His red carnation had dropped out of his buttonhole and fallen on the carpet. He picked it up with a quivering hand and sniffed at it. "Nothing doing," he said. "Mind you, I toyed with this thought longer than I care to remember. But there was no motive, money-wise. Tom's wife is quite wealthy; they have a beautiful house, and they even went so far as to offer me money to pay the ransom. Besides, even if he had been responsible for kidnapping Lilly, he couldn't be involved in any way in taking *your* wife as a hostage."

"Why not?"

"A month after I saw him he died of a heart attack, that's why not."

Harry jackknifed bolt upright. Of course, it was just a hunch he had had. But somehow he had hoped as he was playing Sherlock Holmes that he was well on the road to solving the whole case where the mighty FBI and New York Police Department had failed five months earlier. And now the little mound of hopes he had built up so laboriously crumbled, collapsed with a sickening thud. He stared through his tired bloodshot eyes at Ives who was at his bottle again.

"Okay, how about this?" Harry pursued his desperate trail of amateurish detective deductions. "The kidnapper *didn't* know you had seen the retired cop or any cop for that matter, but was almost sure you would, sooner or later. A few hours before the deadline he let you know that he was wise to your tricks. A kind of bluff, mind you, nothing more. Maybe not so much as punishment for you, as a warning to his next victim—me. He actually does say in my ransom note: See what happened to the May kidnapping, to Ives, by all means go and check with him. Ives played footsie with the police and his wife paid for it. Now you, Harry Bensonny, you try to be a smart cookie, you better shape up and do as you're told. Seeing what happened to Lilly Ives, you don't want the same fate to befall your wife, do you? So you be a good boy now and play ball with me! Get the dough, don't contact the cops and your wife will be returned to you, alive and unharmed."

The two men glowered at each other in silence, each with his own bitter thoughts. Just as Ives started taking a couple more deep drafts, Harry addressed him hesitantly, "Listen, as one man to another, apart from . . . well, the killing . . . I mean was she . . . otherwise molested, your wife?"

Ives lowered the bottle as his eyes burned holes into Harry's face. "Sexually?" he asked hoarsely.

"Yes."

He made a half-hearted attempt at screwing the cap on the whiskey flask. "No," he said, and suddenly rivulets of tears began to course down his gaunt stubbly cheeks. "Autopsy brought that out all right. But . . ." He stopped and wiped his damp face with the ball of his thumb. "But if he had just raped and then killed her with a gun . . . it's a thing you read about every day in the papers and don't even blink at anymore. However . . ." He could not go on and simply peered at the carnation in his hand as the tears trickled down, unchecked.

"You don't have to tell me, Don," Harry said quietly, feeling he had stepped out of line. "I can look it up in the papers."

Ives jerked up his head. "You can keep your fucking papers," he shot back, but the drink had blunted the edge of anger in his voice and the words came out in a blurred tumble not at all consistent with the gravity of the message he tried to impart. "The cops wouldn't let the papers know about his sadism. They kept the details on file so they could trip him up if they should ever catch someone who made a remark about the method used in the murder only he could possibly be privy to and which might give him away as the killer. And they didn't want to frighten the public. You ever hear anything so stupid? Frighten the dumb-ass people who thrive on violence? I was mad as hell for their interfering with my right to speak out, for what he did to my Lilly. Freedom of speech and all this bullshit! But no, these bastards wouldn't let me. Yet what difference would it have made, anyhow? Lilly was gone." Harry noticed that Ives had suddenly crushed the red carnation in his fist. "He slashed off her breasts," Ives continued tonelessly, and Harry saw Ruth standing in front of him, naked, the blood flowing down her body, thick red streams of blood. "God knows what he did with them. Maybe Krafft-Ebing or Havelock Ellis could have told us. They found her body stark naked, in a ditch, where he told me it would be, on Franklin Avenue. He had slit her throat and rammed a fork up her vagina, so far up you could hardly see the handle. And then he . . ."

"For God's sake, that's enough!" Harry jumped up and wheeled in a blind rage from the little man to the typewriter, not seeing it, not seeing anything except Ruth with her throat slit, the throat he had kissed a thousand times, with her breasts sliced off. Where had he heard of such senseless savagery before? Just recently. Yesterday . . . that was it! Last night, when Helga told him about the insensate bestiality of the SS guards as they went berserk and ripped open the wombs of the Jewish camp prostitutes the day before Belsen was liberated. So the SS ran amuck in this country too, without the benefit of a black uniform.

Harry had closed his eyes, seeing behind the private veil of his innermost fears the bloody, mangled, hacked, lacerated corpse of his wife, with a scavenger army of sadistic punks carving their initials into her soft white flesh, ramming ground glass down her gullet, lighted cigars into her eyeballs, and he opened his eyes again to let the sun-lit present swiftly splash reality inside his tormented brain and eradicate the horror of his grotesque vision. He bolted into the kitchen and put a heaping teaspoon of Decaf into his cup, then filled it with the remnants of the water in the kettle.

As he emerged from the kitchen, drinking deeply from the lukewarm black brew, he saw Ives still gazing at the crushed flower in his open palm, tears hanging from his chin.

"I'm sure, now, the killer meant to have your wife serve as an example for the next victim . . . or victims." Harry stopped in front of Ives who finally looked up from the carnation. "I'm perfectly aware the same thing can happen to Ruth . . . my wife. What's he got to lose? Nobody knows where he is, who he is. Maybe she's already dead. As dead as Lilly. I've no doubt now that he must have killed Lilly at once. Could he really have mutilated her like this in the short time it took him to call you after you came back from Tom? *And* have already thrown her in the ditch? Never! He had killed her long before you went to see Tom, or while you were there, and therefore he couldn't have known where you went. That message he gave you, that you had seen the cops, was just a bluff and that's why you can't blame yourself for Lilly's death. But he *had* to kill her as a warning for all his future victims. Don, look at me! This lunatic never had the slightest intention of returning her alive from the outset. It was the only way to make sure his next crime would be foolproof. And Ruth *is* the next crime."

In spite of the grim nature and the ominous portents his analysis entailed, Harry felt uncommonly pleased with the way he had delved into the innermost recesses of the criminal mind. Yet to his amazement Ives merely regarded him stonily, as if doubting his sanity. For a while he didn't say anything, and then shook his head. "God, you and your stupid crackpot theories!"

"What?" Harry felt slightly offended by Ives' uncharitable rebuff, especially when he meant well.

"You're way off track, son, that's what!"

A suspicious frown appeared on Harry's brow. "What makes you so sure?"

"Because she *was* alive. The autopsy proved that, too."

"What d'you mean alive?" Harry did not know what to think anymore.

"I got home, from Tom's, at about two or three in the afternoon," Ives said, sniffling and wiping his nose with a sleeve. "The kidnapper phoned at about five. Naturally, I panicked and called Tom to ask his pals on the force to search the area where I was supposed to find Lilly. By the time I reached the scene they had already found the body. That same night they performed the autopsy and the next day established a very strange thing." His glassy eyes fell on the bottle and he unscrewed the cap and took another swallow or two; it was almost empty. As he set the flask down on the table, long gooey dribbles of the drink trickled down his chin on his soiled suit. "They found traces of peas and carrots and other food in her stomach, stuff she must have been given to eat earlier that afternoon. Around one o'clock they guessed." Harry slumped onto the easy chair and saw the little man's face break up anew. "He meant to keep her alive, Harry," he wept. "He meant to go through with his end of the bargain. You don't feed someone lunch just to kill her two hours later when you could get thirty-five grand. No," he shook his head, raising the drink to his lips. "It was me, me who let him down . . . and her. I double-crossed him. And your cockeyed idea that she was already gone . . ."

"Now, take it easy, will you?" Harry stood up again, trying to retrieve the flask, but Ives was too fast and grabbed it, clutching it to his chest. "It was only a suggestion, Don. I'm only trying to be helpful. Come on, fella, lay off that booze, please!"

Ives rose in a drunken stupor, stepping on the dropped carnation, and hitched up his pants with his free hand. "For crissakes, will you stop telling me what to do," he yelled, pointing the bottle at Harry. "I just about got it up to my gills being told by every oddball how to behave . . . to stop this or stop that . . . like I was some clod with a beanie and a propeller on top . . . I . . ."

"Aw, for crying out loud!" Harry was exasperated himself now. "Why the hell d'you think I asked you over? To listen to your moanings and groanings over Lilly? Shit! You don't solve anything that way, like the sot you've become drinking yourself into a . . ."

"Damn you! Damn you! Damn! Damn! Damn!" Ives shrieked and suddenly raised his arm. The next second the bottle came hurling across the room. Harry ducked just in time, and it smashed into the kitchen door, falling with a loud clatter on the floor. "What do *you* know about losing the only person in the world that ever meant anything to you?" he raved. "You cruddy bastard, your wife will catch it, so help me God she will. She'll end up the way Lilly got carved up, her breasts . . ."

Harry's flat palm exploded on the little man's face. The smack resounded sharply between the walls, and the savage flow of words was cut off like a torn soundtrack. Ives toppled backward, onto the sofa, too unsteady even to sit up straight. He landed sideways on his elbow and peered up at Harry through a pair of glazed eyes. "You bastard!" he snarled. "Hitting a defenseless old man," and the very next second turned from him, burying his face in a cushion, seized by a sudden paroxysm of sobs. His shoulders shook uncontrollably, heaving up and down with the rhythm of the muffled sobs, and Harry stood over him, watching helplessly, unable to explain why he had hit the little guy who was drunk and tormented beyond redemption. Harry knew he was within his rights to flare up, but violence at this stage—goddamn! It sure as hell didn't help his case any, and it definitely wasn't Ives' fault that he was so cantankerous, so desperate. Harry realized he still held the cup in his left hand and that part of the coffee had spilled on his shoes during the outburst. He bent down to wipe the stain away and on straightening up noted that Ives was trying to steady himself again, propping himself against the row of pillows on the sofa and breathing heavily.

"I . . . oh, God, how I curse this putrid world! You don't know how jealous I am of everything . . . that's alive," he muttered at length. "Even your wife."

Harry was glad that the slap in the face seemed to have sobered him up a bit. "Look, Don, I understand how you must feel," he said. "But you're alive, too. You can't go on . . ."

"And I hate myself for it," Ives growled through clenched teeth. "I hate the world, everything."

"And you think hating life will bring her back from the dead?"

For a moment Ives didn't say anything. In the silence they both listened to the pervasive wail and hoot of an ambulance racing down Riverside Drive. "Lucky stiff," he remarked at last. "Even the guy in that meat-wagon is still alive." He made an effort to compose himself. "Tell me, Harry, honestly. You really want her back, don't you, your Ruth?"

"What do *you* think? After all, she's my wife."

Ives uttered a brief sardonic laugh. "Just as I thought," he observed fuzzily but in command of his tongue. He rose with difficulty and stumbled blindly to the other end of the sofa where he collapsed on a heap of cushions. "And exactly what I said to Tom when he asked me the same question. And you know what Tom answered? 'Donald, do you realize you said, after all, she's my wife? You did not say, after all, I love her. Which is a hell of a difference.' And you, too, Harry. You didn't say, after all, I love her. Because you really don't anymore, do you? Who knows—you may even have a woman on the side. Right?"

Harry did not reply, just kept staring at the onerous, emaciated drunk. "Isn't that right, Harry?"

Harry turned from Ives and let himself drop heavily into the armchair. Finally the words came out, but they seemed to be spoken by someone else, a stranger within. "Do you have to still be in love with a person to want her back alive?" he asked, addressing himself as much as Ives. "Don, we don't have to pretend to each other. You had probably been married longer than I have. But even after twenty years you're no longer on your honeymoon. She was . . . she is my wife, and I've taken her for granted, I guess. She was there, and through her I could prove to myself and to the world what a great guy I was. And if in my eyes marriage isn't what it was twenty years ago, that doesn't mean she has no right to live. God knows why I'm telling you, a stranger, all this," he shrugged. "But the truth is time just nibbled away on our love. We simply didn't have to put on an act anymore, the circus of smiles and kisses and blond healthy children frolicking on the lawn the way you see it on vitamin commercials. God knows—hell, I'm just repeating myself, what difference does it make anyway, if our marriage had turned sour? But, Christ! I don't want to feel later that I should have loved her more, in case anything happens to her. Because I *know* she deserved more love. Maybe most wives do. At least that's why *my* wife must come back . . . why I . . ."

But Harry did not get a chance to finish his thoughts. He had gotten up and was pacing up and down in front of the couch on which Ives listened to him, barely awake, droopy-eyed. And then, while his back was turned, he suddenly heard a dull thud and whirled around. The poor little dipsomaniac had pitched forward, hit the corner of the cocktail table with his forehead and was in the process of keeling over, sliding down in slow motion, like a seagull landing, onto the carpet, one arm still half-propped over the edge of the table. The alcohol had knocked him for a loop. Blotto. Ives seemed irretrievably gone.

Harry rushed around the table and bent down, shaking him by the shoulder. The unhappy creature lay face-down on the rug, still as a log, and Harry turned him over on his back and slapped his cheeks the way he had seen it done dozens of times in the movies and on TV, but Ives remained dead to the world. No response. Harry leaned over the drunk's mouth and listened to his breathing. It was deep, regular, redolent of whiskey, a fast unbreakable alcoholic sleep, into which no doubt Ives wanted to escape. To forget. Like Helga the night before.

Harry stood up again and regarded him uncertainly, then knelt once more and gingerly opened the top button of his filthy shirt and rummaged through his pockets hoping to find out exactly where he lived, but all he ferreted out were a dirty handkerchief, some keys, the money he had given him earlier and some loose change.

Harry squatted beside the unconscious alcoholic, scrutinizing him thoughtfully for a minute or two, then made up his mind about his next move. He got up and headed for the phone and dialed a number. For once he had to wait only a few seconds for the party to answer.

"Marty? Okay, okay. Come down for a minute, will you? Yeah, there *are* new developments; just come on down and you'll see for yourself. No, I can't tell you over the phone. Okay."

He hung up and went to the bathroom to tidy up a bit. When he returned to the living room his first move was to pick up the May *New York Times* and the coffee cup he had left on the cocktail table; he intended to wash the mug before Martin's arrival and was about to enter the kitchen when his foot struck an object: the cracked whiskey bottle in the doorway. He lifted it carefully with the tips of two fingers as if in fear of being contaminated by its touch, emptied the few remaining drops down the sink and threw the flask into the garbage pail. Next, he wiped up the puddle of whiskey that had spilled, and then shoved the newspaper into a kitchen cabinet.

The growl in the pit of his stomach reminded Harry that he had had nothing to eat all morning and he took a loaf of Levy's rye bread out of the refrigerator, stuffing half a slice greedily into his mouth. Just before closing the refrigerator, he caught sight of a Saran-wrapped head of lettuce in the bottom glass drawer. Hastily, he peeled off one leaf and returned with it to the living room where he stuck it between the bars of the cage that housed the two parakeets. He threw the old leaf away and returned with some fresh water for them. The whole room smelled of Ives, or more precisely of alcohol, so Harry opened one of the windows a trifle more, and instantly felt the invigorating warmth of the October sun pervade the living room and settle on his face. He took a deep breath of the fresh autumnal air, as if to rid himself of the alcoholic fumes clinging to him, like quantum packages of liquor-sodden clouds. A creepy feeling really, to be alone with a strange, unconscious man stretched out on the floor of your apartment, he brooded as he chewed on his bread and strolled back to the sofa, letting himself down exhaustedly into its cushiony softness. What in God's name was he to do with this odd creature? When he didn't even know where to deposit him . . . and had so much to do today. Hell!

Ives lay a few feet from him, out to the world. Not until now was Harry aware that the drunk's zipper wasn't pulled up all the way. Whatever calamity or stroke of good fortune overtook this world, it probably did not matter one whit to Ives anymore. His whole life seemed to be encapsulated in a cumulus of self-hatred, self-accusation, guilt. It became clear to Harry that life was destined to pass this unfortunate soul by until he had drunk himself to death, or ended up under the wheels of a bus, maybe, or in a Bellevue ward for the alcoholically insane, forgotten, unknown, a non-person in life as in death.

But then life really had always passed by most of Harry's friends, too. Except for Vietnam, the status quo still reigned supreme in people's hearts. Everybody was too much immersed in their own private Spenglerian and Jungian tragedies to be actively involved in the great social upheavals that shook the world. Love, illness, money, death, unemployment, business pressures, job frustrations, family troubles, depressions—these always stood in the foreground. While in the background were riots and demonstrations, wars of liberation, famines, assassinations, racial and civil rights' battles, revolutions and counter-culture gods and goddesses—all merely wedged in audio-visually between Bill Buckley and Archie Bunker, making, marginally, good party talk, or scabrous bilge if a conversation became too heated. For example, when friends came over and Ruth argued with some haughtiness on where Kennedy or LBJ or Nixon or Ford had gone wrong and how she would have decided things differently as a Liberated Candidate if she had been in the White House playing Indira Gandhi and doing what Nixon might have wanted to do but didn't get a chance to. Harry sensed it wasn't very much different in most households throughout the land where people also read the *Times* and the *New York Review of Books* and for the most part discussed politics, movies, books, plays, spicy office gossip, unions, mortgages, inflation, overpopulation, recession, drugs, alcoholism, sex, the raising of children, the Mafia, multinational corporations, and so on. They grumbled about the disastrous failures of courts and jails while surrounded by their Bauhaus or Bloomingdale décor. Nothing seemed to have changed much since the Fifties, except that some of the fashions and the songs were uglier and the kids making life hell for the people in the subways and on the streets were wilder, more vicious. Harry recalled how he used to tease Ruth whenever she . . .

15 ———

The sound of the doorbell slashed into Harry's stream of recollections. He jumped up, almost tripped over Ives' body, and hastened to answer the front door.

Martin crinkled his nose even before Harry had closed the door. "Whew! Did you have a party or . . ." Then he noticed the motionless body on the floor. "Holy cow! What the hell . . .? Who's that?"

"Ives. The guy I phoned last night. Just passed out on me. Drunk."

Martin and Harry stopped in front of the prostrate body. "He arrive in this state?" Martin asked.

"Uh huh," Harry nodded. "Guess he kinda hit the sauce before he got here, but then he kept on swilling the stuff while telling me about his wife. He blames himself for her death."

"Oh?" Martin massaged his chin pensively. He was the only one in the apartment who had shaved this morning and he wore a pair of gray flannels and a clean, cobalt-blue shirt, his favorite "typing-outfit" as he called it. "Why not put him in a cab and . . . Or, listen, how about me driving him home?"

"I still don't know where the guy lives. He doesn't carry anything on him that would tell me. I just went through his pockets."

"Jeez, really tied one on, didn't he?" Martin glanced around the room, deep in thought, then seemed to make up his mind about Step Number One on the spot. "Come on, let's get him in the other room and put him on your bed till he sleeps it off." He gave Harry a mischievous wink. "Ruth and you won't be using it till next Monday, I suspect."

"Knock it off, Marty!" Harry's temper flared again. "Believe me I can do without stupid cracks today," he added testily. Martin was already lifting Ives up under his arms and Harry took the man's feet. "Anyway, after listening to this guy I feel I may never see her again. Alive. So just cut it out, will ya?"

Wordlessly, the two men carried the body through the door into Harry's bedroom and laid him across the width of the double bed.

"Some lush, this guy," Martin remarked, giving Ives a look of unconcealed distaste and revulsion. "I wouldn't take everything seriously, Harry, not in his condition at least. Anyhow, let the crumb sleep it off. Plenty of time to find him a cab when he's sobered up." They turned and left the room.

Harry shut the bedroom door, headed at once for the windows to let in more fresh air, and gazed out on the Drive. As usual, big clumps of black vinyl bags bursting with garbage lined the curb, and in the distance, further down the street, he saw a dozen or so members of the Hare Krishna cult heading for the park in their flimsy robes, much like a flock of flamingos seeking out greener pastures. The faint echolalia of miniature cymbals, bells, and the chant of young entranced men and women came through the nippy morning air into Harry's living room.

Martin relaxed in one of the easy chairs, draping his right leg over the armrest. "Did you get anything important out of him?"

"Only that the kidnapper must have gone berserk," Harry said, looking morosely out across the calm Hudson at the Palisades and finding the world in a state of disgustingly unrealistic normalcy and calm despite the black horror that was enshrouding, suffocating, his puny life. "A real maniac we have to contend with, Marty. He thought that Ives was double-crossing him and then proceeded to mutilate his wife before calling him to say where he could find her, or rather her cut-up corpse. He wasn't even interested in picking up the money by then."

Martin reacted with a low whistle. "Sorta gives you the willies. Must be a real kook we're dealing with, a sickie," he said, watching as Harry slowly turned from the window, engrossed in his own private thoughts, and walked over to the sofa. There were dark circles under his eyes and a day's growth of stubble on his face. "Looks like you had better go through with his bargain then, huh?" But Harry did not answer, still far away with his thoughts as he let himself go limp on the sofa. "You get hold of that other guy, the one about your house?"

At last Harry looked up, visibly perturbed. "My house?"

"Yeah, you know. You told me last night you were going to give that girl-crazy fellow a ring about selling your cottage in the country."

"Oh him! Hell, you're right, so I did!" Harry slammed the flat of his palm against his forehead. "I clean forgot all about him."

A second later his finger moved down a page inside his little address book, then dialed Ed Blakely, his realtor friend. Luckily, this time he was in.

"Ed? Ed, it's me, Harry. Harry Bensonny. How've you been?" He winked conspiratorially at Martin. "Long time no hear. Oh, okay I guess. No, as a matter of fact, everything is kinda loused up. Ed, the reason I'm calling is I have to talk to you. Today. No, I can't on the phone. It's too much of a snafu. It's sort of personal. That's why I thought you might . . . What's that? . . . Gee, that's great! If you're coming down in any case, you simply *must* drop by and see me. It's . . . No kidding, it *is* a matter of life or death. No, I can't I told you . . . not on the phone."

"Harry," Martin leaned forward, whispering to him urgently. "Mention you've got a broad lined up for him."

Harry stared at his friend and nodded. "Listen, Ed, I've got a special surprise for you if you come. How d'you like to meet the most luscious, sexiest, man-crazy broad this side of the Sea of Tranquillity? No, no, not in the Adirondacks, it's on the moon. Yeah, I told her a lot about you and she's all hot just to meet you. Hey, that's more like my old boy," he grinned. "Sure, I'll be home. Right, I'll tell her you're coming today . . . Oh, you dirty old man! Okay, but get here as soon as you can, right? Good. Be seeing you then. Take care."

Harry hung up and slumped back on the sofa. "Well, I'll get that sex-starved bastard fixed up," he sighed, rubbing his eyes.

"You think you really can swing it?"

"You mean with a girl?"

"That too. But I meant the thirty grand."

"Well, I figured on the stocks and bonds, that *can* be converted now, or fall due, the savings and checking accounts on Monday morning, and maybe a thousand below cost for the car. Should add up to . . . oh, I'd say about eleven or twelve thousand. That leaves nineteen thousand for the house. Now, twenty-one years ago they put it on the market for thirteen-five, so equity stands at about twenty-two thousand today, or not too much more since it's way out in the sticks, so that the difference I need, nineteen thousand, shouldn't be too much sweat for Ed."

"Provided he or a client can scrape it together by the Monday deadline," objected Martin. "Are you going to level with him about Ruth?"

Harry shrugged and gazed at his fingernails. "I don't know, it depends," he said. "If Ed gives me a lot of bull I suppose I'll have no choice." He looked up suddenly and bunched his hands. "Hell no, I can't! I just remembered, like Mickey Glumm, he's the world's biggest blabbermouth. I can't take the chance."

"And what about the date?" Martin grinned. "The lady who has the hots for Ed?"

"Oh, God. Another headache. What do you think? You know anyone around here?"

"You asking me, buddy?" Martin pointed at himself as if he would be only too grateful if Harry could fix *him* up with some nice girl.

For a few seconds Harry looked glum. Then his face lit up. "Hey, Marty, what about that babe on the third floor? In one of the apartments under yours. Miss Collington. Or . . ."

"Miss Collins? You don't mean shockingly frank Miss Collins?"

"Yeah. That's the one! Miss Collins. She's great looking, and the super told me once she could be had. For fifty bucks. What do you thi . . ."

The chilling ring of the telephone bell froze the question on his lips. The two men stared at each other. Could it be the killer? A sickening steel-heavy feeling came over Harry as he reached for the receiver.

"Hello." His voice came out dull, lifeless. "Who? Oh, Betty . . . Hi! No, I'm afraid she isn't in. . . . No, I'm sorry I don't know when . . . What's that?" A scintilla of concern registered on Harry's face as he leaned forward. "You mean yesterday? Ruth was supposed to call you at four o'clock about a bridge party next week?" He gave Martin a meaningful glance. "Gee, I'm sorry, Betty, of course she should have told you but, well, the truth is something came up sort of unexpected. You know her mother's up in Maine, and well, she's sick—they think it's a heart attack, and Ruthie thought she better go up and be by her side. Yeah, yeah, she should have had the presence of mind to call you, but I guess she just forgot all about it . . . you know, with rushing to catch the plane and packing, and all that. Sure, sure, you bet. I'll let her know that *you* didn't forget. . . . Okay. Thanks for calling. No, I won't forget. So long." He slammed the receiver into the cradle, clearly rankled. "Bitch! You remember Betty, don't you, that dinner in August—the' dame with the blue and purple tinged hair, about sixty-five with four-inch skyscraper heels, fake double-row lashes? Looks like the Eiffel Tower in drag."

Martin stretched out lazily in the armchair and yawned. "Never mind Betty now, except that we know Ruth was supposed to call her by four and didn't," he said. "Much more important is that *you* had the presence of mind to think up a pretty good excuse for what *might* have happened to Ruth. For future reference. Friends of yours know her old lady's in Maine, so it's not that far-fetched to say she went up to see her suddenly . . ." He braked himself to a stop in mid-sentence. "A funny thing, though, occurs to me, Harry. If Ruthie went out, with bags or with anyone strange, don't you think there's a chance that someone might have seen her leave? Did you ever check with the super?"

"Not so far. I can still do it, but you know as well as I do that Saypool is never around when you want him."

"But there's no harm trying . . . always a chance that he *may* have seen her," Martin insisted.

"Okay, okay, I'll check," Harry was irritated by his friend's persistence to pursue a course of action that to him seemed fruitless. "It just strikes me the kidnapper would be smarter than that. The whole thing is so perfectly timed, so meticulously planned, that I'm sure nobody saw him come or go. Even here, Marty," a grandiloquent sweep of his arms spoke volumes, "take a look for yourself. Do you see any sign of a struggle? Not a thing upset. And I can assure you the guy wiped the furniture before leaving, to remove any fingerprints. Except maybe on the ransom note. How he got in, under what pretense, I can't figure out. Normally Ruth wouldn't let anybody she didn't know into the apartment."

"Well, that shouldn't be much of a problem for somebody who's determined to get in a place, *any* place. Don't you recall the case of the Boston Strangler? The whole world knew about the danger the people in Boston were exposed to—warnings on radio, TV, in the press. People were scared stiff to open their doors to anybody; they couldn't find enough bolts and locks to barricade themselves. And the result? The maniac always found a few suckers only too willing to let him in.

And right now in this city of ours there's no special panic about some nut kidnapping women, except for that case last May. So, it shouldn't have been that hard for someone to finagle his way in here. Maybe he said he was from the gas or the telephone company, you can always hoodwink somebody to . . . "

"Oh, I don't doubt it for a moment." Harry agreed. "Getting in isn't too hard. But how in hell would he get Ruth to go out with him, perhaps into a waiting car, and drive off unnoticed, without her putting up some sort of a struggle? And all this in broad daylight. You figure that?"

Martin shrugged, a trifle vexed at being outsmarted by Harry's logic. "Jesus, how should I know? I didn't start writing at my window till around four. I never saw 'em. And anyhow, who gives a damn these days in New York about people fighting in the street? Anyway, the guy probaby cased this joint first and planned everything down to the most minute detail, even the amount of money you're capable of raising. Who knows, perhaps he attacked her when her back was turned and then chloroformed her and carried her out."

"Without anyone noticing them?" Harry gave a bitter, sarcastic laugh. "Your imagination as a writer leaves a lot to be desired, Mr. Mottello. Carry her out, over his back, between three and four in the afternoon?"

Martin narrowed his eyes. "Okay, how about this? Suppose he . . . what about him rolling her up in a carpet, after she's chloroformed, and then dumping her into the back of a delivery truck? Or a moving van?"

"You watch too many whodunits, Marty. In the first place we didn't order a carpet and she would never have let the guy in with . . ."

"All right, then he got in first under some other pretext, next chloroformed her, and when she's unconscious, gets the carpet from outside and lets himself back in through the door he left ajar."

But Harry looked dubious. "I just can't believe it worked that way. Too conspicuous."

"Don't see why it should be. Anyway, I only say it may have . . ."

A long buzz jolted the two men for the second time, but now it was at the front door. They looked at each other.

"You expecting anybody?" whispered Martin.

Harry glanced at his watch. "Only Ed, the guy about the house. But he can't be here yet. Wait!"

He got up and headed for the door just as the buzz was repeated. A brief glance through the peephole caused Harry to hunch his shoulders as if to ward off an assault awaiting him on the other side of the door. He opened it and confronted Mickey Glumm.

"Hi there, you two-timing old Romeo," the pint-sized promotion director grinned. He was dressed all in white—pants, white sneakers and a white turtleneck sweater. "What's shakin', baby? How ya doing?"

"Oh Mickey, I forgot all about you." Harry greeted him half-heartedly and with an element of unconcealed dismay that immediately turned to impatience and inhospitality. He had no desire to get involved with this clown in his present state of mind.

"Well, that's what I'm here for. To remind you. Spare a few minutes?" Mickey advanced a step but Harry made no effort to get out of his way. The deliberately unfriendly rebuff took Mickey by surprise.

"Hell, Mickey, I really wish I could spend a few minutes with you, but something unexpected came up."

"Look Harry, it'll only take ten minutes. That circular, you know, the sales coupon, the order form I talked to you about last night was a real ballbuster and I think I almost got it licked but just wanted to check on a few . . ."

"Say, Mickey, I have a great idea," Harry put on a jovial air, pretending to be full of cheer at his own suggestion. "Why don't we kick that around some time next week, when I've really got the time to spare? Right now I'm up to my neck."

But the little fellow from the top floor wouldn't take No for an answer. Suddenly his hand was on Harry's shirt, toying with one of his buttons. He swivelled around, half-circle, à la Brando, evading Harry's eyes, part oleaginously polite, part threatening. "Harry, listen, this means a great deal to me. You know I'm the last person in the world to pull rank, and I'm not now, don't misunderstand me, but Uncle expects something big to come out of yours truly, and I think this is the best thing I ever did, even if I must say so myself. A real smasheroo. I know you've got a lot on the ball and Uncle said he wanted me to come up with a real humdinger by Tuesday noon. Or else."

"Or else! What the hell would the boss do to *you*? From what I hear you're doing a pretty good job. He wouldn't fire his own nephew."

"Well, maybe not fire," Mickey dropped his hand and stood on his toes, peeking over Harry's shoulder into the apartment. It happened that the living room was deserted because Martin had slipped unnoticed into the bathroom. "No, I don't think he'd tell me to f.o., but he might push me further down the ladder, like to the warehouse, if I don't come up soon with some real bright idea."

"Mickey, don't get me wrong, I understand only too well," Harry frantically tried to weasel out of this new quandary. "There's nobody I'd like to help out more than you and you know it. But I had a pretty rough night. You see, Ruth's away, on doctor's orders, since early this morning. And then her mother's sick, with cancer . . . and a heart attack, up in Maine—that's where both of them are—and with one thing or another I'm just not up to it," he shrugged helplessly. "I wouldn't be any good to you today. I've been up most of the night myself, sick as a dog, but I promise you first thing next week, Mon . . . Tuesday, before noon, we'll go over that promo of yours and we'll . . ."

"Sure, sure, sure, I believe you," Mickey said with little conviction in his voice but an open betrayal of hurt. "You think you got a pal, but no dice. Ten lousy minutes to run through it and you nix the whole . . ."

As he spoke, Martin appeared behind Harry, wiping his wet hands on his flannels. "I think I better be going, Harry," he said. "Got to get some work done."

"Aaah, look what we got here!" Mickey exclaimed, suddenly stepping back as if disgusted by Harry's presence in the doorway, by his whole personality. "The big man felt sick as a dog all night but he found a nice companion to while the hours away with when the little woman's gone all the way to Maine, huh? And what about last night, Harry old buddy? You coming out of that broad's apartment next door, remember? Getting matches for that pilot light in the kitchen, right?"

"Look, Mickey, you got this all wrong!" Harry felt the warm flush of blood darken his cheeks. "Marty Mottello here, you know him, from the fourth floor. He wrote two books for your uncle, before you started working for him. Hell, he came down to help me this morning. You know what I mean, he got me some food from the supermarket because I felt too damn sick to go out and . . ."

"Sure, sure, don't overdo it, I believe you," Mickey interrupted, unable to repress a little sneer. "And I really love that boozy smell you got in there. That's heavy! Real expensive stuff, too. You're a real prince among men, Harry, and so is Mr. Mottello. Uncle thinks the world of him."

"Look, Mickey, as I said . . ."

"No, don't worry, old pal," he snapped, obviously irked, and retreated crablike to the elevator. "I know when I'm licked. Just let me give you one word of advice, though, for your own good. Don't ever bother to come to me, fella, when *you* need a favor. And believe me there will come the time when you wished you had . . ."

"Harry, I think you have everything now. I put all the food in the kitchen," Martin broke in, squeezing past Harry into the hall and advancing toward the elevator. He had gathered from the tone of the conversation that Mickey might spell trouble, and was more than willing to play Harry's game. "Just give me a call if you need anything else. Ciao."

"Thanks again, Marty." Harry stood irresolutely in the doorway, looking after the two men, one of whom he needed for his livelihood in the office, the other as a friend to talk to about his wife's abduction. He shut the door quietly and leaned against it, closing his eyes. He had to get things straight in his mind. All he needed now was to have Mickey go to his uncle and complain about Harry and he'd end up on skid row. He could hear the voices of the two men echo on the landing as they waited for the elevator.

"So you've been playing nursemaid to old Harry," Mickey was saying in a mocking voice.

"Well, you know how it is," Martin replied in a much lower tone.

"Sure do. When the cat is gone, the rats will play, you dig?"

"No, I do not. What's that supposed to mean?"

"Forget it. Ah, at last!" The elevator door squeaked open "Coming up?"

"Uh . . . No, you better go ahead. I still have to look for the mail. Don't bother waiting for me."

"Jerk!"

Harry heard the elevator door thump softly as it closed and the electric hum as it moved up, then Martin's footsteps passing his door in the direction of the mailboxes.

16 ──────

Harry still had to see if there was anything waiting for him in the mail that might give him some clue as to Ruth's whereabouts. He glanced at his watch. It was just after half past twelve. A feeling of hunger in the pit of his stomach tugged at him with sudden unexpectedness. The irony of it was that after that game of pretense in the entrance hall with Mickey and Martin there was precious little to eat in the house. A couple of slices of Kraft's Swiss cheese came in handy. He folded them like a letter and stuffed them into his mouth. The full container of milk must have been bought by Ruth earlier the day before. He poured himself a tall glass and took a few cuts of salami out of the plastic wrapping and a banana from the bottom drawer.

While he was eating, and hoping the salami would not disagree with his ulcer, his mind tried to cope with the inchoate time schedule he was planning for this day. But no great strategic plan emerged from his ponderings. Next to nothing could be done on weekends in terms of getting the money. This madman kidnapper would not care how he secured it as long as no one got wind of the scheme. Under no circumstances could he entrust Ed Blakely with the secret of *why* he needed the money, that much was clear. Ed Blakely! Great conniving Caesar!

Harry remembered he had promised Ed a woman. Without a chick, that touchy so-and-so Ed would never make a deal for buying the cottage right away, and getting the cash ready by Monday night. To set Ruth free, Harry suddenly realized he had to virtually deal in white traffic and pimp. But where could he get a girl at this time of day, unless it was one of those hookers advertised in the back pages of *Screw*? Even the pros in the Fifties with their postage-stamp mini-skirts and bleached, lacquered beehives didn't show up till well after five.

And then he recalled Miss Collins on the third floor. He only knew her from seeing her in the lobby and on the street; he had never exchanged small talk or pleasantries with her, only greetings. She was rather nondescript, in her mid-thirties he guessed, pretty in a harmless, almost indifferent sort of way. She made no special effort to accentuate her attractive features, although her figure was slender and well-turned.

In all the years Harry and Ruth had been living in the building no one there except the super had ever even mentioned Miss Collins to them. Until Martin today. Could he really risk it and go up to see her and confront her with this proposition? Which she could refuse point-blank, and to top it, get him into hot water. Yet if she *was* agreeable, how much would she charge? Fifty bucks? Seventy-five? For an evening? A throw? But with thirty grand going to the lunatic kidnapper, seventy-five dollars for turning a trick surely could be written off as a mere business expense. He could write her a check. Good God, no, better give her cash.

Okay, that was that. Steps had to be taken to avoid having Ruth killed like that wife of poor old Ives. Ives!

Harry had totally forgotten about Ives. He rinsed his glass, dried his hands and then took a look into the bedroom. Ives was still lying on the bed just as he and Martin had laid him out, fast asleep, breathing deeply, regularly. For half a minute Harry regarded him with a mixture of distaste and sympathy. Whatever would happen in the next few days, Harry clung with all his might to the hope that he would never have to end up like Ives, a monumental wino, his clothing maroon-streaked with vomit, dying in puddles of guilt, nightmares, and urine, every minute of his life. All he could do was to try his best and leave the rest up to fate.

He left the bedroom quietly, closing the door behind him. The way things looked at present, Donald Ives could be assumed to be out to the world for at least two more hours. For the time being Harry didn't have to worry about him and for his next step beat a path to the roll-top desk where he found his checkbook in the top lefthand drawer. He might need it for Miss Collins. As he closed the tiny drawer his eyes fell for what seemed to be the thousandth time on the ransom note. It was a well-phrased warning all right, each word selected for maximum effect, cool, succinct, hitting the message home, with no superfluous nonsense to it: the professional abductor's touch. He must have shadowed Harry and Ruth for a long time to be so damn sure of everything, including the amount Harry could clear. Ives could just make it with his savings and Harry knew so could he. Or at least so he hoped, if everything worked according to plan, especially about selling the house. And if worst came to worst, maybe Ruth's mother could be called upon to come up with the balance. After all, Ruth was her daughter; the two were uncommonly close and there would be no sacrifice too big to prevent her from doing everything financially possible to save her daughter's life. There was even an off-chance, Harry figured, that the kidnapper had her mother in mind too in case somewhere along the line Harry couldn't swing it on his own.

Of course, approaching Mrs. Kirk at this early stage of the game might be premature. Then, suddenly, unreasonably, Harry felt like talking to her. Why, he didn't know. True enough, he had always liked the crusty old dame. But that wasn't it. Symbolically, of course, she was part of an extension of Ruth, part of her own flesh and blood, and he felt that if he could hear Mrs. Kirk's voice, it somehow, possibly, might conjure up in his mind the certitude that Ruth was still alive. The problem was what sort of pretext could he invent for calling the old lady at this unearthly hour—unearthly not so much in the sense of early as of being unusual—because neither Ruth nor he ever really had any reason for calling her, except on holidays. Besides, with few phones on the island, Mrs. Kirk had to walk to the general store down the road to speak to her daughter and there was little reason to put her to that trouble except when necessary, like the time Ruth came down with her heart ailment, for instance, and Harry had to call her up, or for any other emergency and . . .

Emergency! That was it! How stupid of him to forget! During the night and before he went to sleep, Harry had listened to the radio and heard several news bulletins on WINS and WCBS about the hurricane brewing up near the Maine coast. He could inquire how she was doing, whether she needed any help. Besides, calling her could be used as a softening up process about how much he was concerned over her welfare and make it that much easier later to . . . although, on second thought, this was not really necessary and any effort at buttering her up could be dismissed at the outset. In case the old lady asked for Ruth, Harry could always say that her daughter was out shopping, or at the doctor's for her Pap test.

He looked up the grocery's phone number and dialed the Monhegan area code and then the private number. After two or three rings, an operator asked what number Harry was dialing. When he had read it off to her from the little black address book the operator explained that she was very sorry that the lines of communication with the island had been disconnected since early yesterday because of the hurricane which had already caused enormous damage, uprooting telephone poles all along the New England coast, hadn't he heard it on the news? Harry couldn't get his thoughts straight for a few moments, then inquired when the service with Monhegan could be expected to be restored and was informed that as long as the storm maintained its present intensity there would be no point in trying to establish contact with the island and that unfortunately the weather forecast so far saw virtually no lightening of the storm until late Sunday night. If everything worked out according to the most optimistic views of the meteorologists, telephone crews would no doubt start trying to repair the damage early Monday morning and the earliest that contact with Monhegan could be anticipated was Tuesday morning, provided of course that everything went according to the weather men and the storm really subsided by tomorrow night.

The receiver fell heavily into the cradle. In a flash Harry realized that the first of his lines to direct financial aid—even if it turned out only a tenuous aid at best, to be taken as a last resort—had been cruelly cut off by the blind unreasoning force of nature. He gazed off into space but soon took cognizance of the fact that feeling sorry for himself and accepting defeat because of one setback would do him precious little good in collecting thirty thousand dollars in forty-eight hours. He had to start moving, moving, moving fast.

He got up quickly, and with this jerky motion seemed to have set all his braincells back into high gear. In fact, even before "procuring" Miss Collins for Ed Blakely, he would look if there was anything for him in the mail and then try to find Saypool, the super, as Martin had suggested, to learn from him whether he had seen Ruth the day before leaving in the afternoon between three and four. No, dammit, this was the wrong way to go about it, a dumb way of phrasing the question. It would only arouse Saypool's suspicion. He could give him the same line he had given Betty on the phone, about the sick mother in Maine and since there was no telephone connection with Monhegan Island he wanted to know from Saypool whether a friend of his had actually picked her up and taken her with him to the airport where they were both to embark for Bangor. If Saypool had seen them, he could question him about the looks of her companion, simultaneously shoving a couple of dollar bills into his hands. There was nothing like buttering a palm with lettuce, and Saypool loved money—key money, money for repairing doors that did not close properly, money for changing washers. Christmas money, birthday money, just money, any time, anywhere.

Harry reached for his wallet and noted with some satisfaction that it was pretty well stuffed, Friday having been payday at old Glumm's. He returned the billfold to his hip-pocket, helped himself to a pack of Kools and left the apartment to go for the first of his assignments: to get the mail.

For a change, the postman had already made his delivery. Through the crenelated cutout in the box he could make out that some mail was waiting for the Bensonnys. He opened it and retrieved two items: the Con Ed electric bill and one of those pally contest circulars that was just too eager to shower the Bensonny family at their Riverside Drive address with a First Class trip to Switzerland, France, Italy, West Germany and England, or $10,000 in cash, if they would only fill out the enclosed form and enter a trial subscription to a home repairs magazine at an unheard-of-low initial price for 42 weeks. These come-ons burned Harry up. If he had not spent postage on their business reply envelopes, sending the forms back before the deadline, duly filled out, and subscribed to a thousand and one magazines that he mostly gave a cursory glance and only cluttered up the apartment, Harry felt convinced he would be ten thousand dollars richer by now and perhaps not have to go through this ordeal of trying to raise the ransom, or rather the release of his wife.

He bunched the unsolicited envelope unopened in his fist—certain he would not win this time just as he had never won in the past, and stepped out of the building to throw it on top of one of the black vinyl garbage bags lining the curb. The October air smelled fresh, laundered by the torrential cloudburst the afternoon before, and even the crisp yellow autumn leaves in the park across the road looked more succulent and Renoir-romantic in the bright sunlight than the season warranted.

Through the umbrella of the foliage, the rocky cliffs of New Jersey's Palisades looked back at him across the river, stoically and stolidly impervious to human frailties and fortified with the essence of permanence. Harry shook his head in envy wishing he were part of this rock formation, not to have to worry about job security and that horse's ass Mickey upstairs and a wife who had been abducted and now the need to sacrifice a lifetime's savings to bring her back alive. Oh, to be part of eternal rock, outlasting homo sapiens, outlasting Australopithecus, outlasting dinosaurs and brontosaurs, and just watching, watching, with smug crustaceous hauteur, the comings and goings of species, never to be afflicted by pain or grief, just watching . . .

As Harry idled back to the lobby of the building, it occurred to him that Saypool might be down in the garage or the adjacent boiler room which were a few feet along the street and accessible through a side entrance. A flurry of pigeon wings across the drive diverted his attention for a few seconds as he walked down the sidewalk. Obviously the clash of cymbals and the Orffian choir of the Hare Krishna congregation disagreed with their feathery disposition. The religious group was still gathered in a knot of blissful togetherness chanting its Ooooooom songspiel and other mantra recitals and tilting left to right on their sandaled feet before bobbing again right to left as others of their commune brazenly approached passers-by for alms, walking along with them for as much as a hundred yards to palm off some colorful brochure about the benefits of belonging to their mendicant sect and in return demanding hard cash for the gratuitous offering while publicly and pertinaciously advertising their contempt for the materialistic society on which they sponged for support. In short: the everyday rip-off. Everybody played mini-kidnapper, demanded a piece of the action: the pious, the politicos, the brash, the doctors, the White House, right down to the welfare recipients and the importunate audioanimatronicising cyborgs of Walt Disney World.

The garage door was open and Harry strolled down the pedestrian catwalk into the gloomy cavern. Here the double-lensed automobiles were facing each other motionlessly in gasoline-fumed splendor, like mute phalanxes of Kafkaesque robots. A car was just backing up from one of the two opposing rows, then went into forward gear and glided majestically, with almost feline soundlessness, past Harry. He had seen the car in the garage many times, a white Mercedes SL 300, but never before its owner, a foppish middle-aged pink-cheeked man wearing a checkered fawn vest and a red Sulka tie.

Of course, Saypool was nowhere in sight, so Harry decided to take a look at his own car at the far end of the garage to assure himself that everything was all right. He had not used it for at least ten days, and since Ruth did not drive at all anymore because of her heart condition, nobody had checked on it in the intervening period, so this was as good a time as any to make an investigation. He did not open the doors, but strained his eyes in the dark, squinting through the rolled-up windows to convince himself that nothing was amiss. It occurred to him that just possibly the kidnapper might have left another note inside his Dodge Dart, but nothing seemed out of the ordinary, everything was in its proper place, the plastic Kleenex tray, Rand McNally's Road Atlas, a rag for the windshield, the carton of pre-moistened disposable wash cloths. Satisfied, Harry made his way back to the street.

Saypool lived on the ground floor, like Harry, but this floor stretched along the entire length of the block and his apartment was not near Harry's—eleven doors away to be exact, around the L-shaped corner from the Bensonny's.

Harry really had nothing against Saypool's mercenary nature. He knew that in a world that often judged a man by the creature comforts he could amass and show off to his friends and neighbors, Saypool was anything but unique. In fact, he was a most efficacious janitor, keeping the house in top-notch shape, clean, and the apartments in as good a state as was humanly possible with the help he had at his disposal. In all the time Harry had lived there he had never had a run-in with him. Saypool's appearance in no way connected him with the upkeep and maintenance of an apartment house (indeed, he always referred to himself as "maintenance engineer" rather than "super"), but more with the sort of leading man one would expect to step out of Buñuel's imagination. In short, a real middle-aged Romeo type. Actually, some women did go wild over him, and he could turn on the charm whenever a good-looking female tenant wanted something from him—which was frequently.

The building was filled with a fine assortment of black, white and Oriental women, and fairly often one of these lovelies complained to him about a defective faucet or toilet and Saypool always came to the rescue with a smile and a helping hand. He was married and everybody in the house genuinely liked his wife. Often, Ruth had compared her to Shirley MacLaine, a lovely, sexy, high-spirited gal, and it never occurred to anyone that Mr. Saypool would ever forsake his wife, even though he was known to fool around a bit on the side. But the unexpected did happen one day.

Mrs. Saypool became seriously ill. Tests indicated heart surgery. Her ordeal spread over eighteen months, because prior to surgery she had to try to build up her strength, and finally when the day came for her operation, the doctor informed Saypool that she would have to live for the rest of her life with the batteries of a pacemaker. She had lost a great deal of weight, and where she was once assured of a good double-take by any red-blooded male passing her on the street, she now dragged herself from room to room, the skin tautly drawn over the bony contours of her skull, the once-bright impish eyes deep-set in hollows, unsmiling, burned out and exhausted. A year of this and Saypool could take it no longer. His pity and compassion spread butter-thin across the span of twelve months, and emptied his reservoir of love.

He had a house near Red Bank in New Jersey and gave it to her, plus his brand-new car and twenty thousand dollars. She in turn was happy to get out of the city and away from his "tom-catting" as she called it, and they divorced. They had no children, so the break was clean and final.

Mrs. Blagger, who had a studio apartment on the 10th floor, was a widow, about five years older than Saypool, and one of the ladies with whom he regularly indulged in a tryst whenever she summoned him to fix something in her place. It was she who finally snared him and replaced the first Mrs. Saypool.

Harry rang their doorbell now and the new Mrs. Saypool answered it. At once his entire field of vision was taken up by the woman's carp-eye buttons and calico print dress straining mightily against the bulging protrusions confined behind them. In her presence, Harry almost felt like Rizzo of "Midnight Cowboy."

After clearing his throat of a nervous tremor he asked if she knew where he could find Mr. Saypool.

"Why?" she challenged him immediately. "Anything wrong in your apartment, Mr. Bensonny?"

"Well, not exactly," Harry flashed his most ingratiating smile. "It's really something private, Mrs. Saypool."

"Private?" She touched her absurdly bleached Harlow-coiffure. "Can't it wait till later today, Mr. Bensonny? You see he's having his lunch right now and I don't . . ."

"Oh I'm sorry, I wouldn't want to disturb him, but it's terribly important and I'd be most grateful if you'd let me speak to him, just for a minute. It doesn't involve any work, only a question I'd like to ask him. It is really important."

Mrs. Saypool grimaced as if displeased by the urgency in Harry's voice, but Christmas was not too far away and a certain flexibility on her and her husband's part at this point in time might not be altogether uncalled for.

"Well, all right," she agreed with a big-hearted grin as phony as the Christmas-homage soon to be offered by the tenants, and she turned her head, shouting back over her shoulder, "Ducky-boy, will you come here a second?"

"Christ, I'm having my lunch, Eleanor," came the half-muffled, mouth-full reply. "Can't it wait?"

"It'll only take a minute, hon. It's Mr. Bensonny. He says it's very important."

Harry heard Saypool grumble and the scraping of a chair as he got up. He was wiping his mouth with his sleeve as he appeared in the living room behind his wife, still chewing.

"Honest, Mr. Saypool," Harry apologized, "I wouldn't bother you at a time like this if it weren't so important, but . . ."

"It's all right, Mr. Bensonny," Saypool said, putting his arm around his wife's waist. She didn't move and plainly was as eager as anyone to listen to what Harry had to tell to her husband that was so important. "Don't worry! A minute or so away from my lunch won't kill me. What can I do for you?"

"Well, it's a little complicated," Harry started, determined not to give himself away with any slip-up in mendacious and circumlocutory phrasing. "You see, while I was out at work yesterday I got a phone call from my wife—around one in the afternoon—that her mother in Maine had taken sick and she was going to fly up and call a friend to take her to the airport. But I can't remember for the life of me who it was and I wanted to call the friend to find out more about her leaving in such a hurry and other details like . . ."

"Why don't you simply give your wife a ring in Maine?" Mrs. Saypool broke in indignantly.

"Mrs. Saypool," he smiled. "Please don't think I haven't tried. But you may have heard on the radio that there's a hurricane blowing up north and we can't seem to get through from New York. Power lines are all down and won't be restored till Tuesday at the earliest. That's why I thought you could give me a hint, Mr. Saypool, if you could describe who might have picked up my wife."

Saypool scratched the back of his head and swallowed the last bit of food in his mouth. "Well now, let me see," he said. "Yesterday around lunchtime you say . . . What time did I get in for lunch yesterday, hon?"

His wife tugged at her girdle, knitted her brows and screwed up her eyes. "Now, that's a hard one. I think it was about . . . Hey, didn't you have to do something on those circuits . . . the electric meters in the basement?"

"That's right. You even got mad because you said that could have waited till after lunch. But let me see now. Seems to me there was something that did happen. If only I . . ." He scratched the top of his head and his features brightened with a Gable-like flash of his teeth. "That's it! Of course! I remember now. On my way up from the basement, I was humming "Some Enchanted Evening"—I hate this hippy rock'n'-roll—I think it was around one-fifteen or so. I saw one of those fellows, young, neatly dressed in a dark suit, white shirt, black tie, carrying a bundle of . . . Oh yeah, that Watchtower stuff. One of those Jehovah's Witnesses, and he was at your door and talking to your wife. No, come to think of it, your wife was talking to him. She seemed pretty excited, and she was talking in a low voice so I couldn't make out what it was all about, and then he said something just as I passed them, also in a low voice, like they were sharing a secret, so I didn't interfere or anything. I thought he was a personal friend of yours and your wife's since they were talking like that. You know, Mr. Bensonny, we don't like to have any of those fellows, or anybody else soliciting in this building. This is a respectable place. But since they were so deep in their talk I thought it was just a friendly chat and nothing that might cause a religious argument. So, I didn't say a word and went on my way to lunch. And that's the last time I saw Mrs. Bensonny."

Harry gaped at Mr. Saypool, completely taken aback by this new revelation. A Jehovah's Witness? Impossible! Whoever heard of a Jehovah's Witness kidnapping a woman? Unless he only posed as one!

"Yes, I see," he said in a daze.

"Anything wrong, Mr. Bensonny? Aren't you feeling well?" the super's wife broke through to him.

"Sure, sure, I'm okay." Harry pulled himself together. "I was just trying to recall if any of our friends were members of the Jehovah's, that's all. Mr. Saypool, do you remember what he looked like? I mean, his face? Was he fat?"

"Fat, no. Thinnish I'd say. But I didn't pay much attention to him,

Mr. Bensonny. I only saw him for a few seconds and when my tenants talk to friends I don't really spy on them, if you get my point. That's not my business."

"No, of course not. I understand . . . Well, can you tell me if he was young, a teenager, in his twenties, or older?"

"That's hard to say . . . About thirty I guess. I remember he had black shiny hair, sort of Tyrone Power-like, if you know what I mean, like he used Vitalis. Greasy kid-stuff. And he was neatly dressed. Clean-cut. Nothing hippyish about him. *That* you got to say in their favor, these Jehovah's Witnesses. I don't like their soliciting, but at least they're better than the trash you meet on the street nowadays. Never catch any of *them* mugging people, or slipping a shiv between people's ribs . . . to hasten the end of the world they always talk about," he laughed.

"Oh ducky-boy!" Mrs. Saypool chided her husband with a grin.

"Well, I hope I've been of some help, but that's all I remember," Mr. Saypool shrugged regretfully.

"Yes, of course you have," Harry said quickly, dipping his hand into his hip pocket. The word "help" was the green light, the cue. He withdrew his wallet and removed a dollar bill. "You were most helpful, Mr. Saypool, and I hope you won't be offended if I . . ."

"Come on now, you really shouldn't," the janitor said, taking the money out of Harry's hand. "If I can be of help to my tenants I'm as happy as the next fellow."

"Yes, why don't you come on in and have a bite to eat, Mr. Bensonny," his wife suggested, opening the door a bit further. "You look as if you hadn't eaten since your wife left yesterday. I always say you men are helpless without us women."

"Ha, just look who's talking," laughed Mr. Saypool.

Harry looked into the super's apartment. Everything was virgin-white and gold. A white trellis a few steps inside the apartment opened up on a white sofa wrapped in diaphanous dust covers; a huge reading lamp, with the striped white and gold lampshade still in its plastic wrapper, faced a large white table topped by a cluster of white edelweiss under a bell jar.

"No, thanks, Mrs. Saypool," Harry said, buttoning his hip pocket. "That's very nice of you, but I have enough at home and I've really got to be going again. Just wanted to check, that's all."

"Well, hope I've been helpful," Mr. Saypool smiled.

"You have indeed. Thanks again. Both of you. So long."

17 ⎯⎯⎯⎯

They shut the door and as
Harry started walking back to his apartment, deep in thought, he could
hear the Saypools giggle behind their door, whether at Harry or at
Saypool's pinching his wife in a private part, Harry couldn't tell and
didn't care to speculate on.

More important, what in hell was this with the Jehovah's Witness
guy all of a sudden? Maybe he would check with their headquarters in
New York later today, after Ed Blakely had gone. But why the
whispers? Never once in their married life had Ruth let herself get
involved in any of those futile religious discussions. Usually she slammed
the door in their faces. Then why these friendly or animated whispers
Saypool had observed?

In his extreme nervousness and agitation Harry had passed his own
apartment door and was walking in the direction of the basement now,
not even sure why his legs carried him there. He simply had to walk, to
think, and maybe to meet someone else in the house who might have
seen his wife yesterday. He looked up and down the street. There was
not a soul in sight anywhere. Nobody seemed to be staking out his
home either, watching him, the way Ives might have been covered
when he went to see his friend Tom, the retired cop. But where in hell

was the kidnapper? How could he keep tabs on Harry if he *really* were to report the abduction to the police?

No, he dismissed this idea at once. It was too risky after what had happened to Ives' wife. Harry absolutely refused to chance it. His mind reverted once more to the Jehovah's Witness, but hard as he tried he did not get any closer to unraveling the mystery of the religious imposter.

He suddenly discovered himself sauntering along the subterranean passages beneath the fallen plaster and tubular plumbing that had always reminded him in the past of a ship's corridor with its vital pipelines clasped to the ceiling overhead. He passed the laundry room, where he first had met Martin, the service elevator and the meter boxes on the grimy wall that Saypool had worked on the day before sighting the Jehovah's Witness. The whole thing was so bizarre it staggered Harry's imagination. The more facts he accumulated, the farther he seemed to be removed from anything resembling a denouement to this Chinese puzzle.

It smelled foul underground, of garbage and urine, and Harry realized that this walk had served no useful purpose. He went up again, trying to recall who among their acquaintances and friends looked like the Tyrone Power portrayal so graphically depicted by Saypool. In his thirties, greasy hair, dressed conservatively, but he couldn't place anyone who fit this description. What puzzled Harry most of all, though, was why Ruth would have brought him into their apartment. Not that Saypool said that she did, but if this J-W really turned out to be the kidnapper, just how did he wangle himself into their apartment? A total stranger? Especially when Ruth was an agnostic and repeatedly stressed the point that she never wanted to have anything to do with such fanatics.

Harry opened the door to his apartment and stopped in the foyer, undecided, hearing the door click shut behind him. To check up once more, he went into the bedroom, and saw that Ives could still be expected to sleep it off for another hour or two before emerging from his drunken stupor.

In the kitchen, Harry helped himself to more slices of salami and opened a can of cling peaches. While he was spooning them out, his eye caught sight of the African violets on the window-sill and he filled a cup with water to moisten their soil, recalling Ruth's warning never to drown them. This, too, was part of the unsung drudgeries of marriage, the commonplace things. Iris Murdoch's baroque characters did not live like this, so plebeian, nor the sophisticates peopling *Playboy*. How contemptible the middle classes of Pinter's and Simenon's world turned out to be! Workers united, and the wealthy conspired—only the jerks in the middle classes got the shaft. From both sides. And by the IRS.

A package of birdseed lay next to the potted plants, so Harry strolled into the living room to fill up the small dish of the two chattering parakeets.

It was already long after one o'clock, the time the mail normally arrived. The mail! With a start he remembered the Con Ed envelope that had been delivered in the morning, and he pulled it out of his pocket. Goddamn—would Françoise Sagan or Capote or Vidal ever bother with such Dickensian trivia when love affairs and opulent surroundings crowded their cinematic imagination and novelistic projections? It bugged Harry that he should even bother to open the envelope at a time like this when so much was at stake. His thoughts, his confusion, his actions made no sense to him suddenly. Who cared how much Con Ed charged for last month's electricity!

In disgust, he slit the envelope open with his index finger, glanced at the bottom figure on the computer punchout card, and uttered a curse. Forty-six dollars and eleven cents! Hell, they didn't use that much, not even half that amount! They had needed no air conditioning in four weeks, having spent most of September in Maine, and with daylight still lasting through most of the working day very little electric lighting had been used. This proved once more that the common mortal, the little guy, was at the mercy of diabolical giant corporations, of bestial but indifferent machines, robots, computers, with whom it was impossible to argue.

In a nakedly open confrontation with programmed computers which boasted no brains and no hearts, all the urban dwellers, the little men and women in their concrete caves, the Schweiks of the Seventies amidst their Mort Sahl and von Karajan records, the new "Britannica 3's" and Bell & Howell projectors, became veritable Woody Allens.

Harry felt like roaring out loud—feeding time at the lion house—like stenciling a couple of additional square holes next to the punched oblong rectangles that perforated the return card. The Woody Allen in Harry verbalized the mutilation-threat in mute wrath, but, of course, nothing came of dormant anger being translated into the pragmatism of decisive action. Life was too short to metamorphose the nearly impossible into individualistic victory. As on so many occasions, in households across the land, the interior Henry Aldrich gained the upperhand of the

Napoleonic exterior and Harry dropped the bill meekly next to the ransom note. His immediate duty was to save his wife, who had loved and been kind, understanding, compassionate with him for two long decades. No Hedda Gabler, no Nora, she, merely a modern, ordinary woman, a household statistic. Harry vowed to retrieve what he had lost, and to let Karen Horney figure out why later. All he knew at this juncture was that it was not a matter of love or of returning kindness for love bestowed that prompted him to do everything in his power to save Ruth's life but plain common decency, a thing that had to be done, a component of human nature too little exercised in his own life, an ingredient that he hoped had not been altogether extinguished in him.

In the light of this, he had to act now. Ed Blakely would be here in an hour or so and Harry had promised him a woman, so no more time could be wasted. All he needed to recruit a willing female, Harry held, was an essence of Hemingwayesque machismo . . . wherever, within his depths, this chauvinist integrant was likely to be found.

18 ━━━━━━

Earlier in the day, Martin and Harry had briefly discussed a Miss Collins living on the third floor and Harry decided that he had to risk it and attempt to invite the woman down to his place.

He locked his apartment door, and waited for the elevator. When the door opened, a man in a wide-brimmed Stetson stepped out, greeted him with a friendly, "Howdy," and Harry entered the elevator thinking vaguely that at least New York offered an exhilarating variety in life. It still served as an exciting stimulant second to no other city. Only today, Harry felt, this minute—as on other occasions—life threatened to leave you with a kind of post-coital depression that could do with a bit of cheering up.

Harry pressed the third floor button without knowing where on that floor Miss Collins lived. It came as a shock to him as he walked down the cabbage-reeking hall, glancing at the name-plates under each peep-hole, that he had never bothered to get to know the names of the tenants who shared the building with him since the Fifties. This was an old story, though. Each family lived its own existence, with its own

Wilde troubles, Tom Stoppard laughter, Strindbergian tears, Chekhovian ennui and Ibsenesque ecstasies and deceits, hiding behind bolted and padlocked doors and working out its own problems and envies and hatreds as best it could, isolated from and suspicious of its likeminded, yet oh, so different, neighbors.

At last he found it. Miss Collins lived in Apartment 3N. Harry planted himself akimbo and machismo-wise in front of her door and as he pressed the buzzer the first thing he discerned was that his heart leaped into his mouth, thumping wildly against his jawbone, and he could taste the bile of excitement and tension on his tongue. Too late he realized that it was a grave mistake to have come unprepared, leaving all to Lady Luck. He somehow sensed he would be awkward propositioning a young woman he didn't know, and inviting her into a liaison with a perfect stranger—one at least twenty or thirty years older, at that.

Harry waited, but there was no answer and he was torn between an urge on the one hand to try and risk everything to keep Ruth alive and ring the bell again, and on the other hand to let his fear and embarrassment get the better of him and desert his post like a rat and run for the hills. But his hand was already on the button and against his better judgment he leaned against it and shut his eyes, hoping, hoping, hoping she would not be in.

Then he heard what sounded to him like the scraping of footsteps of a tired old person dragging feet slippered a size or two too large across a parquetry floor. Was this the wrong apartment after all? Harry took a fast, close look at the name-plate again just as the door was pulled open. He jerked his head back and stared at the woman who stood in the doorway.

"Miss Collins?" he inquired.

"Yeah," said a blank voice.

"You don't know me, probably. I mean you may have seen me many times. I live downstairs, in 1E." He groped for words, trying to assess her reaction and simultaneously figure out how best to get to the core of his message. "You *have* seen me before, haven't you?"

Miss Collins narrowed her eyes. It was dark on the landing where Harry stood because one of the bulbs near her front door had burned out. She leaned slightly forward as if short-sighted and held the top of her bathrobe together under her chin. Then, almost frightened, it seemed to Harry, she pulled back.

"Yeah, I remember you now," she muttered. "You're from downstairs."

Harry's throat tightened. "Yes. I . . . er . . . I was wondering if I could have a few minutes of your time. It's sort of personal."

The word "personal" struck her like lightning. She stiffened and blinked nervously. "What d'you mean personal?"

Harry felt totally at a loss to explain, almost like a little boy who had been caught playing with himself. The incongruity of the situation made him fumble for words and his palms became uncommonly sweaty. "Miss Collins, do you mind very much if I talked to you in private. I don't want you to think that there is anything wrong, I mean, improper. If you'd rather, you can come down to my place and we can talk it over there."

"Talk *what* over?" she demanded. She certainly did not make things easy for him. "What're you trying to say?"

"Look, I can't talk about it here in the hall, honestly. Isn't there some place where we can discuss this in private? It'll only take a few minutes. And I assure you it's something of great interest to you."

Miss Collins stared at him hard in the dim-lit corridor, obviously trying to get behind his noncommittal appearance and words.

"Well, all right, if it's that important," she said at last and made room for Harry to pass into her foyer.

Harry entered with a brief smile and a mumbled "Thank you" and immediately took note that it was a one-room studio. Two very large windows overlooking Riverside Park and the Hudson were open and flooded the spacious room with radiant mid-October sunlight. But the place looked a mess—and probably hadn't been tidied up in a week, making it the sort of room Ruth would have loved to scrub clean till it turned as sun-bleached-white as a shrine on Mikonos.

"I thought you were married," she remarked as he passed her.

"I beg your pardon?" Harry stopped and looked askance at her.

"Well," she elaborated, "I think I've seen you with your wife. Once I even met her. Last summer at the block party."

"Oh sure, sure. It's just that Ruth . . . my wife, isn't home this weekend; she had to fly up to see her sick mother in Maine."

"I see." They regarded each other in the middle of the studio like two prize fighters meeting for the first time, trying to appraise each other's strong points and weaknesses. Then she broke out of the audio-clinch. "Here, let me make this place a bit more comfortable . . . you know, presentable."

"No, don't worry! I really don't mind, Miss Collins."

"Charlotte. Now that you're in the lion's den you might as well call me Charlotte. All my friends call me Charlotte."

"Okay, thanks. My name is Harry." He smiled. "At least that's what my friends call me to my face. God knows what they say behind my back."

"Oh I wouldn't know," she said, starting to fuss around the room. An unmade bed stood under one of the open windows. She smoothed the sheet and covered it up with a Cactus Rose-patterned quilt from which, at one end, some white cotton batting peeked out. It was at this point Harry was struck that not only the bed with the 19th-century quilt manifested a segment of Americana, but that she seemed to be nuts about American folk art. The entire apartment was studded with artifacts from pre-20th century America that she must have picked up at auctions or by ransacking old barns and attics all over the country. Harry thought Channel 13 could have devoted a half-hour to it, or maybe radio station WNYC. Opposite her bed, kitty-corner to the wall, serving as a room divider between the studio and the kitchenette, squatted a huge lacquered Pennsylvania dowager chest, with three crackled panels displaying Redcoats and Indians. The walls of the apartment were covered not with paintings but with samplers, macraméd chevron wall-hangings and finger-woven arrow-head Shoshone mats. On a rough-hewn natural wood end table at the head of her bed Harry saw five corn-husk dolls encircling—of all things—a 20th-century icy-white vibrator, standing upright like a moonrocket ready for take-off. At the far end of the room, old morocco-bound volumes and yellowed mail order catalogs were lined up, row after row, on a rose-painted bookshelf.

Moreover, Harry understood now why he had heard Charlotte Collins dragging her feet across the floor; there was no carpet or rug anywhere and she wore a pair of handmade Iroquois moccasins intended for a man, about twice the size she needed for her small feet. She pointed to one of the few modern pieces of furniture in the room, an upholstered lounge chair, after she had cleared it of copies of *Viva*, *Penthouse*, and a dog-eared book—Erica Jong's "Fear of Flying."

"You read it?" she asked, as Harry eased himself into the chair. At once a steel-pronged spiral twanged into his buttocks.

"The book?" He shifted his weight away from the offending spring, craning his neck to look at the sexy cover of the paperback she held out to him. "I haven't, but my wife has. She thought it was the most disruptive and honest thing she'd read in years."

"You should read it too. Some woman that Jong. Sure understands women's nature better than anyone else in America. Maybe she'll be our Doris Lessing one day. I once heard her on WBAI, reading some

136

of her poetry on overseas Indians solving the problem of their protein shortage. By engaging daily in fellatio."

Harry's heart skipped a beat or two at the mention of the last word. At least Charlotte Collins, whose judgment of Jong's novel seemed more charitable than that of most critics, did not mince words. Small wonder that Martin had called her shockingly frank. "That must have been interesting," he said, hiding his shock at her crassness behind the flicker of a smile. "Sorry I missed it."

"Yeah, I know," she sighed, letting herself plop down on her bed. She sprawled across it and propped herself lazily on an elbow. "Most men love it."

"Jong's poetry?" he asked with feigned casualness, knowing only too well what this plebeian Xaviera Hollander meant.

"No, fellatio. A recent poll by *Redbook* claimed that 89 per cent of all couples engage in it." She smiled. "Just listen to what Julie Christie has to say about it in that movie "Shampoo," and you'll see what I mean." She brushed a wisp of hair off her forehead and Harry could see, now that she was more at ease, with the sun shining on her profile, she was much more attractive than he had remembered her from the street, a bit listless perhaps, looking like a youngish, un-Revlonized and very pale Vivien Leigh, although in sensual outspokenness about as refined as a 90 proof Al Goldstein. The robe she had on plainly needed laundering and ironing, that much was obvious even to a man who did not pay too much attention to externals, except on occasions like this when he became aware of a conspicuous absence of the neatness to which he had become accustomed in his own household. She did not even hold the lapels of the robe wrapped around her neck any longer so that one side slid down a trifle, revealing the cleavage of her breasts. The belt of the robe was fastened securely around her slender waist and it wouldn't have surprised Harry a bit if she had nothing on underneath. Since she obviously hadn't been expecting company, there certainly appeared to be little need for an undergarment.

Harry moistened his lips. "Yeah, I guess so," he said, glad that the conversation had so soon taken a ribald turn, and hoping that it would make it that much easier for him to steer the talk in the direction of his carnal request. "Men like it but I don't think all women are exactly averse to it either."

"Hell, no! I had a girl friend, back in the Fifties in high school, a Catholic, up near Bliss Street in Queens. She went to confession every Saturday afternoon and never had to confess about having intercourse with a boy because all she ever had with her boyfriends was oral sex."

Harry forced out a brief, self-conscious laugh. "Who knows, she may still die a virgin."

"That's what I told her. At least she'll never get pregnant that way." She placed a hand between her thighs as if protecting it from the cool breeze airing the room. "Okay, Mr. . . . what was it again? Charlie?"

"Harry."

"Well, what is it you came to talk about that is so private, Harry?"

Once more he wet his lips and opened his mouth. His mind went blank. "Right. Well, er, you *are* right, it *is* private, sort of. After all, what you just told me . . . I'm sure you wouldn't have wanted to mention any of this in the corridor outside either." He waited for her confirmation of this, but she just leveled her greenish gray eyes at him. "Well, you see, Miss Collins, I . . ."

"Charlotte. And you're right."

"Right?" Her statement broke the thread of thought he was preparing in his mind.

"I wouldn't have talked about fellatio in the hall."

"Oh. Well, as I mentioned before, my wife is out of town and I . . . there's a friend of mine who's coming to visit me later . . . a nice guy, Ed Blakely, a very unhappily married man. And I was wondering . . . well, you not being attached and so on, if . . ."

"Now, just a second, what makes you think I'm unattached?" Charlotte asserted herself indignantly. She sat up, fishing with one of her feet for an over-sized moccasin that had dropped off the bed.

"Well, I . . . you have this apartment . . . I take it you live alone. You aren't married."

"Now there's a laugh! A woman has to be married to be attached to someone?"

"No, no," Harry corrected himself hastily. "No offense meant. It's just that I've seen you often in the building or on the street and not with a man, so I thought you might like to come down later and maybe have a drink, and a nice time with my friend."

"I see." The woman merely sat there, ramrod-stiff, arms folded like a cigar-store Indian and fixed cold, unsmiling eyes on Harry. "Forgive me for asking, what exactly would this 'nice time' entail, the nice time you're talking about?"

Harry felt the blood pounding in his ears. This was the moment of truth. "Really, I don't know, Miss Col . . . Charlotte. I mean this would depend on you and Ed. Not on what *I* have in mind."

"But I'm curious to know, Mr. . . . Harry. What exactly is it you have in mind . . . if you were in . . . in Ed's place?"

Harry made a grandiloquent gesture with both arms as if to say that the answer was written in the stars. To his dismay, though, the tip of his index finger touched a wooden whirligig standing on a small table to the right of the armchair and before he had a chance to reply the object came crashing down with a loud rattle on the parquet floor.

The sudden clattering sound shot like a thunderbolt through Harry. "God, I'm so sorry." He was all thumbs as he got up and knelt down, picking up the colorful 19th-century toy and putting the pieces back on the end table. A part of it had become detached or broken off in the fall and rolled off the table and clattered to the floor a second time. In a way, he was grateful for the interruption because it gave him time to come up with an answer for her.

"Quit faking it, Harry! Just leave it on the table," the woman's voice broke into his train of thought. "I'll put it together later. Now tell me, from a male point of view, what do you think your friend would expect me to do?"

A real cat-and-mouse game, this, blitzed through Harry's mind as he slithered into the lounge chair, forgetting the faulty spring. The whirligig lay in a sorry heap on the table.

"Oh, I guess he'd like to talk to you a little. Maybe if you want to he'll take you out for a drink or . . ."

"I don't drink," she said primly, and somehow incongruously at this point.

"Well, maybe he'd like to take you to a show, a nice restaurant. At least, if you haven't anything planned for tonight. He's well off and I'm sure could take you any place you want."

"Okay. And then what?" She began to relax again, and lolled lazily on the bed.

"Then?" The little bitch knew, he gathered, but she wanted to drag it out of him, word for word. "I . . . I don't know . . . whatever else the two of you feel like doing after . . ."

"Never mind us two. I'm not interested in what your friend has in mind for me. I want to know what you would want to do after dinner if you were in his shoes. After all, your wife isn't in town, you said."

A nervous smile tugged at the corners of Harry's lips. "Well, it doesn't mean just because my wife has left town for a few days that I'd take another woman out to dinner or the theater the minute she's gone."

"Perhaps not. I don't know how happily you're married, but you said your friend, what was his name? Ed? That he was unhappily married. Are *you* happily married?"

"Me?" Harry repeated inanely. He had come to ask Charlotte a simple question and now she was turning the tables and cross-examining him. Probably a lot of practice, Harry decided.

"Yes, you."

"Well, you know, we never really had a big fight, not in all the years we've been married. We never even yelled at each other."

"How boring!"

"Oh I don't know. I would've thought living peacefully side by side all these years wasn't exactly a bad sign."

"It could be indifference. The end of love. Just living side by side, without touching each other . . . I mean inside."

Why was she doing her best to elicit his private feelings when all he wanted was for her to get laid by Ed? Was this so hard to understand? For a woman who made no bones about airing her vulgarity?

"My God, you sound like a shrink." Harry made an attempt at laughing her off. "As if you were trying to patch up a broken marriage."

"Who knows, maybe you *have* a broken marriage," she shrugged. "And as for me, I make no secret of it, I sure got enough experience with shrinks to know . . . to come face to face with *my* problems . . . having gone to a couple of them for almost six years. Frankly, I think all of us New Yorkers should shop around till we meet the right analyst. Don't you?" Harry only shrugged, trying to understand this strange woman's character, for his own sake, and Ed's. "To help them uncoil, dissolve their tensions. As long as they don't overdo it. Like me." She paused, just long enough to send Harry a self-deprecating smile. "And wouldn't you know, with my luck I'd have to end up with a shrink who tried to make it with me? Which wouldn't have been so bad if the shrink hadn't been a woman. She thought she could cure my penis envy by subjugating my body to the game of little old me playing slavey to her Sappho."

Harry's heart skipped another beat or two. What kind of unsavory fish had he hooked here? "Wonder what Anna Freud or Helen Deutsch would have to say about this?" he commented nervously. Why did lonely New Yorkers always have this urge to communicate their innermost secrets to strangers who couldn't care less? Maybe it was that—*because* they couldn't care less! Pseudo-therapy. With no financial or emotional strings attached.

"She said she was bisexual," continued the 'queer fish,' "that she had the best of both worlds. Well, this wasn't my bag. And d'you want to know something? I didn't feel too good about it. Because she *was* a nice

140

person. Anyway, never get involved with your analyst! So the last couple of years I got a gay therapist and he confides in me and I confide in him. Makes us both feel better. Now we both realize we're not suffering alone."

"Who *is*?"

"Oh, *you* suffer too?"

Harry stared at her. Here she goes again. The two shrinks had been a perfect foil for her inquisitive mind.

"You do suffer, don't you, Harry? You also belong to the human race. Your pal Ed. Me. You. We all have our problems. Never to have a fight with the woman you've been living with . . . How long you been married?"

"What difference does that make now? All I came . . ."

"Now please, answer me! You came up here with a kinda strange request. I am a woman of good repute and I think I got the right at least to ask you a few questions myself, just to check on a number of things, after what you asked of me."

"Christ, all I want is to find out if you'd be willing to go out with Ed tonight, that's all."

"Bullshit! Why the hell don't *you* go out with him, if all he wants to do is gnaw on a few spareribs and drink Valpolicella? No, you tell me about your wife. How long you been married?"

Harry leaned back into the chair, resigned. "Twenty years. Satisfied now?"

"Twenty years! Godalmighty! And never yelled at her?"

"Well, as it happens, she's sick. She got something with her heart. Once in a while has to take digitalis. Or nitroglycerine tablets she lets dissolve under her tongue . . ."

"Okay, you've been married to a sick lady. A good companion, right?"

"Right, a *very* good companion."

"Thanks for an honest answer."

"But why should all this matter to you," Harry appeared perplexed, "whether I'm happily married or not?"

"Because you come up here with that screwy story about some guy named Ed when it's plain as the nose on your face that it's you who wants to get . . . you know what."

Harry sat up straight as a board. "You got me all wrong," he objected strenuously. "There really is a guy by the name of Ed Blakely and he'll be here in an hour or so and it's for him I came to see you, so help me, God, it is."

"Okay, okay." A smile already mellowed her marble-cold features. "How old is he?"

"Ed? I'm not sure. I guess in his late fifties or early sixties."

"Well, that won't take all night, I suppose. Really should be pretty easy stuff."

Harry leaned forward on his elbows, thinking the gentility of a Jane Eyre you have not, maybe her body, but more of the soul, the patois of a Stanley Kowalski. "Look, Charlotte," he said. "Ed is my friend and he's coming to see me as a favor, and I want to do *him* a favor. I promised him a nice young lady who might want to go out with him. So I don't want him to be under any financial obligation. In other words, I want this whole thing to be on me, if you follow me."

"Oh." She rose again from her bed and idled over to Harry, stopping just short of his chair. "How much did you have in mind?" she asked folding her arms.

She certainly had a genius for putting him on the spot. "Well, I don't know what the usual . . . well, fee is for such an occasion." He furrowed his brow. "To be honest, I've never been in a situation like this."

"Fee sounds like I was a call girl or something. Let me make this absolutely clear, Harry, I'm no hooker, no common prost . . ."

"I didn't say you were. It's just that I thought you would let me know what you considered a reasonable price for the night out."

"And night in," she added, winking lewdly. "Let's see now . . . I'm still paying off on that root-canal work of mine. On top of that, I'm between jobs and in a way depend on some extra change now and then, and with inflation, you know, everything is expensive . . . I'd need something to tide me over . . . at least till I get a job."

"You're not working?"

"Well, it's those damn amphetamines my shrink prescribed. I suffer from depressions once in a while, and he gave me these bennies . . . you know . . . the pills, but sometimes they make me feel *more* depressed afterward than before I pop them. Don't ask me why. But I've been so much in the dumps lately that I missed too many days on my last job, a new job, too, and had to stay home. My system got so fouled up I didn't even have the energy to call the office and tell them I wouldn't make it. A map-maker company." She shrugged helplessly. "So they fired me."

"Are you still on them? The amphetamines?"

"I can't live without them. I've taken them for eight months now and the more I take them the more I need them. Couple of months ago it got so bad I put myself in St. Vincent's, you know, on 12th Street, to try to kick it, but after two or three weeks I asked to be released on my own recognizance, because I was ready to go out of my skull there. Trouble is, legally I can only get a certain amount of uppers a month, unless I go to another shrink and also ask him for a prescription, but they register the intake per person somewhere—in Albany I think—and I can't risk that. So, I'm out of pills and can't get hold of any till some time next week. God knows how I'm going to live through the next five days or so."

Harry regarded her closely. "You mean you might take a dive anytime and plunge back into a depression?"

"That's about it."

"When did you have your last upper?"

"This morning."

"How long do they last now?"

"With luck eight hours."

"I see." He had not reckoned with this sudden bolt from the blue. "But wouldn't that mean you'd be in no state to see Ed, or anyone, once the effect of the drug has worn off? If he takes you out at eight tonight, for instance, you might be in one of your . . ."

"Harry, what am I going to do?"

Before he realized it, she had burst into tears and was on her knees, burying her face in his lap. He sat there, immobile, not knowing what to do next. This crude, self-righteous little Amazon that he was about to hire for his friend Ed turned out to be a manic-depressive nut. Sex probably was the only way out of her despair, as good an emotional and sensual outlet to deflect from her mental psychosis as any. But it was only a palliative to smother the symptoms, not to cure the root of her psychological ailment. To her, the rewards of promiscuity appeared to be an orgiastic means to a temporary positive end. But as far as Ed—and more indirectly Harry—were concerned, they sure were up the creek. Almost without realizing it, he placed his hand gently on her head. The hair did not have the smooth silky sheen of Ruth's. In fact, it felt kind of stringy, hard, as though she had not washed it recently. It fitted all so well with the rest of her appearance, the filthy bathrobe, the untidy room, even the leaning tower of dirty dishes about to topple in the sink in the kitchenette. Although she was unemployed and had plenty of time to look after the room and herself, the psychological lethargy most likely affected all of her actions, or rather lack of actions, and kept her in a state of languor, of sluggish passivity. He stroked her hair tenderly, not saying anything. What *could* he say?

Charlotte looked up through her wet lashes and encircled his waist with her arms in a desperate gesture. "Harry, what am I going to do, what am I going to do?"

His eyes swerved around the room as if to retrieve some answer from the Americana, the clean country primitiveness with which she had surrounded herself. Plainly, only in the innocent past and its relics could she find the true soul of her innermost being, the pristine purity of virgin territory. From where he sat, he could see the top of the autumnal trees lining the walks of Riverside Park, and then his eyes fell on the Oglala Sioux deerskin skirt, the Shawnee shoulder bag, two Paul Revere silver pitchers and a scrimshaw paperweight, and again on the vibrator, septic and milky-white as a moon rocket, in the circle of corn-husk dolls. And then, there at his feet, the crying young woman in the soiled robe. It was all so absurdly out of place.

"I don't know, Charlotte," he said. "I'm no doctor. I suppose we all have to bear our crosses somehow...But ... Look, Charlotte," he wiped her tears away with his finger—the second time, it struck him, he had to do this with someone in the last twenty-four hours—"What are we going to do about Ed?"

She shrugged. "I don't know."

"I mean, can you make it with him? Tonight?"

"I don't know, Harry. When it hits me, all I want to do is to go up to the top of the building, to the roof, and throw myself off."

"Jesus!" He stopped stroking her. Hell, he had a Judy Garland syndrome on his hands.

"Harry, when I'm in that state I don't even feel like touching a man. I'm a corpse. Cold, washed out, and the best in the world can't get me excited. I have no orgasm and don't give a damn if the guy with me has one or not. It wouldn't be fair to him. Not with what I charge."

Aaaah, here it came, the clincher. The "no-call-girl" asking for a lot of bread. Harry looked at her. "And what *do* you charge?"

"For the night?" she asked spiritlessly, and he nodded. "Ninety-five." Harry raised his eyebrows. He had read about pros making five times that a night, hookers asking for twenty-five a trick—in hotel rooms, or the quickies in a phone booth standing up, but spending that for another man seemed pretty damn steep. His gut reaction was a low, long whistle.

"Harry, I need it, honestly," she added quickly. "When I'm in top form the guy can do anything he wants and I'll do anything he wants. But right now I need the money, and with the shrink, and the rent and the dentist and food, and you know I don't have a job . . . so I . . ."

"It's okay, don't worry," he placated her, against his will. "You don't have to make any excuses to me. The only thing that troubles me is . . . well, ninety-five dollars ain't hay. Especially when it's for another guy. When Ed comes, what am I going to tell him? How do I know you'll even show up? It's not that I don't trust you, but you said yourself that you took the last upper this morning and you know, by the time Ed wants to take you out you'll be down in the dumps and I'll be left holding the bag. And it's clear, he expects to get laid."

For a minute he thought very hard as her pleading eyes fastened on his. "Of course, I could give you the money when you come down tonight, or give you a ring first and find out what state you're in. If you're okay, and you can come down to meet Ed, I'll give you the dough in cash. If not, well . . ." He shrugged a fatalistic shrug.

"It'll help me so much," she whispered fiercely. "I think I can make it because God knows how I need the money!" She smiled. "You're quite a guy, you know that?"

He returned the smile. "All in a day's work, ma'am."

Charlotte's greenish gray eyes were round and bright and for a full minute she gazed into Harry's face. "If you want to," she whispered as her hand moved from his waist and began massaging the inside of his thigh. "If you want to, you can have me, now, for a few minutes, on the house because you're such a sweet guy . . . a real sweetheart." She had located his penis through his pants and was stroking it gently with experienced fingers. Harry's heart pounded against his ribs; he did not have the strength nor will-power to remove her hand, as his genital started to grow under her sensuous touch, and as it did, she smiled and suddenly sunk her white pearly teeth playfully into his thigh, only an inch or two from the meaty swelling under his trousers. She lifted her head, continuing to rub his erect penis through the cloth. "After so many years I think you're entitled to a fling. Harry, don't you mess around with someone on the side at all?"

He gave Charlotte a long pensive look, unable to answer her, to find the right words.

"Harry," she said, softly, and expertly pulled down the zipper of his fly as if it were part of the erotic foreplay and the deliberate undoing of Erica Jong's Zipless Fuck. "Why don't you take your clothes off? Ten minutes won't hurt . . . while I get the music going."

With that she stood up and undulated suggestively back to the bed, on the way untying the knot of her belt and taking off her robe. She was stark naked. Seeing her like that robbed him of speech. He hadn't known what she meant by her remark about getting the music going and now he didn't really care. All he knew was that her small figure was overpoweringly enticing. It almost drugged his senses, his blood, everything.

As she turned to Harry the sunlight framed her figure like a Renaissance Madonna. His eyes drank in her classic beauty, the voluptuous soft round contours of the woman, the symmetry of the firm little breasts with their hard nipples, the smooth marzipan belly and beneath it the dark forest of hair masking the innermost warm allure of her innate womanliness. She was new to him, and thus it was as if he had never seen a nude before in his life. She was a continent stretching before him, unexplored. He rose from his chair, thoroughly aroused, and started to unbuckle his belt as she laughed and flung herself into his arms, throwing hers around his neck and kissing him wildly, pressing the entire length of her warm body against his. She kissed his ears, his eyes, the tip of his nose, asking him if he liked what he saw and before he could answer he felt her tongue flicking greedily inside his mouth. His arms encircled her waist. One of his hands lowered itself to her firm buttocks—the shape of small mandolins—and then the other worked its way around to the front of her body.

At this point she gently struggled out of his arms and backed away, to her bed, wagging her finger as if chiding a boy who had tried to steal his dessert before mealtime.

"Harry, my love," she cried out triumphantly. "You'll never have a better fuck than you are going to have with me right now. And then you can tell anybody you want to who's the best lay in town. Let me get the music ready first."

Harry did not move. He realized that Charlotte Collins was going to have intercourse with him, with a vengeance. That she expected him to brag about her sexual feats as a mistress. Harry's hand froze on his belt. In a way, this woman was laboring under a misapprehension that not even his own wife, Ruth, had ever been capable of giving him a good time in bed. Ruth was fabulous, or at least had had a euphoric effect on him until he embarked on his affair with Helga. Charlotte also seemed to think she was going to outdo his secret paramour with her sexual know-how. While admittedly some women were more skillful than others in bed, more responsive, more passionate, more geared to each nuance of their partners' sexual idiosyncracies, there wasn't that much difference in experienced women, at least within the context of normal satisfaction that stemmed from true love or uninhibited love-making. Sex to Harry's way of thinking anyway was situated as much in the mind as in the groin. With the right attitude and conjuring up the right lusty desires engendered by the right partner and a lot of understanding for each participant's sexual flaws and moody weaknesses, the carnal union in every case could be just about perfect, take a degree here and there. There was this wonderful thing about sex, that even when it was pretty bad it was rather good.

Charlotte had pulled a record player from under her bed and left it on the parquet floor near the head of the bed where she was now fluffing a pillow. Next, she put a record on the turntable and flicked on a rousing rendition of "Glory, Glory, Hallelujah." Then she reclined on her bed, nude, watching him, and propped herself up on an elbow like a Roman courtesan awaiting her lover. "Come on, what're you standing there for, slowpoke?"

He stared at her dumbfounded, then at the record player blasting the American battle hymn through the open windows, and back at her again.

"That music. Why? Just when we . . ."

"Because I can only screw with music. At least the first half hour or so. 'John Brown's Body,' the 'Star Spangled Banner,' Sousa's marches. It really gets me. C'mon!"

Harry simply stood there in the midst of the Americana, like a totem pole, a wooden Indian, among tavern signs, horse weathervanes, and the stirring sounds of "Glory, Glory, Hallelujah"! He felt like a damn fool and went limp. His hands tightened the buckle of his belt.

"Well, I can't screw *with* music, least of all a marching song," he said, pulling up his zipper. "I'm sorry, Charlotte, it's not my bag. I'm sure Ed won't mind a bit, but if you don't mind I'll take a rain check on it."

He immediately saw the pinch of pain draining her face, one of her hands digging like a claw into a snow-white thigh, and he regretted having said the wrong thing.

"Try to understand, you're too damn appealing to me, to any man, but my wife just left, her mother is sick and I just . . . well, can you understand what I'm . . ."

"No," she cut in icily, not moving. "I do *not* understand. I've known many men in my life, slept with some real dogs, but nobody, nobody has ever turned me down flat, after he got an erection and I took my clothes off."

"I'm not turning you down, Charl . . ."

"I don't see you humping me exactly, Buster. What are you anyway? A queer or something? Here I offer myself to you—you don't have to pay me a nickel—and you son of a bitch, you turn me down."

"I told you I'm not turning you down. Later I'll be only too happy to . . ."

"Sure. Later. When your wife is back. A perfect example of manly timing. Hell, you seem to think you're doing me a big favor! What sort of a fool do you take me for, Mister? *You're* not faithful to your wife, you bastard!" She sat up naked on her bed. "You're faithful to your mistress!" She bent down and lifted the needle off the record, then leveled her cold eyes at him accusingly. "Whoever she is."

The words hit him like the verdict of guilty to a man accused of murder. She had figured him exactly for what he was, a chiseling double-crossing adulterer. The room that had filled with silence suddenly broke with a slight click. The arm of the phonograph player had dropped back on the record. Harry stepped forward quickly and fastened it into its clip, then faced her, leaning forward with his hands resting on his kneecaps. Her features did not change, still cold with the hurt of rejection. And he knew that soon the amphetamine would cease working inside her and she would be all alone again in her misery. Slowly he let himself down on the bed beside her and took her face into his hands and kissed her softly on her lips. She did not resist but did not respond either. Her cheeks were stone-cold, her mouth dry, and she was exposed in more ways than one. Harry had snapped shut her escape hatch from the cruelties of life that surrounded her every-where in the heartless city. Perhaps sex, the only natural panacea she knew, meant warmth, affection, protection to her, even without love.

"You are probably one of the smartest women I have ever met," he whispered. "And you must believe me when I tell you that I have never grown so fond of a woman so quickly."

At last her hurt eyes crinkled into a little smile. Her arms came up around his neck as she pressed her lips in a hungry tongue-flicking frenzy against his. Only a few seconds passed and his right hand started wandering down her warm supple body, past the firm hard nipples of her breasts, coming to rest between her smooth thighs. "Charlotte, you understand more about life than I do," he said in a low voice. "I bet you can see through any man. Women are so much wiser than men."

The kind words warmed her frozen, unhappy heart. She kissed his eyelids, cheeks, mouth. They were dry, loving kisses and she gazed at him through her large eyes. "Careful, Harry. You're so naive. Don't think for a minute your wife doesn't suspect. You're a pushover."

Harry shook his head. "No way. She doesn't. Of that I'm sure."

"One day you'll see who's right, you or me." She removed his hand gently from her pudenda. "Now you run along! And if that friend of yours wants to put up with a zombie, try and give me a ring. I may have taken so many sleeping pills, though, so many downers, I can't promise anything. If I get too depressed, all I can do is escape into sleep."

She cupped his face in her hands and kissed him lingeringly, sweetly, then released him. He stood up, undecided whether to have sex with her after all—with the music out of the way (how could he ever listen to the "Star Spangled Banner" again with a straight face?)—or take her at her word and leave. On second thought, he probably wouldn't be much good in bed now, anyway.

"No, honey, you better go," she smiled, having guessed from the look on his face what was going through his mind.

He nodded glumly and straightened his tie, then went quickly through his hair with his pocket comb, smoothing it down.

"Guess you're right," he said. "Thanks anyhow for everything . . . and tonight. Well," he placed a peck of a kiss on the tip of her nose, "be seeing you . . . I hope."

"You bet," she whispered, almost inaudibly, as he headed for the front door.

His hand had already curled around the doorknob when he remembered something. He turned around and saw her standing in the middle of her fleamarket collection of duck decoys, carved eagles and Cape Cod seashells, putting on her bathrobe.

"Charlotte, there's something I meant to ask you . . . were you home yesterday, in the afternoon?"

She tied a knot in the belt of the robe and gave him a quizzical look. "Yesterday? Why?"

"There's something I wanted to find out. It's nothing to do with you personally . . . It's . . . well, indirectly it's connected with my wife."

"Oh? You were fooling around with your girl friend yesterday?"

"It's not that either. In fact, I promise I'll tell you about it next week. But were you actually here, in your apartment?"

"Let me see now. In the afternoon? Yes, I *was* home. I had bought two magazines in the morning and was reading them in the afternoon."

"Okay. Now, did you have anybody here? I mean, did anybody come visit you, or ring the doorbell, let's say about twelve-thirty or one?"

"Hey, don't tell me you're jealous already, hon! After all . . ."

"Come on, I'm serious, really! It's very important. Did anybody call on you during or after lunch, or up to about six last night?"

Charlotte knitted her brow, then shook her head. "Not that I recall. No. But why?"

"Are you sure? I mean anybody, salesmen, what-have-you?"

This time she waited a bit longer before making up her mind, impressed by the urgency in his voice. Still pondering, she entered the foyer where he seemed to be waiting for her by the front door. "What is this anyway, sweetie? I told you there was nobody here all afternoon, or night—I'm sorry to say."

She had reached him and he put a hand on her shoulder, conscious at once of the frailty of her bones under the robe. "This is more important than you might think. Try to remember: about one-thirty or two, did you have a caller from the Jehovah's Witnesses?"

"Jehovah's . . . You trying to be funny or something?" she laughed. "Why . . . Hell, wait a minute!" She gaped at him, open-mouthed, as if seeing a ghost. "How in God's name did you know? I thought you were working then. Sure, now that you mention it, I *do* remember. About two-thirty or three o'clock I was on the phone talking to an old flame of mine from Chicago who was on his way through New York, when the doorbell rang. I answered it and there stood this tall, dark, handsome stranger. He whispered something. He sounded hoarse, as if he had laryngitis. I even leaned forward to hear him better and wouldn't you know I began whispering myself asking what he wanted and he told me something about the kingdom of God and I explained to him that I was on the phone and that I would have been only too happy to let him come in—so I could have given him a display of *my* idea of the kingdom of God—but he whispered that he made it a rule never to enter anybody's apartment because he didn't want to be exposed to temptation. Then he gave me this little religious leaflet threatening hell-fire to all who didn't believe in God and saying that there was going to be some meeting to which everybody was cordially invited. Well, I threw it away, but of course he didn't know that because I shut the door and then heard him ring the buzzer of the Levins, next door. But it was so funny, Harry, both of us whispering for a couple of minutes like we had some terrible secret to share when I didn't even . . . Listen, is that what you were after?"

Harry breathed a sigh of relief. "Yes." He kissed the tip of her chin, smiling. "You may not believe this, sweetheart, but if you had said that there was no one ringing your bell yesterday afternoon, I would have called the Watchtower Society right now, to make some inquiries."

"What?" Charlotte was genuinely baffled. "You kidding me, Harry?"

"Uh-uh. Next week, I promise." He settled another kiss on her forehead. "I'll explain it all next week. Take care!"

With that he turned, opened the door and slipped out of her apartment unnoticed.

But already, on the way to the elevator, doubts assailed him. He was not so sure whether to call on Charlotte's services after all for Ed Blakely. Perhaps he had been unwise in letting himself be trapped into giving away the secret that indeed his wife was not the important woman in his life, if only by tacit inference that there was somebody else. But the damage had been done. Waiting for the elevator, he cursed himself for being such a pushover as she had rightly called him, and he wondered if other men in a similar predicament would have behaved the same. Men were mere horny beasts whose endurance records for keeping their innermost secrets to themselves always tended to falter at the sight of a piece of ass, especially when it was so lewdly served up by a marching-song freak like the lascivious Miss Collins of 3N. Little wonder Mata Hari was such a raving success. What hung between your legs always influenced in some mysterious way what you had between your temples.

19 ———

The elevator arrived and Harry stepped in, finding himself in the company of a haughty Margaret Dumont type of *grande dame* with a big Edwardian hat and two long-haired boys in their late teens, one of whom had a huge Doberman pinscher on a leash. The two youths sported George Carlin-type ponytails and Indian headbands and wore Levi's and flower-patterned shirts, open to the waist. They obviously had been listening to an "outasight" recording of Bob Dylan's upstairs just before coming down because they were raving about the singer having saved their lives. Christ, if the world would only take Bobby's lyrics to heart, everybody could be expected to sit pretty in the Greening of America, they maintained, and love would return where it belonged, in the ashram or the commune, and there'd be free grass and karma and Kansas wheat for the Indians and the end of fucking free enterprise.

The door slid open on the ground floor and the dowager sailed out of the elevator. As she stepped off she turned to the two day-dreaming lunkheads, her face beetle-red with anger, and snapped, "Commies, why don't you go back where you belong? To China! Or Israel!" (Why was it, Harry wondered, that people always tended to equate personal frustrations with social imperfections?)

The Doberman tugged anxiously at the leash. One of the spaced-out youths made a peace sign while the other muttered something about old fascists who should be subjected in as painless a way as possible to the treatment of euthanasia. Strange, Harry thought, how each in his own way seemed to be indoctrinated and worn down, like the Red Guards and Hitler Youths, by the psychological assault of mass-propaganda, the rape of mass-worship.

He followed the mixed triumvirate slowly down the hallway, past his door, and stood undecidedly under the fanlight of the entry, wondering whether to go to the corner and maybe halfway up to West End Avenue to see if Ed Blakely was on his way, or wait for him in the apartment. He watched the Doberman pulling its master to the curb where it proceeded to press out a gargantuan sausage, while a few steps farther down the sidewalk Harry saw the man he had observed earlier in the day in the white Mercedes in the garage, standing at the curb scraping dog turds from the soles of his shoes. Not surprisingly his attention was drawn to the enormous Doberman doing its duty and he scowled at the big beast, moving his lips in silent supplication that by some divine grace all dogs be put to sleep at once. Everybody wanted everybody else dead: the young the old, the old the young, the rich the poor, the poor the rich, some people all dogs, mistresses the wives of their lovers, and lovers . . .

A few steps away, at the corner of the Drive, Saypool was engaged in an animated conversation with the janitor of the building from across the street. And above, poised like flyspecks in the cobalt-blue sky, a squadron of skywriters squeezed out their fluffy white letters.

The slam of a door nearby startled Harry. He looked in the direction from which the momentary disturbance came and noticed a heavy-set man locking the door of a rain-splattered Oldsmobile. His back was turned to Harry and not until he straightened up to gaze at the friendly and cloudless October sky did he recognize him. It was Ed Blakely. His friend's appearance came as a shock to Harry. He hadn't seen the realtor in about three years and never expected him to have aged and grown so fat in so short a time. He looked ten years older than the late fifties he calculated him to be and the strands of hair topping his jowly face were so sparse they had been strategically combed to cover as much of the shiny bald pate as was humanly possible. Suddenly it occurred to Harry that even as lusty a nymphomaniac as Charlotte Collins might have second thoughts and not take to him that easily and, in fact, turn him down altogether. His pudgy hands brushed back the sweaty streaks of hair as he headed for the building's street entrance where Harry was still watching him. When Blakely became aware of his friend's presence outside he stopped in surprise, then a broad grin spread across his doughy face and his arms semaphored a cordial salute.

"Hey, Harry, you old dog!" he exclaimed, genuinely pleased to see his host. "You been waiting for me?"

Harry shook Ed's hand and in the fashion of two pals meeting unexpectedly dealt Blakely's beefy shoulder a couple of hale and hearty slaps. "Thought I'd be your welcoming committee," he said with forced joviality. "How's old Ed?"

"Can't complain, Harry-boy." They walked side by side down the cool tile-covered lobby to Harry's apartment. "Came as fast as I could. Traffic was awful, though, with those flash floods, and tailgating half the way. Just about kills me. I can feel I'm not getting any younger. But then I had to come to town anyway."

"Glad you could make it, Eddie," Harry said, opening the door to his place. "Come on in."

Blakely waddled past him, loosening his tie, and thumped down the three steps into the large living room. He sniffed the air and turned around, the same moony grin on his face Harry had observed on the street. "Hey, what is this? You having a bash or something?" But before Harry had a chance to reply, Blakely's eyes lit up. "You know, if there's an orgy going on, Ed Blakely is always game. And talking of orgies, Harry-baby, you did promise me a little fun on the side, remember? Now you wouldn't . . ."

"No, no, no, don't worry," Harry assured him, pointing to a chair for the plump man to settle into. "It's all been taken care of. I have just the right broad for you. Right here in the building. Only a few steps away."

"That's what I call service." Blakely made himself comfortable in the easy chair and beamed with happiness. "I bet she's a knockout, huh?"

"You bet. Wouldn't pick anything else for an old buddy of mine. The truth is, she's a real-life nympho."

"Jesus!" Blakely shook his head in unabashed admiration for Harry. "Got to hand it to you, pal. Never let old Eddie-boy down yet, have you? Hey, what about Ruthie? Ain't she home?"

Harry sat on the sofa. "Oh, I forgot to tell you. Her mother took a turn for the worse and she flew up to Maine to see her last night."

"Sorry to hear about that. But it sure as hell explains it."

"Explains what?"

"Well, if *you* can't smell it, I sure as hell can. Like something from the garden of Four Roses. And I don't mean the botanical ones."

"Oh, that." Harry cursed himself for forgetting all about Don Ives again, still sleeping it off in the bedroom. He wished the old buzzard would simply wake up and take off. He grinned back at his friend. "Well, you know how it is. When the cat's away, the mice will play. Had a couple of guys over for drinks last night and the party lasted until this morning."

"Wow! Must have been some corker. And no hangover?"

"Naagh."

"Broads with the booze, too?" Blakely was virtually salivating at an image of naked dancing girls gamboling all over the living room.

"Sorry to disappoint you, Eddie." Harry wanted to get Blakely off the subject of sex and start the conversation rolling into business straits. "By the way, ever hear again from Clara?"

The realtor's heavy face clouded over as if he had been handed the death sentence. "Why bring that bitch up, Harry? You know she's dead as far as I'm concerned . . . except for the damn alimony, the goddamn bitch!"

"Oh I'd forgotten the separation became final. After all, I haven't seen you in almost three years and . . ."

"Well, I haven't seen her, so let's talk business, huh?"

Harry recalled now how touchy Blakely was, not only about his estranged wife whom he hated with all his heart, but about everything. He knew he had to treat him with kid gloves, to humor him along. But at least the conversation had turned to the matter at hand.

Harry leaned forward, his face all business. "Eddie, I'll put it to you square and straight: I want to sell my house."

Blakely stared at his friend in bug-eyed disbelief. "And for a chickenshit trifle like this you gimme a four-alarm ring and bring me all the way here?"

"You said you had to come into town, anyway."

"Sure I did, but what about this thing that you couldn't tell me about on the phone? Jesus, you know that's how I make my living— selling and buying homes—with a lot of the business done over the phone. Especially when I'm familiar with your lot."

"Ed, you don't understand." Harry got up and planted himself squarely in front of his friend. "I want cash for the house. And I want it right away. Equity must . . ."

"What d'you mean, right away?"

"Monday, Ed. At the latest Monday, by two in the afternoon."

The realtor gave him another look of bamboozled stupefaction. "You must be out of your cotton-pickin' mind, Mister. Where do I get a load of lettuce like that in less than forty-eight hours? With a Sunday in-between? And no firm takers?"

Harry turned away, groping for the right words. When he faced him again, all he could think of was to offer him a drink.

"Never mind the drink, pal!" Blakely was all business now. "What I want to know is how the hell you expect anybody to put up cash for your property by Monday?"

"Eddie, have I ever let you down? About anything?" Harry stopped short in front of Blakely, bending forward and resting his hands on his kneecaps. "Be honest now, have I? No, let me finish! I asked you to come down here, even lined up a dame for you. So help me God, she's a real beauty. One word from me and she'll be here in less than a minute and no . . ."

"Can it, Harry!" Blakely had ears only for the business deal now, not women. "Things like that take time. You're smart enough to know better. It's not just a matter of raising money but other things, like having the heating and plumbing inspected. And then there's the paperwork. Registration of deed, escrow, appraiser's estimate, bill of sale, binders, title search, a thousand and one details that make up a real estate transaction. You can't just take your bundle of dough and run. Not with today's tight money."

"But you can *cut* the red tape," Harry persisted. "It's in the most idyllic spot you got—at least you always told me it was an ideal location, even if it *is* 140 miles from New York—and equity must be worth twenty-three thousand at least."

"And you expect me to cough this up by Monday? Just like that?"

"No, I do *not*! The real estate right now should sell for twenty-five thousand and you know it. Even though I got it for thirteen-five."

"You still owe quite a few thousand on it, don't you?"

"No. The mortgage is almost paid off. Except for a thousand at $5\frac{1}{4}$. Meaning there are virtually no liens outstanding against the property. That's why I say it's worth at least twenty-three grand. With the improvements I made—the tool shed, adding a garage and the patio. And I've got the variance to show it's all above board. With that fresh paint job and brand new shingles and storm windows, that cottage is worth every penny I put into it and some more. How about all the winterizing and landscaping jobs I did? And let's not forget the neighborhood. It's been built up and is near a lake, giving it an extra . . ."

"Spare me the details, I know all about it. What you're trying to say, though, is that you should clear twenty-three thousand easily."

Harry straightened himself, stretching his numb arms, and looked at Ed Blakely long and hard. "Eddie, I'm not asking for twenty-three thou, even though I could get twenty-five I'm sure. No, I want to put it on the block for eighteen and not a cent more."

This time it was Blakely's turn to stare hard and long at his friend. "Are you nuts or something? After all the build-up you gave me about the capital improvements and the location, and I grant you could easily clear twenty-five, more even, and then you tell me you want to take a loss? It just doesn't make sense."

"You heard. Eighteen. I'll put it in writing."

Blakely rubbed tiny beads of sweat off his lobster-red neck with a dirty handkerchief and shook his head incredulously.

"And I thought I had heard everything," he mumbled, returning the damp handkerchief to his pocket.

"So what d'ya say?" Harry asked anxiously.

"Why, Harry? Why?"

"Never mind why, just gimme the word. Will you do it or do I have to contact somebody else?"

The realtor raised and dropped both arms in abject resignation and scratched the top of his thighs nervously.

"Well, to be honest, there've been a couple of guys making inquiries about the house. They were quite interested and willing to put down more than eighteen. So that should be no difficulty. But . . ."

"Okay—then give it to one of them for eighteen—whoever can put it up by Monday noon. Goddamn it, Eddie, you know the title is sound. The details can wait till later. The guy prepared to buy it simply will have to take your word for it. Once he has written a check out for it— a certified check—*then* you can go ahead with the red tape."

The fat man gaped at him slack-jawed. He still couldn't trust his ears. "I don't get it. For Chrissakes, Harry," he expostulated, "that's absolute madness, putting the house on the market for eighteen now when you're bound to wind up with twenty-five, maybe thirty thousand by the end of the month. I can't go along with that. Why not think about it for another week or two before you . . ."

"But I need it *now*, damn you!" Harry shouted. "Why're you so fucking pig-headed?" A bolt of hurt struck Ed Blakely's face. Like a rock. His dewlap-jowls quivered as if he had been punched hard on the nose and required a full minute to recover, to reorientate himself. Harry knew at once he was defeating his own purpose, after he had sworn to himself to remain calm. What on earth had gotten into him? Why did he flare up constantly today? . . . Yet all he could do, could think of at present was to apologize, for his tactless blunder, even though the shock of pain was bound to linger in Ed Blakely's stunned face and serve as a reminder of this dreadful faux pas throughout the rest of their talk . . . whatever he could still salvage of it.

"I don't know what came over me, Ed," he apologized lamely. "I'm sorry. I didn't mean to . . . Just nerves, I guess, with one thing or another . . . If only you knew . . . I've been going through rough times."

A trickle of sweat coursed down the side of Blakely's blue-veined cannonball head and he grabbed for the greasy handkerchief again and dabbed at his perspiring temples. "But why Monday?" he asked hoarsely.

Harry returned his gaze steadily, his mind working overtime in a feverish attempt to undo the damage done and make the next lie palatable to this man who refused to be a patsy. "Okay, I'll level with you," he said finally. "I've got a chance to really clean up—I mean make a *fortune*. A deal I've promised not to talk about, discuss with anybody. An investment. There isn't the slightest doubt in the world that it's the safest thing I ever did in my life."

Ed Blakely folded the mucky handkerchief carefully and wiped his palms with it. "An investment?" He looked up. "At a time like this? When nothing is safe, no stocks, shares, bonds, funds. You must be crazy . . ."

"Eddie, I know it's as good a deal as anything I ever . . ."

"Chrissakes!! The only way you can strike it rich today is to buy 9 per cent government notes, or get bundles of short-term treasury bills, or strike oil. But I don't think for one minute the big boys at Exxon are standing around waiting for Mr. Harry Bensonny to sink his dough into an oil well before going ahead and . . ."

"Listen, Ed, don't force my hand," Harry worked his jaws, feeling cornered again. "You've simply got to trust me when I say . . ."

158

"And *I* say you are gambling away a cottage into which you have dumped most of your savings, blowing it all on something you may lose your shirt on."

"You may not believe this but there is absolutely no risk involved. It'll give me a quick turn-over on my money. All it requires is timing."

"No risk, my foot!" Blakely retorted derisively. "Somebody's got your number all right. No risk, Harry, except for your property and I wouldn't be surprised your savings too." He drew in his lips and shook his head. "God, you're more naive than I took you for, Harry, a real-life sucker. And whoever is responsible for this deal knows it. You are . . . Hey, it's not you alone, is it? I mean you have to consult Ruth too, don't you? I can't do anything without her consent, Harry, and you know . . ."

"Not as far as the house is concerned. The deed is in my name only. She has nothing to do with it. I acquired it before we got married. I can do with it as I please."

"Oh! And she knows about this? Your plan to sell out? At a loss?"

"Of course she does. What do you think? You don't imagine I'd try to do it without her go-ahead and sell out behind her back?"

"Well, okay. If that's the case I can't . . . No! You let me speak to her first and make sure. I don't want to get it in the neck from her later, making me out as some sort of an accomplice in this . . ."

"Eddie, there's nothing I'd like better than to let you talk to her. Right this minute if you want to. In fact, there's nothing I'd like more than to hear her voice myself, this instant. Only trouble is, where she is in Maine all connections with the mainland have been cut. Did you hear about the hurricane off the coast of New England? I tried to get hold of Ruthie a couple of hours ago and was told that they won't be able to repair the lines till sometime on Tuesday, if they're lucky and the storm subsides by then."

"I . . . You know, Harry, I just can't believe it."

"Go ahead! There's the phone. Ask the operator to connect you with the store on Monhegan Island." He picked up the address book. "I'll give you the number. It's . . ."

"No, it's not that. I believe you about the lines being down. What strikes me as fishy is this sudden need of yours to lay your hands on every single penny in a hurry before Ruth gets a chance to return to the city. I thought I could trust you, Harry, but I see now that obviously I can't. Whole thing sounds so goddam shady to me I'm sure you're up to some dirty trick. Who knows, you may even blow town, leave with some broad and take all the dough you can get hold of with you before poor little Ruth ever gets wind of . . ."

"What's the matter with you? You gone crazy or something?" Suddenly Harry saw red. His desperate hope of making it with the house, his trump card, was going up in smoke, and before he knew it a demonic fury possessed him as, almost against his will, he flung the little address book at his friend. It struck Blakely in the left eye and he reeled back, then folded over into a crouch with a cry of pain, the messy handkerchief dabbing away like mad at the injured eye. "My God, you've got some nerve!" Harry exploded self-righteously. "Since when did I ever give you cause to believe that I'd be capable of leaving town with some broad and abandoning Ruth? The unmitigated gall!"

Blakely blinked up at the raving man. "You're sick," he muttered.

"No, *you're* sick." Harry yelled, beside himself. "A guest in my house and one innuendo after another that I'm selling the house to beat it with some floozy." Here he went all out for Ruth, prepared to sacrifice every cent of his life's savings for her, and now this lecher suspected him of nothing less than infidelity. "The unmitigated gall . . .the . . . the . . . me double-crossing my wife!. Goddamn you, you've got no right casting such aspersions, d'you hear? Hey, look at me! I'm talking to you!" he shrieked, enraged beyond endurance that he should be suspected of two-timing Ruth. "As God is my witness, it's for her most of all I want this money. And I want it now. I want it on Monday. Jesus Christ, is that so hard to understand when I'm willing to make it worth your while?"

Ed Blakely looked up, still patting his now inflamed eye with the handkerchief. His bovine jowls quivered like Jell-O, his mouth fixed agape in frozen bewilderment, but he said nothing. A blood-pounding silence between the two men stretched unbearably as they appraised each other with unconcealed hostility.

After a minute of this, Blakely stirred and got to his feet, rising with enormous difficulty from the easy chair. He put the handkerchief back in his pocket and with shaking hands straightened his tie.

"That's the second time this afternoon," he said with a deep rumble in his voice. "I don't have to take this crap from anybody. I didn't come here to be . . ." His lips moved, but no words came out. He stared uncomprehendingly at Harry, then turned from him and shambled heavily, like a wounded hippo, in the direction of the foyer. "There's nothing further to discuss."

Harry was breathless, his heart pounded achingly inside his chest, and a nerve throbbed wildly in a vein in his temple. He stared after Ed Blakely, not moving, rooted to the ground like a block of wood.

"But what about our deal?" he asked feebly.

Ed Blakely stopped and turned. "There never was any deal between us, sonny-boy. You go ahead and sell the house any way you like. But not through me. There are plenty of other agents you can get listed with." And with this he raised his right foot to haul himself up the first step to the foyer.

That was all Harry needed now, to be left sitting high and dry, without the ransom money. It sure as hell was the death blow for his wife. And it was *his* bloody fault.

"Ed, the house is yours!" Harry was panic-stricken, his voice shrill, strident with despair as he bolted past the armchair and grabbed Blakely by the elbow. "You can have it for twenty thousand. Forget about the other guys. It's yours for twenty and you can sell it to the first buyer for twenty-five, thirty-five, forty thousand once the deed is yours. All you got to do is change the deed to your name, with my signature validating it all, on Monday, at the bank."

Blakely peered up at him through the red-shot eye, sweat pouring down the white layers of his face and staining his dank collar.

"Leave me alone," he said in a tired voice.

"Ed, if twenty is too much I'll take eighteen from you. For God's sake, pal, can't you see how desperate I am? The papers can be drawn up today; all perfectly legal, and on Monday you can give me a certified check for eighteen. Surely, I'm not asking the impossible of you. Especially when you know how you can clean up on this deal . . ."

"Eighteen?" Blakely asked, his interest suddenly revived. His voice showing more life, he said, "Me? For eighteen? You're not putting me on or something?"

A faint smile, half of relief, half of sheer exhaustion, untensed Harry's set features. He placed a fraternal hand on his friend's shoulder. "Ed, I know I blew my top," he said conciliatorily. "There was no excuse for it and to say I'm sorry won't make it any better. Maybe even offering you the profits on the sale is an insult. But . . ." He looked at the mystified, sweating face of the realtor who no longer knew what to make of the whole situation, of Harry's sudden irrational fits of violence. "Ed, all I can say is that a week from today you *will* understand . . . understand why I acted this way."

Ed Blakely returned Harry's gaze steadily, then removed the hand from his shoulder and shuffled with a tired slouch back into the living room. There he stood stock-still, ostensibly regarding his scuffed shoes, and at long last turned around to Harry who was standing on the second step to the foyer, watching him anxiously. "Okay. As long as it's kosher, and you make sure there's nothing unethical about this transaction, okay, maybe I'll go along with it. For eighteen."

Harry shut his eyes. He was overcome by a sudden dizziness. He thought the furniture was whirling around in concentric circles in the dark whooshiness inside his cranium. He opened his eyes again and slowly strode over to the fat man, extending his hand. Ed Blakely looked at it glumly, not sure whether he might be sealing a deal he would regret later, but he grasped the proffered hand and shook it limply and without much enthusiasm.

Harry leveled his eyes at the realtor with great difficulty. "Gosh, Eddie, what can I say . . . except that I knew I could depend on you . . . and that you won't regret it. You can't possibly go wrong. All you've got to do is change the deed to your name, have it notarized with my signature and . . ."

"Just cut it out, pal, I don't feel like talking about it right now," Blakely replied dourly. "It's a bit more complicated than that and I need some of your papers later, like the title deed, encumbrances, and your tax forms, to see that you're clean, but I think I can swing it, the closing, by Monday noon. I'll also want to take a look at your lot— maybe tomorrow. But let's get one thing straight once and for all, and you better pay attention to me. You raise your hand against me just once more, or gimme any of your lip, old buddy, and you can kiss the deal good-bye. *And* I'll have you thrown in the slammer for assault. I've got enough headaches of my own without being insulted like this and wasting my time hanging around some clown blowing his top every few minutes. Life's too short for . . ."

"Ed, I've told you I was sorry. I don't know what got into me. Maybe next week you'll understand why I lost my temper. But it won't happen again. Scout's honor. Promise. Cross my heart and hope to . . ."

"Okay, okay, cut the comedy! Just as long as you know what the score is."

"I got the message, don't worry! Listen, why don't you sit down, make yourself at home while I get us something to drink and baptize the deal."

At last Blakely began to climb out of his down mood. His pasty complexion was rippled by a relieved little smile and he slumped back on the sofa. "Don't mind if I do," he said, sighing deeply but shifting forward a moment later, perching on the edge of the sofa as if ready to ward off the next blow. "After this little to-do I'm about ready for anything."

"Sure thing." Harry forced himself to grin back, then headed for the kitchen. "Got some French brandy left that'll tickle your palate. And as a special reward, after the drink I'll just step outside for a minute and get you that gorgeous chick I promised." He stopped in the kitchen door, blessing the turn of events the afternoon had taken after such a wretched beginning. A woman for Blakely, and eighteen G's for the house, and his worries were over. The rest of the money he could withdraw easily on Monday from his savings and checking accounts, maybe sell his Dodge Dart, and cash in his stocks and, perhaps, his bonds. As far as the ransom was concerned Ruth seemed as good as safe.

"Outside?" The wobbly contours of Ed Blakely's face looked puzzled. "I thought you said she lived in this building, just a few steps away."

"She does. In shouting distance even," Harry said. "Provided you yell loud enough. I'll see her after I give you my papers and get everything settled for you for tonight. And let me tell you, Eddie-boy, this broad will do anything, night and day, if you can hold out that long."

The lewd promise served Ed as a shot of insulin to a diabetic. A Picassian leer broadened the mountainous face even more. "Boy, I bet she'll make all this worthwhile yet," Ed chuckled. "I bet you've had her yourse . . ."

A loud thump, as if somebody had fallen on the floor, broke into the now convivial atmosphere of the living room.

Ed Blakely heaved himself from the sofa and spun around in the direction of the noise—the bedroom. "What the hell was that?"

"Jesus Christ, I forgot all about him!"

Harry darted through the living room as the shocked broker froze to the spot.

"Who?"

Before Harry reached the bedroom door, it flew wide open, smashing into the wall, and Donald Ives tumbled out, pitching forward blindly, catching himself and falling heavily against the bathroom door.

"Who in God's name . . .?" Blakely pointed, white as a sheet, at the disheveled figure.

Ives belched and rested with his forehead against the coolness of the wood.

Harry's eyes flitted desperately between Blakely and Ives. "I'd forgotten all about him, Eddie," he explained, moving gingerly toward the drunk to hold him up under his arms. He turned with a sheepish grin to his friend. "You know how it is, Ed. The party last night. When the cat's away, the mice will play, right?"

"Been holding out on me, Harry, huh?" Blakely this time believed Harry hook, line and sinker, as the evidence and the fragrance of whiskey manifested themselves in front of him. "Must have been some bash you had. Guy sure is plastered."

Ives lifted his head with what amounted to a superhuman effort and tried to focus his eyes on the realtor. "Pashtered, my foot!" His speech oddly enough was more leaden now than earlier. With his head bobbing up and down, he turned to his host. "You, man . . . whazzyaname? . . . Whyn't you gimme a li'l drink, thasha good feller . . . Just a li'l ole . . ."

Ives was about to sag to the floor again and with great difficulty Harry managed to keep him up on his legs, steadying him now against the living room wall. The guy had to leave. And pronto. Not only was he of no further use to Harry, but in his present state he could give away the secret of Ruth's disappearance. Blakely had a mighty reputation for gossip and this was about the last thing Harry needed at this moment when he was so close to clinching the deal and securing the ransom. With luck—if anything in this situation could be called luck—with luck favoring him at last he had no intention of having the rug pulled out from under him by this lush. It certainly wasn't Harry's fault if fate had dealt Ives a raw deal.

Harry glanced over his shoulder at his portly friend who stood in the middle of the living room not quite sure whether to come to his aid or to just watch the sorry spectacle.

"Ed, listen. Let me take care first of old Don here. I'll just help him find a cab. Why don't you look after yourself in the meantime? There's some brandy in the kitchen cabinet, right over the sink. Just help yourself, will you?"

Blakely did not need a pair of binoculars to see that Harry had his hands full maneuvering Ives through the living room without the poor sot bruising himself on furniture or buckling under the weight of his uncontrollable torso and limbs. Ives' left leg had the annoying habit of moving timorously forward, pausing in mid-air, and, instead of advancing, changing its mind and moving diagonally in front of the right leg, which forthwith stumbled over the left. A slow-motion pas de deux.

"You sure you don't want me to give you a hand, Harry?" Blakely made a half-hearted attempt to help, but the last thing Harry wanted was to have him around when Ives might still spill the beans about Ruth.

"No, honestly, Ed. You go ahead. Shouldn't take too long. Here . . . take it easy, one step at a time," he addressed himself to the bungling effort of Ives negotiating the steps to the foyer. "That's better. See, Don, we're almost there. Fresh air will do you a world of good." At the front door Harry rotated once more out of Ives' half-nelson toward Ed Blakely who kept watching the two with an air of distress and indecision. He gave the realtor a wink. "I may have to go to West End Avenue, or as far as Broadway, to get a cab. But it shouldn't take too long. Okay?"

Ed Blakely returned his friend's wink. "Just take it easy! Don't worry about me!"

20 ⸺

Harry eased out of the front door, pulling Ives along. He lifted one of the drunk's arms and draped it over his shoulder, holding onto his hand so that the arm would not slide back again, and supported himself for balance with his other arm by winding it halfway around Ives' waist. Indeed, Harry was so involved in steering Ives safely out of the building, out of his life, that he never noticed he had forgotten to pull the door shut after him. Or perhaps he thought that Blakely would have enough brains to close the front door himself, but the realtor was so relieved at being left alone for the first time this afternoon since the frightening experience with wild-tempered Harry that he headed at once for the kitchen where the promised French-imported brandy hopefully would mellow his rather shattered nerves and restore his equilibrium.

Harry, meanwhile, escorted the drunk down the cool, checker-square-tiled landing, constantly speaking encouragement to him not to drop off again.

"You know, Don, you better let me have your address, so I can tell the driver where to take you."

Ives wanted very much to stop walking so he could focus his full attention on Harry, but he couldn't—he was being forced to keep moving, to stay awake.

"Come on, move!"

"This headache . . . Chrissakes . . ."

"The address, Donald . . . Where do you live?"

Harry had to stop for half a minute. His arm was almost numb. He rested Ives against the mail boxes near the street entrance and kept him up with one arm. Ives drooled ribbons of sour saliva down his bristly chin and gazed glassily at his host.

"My addresh?" His tongue lolled without control. "What do you care . . . where I live . . . with your wife half-dead, why . . ."

"Never mind that now," Harry countered angrily and again pulled Ives' arm over the back of his neck as they staggered toward the door. "Just give me your address . . . for the taxi."

"Ha . . . you think . . . your wife . . ." He belched. "Gotta go to the john."

Harry didn't care. They had walked down the stone steps and almost reached street level and he had no intention of taking him back to his apartment for a leak. Let him wait till he gets home, Harry decided.

By now they were only a few steps from the sidewalk, when all of a sudden a shadow darkened the stoop leading into the lobby and somebody entered the building carrying an overloaded shopping bag. Harry looked up to avoid a collision. It was Helga. She stopped, startled at the sight of Harry staggering along the wall with the soused little man on his arm.

Harry halted in his steps, too, and stared at her, speechless, aghast, the blood thudding again in his ears. He had not seen her since the night before when he first learned of Ruth's disappearance. She didn't even know about the kidnapping. Their eyes met in stunned silence. Only Ives was unaware of another presence, much less the glances being exchanged.

"You think you're so damn shmart . . . doncha?" Ives rambled on as Harry strove desperately to hustle him out into the street, away from this building, speedily, unnoticed, before further damage was done. "But you won't . . . you won't shee her again . . . hear? . . . You'll never shee your wife again . . . never . . . alive . . ."

Harry felt like strangling Ives. He dealt him a sharp jolt in his side with his elbow, to keep him moving. Helga had to step back to let the two pass through the door. Harry's face was flushed, both from the effort of handling the drunk and the dismay over Ives' remark in front of Helga and getting caught in this awful predicament. At last, though, the two men reached the street. Harry cast a quick furtive glance back over his shoulder and was just in time to see Helga give him a totally uncomprehending look. Harry could only shake his head, emphatically, as if to say that the man is mad, don't you believe a word you heard. But whatever Harry's impassioned reaction, this was not how Helga interpreted Ives' words. She still riveted her eyes on the street, although the two men were no longer in sight, and then frowned, trying to make sense of the snatch of conversation she had overheard.

Very slowly she turned from the entryway and moved up the steps and then down the hallway, past the mail boxes, deep in thought. What on earth did the drunk mean by 'You'll never see your wife again'? And had he added 'Alive'? Or was she only imagining this? And who was he, anyhow? A friend of Ruth's? A member of Harry's publishing firm? Who . . .

With some alarm Helga realized that she had actually passed her own door and was already well on the way down the corridor to Harry's apartment. In all the years she had lived here this had never happened to her. This lapse irritated her. Perhaps an unmistakable sign of getting old. She was about to turn back in the direction of her own place when she noticed, from where she stood, that Harry's apartment door was wide open. She kept looking at it, not sure whether she was dreaming or not, not even conscious of the weight of the grocery bag in her arms. You just didn't do such things in New York. Nobody in his right mind left his apartment door open for anyone to walk in, not with all the break-ins, muggings, rapes, murders, mayhem, and the police statistics of the city's increase in the rate of killings over last year's. But there was no doubt about it. The door was wide open and as far as Helga could make out no sound came from inside. And then she remembered the drunk's statement once more, about the fact that Ruth would never be seen alive again by Harry.

Without wasting another moment, Helga dashed back to her apartment. Her free hand dug nervously for the keys in a pocket of her fawn cabretta-leather coat and she let herself in. In the kitchen she quickly deposited the groceries from the bag, stowing them in the refrigerator, with Schrafft's vanilla ice cream going into the freezer. She then jammed a package containing her laundered bed sheets into the linen closet adjoining the tiny hallway between the living room and the bedroom. A trip to the bathroom to wash up revealed that her lips needed a dab or two of Charles of the Ritz's modest red. Her heart was racing as thoughts plunged helter-skelter through her confused mind, thoughts that had started in the lobby when she bumped into Harry and the dirty little drunk with the bloodshot eyes. Who could he be? Harry had never once mentioned an acquaintance of his who even faintly resembled him. But much more puzzling was that remark about Ruth. She simply had to find out what had been happening since the night before.

A last glance in the mirror more than satisfied Helga that her features bore up remarkably well in spite of her forty-four years, that the raw material of nature had copiously endowed her face with a hypnotic symmetry which concealed the essence of toil without sacrificing the underlying surges of strength, sadness, humor, tenderness. But her large expressive eyes could never hide the fact that she had lived through one hell of a lifetime.

No more time could be wasted. Helga took off her leather coat and hung it in the hall closet, seeing to it that the housekèys were transferred to the small pocket of her Cardin pantsuit.

Nervously, she locked her front door and walked down the hall to Harry's apartment. The door was still wide open. She cast a brief glance up and down the corridor to make sure she was not seen entering, although at this juncture it should hardly have mattered, but not a soul was in sight. She stepped gingerly into the foyer of Harry's private domain, and stopped. Once, while Ruth was staying at the Presbyterian Center for a physical check-up, Harry had invited her in, just to look around. He showed her around briefly and then both retreated again to the safety of her apartment where they had no fear of being interrupted in their love-making.

Virtually nothing had changed in the scene Helga had committed to memory. The windows were wide open but despite the cool breeze blowing in from the Hudson there was the unmistakable suggestion of alcohol in the air. She frowned. Not a sound came from any part of the apartment. It seemed deserted. A little black address book lay on the carpet, near the sofa.

Helga made up her mind she simply had to find out what was happening. She cleared her throat and emitted a birdlike, "Mrs. Bensonny!"

There was no answer. She advanced a couple of steps, to the very edge of the stairs leading from the foyer into the sunken living room.

"Anybody home?" She waited a few seconds, then raised her voice a couple of notches. "Hello! Can I borrow some matches, Mrs. Bensonny?"

The sound of her voice must have carried this time into the kitchen and reached Ed Blakely. Because the next second she distinctly heard steps, and then a squat mountain of a man in a rumpled suit and gaudy tie emerged with a glass in one hand, the other hand smoothing the disheveled wisps of hair over his bald crown.

A happy grin spread at once over his face. "Is there anything I can do for you, young lady?" he asked.

"Oh." Helga was caught off-guard. Another stranger! What *was* going on here? "Well . . . I . . . I came to see Mr. and Mrs. Bensonny about something."

Ed Blakely took a few steps towards her. "Mrs. Bensonny is out of town, I'm afraid. So she won't be able to help you very much."

"Oh, she is?" This came as a surprise to Helga. Harry had not mentioned anything the night before about Ruth going away. Why hadn't he gotten in touch with her and told her about it today? Then, again, the old drunk's odd statement crossed her mind.

"However, I'm not Mr. Bensonny," the realtor's voice broke into her train of deliberation. "He should be back in . . ."

"Of course you're not," she smiled, stepping down into the living room. "I know Harry quite well."

"Harry? Oh, then you're a friend of his?"

Helga began to feel quite giddy at the prospect of Ruth being out of town and having Harry all to herself today, even if it meant that the hour of confrontation was delayed again . . . unless . . . had he already told Ruth the night before about his plans to marry Helga? Was this why she has left town? In a huff? But then, why these two strange men in the apartment, the fat man and the drunk?

"A friend?" Helga smiled, teasingly. "You could say so, yes."

"Well, any friend of Harry's is a friend of mine," Ed Blakely said and shook her hand. "I'm Ed Blakely, from Sullivan County. Harry may have mentioned me to you if you're a friend of his . . . Have you known him long?"

Helga had some difficulty retrieving her hand from his sweaty grasp. "Long enough to . . ." she started, then thought better of it and smiled the demure smile she usually trained on men to make them forget what they were planning to ask her. "Well, let's say we're neighbors, Mr. Blakely. And it's quite possible Harry did mention you to me. Or me to you. You see, we're quite close neighbors. I live in this building, only a few steps away." She rendered a harmless, carefree laugh. "And here I am."

A few steps away . . . and here she was! *The* cue! Ed Blakely's pudgy face quivered with excitement, and so did the drink in his hand. "You live in this building? Jesus Christ!" he exclaimed jubilantly, looking for a place to put his drink. "He sure as hell mentioned *you* to me, lady."

Helga's smile vanished in a flash. "He did?"

"Sure did." Blakely hastened over to the roll-top desk and placed the glass on it, next to the typewriter, still containing the ransom note. He turned back to Helga and approached her. "Whatever your name is, young lady, he sure hasn't been holding out on me about you. Everything he told me about you is true. You sure are a lovely woman."

Helga, instantly suspicious and upset, felt the sphincters in her entire body close up. How much had Harry confided to this stranger? And why? It wasn't at all like Harry to shoot his mouth off. An uncertain half-crooked smile did not help to relieve her tension either, nor soften her hardening features. "Well, thank you kindly, Mr. Blakely," she said. "What other fascinating things did Harry tell you about me? I hope it wasn't too bad."

"Honey, perish the thought! How could he? A lovely creature like you!" He stopped short of Helga and without a warning grabbed both her hands in his damp palms. They shut like clams around her thin white fingers. "Gal with a cute accent like yours couldn't do anything bad." His wet toothy grin seemed to stretch from ear to ear. The bags under his eyes hung like dark awnings over his plump cheeks and his cognac-sodden breath swept over her face. A rumbling laugh rose from his inner depths. "Unless, of course, sex can be considered bad." He punctuated this statement with an overly familiar squeeze of his hands and a lecherous wink.

Helga felt herself go ice-cold. Had Harry gone stark-raving mad telling Blakely about their intimacy? She tried to withdraw her hands from his fleshy clutch, but to no avail. "I don't . . . understand, Mr. Blakely. What do you mean, sex?"

"Aw, come on now, sugar. You don't have to pretend to Uncle Ed. I wasn't born yesterday."

"I am sure you were not," she shot back edgily, momentarily imagining an SS uniform on this hulking man. Once more she attempted to extricate her hands but only felt the thick sausagelike fingers close

171

pincer-tight around her wrists. "But forgive me for being so dense. I still don't understand your remark about sex!"

At first he had held her hands, then her wrists, now his hands were stealthily climbing up and massaging the upper part of her arms. "Honey, what's to understand about sex? I'm sure you're old enough to know what it means to have a meaningful relationship, huh?"

Helga could not trust her ears. "And that's what Harry told you?"

"And why not? You don't have to be ashamed about enjoying sex. Everybody does."

She tried very hard now, without making any pretense, that she meant to be released from his grip. "You know, Mr. Blakely, I find this topic exceedingly unpleasant. After all, we do not even know each other. Now will you kindly let me . . ."

"That's something which we can correct pretty quickly, sweetiepie. After all, we *are* sort of birds of a feather, aren't we?"

"We are?" Helga made no effort to conceal her bewilderment, her revulsion. "I don't follow you, Mr. Blakely."

"Don't you, honey-bunch?" He began to tremble now with excitement and grabbed Helga by her shoulders, trying to press her gently closer to himself. "You don't have to pretend to me, angel. Really. As I was saying, we're sort of cousins under the skin, because I feel the same way about sex you do. Harry said so. You and I . . ."

With a sudden unexpected yank, Helga wrenched free, and stepped back quickly, rubbing her arms to stimulate the circulation. "Now look here, Mr. Blakely, I don't know what Harry . . ."

"Aw, come on, baby! Harry told me all about you, the good times you can give a man. So why . . ."

"He *what?*" she exclaimed, refusing to believe what she just heard. Had Harry gone mad, betraying their most sacred moments together? "He actually said *that!*"

"What's the matter with you? Relax! There's no need getting all uptight. Everybody screws around. You've done it. He said so himself. Relax!" He lunged forward, seizing her violently with both hands, then sneaking one arm around her waist and drawing her close to him so forcefully their heads collided.

"Let me go!" she screamed, struggling in his vicelike clasp. "Will you let . . ."

"Come on now, loosen up, stop acting like a goddamn virgin!" Blakely finally got impatient. Enough of this coyness, he thought. "Harry said you're a nympho. So how about a kiss, sweetie . . . for

172

starters?" One of his hands quickly stole around to the front and snaked up to the top of her unbuttoned jacket. A second later a big pudgy hand grasped one of her breasts, with such clumsy savagery that she cried out in pain. "Just one little kiss," he rumbled hoarsely.

His wet brandy mouth forced itself over her tight lips and strove to pry them apart with his tongue. One of Helga's hands had been freed while his own was exploring the front of her body and with all her strength she dug the tips of her fingernails into his round fleshy dome, scratching them down hard across his inflamed eye, cheek, nose. But he was too strong, too drunk with lust to notice. She breathed hard, trying to catch her breath, and in a desperate gesture of resisting his advances she opened her mouth wide and sank her sharp teeth into his lips. Like a wounded elephant, he released a trumpet's blast of pain.

The slam of a door exploded in their ears. As though struck by lightning, the two bodies split apart. Harry stood in the foyer, aghast, his eyes taking in, yet rejecting what they saw.

"What the hell . . . What's going on here?"

"The bitch!" Blakely's hand darted to his face. A trickle of blood oozed claret-thin from the corner of his mouth. "That wildcat . . . you weren't half-kidding. She really bites!"

Helga staggered back, faint, her pantsuit in disarray. "What is this?" She could scarcely catch her breath and wiped her face with the sleeve of her jacket. Then she turned on Harry, anger and reproach brimming in her voice. "What sort of friends have you *got*? This son of a bitch grabbed me and would have raped . . ."

Harry had heard enough. In a flash he jumped down the three steps. "Have you gone mad?" he shouted, enraged as the pieces began to form in his mind. "You let go of her! At once! You touch her just once more and I swear I'll brain . . ."

"Hey, now take it easy! Let's not start *that* again!" Blakely raised his voice, alarmed and bewildered, dabbing with the smudgy handkerchief at his blood-smeared lips.

"He said you'd understand," Helga spat out bitterly at the man she had trusted and loved. "That it was all right for him to screw me, that you told him about the good time I give men and . . ."

"That's it, brother! Lay off her! And get out of here! Now!" Harry shouted, bolting past Helga. He grabbed Blakely's elbow and spun him around, catching him unawares as he was drying his damp face.

"That does it!" the mountainous man flew into a rage. He jerked his arm free, backed away from Harry, rearing to jump at him, his eyes filled with hatred. "That's the third time, you bastard! The third time this afternoon . . . after I warned you to lay off me. First telling me about the broad screwing like she couldn't have enough of it and then . . ."

"What!" Helga's eyes burned with contempt. "Harry, what is he . . ."

"He's twisting everything. I wasn't talking about . . ."

"I'm not twisting nothing, and what's more, both of you can go to hell!" bellowed the incensed broker. "You lay your hands on me just once more, you son of a bitch, and so help me God I'll break every goddam bone in your body, strangle you with my bare hands. And as for this foreign bitch . . ."

Harry grasped Helga by her wrist and in a sudden protective move stationed himself in front of her. "Don't you blame me for your mania, your satyriasis, you sick old fool!" Harry overshouted Ed Blakely. "Coming in here and trying to rape the first woman in sight . . ."

"You go to hell!"

"No, *you* go to hell! I told you I don't want you around any more. This wasn't the woman I had for *you*. And even if she were you had no right to touch her here in my apartment."

The two men confronted each other full of loathing, their breath coming in swift little gasps, each appraising the other's physical condition in the manner of sparring partners. Helga stood behind Harry, shaking with fright, digging her fingers into his jacket, again seeing the flash of black SS uniforms.

At length Blakely broke the horrible silence. "You and your broads!" he said hoarsely, putting his handkerchief away and tucking the bottom-end of the gaudy tie under his belt. "The minute Ruth's out of the way it's booze and orgies and whores like her. And that dame you promised. And I can tell you I've seen better on the Bowery."

"For the last time: get out!" Harry pressed the words through clenched teeth. "Or do I have to throw you out?"

The realtor shook a fist under Harry's nose. "You just try and touch me once more . . . and you know what'll happen."

"Then get out!"

Ed Blakely wiped the rivulets of sweat from his forehead with the back of his hand, regarded the two for a few seconds longer with unconcealed detestation, then moved heavily past Harry, in the direction of the front door. Suddenly, before reaching the stairs, he made a swing around, and took a grab at Helga's arm, pulling at it savagely.

"You coming along?" he importuned gruffly. "If it means anything to you, I can pay better than he does."

Harry's hands flew up at Ed Blakely's offending arm. He spun him around and dealt a vicious blow to the seat of the fat man's pants with the sole of his shoe, causing him to pitch forward onto the steps. "For the last time, beat it, before I tear you apart!" he yelled.

Blakely lay there for a few moments, stunned, then stirred and raised himself with a huge effort, defeated. He dusted himself off, tugged at the ends of his jacket, and lumbered up the steps, shakily, staggering into the foyer. There he turned, white as a ghost, and leveled an accusing finger at the man and woman staring up at him.

"You think you're the horse's ass, don't you, Harry?" he said menacingly, his jaws clenched. "Well, maybe you had me fooled for a minute with all that jazz about your house. But let me tell you I'm nobody's fool. As far as I'm concerned the deal is off. No s.o.b. calls me a maniac, then decks me and insults me right in front of a low-down hooker, and gets away with it!" He turned away, lurched toward the front door and opened it; then changed his mind and again confronted Harry and Helga who stared after him. "And if you think Ruth isn't going to hear about *her*," he pointed to Helga, "about this chippy of yours living right here under Ruth's nose, you've another think coming to you. I'm wise to your tricks, mister; you want that dough so you can split with this fucking broad. But not with my money you won't! Nosireeee! And that's what I'm going to tell Ruth!"

With this threat he stepped out into the hallway and slammed the door after him.

21 ———

Silence, absolute, deafening silence, filled every particle of the living room. The two kept gazing at the shut door as though half-expecting Ed Blakely to come back and say he didn't mean any of it, that it was all part of a nightmare, a misunderstanding. But of course nothing of the sort happened. The stillness became unbearable, and the couple turned to each other, the violence of the last few minutes etched in their faces; and it was only then that Harry moved away and disappeared into the kitchen. Helga did not stir, not knowing how to react nor how to put any of the preceding bits and pieces together.

After only a few seconds Harry emerged from the kitchen, gaping at an empty brandy bottle in his hand. He passed Helga, blindly, as if she didn't exist, stopped in the middle of the room, shaking his head at the bottle in utter disbelief, then slammed it down on the coffee table.

The crash went through Helga like an electric current. She looked at Harry hard, searching for a reason for this strange behavior, but his back was turned to her. Even at a time like this, dazed and bewildered as she was, she could not help but notice that he still wore the same shirt, the same suit he had taken off the evening before in her apartment and put on again. He usually changed his clothes every day, without fail.

"What's happening, Harry?" she asked in a frightened voice. "Who *was* that man?"

Harry wheeled toward her, his eyes ablaze with anger. "What *I* want to know is what the hell *you* are doing here."

"Me? . . . I . . . well, I . . ." She groped for words, shocked by his tone of voice. "That man, he suddenly grabbed me and . . ."

"Dammit, I asked you what you are doing in my apartment," he shouted at her for the second time.

She tried to remain calm and ignore his raised voice. "The door was open," she replied quietly. "It was open after I saw you with that drunk outside, the one who said your wife will never come back." For a moment she waited for him to say something, and frowned. "Harry, what did he m . . ."

But he wasn't listening. "Helga, for God's sake, I told you a thousand times *never, never* to come here. Suppose someone saw you come in here. There'd be hell to pay. You heard Ed's threat."

"Darling, I didn't . . ." Again she struggled for the right words. What was the matter with her? Tongue-tied! She, a prize-winning author! But she had never seen him like this. For a moment she debated whether to take him into her arms, try to calm him, letting him feel the warmth, the intimate softness of her body. But she decided against it. Instead, unaccountably, her voice steadied. "Harry, tell me, what did he mean, the little guy in the hall, that your wife won't come back? Alive. And this fellow Ed, he said she was gone too."

"That fellow Ed . . ." Harry's hands clenched at the memory of what had occurred here minutes earlier. "D'you realize what you did, you damn fool? You loused up a deal! Something that may cost me everything." He smacked a fist into his open palm. "God, you fouled me up all right *this* time!"

Helga simply refused to believe what she was hearing. Suddenly everything was *her* fault . . . when all she had done was almost get raped by a stranger in Harry's apartment.

Still wobbly from the shock of the encounter with Ed Blakely, she let herself down on the edge of the sofa, never taking her eyes off Harry. "What *have* I done, Harry?" She spoke in an almost inaudible voice. "A man says in front of me that Ruth will never come back; I run over here to help you, to find out what was happening . . . because I love you, and the door was wide open . . . I pretend to ask for matches to get into the apartment . . . this big ape comes out of the kitchen and paws me . . . and you say it's all my fault . . ."

"Aw, cut it out, Helga, don't gimme that innocent routine!" He glared at her, still smarting from her interference and the resulting blow-up with Blakely that could ruin all his efforts to secure the ransom money. "Next you'll come up with the line that I don't love you anymore. Not even Ruth ever gave me that crap . . ."

"She didn't have to," Helga said softly. "You told her so yourself."

Again, he appeared not to have heard what she said. "Helga, I needed this deal," he persisted, beginning to pace the floor in front of the sofa. "Ed was ready to lay a lot of bread on me, thousands of dollars. I told you a million times not to come here. And the one time you do you mess everything up. How often, damn it, have I told you that we can't afford to be seen together? Not now—not ever!"

His last words cut through her heart, like the blade of a dagger. "Not ever?" she repeated dully.

Harry realized that he had gone too far. By the same token he realized he could no longer undo what he had said. Besides, he felt a strange anger rise within himself. Even the outbursts with Blakely and Ives were something totally alien to his nature. What *was* happening to him suddenly? He turned from Helga and gripped the neck of the empty brandy bottle on the table. "Well, anyway, you loused up perhaps the most important deal in my life."

He had not even bothered to answer her last question and again the stiletto penetrated her heart. She could feel the hot sting of tears burning in her eyes. Had he already forgotten last night's sacred promise? "Darling, please, will you tell me what the drunk meant in the hallway about Ruth being gone and not coming back again? Don't you think I'm entitled to . . ." The bottle came down with a shattering crash on the coffee table. Shocked, she waited a full minute but he didn't speak. "Didn't you tell Ruth about us?" she whispered. "Last night?"

He whirled on her, his face aflame with rage. "Goddamn you, no!" he exploded. "Christ, I never even got a chance to . . . I never even saw her after leaving you last night."

"You still haven't told her about us?" This time it was her turn to be insulated in the cracked shell of misery. "You went back on your word."

This further infuriated Harry. "Why the hell don't you listen to what I'm saying?" he screamed. "How the hell could I speak to her when she's been kidnap . . ."

The last word, half-uttered, froze in his throat, in mid-air. But too late. Harry had never meant to tell Helga, feeling somehow that no good would come of it. He was sure everything would end up cockeyed, and the result would be hysteria and misunderstanding. He stared at her, shocked at the sound of the dreaded taboo verb, at his own carelessness, and she at him, stunned, unable to ingest what she had heard. Ice-cold showers of pinprick-goose pimples spilled down her spine, into her thighs, her hands, fingertips. Outside a car was passing with a radio blaring forth a strident hard-rock sound; then its tires ground to a stop at a traffic light.

"She . . . *what*?" Helga froze, hardly able to breathe.

His strength was spent. The restless night, the mental strain, the entire bizarre chain of events since waking in the morning had all taken their toll, sucked everything out of him, and he just stood there, totally exhausted. "Maybe now you understand why I blew my stack," he said thinly.

"Kidnapped?" She shook her head, incredulous, unable to accept the hideous word. "You're not putting me on? But where? How d'you know she's kidnapped?"

The secret was out and he figured he might as well tell her the truth. What difference did it make now? After all, Martin knew too, and what reason did he have to trust her any less than him.

"Okay, that's how I know." He took her by the wrist and pulled her roughly from the sofa, leading her to the roll-top desk. "But whatever I show you, Helga, don't touch it, and not a word to anyone! Above all, keep your hands off! The kidnapper may have left his fingerprints on it. Just read it!"

Like Harry and Martin before her, she rested her hands on the back of the Hepplewhite chair and started reading the extortion demand.

"Oh my God!" Her hand flew to her mouth and she looked at him, then back to the note as her eyes consumed every word of it. She read the entire message twice, letting each word sink in, then looked up at Harry. "When did all this happen?"

"I know as much about it as you do," he replied, having calmed down somewhat while she was reading the note. "I found this last night in the typewriter after seeing you . . . Listen, did *you* see her yesterday?"

"Me?" Helga shook her head. "No. Sometimes weeks go by when I don't see her. I certainly didn't yesterday. Harry, the note says you're not to contact the police ."

"I haven't and I'm not going to."

"But how on earth are you going to find her?"

"It's not a question of finding her but raising the money and waiting for instructions from the . . . whoever it is."

"And . . . you were trying to raise the ransom . . . when I came in?"

Harry returned to the sofa and let himself slump on it, gray with fatigue. "That was Blakely," he muttered dejectedly, "who could have swung eighteen thousand clams in my favor."

"But who *is* he . . . that awful man?"

"Real estate agent . . . an old acquaintance of mine . . . he could have done it by selling that cottage I have in the country . . . Well, I owe him quite a few favors . . . and this was an extra one I had for him."

"This? . . . What favor?"

"This, what happened to you. He thought you were a woman I had promised to let him ball. Case of mistaken identity . . . I just saw red seeing you being pawed by another man."

"Oh." Helga regarded him from the roll-top desk, clamping her cold hands under her armpits. Never in her wildest imagination could she picture Harry as a pimp. But she did not feel like going deeper into this sordid issue. As far as she was concerned it was over and done with. "So what're you going to do now? Eighteen thousand. The money's due . . . When is it?"

"Monday, five p.m. Then I'm supposed to get further instructions."

"But can't you stall him on the phone and have the call traced?"

"Helga, please!" He cast her a reproving glance. "Criminals are wise to such childish tricks. *They* are the ones who call the shots. They talk to you on the phone, give explicit instructions, and then hang up, and if you didn't get the message, it's just too damn bad. Besides, I can't afford to get in touch with the cops—not even a P.I."

Helga gave him a baffled expression. "A what?"

"A private eye. That's where the little drunk in the hall comes in."

"The one who said your wife will never come back . . . alive?"

"Yeah," Harry nodded grimly. "That was the husband of the first victim. A woman abducted last May. At least the kidnapper gave me that much of a warning of what would happen to Ruth if I *did* play footsie with the cops."

"So *that* was him." A dent of worry appeared between Helga's brows. "*He* went to the police?"

"Not really—just an old pal of his who had retired from the force years before."

"And the kidnappers found out?"

Harry then told her exactly what Donald Ives had confided to him and the fact that Ives had gathered the money and was prepared to hand it over to the madman.

For a few moments Helga buried her face in both hands, shaking her head. "God, how awful!" she mumbled and dropped her hands. She took a deep breath and tried to think. "But, Harry, I don't understand, this kidnapper, why should he pick on you? I mean Getty, Bronfman— that I can understand—Hearst—okay. Even a Berlin politician. But a guy who's barely making ends meet, really a middle-class nobody, I don't get it."

"That's just it! You put your finger right on it," he said emphatically, becoming calmer and more composed. "A nobody, a guy who doesn't rate space in the press. Nobody gives a damn about Ruth. Ruth's not wealthy, not a sex symbol, and she is nobody important, so the heat is off the abductor. There's been a rash of kidnappings the last few years and except for the big headliners like Patty Hearst and Bronfman, an ambassador's daughter in Mexico, the Dutch industrialist in Ireland, most of them end up on the back page, if there. So," he sighed, "like you, I asked myself that question a thousand times, Helga—yet the fact remains: this time it's me."

"What I really don't get, though, is why he's so sure you'd be able to come through with thirty thousand dollars," Helga puzzled.

"Because he knows I *can* make it. This son of a bitch must have cased me thoroughly. He must have worked out every last detail of my financial resources to a split-second schedule—that's the way he kept tabs on Ives . . . the drunk you saw in the lobby. All of his assets— stocks, savings, and the furniture just about came to what the kidnapper demanded—thirty-five thousand—five grand more than he knows I'm capable of handing over." He searched his pockets for a cigarette. "With *everything* I can possibly rake up I'd be able to meet his demands. This maniac really studied us. He knows I'm too scared to say boo and go to the cops."

Helga observed him closely as he lit a Kool. "But what are you going to do now?"

"Well," he shrugged, "stocks and checking and savings accounts I can convert to cash on Monday. Tomorrow I'll try to sell the car."

"Tomorrow? On Sunday?"

"Sure, Sundays are the best days for used-car dealers."

"But even so, with what happened this afternoon, you'd still be eighteen thousand short, wouldn't you?"

"I guess so," he nodded. "That's where I goofed—with Ed. Eighteen grand down the drain."

"It was my fault, Harry."

He wanted to say something but paused and for the first time since Helga entered his apartment regarded her calmly. Standing there by the roll-top desk in her chic herringbone pantsuit, the smart tight-fitting slacks hugging the contours of her beautiful legs, she looked tantalizingly attractive. He knew he had been grossly unfair, almost to the point of brutality earlier in accusing her of muffing the chance of closing the deal with Ed Blakely. "How could you have known?" he said at length. "Not your fault Ruth's been kidnapped."

"But how're you going to pay him off by Monday night? And in non-consecutive serial numbers? Even if you get everything else converted to cash, won't you still be eighteen thousand short?"

Again Harry glared at the empty brandy bottle, suddenly grabbed it by the neck and once more slammed it on the marble surface of the coffee table. "Goddamn!"

Helga pursed her lips. "Harry, if you want a drink, to relax, I have some champagne."

"For God's sake, Helga!" he cried out, shocked. "Champagne! I don't feel like celebrating now."

"I'm sorry," she whispered, cursing herself for saying the wrong thing. "It was only a suggestion . . . because the brandy's gone and all I have is . . ." Again he focused his full attention on the empty bottle as Helga thrust herself from the Hepplewhite chair and approached him, stopping at the other side of the low table and facing him. "Harry," she started hesitatingly, "may I be absolutely honest with you?"

He looked up at her. "Honest?"

She was visibly ill at ease. "I mean . . . you won't take offense at what I'm going to ask you?"

He gave her an indifferent shrug. "I'm past taking offense."

"Are you sure . . . Ruth never suspected anything?"

"That she was going to be kidnapped?" Her question plainly struck him as stupid.

"No, I mean about us?"

"Come off it, Helga! What's that got to do with . . . this?" He gestured in the direction of the ransom note.

"Perhaps more than you think."

He didn't like the Miss Marple-like line of sleuthing her logic was obviously about to embark on.

"Well, do you mind keeping it to yourself?"

"No, Harry, please, I'm serious," she pressed her point. "It may be nothing more than a hunch but you've got to consider everything."

Abruptly he rose from the sofa and headed for the kitchen. Without pretense he tried to break her train of thought. "Coffee?"

"Thanks." But Helga would not let herself be put off that easily. She followed him and leaned against the jamb of the kitchen door, watching him as he put a water kettle on the stove. "Suppose, just suppose she found out about us, only never let on to you."

"Yeah, I know, don't bother to finish!" Without turning, he gave her his counter-reasoning while getting out two cups and putting a heaping teaspoon of Decaf into each. "She finds out about you and me and in order to get even with us she has herself kidnapped, or made it look like a kidnapping, soaks me of everything I own and never shows up again. To teach me a lesson—that what you're driving at?"

For the first time since asking Helga whether she wanted any coffee, he turned and faced her, a sense of triumph on his face at having outsmarted her at her own detective work. "Not quite, Harry," Helga said as he poured some boiling water out of the kettle into the two cups. "Let me go one step farther. For you to get instructions from the kidnapper on the phone—and I'm sure it'll be a man—she'll need the *assistance* of a man . . . Thanks." He had offered her a cup of black coffee and both proceeded back into the living room where they settled on the sofa and easy chair respectively. "Harry, tell me, what makes you so sure," she continued doggedly and with great emphasis, "that while you were working your guts off editing a semi-porno novel for Old Glumm and not being the attentive, virile husband any married woman in her forties would expect in the sack, and out of it—what makes you so certain that she didn't look for greener pastures? Remember, she's still very attractive, could get any number of men, and what's more she's at an age where women can be driven crazy with sexual desire if they don't get enough from the men they love. Believe me, women in their forties fall in love, too. Maybe some man has coaxed her into deserting you, and she'd do practically anything short of murder to hold onto him and at the same time try to get back at you for the way you neglected her these last two years."

He put down his cup of coffee. "You must be mad! Not every kidnapping has a Patty Hearst twist, you know."

"Wait! Once you've complied with his instructions on Monday and deposited the money at a pre-arranged place," she pursued her point undeterred, "all they have to do is to pick up the bundle of cash, and it's goodbye forever. No more phone calls. Nothing. No greater revenge than that of a woman scorned. And Ruth will have the added satisfaction of knowing that finally you will have paid your debt for the torment you caused her during the last year or two when she had tried everything in her power to hold onto your love and to . . ."

"Aw, shut up, please! Whose side are you on anyway?" Harry interrupted gruffly. He took a sip of the steaming hot coffee. "Ruth didn't marry me just for sex. If I had become impotent, like Lady Chatterley's husband, she'd still have the same . . . hell, let's forget it!" he snapped, realizing he had blundered into a self-defeating deadend. "Anyway, I don't believe a word of it, your theory of her deserting me, et cetera, that she'd do a thing like that. There are too many telltale signs that she hasn't been unfaithful."

"Why shouldn't she have been? You were."

"Thanks." Harry tapped his cigarette nervously in an ashtray. "But that's different—at least I had told her I no longer loved her. After all, I'm only a man."

"Oh Christ!" the woman opposite him exclaimed. "Germaine Greer should have heard that! As if only men were capable of human emotions." She put her cup down on the saucer with a loud clatter. "Harry, let me be brutally honest with you. I have no pity for your wife. Because I love you, insanely, unmercifully, as she possibly loves *her* man. And if she's gone through with this scheme—because to me there's no earthly reason in the world why a kidnapper should have picked on you of all the eight million people in this city—then . . ."

"Well, he did," he cut her off curtly. "He had to pick on someone and it's just tough luck it's me. After all, people ask themselves every day, why is it me, God, why me, when there are millions of sons of bitches less worthy than me going scotfree after a lifetime of crime, why must *I* die of cancer?"

"Harry, if Ruth has gone through with this scheme and made it appear like a kidnapping, I can only admire her. It shows a strength of character I wouldn't have thought she had."

"And if it's not her scheme? What then?" He shook his head, grimacing displeasure at her line of argument. "You just don't know Ruth."

"Did the Hearsts really know their daughter? For that matter, do *we* even really know each other? Harry, you rule all this out, don't you? That this couldn't happen to you."

"Any husband would. I can't afford to take the risk of accepting your deduction and relaxing. The consequences are too awesome to contemplate . . . Besides, most women . . . well, Ruth doesn't have that much imagination."

"Most women, eh? Thanks." An edge of disdain entered her voice. "I must write Doris Lessing and Mary McCarthy and Muriel Spark and ask them who *their* male ghost-writers are. Obviously, a hole between your legs means you have a brain-drain. Like Madame Curie *and* Simone de Beauvoir, *and* George Sand. Freud's destiny of anatomy."

"You know very well I didn't mean it that way," he growled, ill-tempered.

"Sure, you men never do . . . once you've gotten it off your chest . . . But don't get me wrong, Harry, if Ruth fights tooth and nail to hold on to a new love let me assure you I can be her equal in *every* conceivable way."

Harry's eyes narrowed with suspicion. "And what is that supposed to mean?"

"That I love you, too, with all your silly little pinpricks and ridiculous chauvinistic remarks, and that I've no intention of giving you up either."

"Who's saying anything about giving me up?"

"*I* am. Because I don't believe you really, truly love me."

"Cut it out, Helga!" Harry turned on her full-face, unconcealedly annoyed. "This is neither the time nor the place for dragging our affair into all this. Besides, I fail to see any connection between this note and your insinuation that I don't love you."

"You don't? After I just told you that maybe she's trying to get even with you? You may prefer to refer to it as an affair, but last night we agreed it was a prelude to marriage. Or have you forgotten?"

"*Adultery*, my dear Helga, cannot in the best of circumstances be graced with the euphemism *a prelude to marriage*."

Their voices had raised and they now faced each other squarely, like soldiers of opposing armies on a battlefield. Helga nervously unbuttoned the last button of her herringbone jacket that Ed Blakely had not been able to pry open earlier, and she pulled at the sleeves of the aquamarine blouse underneath. "Thanks a lot, Father Harry, I deserved this," she said, her voice thick with sarcasm. The next second, she regretted her cynical riposte and changed tactics. "Are you really going to try to raise the ransom?"

"What do *you* think?"

"I asked you."

"Of course I am."

"Why?"

"Why! She's my wife, isn't she?"

"And you've often wished she'd one day up and leave you, didn't you?"

"Of course. But that meant divorce to me. This is different."

"Is it, Harry?" she challenged him, studying him closely. "Remember last month, in bed, you said you wished she'd drop dead?"

"For crying out loud! That was just a figure of speech. And you know it."

"Yes, I know it," she replied icily. "When it hits the truth, your emotional revelations wind up as rhetoric, more or less, don't they? Empty desires." A scintilla of steel edged into her voice. "In other words, you still love her."

He slammed his fist down on the coffee table. "Hell, what do you want of me?" he yelled. "I've told you over and over: No! It is no longer a matter of love. What in God's name do you want me to do? Certify it?"

"No, my dear Harry," she strove very hard to remain calm. "I don't want you to do anything."

Harry bit his lips, and regarded her skeptically over the brim of his cup. "And what precious scheme is going through your pretty head now, *if* I may ask?"

A wan smile altered her pale features. "Exactly what I said," she replied with as much composure as she could muster. "To do nothing. You've done your best, heaven knows, trying to raise the money. Okay, go ahead, sell the car, trade in your stock, withdraw everything from your bank accounts. But you'll still be eighteen thousand short. You tried to sell the house, but the transaction backfired. Maybe it wouldn't have, but it did! Harry, you've done your damndest. And you failed. Even if you stopped now, this very minute, there'd be no need for recriminations. You *have* tried." She let the message sink in, but he only stared at her. "Still don't get it, do you?"

"Correction, my dear woman. I'm way ahead of you. You *want* me to fail, don't you?"

"It's not a question of wanting it. You *have* failed. What's more, I wouldn't love you if I didn't feel that at last fate is trying to be kind to *me*."

Harry cupped the coffee mug in his hands, but the drink had grown lukewarm. He started to put the cup back on the table, but his hands suddenly began to tremble so violently some of the coffee spilled. He tried hard to compose himself. "Helga," he said gravely, "whatever you or I may think of Ruth, above all, she is a human being. I cannot knowingly, wilfully, sentence her to death."

"But nobody is asking you to, you fool," she remonstrated, exasperated. "Can't you see? You *have* tried. *You*'re not sentencing anybody. So, what more can you do?"

"There's a helluva lot I haven't tried, ways I haven't thought of yet."

"Like what, for instance? A bank loan?"

"That crossed my mind, too. It's something I can work out Monday morning."

"What reason will you give them for an advance of eighteen thousand, if you don't mind my asking?"

He peered into his cup, thinking hard. "I'll come up with something."

"They'll ask for papers to back up whatever you want, Harry."

"I know. Thanks. For nothing."

"Don't take it out on me with that insufferable attitude. *I'm* not putting obstacles in your way. *They* will. On Monday morning . . . What about your boss? Can *he* give you an advance?"

"Old Glumm?" Harry considered him for less than a second. "You don't know Glumm. What boss ever advanced an employee eighteen grand? That's more than I make in a year. Even if he came up with it and Ruth was returned, we'd have nothing to live on for more than a year. Anyhow, Glumm's habit is to fire anyone who might tarnish his firm with anything resembling a scandal. Don't ask me why. I know all about the crap he publishes. But that bastard wouldn't advance me a nickel. I've seen some pretty bad scenes in that office, with guys pleading for ten bucks a week more and him turning them down flat, no matter what the reason. You can count *him* out."

"Okay, no dice there." Helga gave a sigh of relief. "But tell me, Harry, honestly, what do you think you *can* do?" He didn't answer, just kept gazing morosely into his cup of black coffee. "Harry, be honest with me now: do you still want to marry me?"

He looked up sharply. "You know I do. But . . ."

"But Ruth won't give you a divorce. Right?"

"I never had the chance to ask her." He stopped short, holding his breath, realizing too late what had passed his lips.

Helga nodded gravely, her hazel eyes fastening hard on him. "I see."

"I mean I didn't bring *you* into it," Harry corrected himself guiltily. "I just said that my love for her had grown cold and . . ."

187

"Don't lie to me, Harry." Her voice was on edge, strident. "Just give me a truthful answer for a change: what in God's name do you stand to gain . . . from a woman who's keeping us apart?"

Harry cracked his knuckles. He felt cornered. "Look, Helga, I love you. I want to marry you, but I don't want to do it at the expense of Ruth's life."

"But you're fighting for her with the kind of ferocity of a man in love with her."

"But I'm not, damn you!" he screamed, jumping up. He walked quickly around the table and faced her. "Now listen to me! I've told you before that I love you. I'm no longer in love with Ruth. If this awful thing hadn't happened yesterday I would have told her about us by now. That's the God's honest truth. But because I don't love her doesn't mean I want her dead!"

"Even if she's the only obstacle in our happiness?"

Harry clenched his fists. "For crying out loud, isn't it enough for *one* of us to have a life on his conscience?"

A moment of shocked silence filled the room. The next second, Helga's hand exploded in his face. Her four fingers burned red-hot streaks on his cheek.

"You bastard!"

Harry's head snapped back, his face darkened with hurt and shock.

It took all his strength to get hold of himself and not to strike back. "Don't think for a moment, Helga," he said with great difficulty, "that your hysteria has any effect on me."

Venom, out in the open at last, flashed in her eyes. "I'm not hysterical," she raised her voice. "Hurt, but *not* hysterical."

A pulse started to pound thickly under Harry's jawbone and in his temple. "How much peace of mind would you have, Helga, lying beside me at night, knowing I was responsible for the death of a wife?"

"Oh?—Laying plans for getting rid of Wife Number Two already?" she ricocheted cynically.

"Don't be an idiot!"

"I'm not the idiot. If I were, I certainly wouldn't be here. Alive."

"Oh, don't be so melodramatic!" he cut her short sharply. "You don't know how sick and tired I am hearing about how superior you must have been to get alive out of that Nazi inferno. The big Germanic . . ."

"Nice, Mr. Bensonny! Really nice! The philistine New World person . . ."

"My dear girl, I'm not yet accustomed to the cultured Old World acceptance of murder. Even if *you* are!"

She struck out at him again but halfway through the motion changed her mind, and dropped her arm, quickly, holding it firmly in one hand. "No—why should I? And give you the satisfaction of losing my temper all over . . ." She raised both hands in a pacifying gesture as if to stave off another of her outbursts. "Okay. Okay, let's stay calm! As I was saying, it's *so* easy," she said deliberately. "All you have to decide is what you value more, Harry: Your conscience, or me."

Harry glared at her a long time before answering. "And what is it *you* value most?" he asked darkly. "Your love for your murdered brother . . . or a conscience that drives you to drink and barbiturates thirty years later?"

She returned his steely look. Then, slowly, her shield crumbled; her lips began to tremble, and she lowered her eyes. Why did he have to bring Fritzi into this? When he had promised her never to talk of it, and certainly not in wrath, nor vengeance.

She turned from Harry and, wordlessly, sank onto the sofa, hiding her face in her hands. Harry watched her silently, making up his mind not to go to her, not this time. Why did she badger him, and hurt him so much at a time like this? And confront him cruelly with an either-or proposition? What had happened to them suddenly? Why should an absent Ruth be more of a danger in breaking up their love than a Ruth living next door? He watched her guardedly when, after a short time, without even looking up, Helga extended her hand to him. He was rooted to the ground, yet almost against his will felt himself drawn to her. He took her hand and the touch rekindled the dormant fire of love that lay in wait, and he raised her cold finger-tips to his lips and brushed them against his eyes, his cheeks.

Helga did not look up but the touch of his hands caused the tears to fall unashamedly.

"Harry . . . why?" she asked softly. "Why do we hurt those we love?"

He did not answer. There was no answer. Everyone went through this torture, the pain of love, of feeling imperiled by the towering edifice of emotion, of needing constant reassurance from those who could give it most readily and in the fullest measure. Love became a permanent testing ground, a tease, a game . . . when it was not withering. And Harry could not answer.

"Harry . . . why . . . how can there still be so much of Ruth . . . in your heart?"

He lowered their hands from his lips but did not let go of hers. A deep, sad sigh escaped him. "I don't know," he said, more to himself than to her. "Memories perhaps, odd half-forgotten moments, with a woman who's been by my side for half of my life . . ." He shrugged. "A walk in the rain through the woods of Maine many summers ago . . . picking raspberries . . . a million such commonplace things, Helga . . . her asking me to scrub her back in the bathtub . . . my working late at this desk and her waiting up till I went to bed . . . or simply watching her read, brush her teeth . . . or my coming home from work, in a foul temper because nothing ever came of the National Book Award speech I'd prepared for the great American novel half-baked in my mind, and her crawling into bed later next to me, even though I was grumpy over my feelings of inadequacy, my worthlessness. Her holding me tight, kissing me, stroking my face in the dark and telling me that even if everybody turned against me she'd still be by my side loving me . . ."

He swallowed hard and looked at Helga's hair without realizing that she still had not raised her face to his.

"So many things, Helga . . . which you only remember when there's a void . . . to be filled with memories . . . like the time she buried a dead robin with a spoon at a picnic at Bear Mountain. Or the nights her pillow was wet after she had been told she'd never have children. Or her body lying naked in my arms, racked with sobs, when I wouldn't make love to her after coming from your apartment."

At this, Helga lifted her face, mascara stains streaking down her cheeks. Only now he realized that she had been weeping. Tortured, he shook his head. "Helga, don't you understand? I *cannot* kill someone guilty of no more than an inability to support the love of a . . . a philanderer."

Gently she pulled her hand out of his and closed her eyes. When she opened them, she scrutinized his face for a full minute. Then she got up, walked over to the other end of the coffee table and lighted one of his Kools.

She drew deeply on the cigarette and exhaled a long stream, watching the smoke disperse and vanish in the spacious living room. "Okay. But answer one question for me, Harry," she said at length, drying her face with the tips of her fingers. "Suppose you can't meet the balance—the eighteen thousand—what then?"

Harry thrust his hands into his pockets, feeling himself go cold all over. "I won't even consider that possibility . . . and I'm *no longer* in love with her. Can't you understand that?"

"And can't you understand that I *am* in love with you," she came back fiercely. "That the only way I know now to get you for myself is by not having her around . . . ever."

His fingers sunk into his thighs. "You *are* insane," he whispered.

"Oh God! I knew you were going to hurl this at me sooner or later," she exclaimed, crushing the cigarette in the ashtray. "Harry, I've gone through hell in my lifetime, but I'm *not* insane, I assure you."

"And what exactly did you learn from your experiences, if I may ask?" he stood his ground. "What is it you've learned from life and books, Helga?"

"I learned plenty. Compassion. Love. And I'm *not* insane."

"A love that is self-serving."

"Goddamn it, whose love is *not* self-serving? You also helped yourself to my love at Ruth's expense. Tell me, Harry, what *do* you want of me? To wish her back? When you're the only thing I have ever truly loved . . . since Fritzi. Do you *really* want me to go insane?"

Only at this moment he recognized, for the first time, that she was not only fighting for him, but for her life, her sanity.

Harry's hands felt as heavy as dumbbells as he took them out of his pockets and walked over to her, grasping her arms. "No, you're not insane, Helga. We're tired. Both of us." He drew her close and kissed her hair. "Terribly tired."

"No! I'm *not* tired." She broke away from him. "Harry, I'm after the truth. And I want you to take a stand."

His arms dropped heavily down to his sides. He felt rebuffed, all his understanding, compassion gone to waste. "You just *will not* give in, will you?"

"No—I won't!" She grabbed her elbows, making a valiant effort to steady herself. "Harry, after all the promises you made to me I think I deserve a decision from you, now: I want you to choose between Ruth and me." She waited for an answer, but he only narrowed his eyes.

"Well?"

"You're a *monster*!" The words cut his breath, stopped his heart momentarily.

Her whole body stiffened. "Oh, sure, go ahead, say it: I'm a Jew-bitch—the discarded woman who should have been sent to the gas chamber—monstrous enough even to deprive you of the eighteen thousand you need." She was infuriated, spiteful. "Or hasn't it occurred to you yet that *I* have the money? It's more than half of my savings but

I *have* it. And it'd put an end to your search in one fell swoop. This never entered your mind, did it?"

Rightly or wrongly, Helga felt she had to let go full-blast with all the might, the emotional mettle she could marshal to let him know once and for all where she stood, no matter what the consequences, and now her eyes fastened upon his, desperately, waiting for the final verdict. But she had to wait a long time before he spoke again.

"I see. And *this* is how you can make sure of my love?" he challenged at last. "Don't you understand that you're forcing my hand now?"

"Forcing your *hand*?" Her throat tightened, and she reached up to open the top button of her blouse. "What do you mean?"

"You could have offered me the money without my pleading for it like a beggar. And I would have loved you all the more for sacrificing your savings for her life, regardless of what you think of her."

"I see. Blood-money," she observed derisively. "For eighteen thousand you get Ruth back alive and I get little old you. A tit-for-tat swap, in other words."

Harry nodded somberly. "Crudely put perhaps, but yes. Remember though, it's a mercenary arrangement not of my making." He waited briefly, then took the bull by the horns. "But of course, you're not going to do it, are you?"

Helga's nails curled into the soft seat of the sofa. "Harry, this is probably one thing you will never understand because you haven't lived through my hell, but . . ."

"Helga, please . . . We're talking about the future now, not the past!"

"Exactly! Maybe now you'll understand why my future actions *are* based on the past." For a moment she imagined that Harry was shutting his eyes with an air of Promethean resignation. "Please, Harry, at least hear me out! The years in Riga, Auschwitz, Bergen-Belsen *have* something to do with your wife . . . Please listen!"

Harry tightened his lips, bracing himself for the new life-and-death battle that clearly threatened to project itself from the past into the present, the future, but in the end he gave in. "All right," he sighed. "If it has to be."

"Yes, it has to be," she shot back, piqued by his blasé attitude. "God, you make it so hard on me, Harry, the way you act. I don't even know where to start . . . I know that nobody who hasn't gone through it can possibly grasp the full meaning of the agonies, of the excruciating atrocities Jews were exposed to for five long unending years. Harry, every minute of life seemed to stretch an eternity, then stand still, and we wondered if by some heinous chance, some vile trick of fate it wouldn't be our turn next to be herded off to dig our own mass grave, to jump into it and be shot in the back by the special Einsatz Kommandos before a layer of lime covered our corpses and the next rows of Jews were forced to jump on top of us. A fate determined only by the fact that we were born of Jewish wombs. This was our crime. Maybe it left me paranoid. I don't know. It's all beyond description. When we weren't killed, it was our duty to wait to be killed, like the older children being used for live target practice. It was Russian roulette, day and night, without stop, for five godawful years. And people in this country speaking of over-subscribed quotas. Harry, all I know is that the carrying out of Hitler's insane orders somehow opened a breach in the human conscience and . . ."

"Helga, please!" Harry whispered, his head bent down, unable to face her bitterness. "I know I can't possibly ever grasp any of this. But it's something you cannot blame on Ruth, whatever you may think of her."

"Yes, Harry, yes, I can," she spat back furiously. "Why d'you think I'm bringing all this up? Look, since then I've been the brunt occasionally of anti-Semitic barbs, usually from sickies, who didn't know what they were talking about, calling us Jews Nazis or Commies or blaming us for the weather or Wall Street. People who would just as soon have had Hitler win the war, instead of FDR and Churchill. People who were not driven so much by hatred for the Jews—most of them churchgoers who proudly announced to me they never met a Jew —but because they needed something to hate in order to survive in the same way normal persons need something or someone to love to give them the strength to go on living. Even if you deny it, Harry, even if you claim she never expressed such feelings in your presence—no, let me finish, please!—it doesn't matter, Ruth's words opened an old wound that had taken thirty years to heal. She chose her words well, last July, knowing exactly where my Achilles heel was. It turned out to be a perfect hit. The look in her eyes, the hatred and contempt she felt for me, I had seen a thousand times in Belsen—it was the perfect punctuation to her insult. And when I asked you whether your wife had read my book you said she didn't finish it because she was bored by it and that the inmates of Auschwitz and Maidanek and Ravensbrück and Buchenwald probably deserved what was coming to them and . . . Jesus! You can give me all the arguments in the world why I should help your wife today, Harry, or on Monday, but every time I see her on the street, or in my mind at night alone, I not only see her but the grinning skull of my mother when she tumbled with twelve hundred other naked corpses out of one of those gas chambers in Auschwitz. Maybe to Ruth my mother deserved what was coming to her. But when I see Ruth I also see myself standing with two hundred other half-frozen bodies of the transport in a completely enclosed freight car ankle-deep in our own shit after being shunted about in subfreezing temperatures without food and drink for four days and nights from Riga to Auschwitz. Oh God, don't you realize, Harry, that when I see Ruth I remember those blue-eyed Aryan members of the master-race tossing babies alive into the ovens or threatening children with death unless they shot their own mothers and . . ."

"All right, I think I get your point," Harry said quietly. He walked, utterly fatigued, around the cocktail table to the easy chair and let himself sink into it wearily. "What it amounts to simply is that we've reached a deadend, an impasse not even a Metternich could resolve . . . I'm at a loss, I just don't know what to say, Helga." He was visibly groping for words, snatching at hope where there was none. "None of us are saints and we just have to go on living and dying, I guess, each in our appointed time and place—you, Ruth, me, our parents, grandparents, everybody. Free will perhaps does belong to destiny, after all, and not to us."

Helga shook her head. "Harry, it isn't only that. Suppose we had never met and I didn't love you, I couldn't save Ruth then. It wouldn't mean anything to me, would it, her disappearance, her life or her death? Oh Christ, don't make me do it, Harry! It's not only Ruth I want out of the way—for our sakes—but the evil, the unspeakable curse of the Holocaust she represents . . . to me at least, the abomination I associate with her."

Harry still did not look at her. He was toying with the little black address book which he had picked up off the carpet, leafing blindly through it. With all her intellect, in the face of such insurmountable loathing, logic and argument were pointless.

God, why couldn't intellect win over matters of the heart?

"That intellect of yours," he muttered aloud to himself.

"What?" Helga was startled by his strange utterance.

"Your intellect." He looked up, seeing the ghostly woman's face opposite him staring back, not understanding, the beautiful eyes empty, drained. "All those lovely words you are capable of stringing together, Helga, fusing them like bright enamel colors in the kiln of your mind.

Here, in this living room. And outside." He paused for a moment. "Take the collection of poems you've written over the last twenty years, that a critic compared to Nelly Sachs, and others referred to in review after review as perhaps the most tragic outburst of poetry a woman had written in the English language since Sylvia Plath turned her mind inside out and twisted words into madness . . . Well, you didn't get rich on the book, but it firmly established you as a Literary Woman. You made your money as a speaker after that and your great theme always was 'to pierce the fierce flame of hatred ignited by man and to see and to seek in evil, behind evil, the seed of goodness that could still be nursed.' "

"Harry, it's no use," Helga squirmed uncomfortably, knowing what was coming. "You *cannot* bring this up now and try to . . ."

"I would think that this is the one time that I *can* bring this up, Helga," Harry went on mercilessly now, seeing his opening and going on the offensive. "Here is the test of all of your principles by which you pretend to live. Unless you mean to tell me your entire philosophy is nothing but a sham."

"Harry, please don't!" She turned from him, clawing her fingers into her thighs. "It was a philosophy for the *world*, for *mankind* to emulate so that others would not repeat . . ."

"Yes, for others," he shot back, angrily, "but not for you! The inferno of torture where every minute, naked in the snow, dragged to a stop before the next minute began, where you saw your loved ones butchered, this roaring inferno, this flame of remembrance has finally spawned a mountain of hypocrisy. But tell me, Helga, where in the name of heaven *is* the forgiveness, where *are* the verities you have always heralded with such acute penetration and insight in your heroic stanzas? Explain it to me . . . Helga, I'm speaking to you! Turn around and look at me!" he shouted suddenly. "For God's sake, at least have the guts to level your eyes at me when we discuss life and death! The death of a human being!"

She turned her bone-white face slowly to the man she claimed to love. Her eyes had dark shadows encircling them, and mascara streaks again seemed to have become prison bars as they had the night before.

"Harry," she whispered.

"You dare talk of barbarians and black-uniformed bullies spraying bursts of machine-gun fire into innocent bodies?" he pressed on. "The massacres of yesterday, Helga, *haven't stopped*. Do you understand me? Right here, in this very room, less than 24 hours ago, there was a law-abiding human being who at this very moment may be begging for her life. Trying as frantically to survive as your mother did thirty-two years ago, clawing at the walls in the gas chamber. Auschwitz had Dr. Mengele and Rudolf Höss; Treblinka, Franz Stangl; Belsen, Kramer. Today, *this city*, has a mad killer, a kidnapper, and Ruth is in *his* hands.

"Thirty-two years ago they snatched a Jewish baby from its mother's arms, held it by its ankles and in full sight of the mother smashed its skull against a brick wall till its brains splattered all over the wall and the blood splashed on the snow. Today a mad kidnapper feels he's been crossed, so he takes his prisoner, jabs a fork up her vagina, grabs a hunting knife and carves off her breasts and then slits her throat from ear to ear. That's what he did to Ives' wife. Ives told me so himself because he had to identify her body. And it destroyed his life. You saw him yourself in the hall. Helga, look at me, damn you!" She avoided his eyes again, this time hiding her face in her cupped palms. "Goddamn you, will you look at me!" he screamed. She let her hands fall heavily on her lap and with a great effort turned her face toward him.

"Now, will you answer me, regardless of what you may think of Ruth with her ridiculous, callous remarks about people: do you really want to be part of a monstrous act, Helga, a savage murderous deed just because you resent the way she has acted toward you? I ask you: do you really want to put yourself on the same level with the wives of those brutish killers in Hitler's extermination camps who knew only too damn well what their husbands were up to and . . ."

"For God's sake, will you shut up!" Helga shrieked at long last, jumping to her feet. "I can't stand it anymore! Bringing *me* into this filthy case, making *me* responsible if anything has happened to her. As if it were up to *me* to come to the aid of every cruddy victim in this city until I become a pauper! It isn't fair, you damn bastard, it just isn't fair! How can I be held responsible by you, by anybody, when I'm only . . ."

"Because you are the only one with the means to help her, that's why," he shouted at her. "You said so yourself; and in one of your poems you stress that hard as the hopeless assignment may sound someone *has* to start somewhere . . . somewhere where goodness overrules ev . . ."

"Will you stop quoting my goddamn poems to me as if they were God's own gospel, for Christ's sake!" she yelled. "You tell me why it ought to be me of all the four billion dumb-ass people in this sordid cesspool of a world, *me* who should be the first to start cutting out the

196

malignant tissue—and *that's* part of my poem *Biopsy*, if you care to reread it—why should *I* remove this malignant virus when the rest of the godforsaken world's body remains ravaged by cancer? Why me, damn you, Harry, why me? Here, look at this! Now I want *you* to look hard at what I'm going to show you, even if you *have* seen it a thousand times before."

She ripped off her herringbone jacket, tossed it on the floor, and rolled up the right sleeve of her aquamarine blouse. Two giant steps took her to where he was sitting and she thrust the inside of her lower arm into his face. At first he was conscious only of the faint fragrance of eau de cologne, then he saw the familiar blue-stenciled A2988657 tattooed on the skin close to her elbow.

"Look at it, you son of a bitch! Do you see it? Of course you do. You've kissed it a million times, haven't you? And can you imagine the irony of the money I have made writing about the horrible experiences of Auschwitz and Belsen, going to help someone who might actually be capable of playing a Dr. Mengele in this country if the occasion ever arose? Isn't that a laugh? Come on, Harry," she cried hysterically, "say it, please, say it's a laugh! The world's funniest joke. Laugh! Harry, why the hell don't you laugh, you damn uxorious bastard?"

She fell to her knees, then, and buried her face in his lap, her body racked with sobs. Harry sat in the chair, not moving. He was almost paralyzed with grief and frustration, knowing that in her own vision of life perhaps she had a right to let Ruth die. He no longer knew what to think; it all seemed so hopeless suddenly. Helga dug her nails into the insides of his right thigh but he was hardly aware of the pain. Everything seemed to be lost. The last source of money he had secretly entertained—an unspoken subconscious wish on which he pinned his every hope, and Ruth's survival—evaporated now. But even then his mind was seeking out a last-ditch rescue, and ten-thousand bewildering thoughts criss-crossed his mind. How to start to string them all together? One supreme effort was needed to sway the only person in the world who *could* help him.

"What's there left to say, Helga . . . except that perhaps you're right not to help," he started off softly, over her choked sobs, not realizing he had begun stroking her hair. "After all, you've only got to look around you to see why we feel the way we do. I don't know, maybe it's our century, New York, this country . . . or the whole world," he continued half-heartedly, "where big-fish-eats-little-fish . . . where all the horrors of warfare and slaughter every day are brought right into our homes, via the tube—fictitious and real Auschwitzes every hour on the hour—and we shrug it all off, consigning the responsibility to others for clearing up the mess. It's little wonder some of us become hateful, neurotic. Nobody is really exempt. Nobody. Not you, Ruth, certainly not me. Only I always hoped when the chips were down people wouldn't abandon one another . . . not altogether. Yet, even *we* abandoned each other, Helga, almost—just now. This is the first time we've seen each other under pressure, and it isn't pretty, is it? Neither of us came up smelling like roses. But I had always hoped that somehow when everything collapsed all around, people wouldn't desert one another for the . . . well, how shall I phrase it? Some people we may not like are still people, like Ruth . . . human beings, but then there are others who kill and those who watch the killing and sit by in silence . . . even though they *can* help . . . and they *aren't* human . . . they are bugs . . . *bugs*, Helga . . . and I was hoping our time hadn't come yet to turn into bug-people."

Suddenly Harry didn't know where he was heading with his argument. In fact, his appeal to the core of her heart was wide of the mark, and he realized with an illuminating flash of recognition why so many people only found peace of mind in accepting the fact that the chaos of life, of existence—the extension of Jasper's, Heidegger's, Sartre's, Camus' Existentialism—was the natural state of affairs, and that good and evil did not exist, and were only a matter of mind.

"Helga," he whispered. "Perhaps we failed too . . . surrendered already what's human about us . . . that we've gone to the dogs along with the rest of the world. Just that I was hoping somehow that the bugs, the rotten bugs dormant in all of us hadn't reached *our* hearts . . . yours and mine . . . that we'd still have time before they took over and we . . ."

Her face came up then, the wet shimmering eyes reflecting their full misery.

She stood up and rolled down her sleeve, then pulled her jacket back on. Harry watched her in silence, no longer sure what to say, certain he had failed with his clumsy appeal. He wanted to take her into his arms, hold her close and tell her that he understood her at long last, and that everything would work out all right, but he couldn't bring himself to.

Helga was smoothing her jacket now, and fluffing her hair. She turned from him, feeling wretched and despondent, a new world she had built up so laboriously crumbling all about her, then walked uncertainly around the cocktail table toward the foyer.

Reaching the top of the steps, she turned around to face Harry. It was already dusk and they could barely make out each other's expressions as they stood, motionless, in the dying light of the October day.

"Harry, haven't we forgotten something?" she asked in a remarkably controlled voice.

A million thoughts tumbled in a headlong rush through his mind, trying frantically to get sorted out. "Have we?"

"That I am carrying your child."

She turned her back on him once more, only to stop at the front door. It was true; he had forgotten about her pregnancy in the turmoil of the past twelve hours. Murder, kidnapping, bankruptcy, infidelity, pregnancy . . . a whole world, a lifetime of struggling and groping for security appeared to be falling into ruin around him. He no longer knew which way to turn, where to start straightening things out. Even his plea to her to listen to reason, that she should not be counted among the bugs of the world, proved to be confused, desultory, floundering, coming from a man who was at his wit's end and could not trust his own integrity anymore. While he felt she was wrong in her blind selfishness, her dark vengeance, he saw little difference in his own show of hypocrisy, his morbid preoccupation with displaying a Christ-like loftiness, playing it off only to downgrade her and in doing so to sway her tormented and weakening spirit to his side. Both had been unable to conceal the gloomier, more barbaric aspect lurking in the human heart. A bit of Hitler was alive, indeed, in each one of us, he decided, and the last few minutes had testified to this sorry fact.

"Well?"

"Yes, of course," he slipped out of his reverie, his voice hoarse and harsh, plunging back into the icy present. "I suppose after Monday we will know . . . what we can do . . ."

"I wonder." Already she had regained her composure. "Yes, we'll see," she said, opening the door, and was about to step out when she changed her mind and shut it again.

"About what you said . . . that the world was being taken over by the bugs, Harry," she furrowed her brow as another little after-sob sent a tremor through her slender frame. "I don't think I would want to be counted among the bug-people."

"What?" He wanted to rush forward and grab her in his arms. Here, for the first time, shone the ray of hope, at long long last, the light at the end of the tunnel he had been fervently waiting for. "Helga, you . . ."

"No, stop!" she exclaimed, cutting him short, so that he froze at the bottom of the stairs, in the living room. "Don't, Harry, please! Let me think. Don't come any closer. I can't think when you're near me. Just let me . . ." Her thought unfinished, died on her tongue, and she turned the doorknob. But for the second time, she changed course in midstream as if reluctant to cut off her contact with the man she loved, fearing it might be the ultimate break, and she faced him once more.

"You know, if she . . . when Ruth comes back," she said, "there's no doubt in my mind she'll never release you . . . No, let me finish! I'm too tired to argue after what we've been through. We certainly can't be any too proud of what we did to each other today, but I guess we're only human. Harry, I know you're a decent, good man . . . even with that wild side I've never seen before. Most of the things you said today hit the nail right on the head, so maybe I just have to accept the inevitable, that you must go on fighting for her, no matter what. I think I do understand now why you have to . . . and, hopefully, you understand why I'm not the monster you thought *I* was . . ."

"Helga . . ."

"No, stay where you are! Please! . . . I see you only as a woman can see a man, and so does Ruth. No wonder she can't afford to lose you." A short tremulous breath escaped her lips. "The point is this, Harry: Once the woman you claim no longer to be in love with is back, she will try to hold onto you with a love so obsessive, so fierce and unbreakable, that I—the outsider—will *never, never* be able to compete with it. You will be trapped in a dead marriage . . . and have lost my love at the same time!"

She opened the door and quickly let herself out, shutting it softly behind her. Harry still rested with one foot on the first step looking at the closed door while outside, on the Drive, the street lamps suddenly lit up and the wailing sound of a patrol car fluttered by in the distance. Then total stillness. Another day had gone. Harry was alone.

22 ———

For the first time in twenty-four hours Harry's stomach rumbled. It rumbled, growled, and fretted with a vengeance. It would no longer countenance the maltreatment of prolonged neglect. For an hour or so after Helga left, Harry was so riled he paced up and down in his living room trying to straighten things out in his head. It had gotten dark inside, but he did not want to be distracted by the sight of anything that might remind him of Ruth, nor of the events that had taken place in the living room since noon. The light from the streetlights nearest the windows cast a butter-yellow runway across the living room carpet, giving him a sufficient skeletal outline of the furniture standing in the nocturnal shadows to prevent his tripping during his nerve-racking perambulation.

After an hour or so, just about the time his stomach began to express itself, he realized that he had been striding about restlessly without having arrived at any conclusion as to how to gain the safe return of his wife.

Somehow he could not focus his thoughts on anything. The pulsing thuds of persistent pain in his temples finally compelled Harry to take a Tylenol—with his ulcer, aspirin was out—and then to alleviate the ache of his whole being, which included the warning growls of his stomach.

The latter indeed had begun to sound more and more like E. Power Biggs pulling out all bass stops at the organ. He had to *go out*, to *get out*, and to eat something. Thirty hours without decent nourishment was about as much as any man could bear. In any event, it served precious little purpose to crown the tragic occurrence of his wife's abduction with an insult to his innocent innards. The theories of Erich Fromm, Ashley Montagu, William Menninger and Frederic Wertham did little to alleviate Gray's anatomical and physiological demands which displayed hardly any interest in social attitudes and environmental peculiarities.

Until tomorrow morning at least, when he hoped to sell his car, there was nothing more to be done tonight other than to pack in a hearty meal, go to bed and, at the very least, try to get some sleep. A good night's rest might spur him on to summon new courage, marshal new ideas, new hope.

Harry changed his shirt and suit in short order, put on a new tie Ruth's mother had given him for his birthday the month before, stepped into his raincoat and then drew the Fiberglas curtains closed in every room.

He knew a respectable Cantonese restaurant on Broadway, and even if in his mind the situation of him sitting back in comfort and supping on won ton soup coincided with his wife's sufferance of physical brutalities and humiliations, what else could he do under the circumstances? It certainly served no purpose whatever to stay home and mope around and, to cap it, starve to death. If he was to get up early the following day to pursue the next step in his schedule, he just had to keep as fit and alert as possible.

The weather had turned unexpectedly chill and damp. Rain was in the air and a low, thin fog transformed the neon-lit waters of the Hudson into a smudged Turner. Harry walked briskly in the cool evening breeze to warm himself, but after a minute or two he had to bury his hands deeply in his coat pockets to fend off the chill.

It was eight o'clock on a Saturday night, and so the Chinese restaurant was filled to capacity, and no one noticed the lone man waiting for a table and removing his coat. Unsmiling waiters moved about in a no-nonsense manner, taking orders, serving, clearing tables of dirty dishes and pocketing tips. Young couples held hands while warm plates, steaming covered dishes, and porcelain pots of piping hot tea were set before them. A party in the back of the restaurant sounded inordinately noisy to Harry, and he wished he hadn't come out at all.

Being among people who were enjoying themselves, while he was almost inconsolably grieved seemed eminently unfair to him, an unreasonable demand in his present frame of mind.

At last, a table-for-one became free when a sad-looking elderly man with dark circles under his eyes and a Maugham-lined face vacated it, and Harry headed for it, wondering what heartbreaking story this relic might tell, if only some living soul were sympathetic enough to listen.

Over the egg rolls he ordered against the better judgment of his ulcer, Harry studied the faces surrounding him in the mellow pools of light streaming from the colorful lanterns above, and suddenly he was struck by the fact that maybe one of these innocent-looking façades concealed the horrible secret that he was trying his damndest to penetrate. Indeed, was it so unlikely that one of these chatty customers might turn out to be the kidnapper or an accomplice who not so long ago had played a vicious cat-and-mouse game with his wife, who perhaps had even brutalized her?

And suddenly Harry saw on every patron in the restaurant a killer's mask, a George Grosz monstrosity. Somehow he could not shake off the nagging suspicion that behind all these sweet and deceptive fronts there lurked the hearts of murderers, of potential kidnappers—not the blasé faces of the inscrutable Westerners that surrounded him, discoursing on the illusion of détente or the brilliant artistry of Liv Ullmann, Ellen Burstyn and Lina Wertmuller—but fiends and foes capable of wreaking havoc upon another's life. Of course, all humans could be counted on to display, if sufficiently provoked, enormous outbursts of temper, berserk tantrums, insane sprees. Harry was only too painfully aware of this very shortcoming in himself. Hadn't he tasted a generous slice of his own blemished nature late this afternoon?

To be sure, he had witnessed a like fault in the "flawless" nature of the woman he loved, and the spectacle emanating from this Laingian showcase of intrinsic cruelty was anything but pretty. The longer he knew women the less he understood them. It struck him that about the only trait predictable about women's nature was their unpredictability.

In the meantime these jackasses around him, with their intent young faces, were still fooled by the Schnitzlerian roundelay of love. Goddamn it, didn't these dumb-ass lovers realize they'd always be strangers to each other?

Over the saber-rattle of dishes and silverware, Harry forced himself to focus his attention on his Lucullan meal, a rich mixture of roast pork, bamboo shoots and onions in cylindrical egg-dough casings, and not on his suspicion of being surrounded by a hostile army out to harm him through his wife. No paranoia please, he prayed silently, not at this stage of the game yet. A good night's rest, and he could face the following day, hopefully with more stamina, and a measure of optimism. The shadows and the loneliness of this night were aliens to him and he hoped to quickly seek his sanctuary in Morpheus' arms.

When he got home, it took all his remaining strength just to shower, to cleanse himself not only of the grime of New York, but to purge himself of all the memories and horror of the past twenty-four hours.

After Harry had put on his pajamas and brushed his teeth, the full impact of Ruth's absence totally and unexpectedly manifested itself and engulfed him in all its immensity. He stood in the door of their bedroom and glared at the large, empty bed. The blue satiny bedspread was stretched across it, not tautly stretched but oddly crumpled. For an instant he wondered why there were creases and dark stains at the foot of it. Ruth always prided herself on being immaculately neat. Then he recalled that almost twelve hours earlier Donald Ives had slept on the bed for several hours. In a micro-second a shudder of revulsion passed through Harry. Jesus! He wasn't about to lie down where that lush had drooled. He rushed to the bathroom, grabbed a can of Lysol from the top shelf of the medicine cabinet and started to spray the hallway between the bathroom and the bedroom, and then the bedroom itself, as if he were exterminating the spirit of the drunken little man with the disinfectant.

When he pulled the bedspread back, the awful silence in the night-filled apartment really closed in on him. Dreading the stillness, he flicked on the radio and tuned in to Jean Shepherd who was substituting for Joe Franklin's "Memory Lane" and reciting one of his inimitable stories of an earlier, seemingly harmless, age over WOR, acting out in his own onomatopoeic way all the joys and mishaps of his boyhood. But half the words bounced off Harry, like pebbles skipped on water, and even though the raconteur's amiable chatter was so comfortingly far removed from the harsh reality of the contemporary scene, Harry could not concentrate and turned off the radio altogether after a short time.

He switched the light off and opened the window just enough to let some fresh air in without inviting a burglar in. The Fiberglas curtains immediately blossomed out full-sail before receding again in slow-motion billows. Outside, a 100-watt bulb over the entrance leading into the courtyard, which the bedroom window overlooked, provided just enough light to cast playful shadows on the bedroom ceiling. Immediately on sliding into bed Harry noted that Ruth must have changed the sheets the day she disappeared because they felt glacier-cold and smelled fresh-laundered and redolent of the lemony fragrance of the sachet she always kept in the linen closet. This only made everything worse.

God, just to escape quickly into the arms of deep unbroken sleep, not to think anymore, to switch off the tiny persistent neutron reminders of the woman who for twenty years had been his bed-companion. Her warm supple body always snuggled closely to his for comfort, cuddling him affectionately, her hands gently caressing his hair, the nape of his neck and on down his spinal column, her fingers playing lightly with his rear end under the pajama bottoms, as her warm clean breath brushed against his lips until they both dropped off to sleep.

But there was nothing now, no one. His hand reached out to touch the pillow on her side of the bed where she always had been. Before turning the light off, she often sat there propped against the headboard, massaging her hands with Nivea creme, pushing back the delicate white cuticle from the crescents of her fingernails with a Q-tip and studying his face. They would exchange small talk about his office, friends, a show at the Guggenheim, or whether they should make reservations to visit Tanglewood or Jacob's Pillow the following weekend, and this idle talk that rarely ended in stubborn stone-walling suddenly assumed a quality all of its own, something of an intrinsic value he had never quite appreciated before. It had become as natural as breathing or eating, and somehow a part of life, slipped in unnoticed, taking on a harmonious sustenance devoid of the melodramatics and passion which alone appeared to give meaning to marriage in the highlights of sitcoms and Jack Lemmon movies. A marriage made in the image of *Good Housekeeping*. If it lacked the blood-letting excitement attending ghetto life and its disadvantaged dwellers with their brushes with the police, the violence that had become second nature to them in their fight to survive the ugliness and crudities of their social and psychoid environs, the Bensonny household—devoid also of children and the constant nefarious crises in bringing them up among the vulgarities and dangers of school life and aggressive peers—at least could boast of well-stocked, amusing weekend parties with friends who kept their relationships viable and nourished by catty gossip about mutual acquaintances.

Each family lived its insulated Mary Tyler Moore episodes of pinprick events that could hardly be expected to make the evening news with Barbara Walters, although each domestic circle nonetheless revealed its share of kitsch and schmaltz and Weltschmerz and even, at times, a bonus assortment of spiteful fights in the marital ménage—all of which appeared to lubricate the liquored up chatterbox production of friends with whom he and Ruth came in contact. And, there were always credible rumors culminating in adulteries, divorces, fatal diseases, sessions with analysts, and occasional spouse-swapping tales. However, jail terms were virtually unknown among the coterie which the Bensonnys entertained—a circle made up mostly of people in the publishing field.

It always pained Harry that he wasn't a Bill Targ or Robert Gottlieb or Saxe Commins and his mediocre abilities could never penetrate the iron ring of big guns in the literary world who found honorable mention in *Publishers Weekly* and who also pitched tent, like him, in the Broadway-Riverside Drive encampment: the Epsteins, Norman Podhoretz, Murray Kempton, the Irving Howes.

Such frustrations aside, Harry's life could only be described as settled, in contrast to the lives of most of his friends who regularly scrapped with their wives or mistresses, and frequently broke up in the end. Until now. These last few hours. If any of his friends had ever suspected that Harry himself had been involved for two years in a torrid affair of his own (which now by all appearances seemed to come to a climax with the impregnation of his mistress), they would have had a field day of seamy gossip. Not that he could really blame them. But it hurt like the devil when you were the one that got hit, Harry concluded, and the smile of smug superiority and disdain was turned against you. To be sure, Helga would be accepted by his world-wise friends; they might even envy him for landing such a delectable and intellectual femme fatale. The point could even be argued whether Helga might not deign it beneath her to be seen in the company of *his* acquaintances. Not that she was a snob; the truth was she would fit eminently well in their midst. At the same time, Harry could not predict what would happen to Ruth if they were divorced. Would he still see their mutual friends, or only she, or could it be settled amicably and both parties continue their relationships as in the past? Or would their friends pair off into pro-him and pro-her camps?

Somewhere in the courtyard an open window emitted the well-modulated, but very loud, voice of Johnny Carson mentioning that he had some good news and some bad news during his opening monologue.

This joke from a rerun of the old "Tonight" show caused Harry to flash back momentarily to the Chinese restaurant where he had opened the fortune cookie at the close of his meal with the firm determination to apply its verbal content to the struggle of getting Ruth back alive, even though he normally laughed off such nonsense. In its usual non-committal fashion the cookie he had opened merely said: "This is the time to accept the bad with the good." Well, at least the maxim did not suggest a specific action. The bad with the good. There was some comfort in the options left open to him. But did this mean that in case anything happened to Ruth he should find solace in the juicy consolation prize of a new wife, cum baby? On a more practical level, Harry was perturbed more by his increasingly paranoiac suspicions. Although the town had its ample share of psychos, he now saw an enemy even in the most innocuous of persons.

The faces in the restaurant had fully pointed this out to him, the nuts rubbing elbows with the innocent. But on second thought who were the innocent and who were the nuts? Who hadn't heard about some dear old trusted Uncle Billy suddenly caught red-handed by a shocked mommy as he was drying off little Lillian, fresh out of the bathtub, with one pinkie inside sweet Lillian's vagina? The country was full of such latter-day Januses—the blue-collar-grandfathers and Uncle Bills who cursed the breakdown of Uncle Sam's judicial system; the local-bank-president Uncle Bills who beat town with their secretaries and half of their banks' deposits. It happened every day. Everywhere.

Harry couldn't figure people out anymore. Not himself and certainly not Helga, the woman to whom he was willing to surrender body and soul. Goddamnit, why was life made thornier once the sexed-up layers of love and lust were peeled from it by time? For two solid years she had wanted to live for him alone, to do anything in the world he would have asked her to do, and now, the first time he pleaded with her to do him a favor when the chips really were down, she gave him a whole megillah, as she would have said, about why moral commitments would not allow her to meet him even halfway. Love truly was two-edged. Pascal had something on the ball all right when he wrote that the heart had its own reasons which reason cannot know. Oh, Helga had a brain all right, plus a lovely body which she knew how to use to evoke the maximum sensual responses from her bed-partner. At the same time the critic who called her the biggest thing in feminine poetry since Sylvia Plath was way off. Not by any stretch of the imagination could Helga be considered a sesquipedalian poetaster, but Marianne Moore and Anne Sexton lived for years after Plath's suicide and there were many women poets today—Adrienne Rich, Diane Wakoski, Gwendolyn Brooks (all of whom Harry preferred any day to the mythological pretentiousness of their male, self-centered counterparts)—greater than Helga Lipsolm. Personally, he liked embittered Nikki Giovanni and the earthy passion of Erica Jong more, with their wild convictions spewing out of dark dungeons of unchained principles.

Erica Jong! The writer whose first novel Charlotte Collins had recommended to him earlier that afternoon. Good God, he had forgotten all about the woman in 3N! How in God's name had she spent the evening after all? Did she wait for Harry to call her to come down and pick up the money so she could get laid by that fat slob Ed Blakely, or was she looking for the nearest high roof to jump off after the amphetamines no longer eased her dreadful anxiety? Whatever, in the meantime Charlotte Collins, like Lady Lazarus in Sylvia Plath's *Ariel*, was condemned to eating men like air.

No wonder, as in Anne Sexton's poem, women today all slept like guerilla fighters, with one eye open for attack, and it would not have come as a surprise to Harry if all women were wary of men, regardless of whether the male confronted them as employer, confidant, father, protégé, lover or husband. Did, indeed, in women's experiences, men assume the image of an ogre carrying a brown shopping bag—as another poem by a feminist proclaimed—filled with turnips and the wife's head, her eyes closed?

Seeking help, Harry now turned his attention to the bookshelves lining the longest wall of his living room. Beckett simply would have reassigned Harry in typical nihilistic fashion to the trashcan. Capote might have interviewed the kidnapper-butcher after the heinous deed was committed and found the human angle of the crime most persuasive and one that could be traced back to a traumatic experience in his childhood. Such fine writers as Doris Lessing and Joyce Carol Oates might have vied for the 20th century George Eliot-Sandian exposé of victim and perpetrator in a psychological and social context without coming to grips with a satisfactory conclusion, let alone solution. Macho Mailer would no doubt dash off some florid, dense fictional treatise relating the crime to an aimless society cooped up in blocks of concrete, to politics, science, boxing and sex as propounded by Aquarius. Updike, by his expatiating clarity of insight and crystal-bright imagery, would cause Harry's character to struggle against an inability to act heroically, and, by the same token, make the killer's internal urges the reader's own, inducing the latter to feel compassion for everything that could be elicited as human. Philip Roth would be acclaimed for stressing in his inimitably funny and wise fashion the elemental conflicts in America's (and Harry's) drab and bitter marriages. Günter Grass and Heinrich Böll might turn Harry's melancholy into a lacerating story of loss and seeking. Pynchon certainly could be counted on to complicate the case even more with a shuffle of finical chapters and players while Genet could be expected to apportion 100 per cent blame to the crypto-fascist heterosexual Harry Bensonny and deliver a wealth of eulogies and accolades on behalf of the anal-oriented hero-killer for his selfless deed in ridding the world of another hetero-capitalist bitch. But nowhere on those shelves could Harry find any step-by-step demonstrations for his next move such as were shown in Chilton's "Auto Repair Manual," for instance.

His mind exhausted, Harry once more reached out for Ruth's pillow, and again only the cool lemon-scented linen was there, icy to his touch. He crushed it to his chest and shut his eyes tight, imagining in the blood-darkness the beat of his wife's heart as rapid as the flutter of a bird's wings beneath the warm ribcage of her slenderness. But there was no heartbeat, no warmth, only the cool resiliency of the pillow, and Harry shoved it from him, helplessly. He lay absolutely still, staring at the ceiling, concentrating upon the warmth of Ruth's body as she held him in her arms, so often, so countlessly often in the past, and he turned on his side, touching the pillow again . . . and fell asleep.

Once during the night he woke up, went to get a drink of water, and on his return heard a radio blaring forth from the courtyard as Candy Jones spoke to Dr. Carleton Fredericks about the dangers of consuming $C_{12}H_{22}O_{11}$ and similar carbohydrates.

Around two o'clock Sunday afternoon Harry woke up.

23 ⸺⸺⸺⸺

It was a raw blustery October day, gray, with dark smudgy clouds sagging low. Harry felt ravenously hungry when he woke and, although it was afternoon, he prepared the sort of breakfast Ruth always had in store for him after he had shaved. A bowl of hot oatmeal with applesauce, wheat germ and half-and-half, two pieces of toast spread with peanut butter and honey respectively, a soft-boiled egg and a small glass of orange juice, followed by a glass of milk reinforced by Tiger's Milk. Ever since Dr. Renner had discovered Harry's duodenal ulcer he had had to stick to this breakfast, but it agreed with him enormously, cleaning up his insides and tasting pretty damned good to boot, besides supplying him with most of the energy he needed for the day on his demanding job.

What had caused the ulcers, almost eight years earlier, Harry could never tell for sure. Except for life at the office and a brief stint with the Army in Korea in the early 50's, he had no aggravations to speak of, was largely free of stress, and his existence anything but hectic. Was it perhaps a matter of genetics? He knew his grandfather had also had them.

Washing the dishes, he grinned and reminisced about the day Ruth took him to an X-ray technician for the Roentgen plates. For about ninety minutes he was subjected to an unearthly succession of degrading and humiliating postures, lying under a huge X-ray machine on a leather-padded table. He had to wear a knee-length crepe paper nightshirt with the sides slit open and joined only by a piece of string. A brigade of nurses instructed Harry exactly how to lie and hold his breath, and in-between shots he had to drink what seemed to him like gallons of pink barium sulfate that he felt was coming out of his every orifice. In the background, Ruth, to his intense embarrassment, watched the entire process with a hawk's eye, making certain nothing harmful was being done to her love. Then both of them had waited for an endless half hour before the verdict came.

Harry had lost twenty-eight pounds in eight weeks and had felt nauseated at the mere sight of food, besides breaking into a cold sweat day and night. Exhaustion had showed in his face, his cheeks sunken and his deepset eyes ringed by dark shadows. When the X-ray technician finally diagnosed a big duodenal ulcer that was curable, Ruth burst into tears. For joy.

Dr. Renner prescribed some pills and a bland diet for at least eighteen months and warned Harry that he would have great difficulty moving his bowels for a few days because of all the barium inside him. However, what Harry had not reckoned with was the fact that for almost five days he had not had a bowel movement and when Ruth finally called Dr. Renner about it, she was told that this was not unusual, but that it would be a good idea for her to give him an enema, and of course to remind him to not forget to continue taking his Combid pills to prevent the nausea.

Harry was aghast. He had never taken an enema in his life, and he felt humiliated at the prospect. But Ruth was adamant and had already bought all the paraphernalia to rid him of his discomfort. For the first time in their marriage, Harry felt really uncomfortable in Ruth's presence and set up a hue-and-cry about not wanting to let her go through with it since such an "extreme" remedy was unnecessarily demeaning. Eventually he lost his temper and heaped abuse on her for bothering Dr. Renner with such trivialities. Lying naked on a mat on the bathroom floor, he heard Ruth merely laugh off his remonstrations, and finally she succeeded in having him submit to her administering the clyster despite his continuous stream of protestations about squeezing the rubber hose and soapy fluid up his rectum. Then she casually washed the soiled mat when the soapy fluid, without warning, began to take its ghastly effect. He spent almost two hours in the bathroom, feeling that about thirty-five years of parasitic sludge was sluicing out of his system.

When the cramps finally subsided he put his arms around her waist and asked her forgiveness, but she only whispered that she loved him and that that was what it was all about.

Maybe Ruth was right, too. That's what marriage *was* all about, not minding the shit and the stench of someone you loved—not just worshipping the self-anointed Bismarckian office hero and Max Beerbohmian cocktail cynosure and raconteur—but loving man with all his weaknesses, shortcomings and flaws. He had admired her for this selflessness then, and surreptitiously, unconsciously *now*, rinsing the breakfast dishes. And he wondered if Helga would be *as* strong in caring for him when and if the need ever arose. But he guessed she would; after all, hadn't she witnessed much greater horrors than someone taking an enema, when she was at Auschwitz and Belsen where the stench of corpses covered in their own excrement was so all-pervasive that even the neighboring communities began to wonder what was happening in the death-camps.

Nevertheless, one thing became alarmingly clear to Harry: he was not cut of the same cloth as Ruth. Because a year after this bathroom incident, Ruth herself was confronted by a similar situation when she had become constipated for more than four days. Again Dr. Renner suggested the same treatment, and Ruth asked Harry to help her with the enema. He started making the most monstrous excuse about having to go out at once and help someone with his manuscript, although it happened to be a Sunday. Ruth just smiled and agreed that his client should not be kept waiting, and said she could cope with it herself and that she could well understand he would rather be away at the time. Not once did she mention that evidently it was all right for *her* to help him but not for *him* to help her in this unpleasant undertaking.

Harry had left the house then in a hurry and walked for hours along the Hudson cursing himself for copping out on her, for his lack of chivalry, or fortitude, or what-have-you. The exact word failed him, until it dawned on him that what he lacked most was compassion, a quality Ruth had shown in abundant measure not only on the occasion of giving *him* the enema but when he refused her. He felt like a worm and walked over to Broadway, found an open florist, and bought a dozen roses to make amends.

When he got back home Harry found Ruth in bed pretending to read the paper, but there were tears in her eyes. She said nothing when he came in, only looked up, saw the red roses, and knew at once he was trying to undo the damage he had done. He sat down beside her on the bed and she embraced him silently. She asked him why he had spent so much money on the flowers and he said because he loved her, that there was no other reason, and then he asked her why she had been crying and she lied to him that it was the pain of the cramps she had had as a result of the enema. But Harry knew better. Ruth was not the sort of person to cry over pain, least of all over stomach cramps, and it was at this point that he knew he had to make a clean breast of it all and he told her quite honestly that he never went to see anybody about a manuscript, that it was a matter of unconscionable cowardice on his part and he had just chickened out, perhaps he just did not want to associate her lovely body with anything as repulsive as excrement. That was the gist of it and the God's honest truth. And he swore to her that if she ever needed another enema he would volunteer to help her with it. Because he realized, inwardly, that true love did not mean to dominate, to exploit or manipulate, but to reveal weaknesses to each other, without fear. And to open oneself to the other's needs.

Only the barrage of mad little kisses all over his face demonstrated that she had forgiven him and loved him more than she ever had. That Sunday Harry was so madly in love with his wife that, after putting the flowers in a vase, he undressed and crept into bed beside her and they made mad love all afternoon and then fell asleep and made still more love later, till late at night.

These little episodes flitted through Harry's mind as he drove his Dodge Dart through the relatively deserted streets of New York in the direction of Northern Boulevard in Queens to see what price he could get for the car. Ruth's face often appeared before his eyes, especially when he had to wait for a traffic light to change, Ruth the Nurse Image, Ruth the Mother Image, Ruth the Housewife Image, Ruth the Mistress Image—images that no doubt would have infuriated the Feminist Movement, but although he did not feel the least bit paternalistic in his relationship toward his wife, or with any woman for that matter, perhaps some of the remnants of a subconscious chauvinism and sexism that had been instilled into his lifestyle since childhood still clung to him when thinking about women in terms of role-playing personalities. Could it be that the biology of testosterone was destiny after all, or that he was the prisoner of his own manmade conceptions? Nevertheless, to him women were still something apart, to be treated differently from men. He behaved toward the latter with a camaraderie and ease that to his way of thinking would be gross and unreal in a vis-a-vis relationship with women. And possibly to this extent the Women's Libbers were correct: men had no right to think of women as something apart that needed special treatment or attention not accorded to their own sex. Or again, as in Harry's case, it was this specific differentiation, this variance and shifting of an inner attitude when facing the female that put him slightly on edge, made life vastly more precarious, exciting, and interesting, to say the least, fraught with a certain amount of risk, of danger, of joyful anticipation, of feeling your way about, of . . .

Red, blue, green, yellow and orange triangular flags suddenly burst onto his retina as they fluttered in the chill breeze, snapping briskly above a brood of shiny cars. Everywhere bunting and banners announced that Crazy Guy, the dealer of the used-car lot, was offering top prices for second-hand automobiles and selling them at rock bottom.

Harry veered off the road and steered his car along a lane buffeted on each side by dozens of limousines, coupes, station wagons that were just waiting for bargain-hunting buyers. The rock-bottom prices Crazy Guy had in store for his clientele were marked in large white figures on each windshield. Harry brought his Dodge to a stop at the end of the lane where a brick wall converted it into a cul-de-sac. He rummaged about in his glove compartment, making sure he had all the pertinent papers with him. The damp frost of the late afternoon made him shiver with cold as he got out of the car. He had not taken his topcoat along and bundled up in his jacket against the wet raw wind. He was looking around for Crazy Guy or an office when he heard, not too far away, the exchange of angry voices, sounding almost like sea lions clamoring for fish during feeding time. Again the louder and more aggravated voice of the two flared up, threatening the other man off the lot. Harry followed the sound of the voices and found its source in another lane in front of a sedan that resembled a Bentley and had a sliding roof over the driver's seat.

"What the hell do I care?" the angrier of the two men shouted. "If you don't like it go down the road and see how much Super-Joe's going to rake over to you."

The other man, a small, heavy-set fellow with a Tyrolean hat, already had his hand on the door handle. "You bet your sweet life I will," he snapped back. "I thought that maybe you would outbid him but he offered me two hundred bucks more than you did, and he'll get my business."

"Go, good riddance," the swarthy tall man who made the most noise yelled. "I get cocksuckers like you all day long and I ain't going to get no ulcers over your chickenshit gig." He stood akimbo, his meaty biceps bulging and revealing the tattoo of a nude on one arm and an eagle on the other. All he wore was a sleeveless sweater and a pair of Levi's and sandals. Probably getting infuriated all day long with his customers kept him warm in this biting cold, Harry figured. He stepped out of the way, letting the Bentley shoot past him like a silent seal and out of the lot. At this point the angry man, obviously Crazy Guy, caught sight of Harry and knitted his threatening, shaggy John L. Lewis brows.

"You want anything, Mac?" he barked.

Harry stepped back into the lane and approached Crazy Guy. "Yeah. I got my Dodge Dart here and I was wondering how much you'd offer me for it."

Crazy Guy strode brusquely toward him and stretched out his oil-streaked arm. "Sure thing, buddy," he said, shaking Harry's hand with a vehemence that made him wince. "Where've you got it?"

"Just down the other lane," Harry declared, leading the way for Crazy Guy past two cars, one of them another Dodge Dart with a fat $1900 painted on the windshield. "I didn't know where else to park so I . . ."

"Don't worry about that, Mac," Crazy Guy said, following him. "You got any verification? Driver's license, bill of sale, I.D. card, insur . . ."

"I got them all here. The car's in perfect condition, you can see for yourself."

"Yeah, I know, I know," Crazy Guy said warily. "Every Tom, Dick and Harry comes in here and gives me the same snow-job that their car's in perfect shape and then you open up the hood and half a dozen vultures fly out."

"Well, convince yourself!"

They had reached Harry's Dodge and Crazy Guy took a brief appraisal of the car's body, surveyed the tires, then checked under the hood. Harry watched guardedly as Crazy Guy poked around the engine. After a time the car dealer began to mutter something about the camshaft and a faulty exhaust valve. A little while later he disappeared completely behind the raised hood but Harry still heard him mumbling, this time something about a cracked piston ring, low battery, faulty conductor cable from the secondary winding. Harry had never been much of a mechanic and had no way of knowing whether Crazy Guy was just giving him a lot of bull, to soften him up for the big letdown when it came to talking business. If possible, he would do anything to avoid an argument, not being in the mood for challenging anybody very much today, and he certainly had no intention of getting down to name-calling and ending up in the cocksucker category like the fellow in the Tyrolean hat. But at least Harry was sure he could clear around fifteen hundred after seeing the other Dodge Dart in the lot selling for four hundred more.

At length Crazy Guy came up from under the hood and slammed the top shut. "Okay, let's take her for a spin down to the office," he said, wiping his grease-stained face, and headed for the driver's seat.

Harry ducked into the car, sitting down beside the car dealer, on the passenger side, and gave him the key. Obviously Crazy Guy wanted to test-drive the car and make sure she ran smoothly. He turned on the ignition, raced the motor for a minute, spoke of a tune-up, and backed down the lane with a daredevil Evel Knievel speed Harry wouldn't have taken on a trafficless autobahn. Then he gunned the motor forward on Northern Boulevard and suddenly slammed on the brakes, causing Harry almost to be thrown against the windshield. Crazy Guy had come to a screeching halt in front of a miniscule wooden cabin from which the white paint peeled off in large blistering flakes. They got out of the car and entered his dingy cabin. The floor was littered with batteries, a stack of tires, some empty cans of oil and a few dirty rags, and in the center stood a large desk with dozens of bills, maps, forms and documents scattered across it. A small potbellied stove kept the tiny room at a well-nigh boiler-room swelter. Small wonder Crazy Guy only wore a sleeveless sweater. The walls of the cabin, except for the two grimy, spiderweb-choked windows flanking both sides of the desk, were plastered with pinups of nudes from *Playboy* and *Penthouse* and perhaps a dozen or so snapshots of Crazy Guy posing with enormous fish he had caught somewhere.

"Okay, make yourself at home," Crazy Guy said, gesturing to a rickety wicker chair. "Let's have the papers."

Harry sat down and handed him all the documents he had relating to the sale and ownership of the Dodge. The salesman gave them a thorough perusal as Harry studied his brutish, swarthy face for a sign that might reveal a measure of appreciation, but none was forthcoming, and Harry could well picture him as the sort of clod likely to come up with a statement like "You wouldn't want no sheenie or spade

216

plowing your sister, would ya?" Feeling that silence in the circumstances with anybody as experienced as Crazy Guy appeared to be in the rough tumble of life and the secondhand car business in particular was the better part of wisdom, Harry diverted his attention again to the pictures on the walls. There must have been about fifty or sixty dream girls in the buff enticingly massaging their thighs or spreading the top of their pubic hair ready for action as they paraded themselves unashamedly around Crazy Guy's desk. Harry got to wondering what really did go through the mind of a man who was surrounded by this bevy of voluptuous beauties for about twelve hours every single working day. Did he still notice them? Did they have the effect of actually blunting his desire, his lust, after a while, so that he was no longer conscious of the feminine form, its overpowering loveliness? Or did he masturbate mentally, letting the women take free rein of his fantasy in his mind's eye and rape him without ever engaging in the pleasure of pursuit, the challenge of domesticity, the pain of rejection, the responsibility of intimacy? He didn't know what to make of a person who was constantly encircled by fleshpots in all their most alluring sexual poses without having them stimulate him sexually to such a pitch that he would indeed have to release his tension, his pent-up desires. Did the withheld stimulus actually project to his real-life erotic responses—so that he could never perform his manly functions properly—and brainwash him to a state of seminal impotence? God knows, maybe he blew off his frustrations when coming into touch with his less accommodating customers, as he had done with the man in the Tyrolean hat.

And yet, on the other wall his own person, in the photos, was surrounded only by types that might best have been described as hefty truck-drivers or has-been wrestlers, all chuckling over Crazy Guy's catch of fish. There wasn't a single woman in those snapshots, just brawny men, fish, and picnic tables loaded with beer cans.

"You ever do what's in the pictures?"

Harry startled. "What?"

"The pictures. You were looking at them. You ever been up to Lake Winnebago, in Wisconsin? Deep-freeze fishing?"

"No, I haven't."

"Well, that's where I head for in winter," he grinned a yellow, nicotine-stained grin, leaning back and scratching his crotch with a corner of Harry's driver's license. "With my buddies. You drill a hole into the ice, with electric-powered augers, get yourself some thermal-layer underwear and an outhouse and then you catch walleye pike,

217

rock bass, lake trout, Michigan smelt. Or you move on to another lake and catch crappies, sunfish, bluegills. All you got to do is get yourself some good bait, live minnows, red worms, silver wigglers, corn borers or ice flies and bingo! You got the nicest vacation a man can dream of. You fish too?"

Harry shook his head. "No, I can't say I do. My wife and I go up to Maine, though, for our vacation; lots of fishing up there."

"Aagh, chickenshit. That's no fish they got there. Who the hell wants lobster all day long?"

"Well, they've got some other fish too I've been told, hake, mackerel, whiting, haddock and cod for instance. Your wife go fishing too?"

"Shit no! No way! She don't care for no fishing. She lives her life and I live mine. Who the hell wants to have the same face all-year-round chewing your ass off if you don't do what she wants. Am I not right or am I?"

Everybody seemed to have his own beef about marriage. Crazy Guy didn't want the same face around all year, but he sure as hell could stand the same tits and cunts around him all year in his filthy hut. The dream girls you could order around at your beck and call in your imagination—that was something else. Real cool! What a sad life, being married to five dozen centerfolds!

"About this Dodge of yours," Crazy Guy suddenly broke into Harry's musings. "Your papers are in order, but you realize that car's got 68,000 miles on the odometer."

"I know. I've driven it quite a bit. But it's in top shape consid . . ."

"No, it ain't. There are a good half dozen items I gotta replace. Realignment and tune-up and all that jazz. Tell you though what I'll do. I'll give you a good price because you strike me as a nice fellow. How would four hundred strike you?"

"Four . . ." Harry sat bolt upright, grabbing the corners of the desk. "Four hundred! You must be kidding. I was figuring on at least fifteen hundred."

Crazy Guy burst out roaring with laughter, almost splitting the crammed space of the over-heated cabin with the volume of his mirth. "Fifteen hundred! You can't be serious, Mr . . ." He glanced at the driver's license. "Mr. Bensonny. Who the hell would pay you fifteen hund . . ."

"What about that Dodge Dart outside? I saw it. You're offering it for nineteen. Why should I give you mine for four hundred?"

218

"Look, Mr. Bensonny," Crazy Guy furrowed his bushy brows again, leaning forward on his elbows and looking like a menacing Edward G. Robinson heralding an impending eruption of temper if Harry tried to cross his ways. "That Dodge you saw outside is last year's model. In perfect condition. Your old heap—here, take a look at the bill of sale—is, let's see, it's five years old. You figure on a thousand depreciation for the first year and six hundred for each year after that. But I'm willing to let you have a break because I like you, even with all I got to repair. Keep in mind, though, I'm not twisting your arm to sell your car; you came to *me*. I made the offer, and if you don't like it, try anybody else and see how much they'll give you. So there it is: the car's book value is four hundred—take it or leave it!"

Harry felt the blood drain from his face. This was the second unexpected financial blow in twenty-four hours. First Ed Blakely and the failure to sell his house, and now this, the car. Four hundred dollars would be of no earthly use to him whatsoever in the overall picture. Better to keep the old machine after all, which to him was useful enough for any number of drives and emergencies of which there could be plenty in the next day or so. But the mere pittance Crazy Guy or any other dealer for that matter was willing to dish out wouldn't even amount to a drop in the bucket. A sudden panic seized Harry.

God, what was going to happen to Ruth if he really couldn't manage to raise the thirty thousand dollars for her release? Would Helga, her self-confessed arch-enemy, who was well prepared to see her dead, really get to see his side of the coin and hand over the money that it had taken her a whole life-time to save up, give up the proceeds of a work dedicated to the memory of her whole family brutally murdered by the maniacal anti-Semites, sacrificing it all for a woman whom she hated—however erroneously—and who stood in the way between her and possibly her sanity?

"You want a shot of whiskey or something?" Crazy Guy gave Harry a quizzical look. "You look kinda queasy, like you could use a drop."

"What? Oh no, no, that's all right," Harry said huskily, and stood up. "It's only that I expected a thousand bucks more. It just never occurred to me that . . ."

"Sorry, Mister," the used-car dealer shrugged, handing the papers back to Harry. "Four hundred smackers as the case stands is more generous than I need be. But don't take my word for it. Go to another dealer, just for the hell of it, and see what he's got to offer. Okay?"

"Yup." Harry sighed.

"Only tip I can give you," Crazy Guy volunteered, getting up himself now and again pumping Harry's hand, "is that you put a sign in your car window that you want a thousand bucks and maybe in a month or so somebody will catch the bait. There's always that chance."

Harry returned the documents to his jacket and nodded. "Thanks anyway. But I need the dough tomorrow."

"Tomorrow!" Crazy Guy released a low whistle through his teeth. "Well, good luck to you, Buster! All I can say is you better strike it rich mighty quick, like in some oil field." The hot cabin once more exploded with Crazy Guy's uproarious laughter as Harry shut the door behind him, leaving the used-car dealer alone with his rock bass, the papery nudes, and the oil cans.

24 ──────────

Harry got into his Dart like a zombie and idled down Northern Boulevard, not even sure where he was heading. Just for luck he tried another dealer who was about to close shop for the day, but this one, a neatly dressed young man who had an arm around the shoulders of a frail Japanese girl with steel hooks instead of hands, wouldn't offer him more than three hundred at the most. Who knows, Harry wondered, perhaps they really fixed a car up nice and fiddled with the odometer, setting it back to 12,000 miles or so and then sold it for a great profit.But even if they did it would not matter much when all he could squeeze out of them was a paltry 1 per cent of what the kidnapper asked.

Harry made a U-turn on 87th Street in Jackson Heights and headed back for the city. Nightfall was coming on by leaps and bounds now, pushing daylight down the equator. In the distance the silhouetted tumble of Manhattan skyscrapers hulked like toys against a darkening backdrop. Way off to the left the two oblong towers of the World Trade Center stood guard while the top of the Empire State Building played hide and seek in a bank of piled up cumulus clouds.

These heavy formations of clouds in the sky already merged with the darkness that began to drape its chilly cloak over New York; it was the kind of weather that tended to depress Ruth slightly, although it had little impact on Harry. Except for today when a blue sky might have cheered him up somewhat, but even the unavoidable cycle of nature seemed not to spare him, to militate against him, as if to demonstrate that fate still was boss over puny man. The mightiest of men had tried to fight the elements, and failed. Not merely the dust-speck jocks with their pikes and paper-broads, nor the dregs of humanity running out of doorways and wiping windshields of automobiles stopped for a traffic light with a dirty rag and their own spittle, not the poor Charlotte Collinses and insignificant Harry Bensonnys and Donald Iveses—of these nobodies one could expect failure. But also the semi-gods in high places and elitist echelons, the Napoleons, Pericleses, Dariuses, Hitlers, where had their empires and dreams sunk? And what about the saddle-shod anarchist-rebels of the 20th century advocating, with Kierke-gaard, the scuttling of the shipwreck with all the cargoes of this earth in order to start afresh? They amounted to less than nothing and accounted only for the noise they made, Harry decided.

No wonder everyone was going nuts. Psycho. Schizoid. Neurotic. Fighting nature, and each other. And in the end the shrink-manipulators of the ego and the id succeeded, at best, only in alleviating the pain of their patients' neuroticism in order to enable them to face that much better the prevalent neuroticism of the other incurable patients.

But life went on regardless of whether Harry tried to submerge his shattered psyche in the comforting thoughts of daydreaming himself into an idealistic society, like Brook Farm, for instance, or in the more realistic yet depressive we're-all-in-it-together syndrome of Big M.A.C.'s New York experience, or whether simply to tool along hoping that the fear of death would finally prove the driving force behind life generally and, in particular, behind his ultimate goal in trying to retrieve the woman who did not deserve to die.

What else could he do now, Harry pondered as he took a spin down Roosevelt Avenue, the tires humming hypnotically on the single-lane blacktop. Sunday was almost shot to hell anyway and his chief project of selling the car had been a total flop. One thing was certain, though: he would not go to Helga and tell her about his latest failure. Not only was it humiliating that the Great Lover had been thwarted in so simple a transaction, but it would most likely set off a new argument, a new plea for Harry not to go through with the scheme, that he had done his damndest, and on and on. A more prudent move for him by far would be to see her about the money the following day, Monday, when the going really would get tough. As a last resort. Inwardly he knew he was asking the impossible of her. The same went for Old Glumm. It was absolute suicide asking him for an advance. And now, instead of being eighteen thousand short, he was nearly twenty thousand in the hole. Where in God's name could he get hold of that sort of money on such short notice? He had no immediate family left. His gossipy friends were of no use at all. His employer and co-workers could be counted out altogether. Glumm did not even care to know about his employees' families, had never met Ruth, nor bothered to ask one single thing about Harry's private life.

In his present condition, Harry hated the idea of having to arrive back home so early, to be with himself in the apartment and keep on mainlining his mind with worries about what tortures and humiliations Ruth might be subjected to at any given moment. He had slept too long already to be tired and find refuge in another deep uninterrupted night of slumber. A movie didn't seem the right thing either. Sitting in a laughing, petting, popcorn-munching audience, while his wife's death might only be twenty-four hours away struck him as something out of Charles Addams—callous, cruel, totally incongruous.

He parked the Dodge on the Avenue of the Americas and sauntered to Fifth Avenue. Most windows already displayed their Christmas wares among glittering lights, pink fir trees, artificial snow and papier-mâché reindeers, although the only shop open at this time of night was the Doubleday's near 58th Street.

Harry entered listlessly, for no other reason than to kill time. A dozen or two browsers and customers milled around aimlessly in the brightly lit store among the thousands of glossy, dust-jacketed books. Only a year or two earlier, as manuscripts, these books had caused giant headaches and angry exchanges in editorial offices, quite apart from the usual side-effects of furious memos being dispatched to printers and binderies, with financial clauses and editorial coaxings fired off like heat-seeking Sidewinder missiles from the plush and cluttered haunts of the literary agents who hovered like anxious mother hens over the whole ugly erudite mess. Idling through the store, Harry realized only too well that even if there was no indication here, or for that matter at Foyle's on London's Charing Cross Road, of the blood and tears spilled prior to the birth of the books, the authors and playwrights always resented seeing their works cut, changed, rearranged, mutilated, twisted, hyped up, toned down, lengthened, or done over by mercenary editors, and that the latter proved to be just as quixotic and erratic in their judgments as anyone else and as able to predict with certainty a book's or play's ultimate fate as the author, critic, or publisher. Thousands of the forty thousand titles published each year vied for the honor of ending up on the best-seller list, and finding front-page reviews in a reputable magazine and seeing their authors celebrated on talk-shows as a second Hemingway or a budding Borchert and Büchner.

But there they squatted now, obediently, on their labeled racks, like children in their colorful Sunday-best, basking in a moment of glory, under headings such as crafts, reference, humor, fiction, history, all the magic mini-masterpieces and cultural pastiches that had cost so much sweat and despair and labor and pain. Yet most just managed to squeeze through one printing, or proved to be abnormally "slow-comers," like Robert Musil, then were withdrawn from circulation, to come to an end in the oblivion of time, in the furnace of out-of-printism, forgotten, offered for a dime with a 1937 *National Geographic* outside a grimy second-hand bookstore on Third Avenue downtown, and which were finally reduced to recycled pulp, unknown, and—except for the Library of Congress and New York's 42nd Street Library—unrecorded.

Harry made a serious effort to lose himself in the fairyland color-plates of the travel book section and the coffee table da Vincis, proceeded to seek out a few thrilling passages highlighting most best-selling novels, passed over Woodward & Bernstein's "The Final Days" and the inevitable interpretational analysis dealing with such mod history-making fat-cats as Mao, Lenin, FDR, Hitler, LBJ, Castro, Stalin, Churchill and Kissinger, and made a sincere attempt at wringing a few laughs from some of the hilarious cartoon tomes which were a compilation of drawings over the last 50 years of the *New Yorker* or a selection of the best of *Punch*. A couple of dungeon-bleak derelicts simply walked around gaping uncomprehendingly at the dust-jackets just to get out of the cold while a number of teenagers passed their time near the stacks of *Foxfire* books and *Whole Earth Catalogs*, loafing among the black magic, yoga, Zen, astrology, TA, est, TM, ESP, SF, Zoroaster and witchcraft sections, or they crowded around the lives and salaamed over works on Mick Jagger and Muhammad Ali and Jane Fonda and Rev. Moon and Kahlil Gibran and Castaneda and Hesse and Brautigan or their own favorite egomaniacal prima donnas that were light-years removed from Kant's concept of a priori realities. Plainly the 1960's and 1970's had alienated the young Doomsday people and acid heads from rationality, diverted them to the mythological never-never nostalgia of Barth, Tolkien & Gardner, then sent the granola gropers marching out of their spurious Eden into the arms of The Exorcist who at least had the easy solution of violent redemption up his sacred sleeve.

Harry began to hate himself for hating everything and everyone again, especially the poor suckers in the store and the young eager kids reaching out for some salvation as they padded around loamy mother earth in their sandaled feet knowing not what to do with their vibes or where to go and differing very little from himself in his present loathsome predicament. He had to get out fast and he was just about to do so when something extraordinary happened, and he stopped.

A particularly strident voice relieved Harry momentarily of his morbid state of depression. Not far from where he stood near a stack of *One Hundred Years of Solitude* and *Zen and the Art of Motorcycle Maintenance* he saw an elderly woman in an oatmeal tweed suit and pince-nez badgering a clerk in a light tan smock for a novel which she maintained was one of the finest books the critics had raved about last year. The clerk obviously was at a loss and could not even recall ever having heard of the title. This had a nettling effect on the woman who up to this point only partially showed her profile to Harry. In describing the book's content to the hapless clerk, she happened to turn slightly so that Harry saw her face.

Without a moment's hesitation, he took a hurried step backward, doing his best to hide behind one of the triangular book-racks bearing whodunits. He recognized the woman as the author of one of Old Glumm's own publications, an awful potboiler of a Regency romance that hardly sold out half of its first printing of 5,000 copies. In fact, after a year or so it was terminated as a remainder at Marboro's and still finding difficulty in landing customers for its burning castles and manor houses, raped twins and the noble Duke of Connaught coming to the rescue only to be slain by one of the two jealous sisters.

So here was the old ploy again, a one-shot author spreading her vaporous fame by spending weekends in bookstores, pretending to herself, and others, that her jejune and puerile drivel was first-rate, trumpeting out the title of her own out-of-print opus to make sure that people would not forget her illustrious work and its breathless contents which she summarized in a shrill voice for the benefit of her captive audience. Furtive glances of some timid Vonnegut children with appliquéd tote bags near the Country & Western record department only helped to encourage the writer of "Sisters of Bad Fortune" in her

225

belief that sooner or later the customers would storm the barricades of other bookstores, perhaps already during the coming week, clamoring for a reprint of the missing title. For an instant Harry could not help but reflect on the comet's tail of the star of fame that most writers, *all* artists, sought and which habitually evaded the vast majority of them. True enough, everybody looked for his own private niche of glorification, enshrinement, adulation, immortality, but it was given only to the select lucky few to stand out as pulsing suns and quasars; the rest soon sank into everlasting darkness and Harry knew he might as well face it that he was among those slipping past the stellar lights into a perpetual void along with this grande dame.

He had to escape this literary showcase with its silent and meek customers and the persistent shrew pouring out her bitter unacknowledged heart before he started feeling more and more sorry for himself and the world or go once more to the other extreme and feel hatred rushing at him at full shriek and learn to loathe those around him, and the heart within.

25 _____

The rain-plump clouds earlier aquatinting the sky now had completely melted into an inky-black starless night. Outside the bookstore, a cab driver was refusing to take a woman to the Bronx, and Christmasy Fifth Avenue suddenly appeared to Harry as one long spurious dreamland light-years detached from Eiseley's idyllic night country. Despite the scintillating festival sights of joy and the rotating carousels and high-wattage candles and tintinnabulating bells heralding the season's greetings, Harry could detect another more morose life today because ahead of all these strollers there stretched, to *him* at least, long vistas of future fears, frustrations, fights, desertions and all those other threadbare bits and pieces attending man on his hazardous journey to the grave that never made the display windows with their pink powder puffs and papier-mâché dolls and plum pudding cottages, but which forever darkened the springtimes and falls of every human.

Once back in his Dart, Harry made up his mind to grab a bite to eat and then head for home and hit the sack. His philosophizing had become thoroughly morbid, angry, contemptuous, akin to unarticulated ghetto feelings, and it threatened to drain him totally of all the understanding and kindness for which Ruth and Helga had once loved him.

Not feeling in the mood to rub elbows with the $35 denim work-shirt crowd at P. J. Clarke's, or dine on a steak tartare at Ma Bell's, he simply grabbed a frank and orange juice at a Nedicks, but the hot dog turned out to be so greasy he had to take a couple of Mylantas to avoid becoming nauseated.

After parking the car in the underground garage, Harry walked pensively to his apartment, recognizing with an increasingly aching sense of emptiness that never before had he needed the company of a sympathizing woman as desperately as he did tonight. He felt cut off from everyone. Even his mother-in-law on Monhegan had deserted him, with Mother Nature blowing up a storm to separate him from her. He stopped for a moment by Helga's door, unbearably tempted to ring the bell and talk to her, even if it developed into another verbal battle. But he decided against it in the end, fearful that in his attempt to be nice to her, to be close and feel the warmth of her body, she would sense his weakness, his camouflaged self-pity, see it as an opening, and that her feelings of possessiveness might reassert themselves and prevail upon him in his hour of vulnerability to reconsider things and undermine his resolve, and worst of all that she might even forget or be tempted to forget not to belong to the bug-people of the world after all. It was too great a risk. His presence in her apartment might undo everything he had been able to wrest from her—for whatever it was worth—with so painstaking and strenuous an effort the previous afternoon. Better to let sleeping dogs lie and have faith in tomorrow afternoon when there was a good chance, or at least a glimmer of a chance, that she would withdraw enough money from her passbook to meet the kidnapper's extortion demand.

The hallway smelled of cabbage, very much as it had on Saturday afternoon when he got off the elevator on the third floor. The odor immediately triggered an association of ideas, culminating in his mind's screen in the image of Charlotte Collins taking off her robe. Should he seek comfort with her? But almost at once he decided against this move. Most likely this sweet sorry creature was in about as bad a psyched-out state as he was. In this case, Harry felt, misery was not company. It wasn't sex Harry craved tonight, as much as somebody to talk to, whom he could trust implicitly, who would understand, be sympathetic, without being possessive or drawing it all into a Lord Peter Wimsey yarn as Martin was prone to do. And the only person who fitted this description was the very person around whom this whole search evolved, his wife.

228

He let himself into his apartment and turned on all the lights. The fact that he was alone was depressing enough; darkness somehow added to his despondency. He drew the curtains, saw to it that the potting soil of the plants was not too dry and added some birdseed and water to the cage. He had forgotten earlier in the day to look after the parakeets and now removed the old lettuce leaf, doubly determined not to forget to give them a fresh one tomorrow, no matter what stroke of misfortune befell him.

It was a few minutes past eight, too early to go to bed. Harry began to feel more and more restless, with nothing to do but to wait till morning to try to scrounge together as much money as possible for the ransom. He simply couldn't concentrate on anything. In the reading rack beside the sofa rested a curled-up copy of the latest *Time* and the previous week's *New Yorker*. One thing Harry was sure of: in his present state of mind he wouldn't be able to stomach the *New Yorker's* Penelope Gilliatt and her 19 page chi-chi celluloid hatchet job (which Harry felt could be summed up just as perspicaciously in two terse paragraphs), nor the quiet sophistry of Elizabeth Spencer and Emily Hahn or John Cheever's exposition of the poor rich feasting on smoked turkey at the Hotel Carlyle. Richard Rovere and Air Force One and the President also would have to wait until Harry's mind had been swept clean of his own capital headaches. He forced himself to thumb through the new *Time*, glancing only at the lead paragraphs which in unmistakable language communicated the Welt-Angst through which the human race had marched in the past seven days and the U.S. in particular, continuing to just drift, uninvolved and demoralized. Lebanese and African clashes, summit meetings in four capitals, oil prices expected to rise next year as a new preliminary for world-wide double-digit inflationary spiraling, West Bank flare-ups, Russia's banishment to Siberia of another of its poets, Uganda's Idi Amin again making a bestial fool of himself, new internal power struggles among leaders of China's Central Committee, a hijacking over Afghanistan, the ozone layer in the stratosphere gradually being destroyed by SSTs, six senseless murders by a farm worker in a small town in Nebraska, new sex scandals in Washington, a Liberation Army kidnapping another American executive, New York public schools vandalized by alcoholic students, race riots in hungry Bangladesh, bombs exploding in Nicosia, London, and Belfast, earthquakes, mass starvation in three African countries, Brazilian killer bees approaching the North American continent, UN racism, snuff movies, Dick and Liz, Saturday night

specials and SALT talks, strikes, no cure for cancer this century fore-
seen by a Nobel prize winner, the swine flu virus, polar caps melting,
and on and on, ad nauseam. Who needed it? As usual, the world was
going to hell in a basket. How did all this differ from the week
before, the month before, the decade before anyway? That dirty 20th
century—the strongarm extension of 1848 and the Industrial Revolution, regardless of Jacob Bronowski's song of praise on the Ascent of
Man, who in between catastrophes managed to produce the Bill of
Rights, Rheims Cathedral, Beethoven's Ninth, Mona Lisa, a Galileo,
Pythagoras, Newton, Willa Cather, Goethe, Mozart, Ralph Nader,
Salk, Einstein and Watson and Crick. My God, Harry reflected, staring
at *Time's* Education Section, the poor youngsters two hundred years
from now—if there were still human survivors around in the 22nd
century—what they would have to add to their storehouse of knowledge, the history, the scientific over-accumulation—hell, every goddamn school child a veritable Herman Kahn! Or Isaac Asimov!

Harry tossed the magazine disgustedly back into the pine-knotted
rack and turned on the television. Within a few seconds shots rang out
from the idiot box and he flipped the dial in a normal reflex to another
channel where a woman screamed: "Don't! I beg you, please don't!"
with tears streaming down her face as a man in a Confederate uniform
snatched a baby out of a crib and vanished through the door.
Another channel revealed an ambulance racing down Geary Street in
San Francisco, its sirens wailing in the wind, and the educational
channel gave him a fix on an articulate psychologist from Harvard
answering questions from alert youngsters on why the occult was a
typical pseudo-religious release in a society that was mechanically
geared and lived daily on a pabulum of unending reports of violence.

Violence, everything was violence, as if it were, like sex and birth,
part of man's neurological mechanism and ran in parallel fashion
within the human mainstream, reinforcing the bloodlust that supported
both death and birth to balance one against the other in an attempt to
maintain a halfway sane population equilibrium. But it somehow did
not seem to work as planned by Mother Nature. Populations grew
unchecked and violence did its damndest to keep the numbers of people
down everywhere, with wars, epidemics, starvation. When did it all
start, this bizarre explosion of brute fury, Harry wondered, as his hand
switched the image on the screen to a snarling Bogart calling some
sniveling cur "Treestump!" and then dealing him a vicious blow. Was
it with Hegel, 1776 or with 1848? Or the French Revolution, Marx

fired from his job at the *New York Tribune*, or later with the unleashing of Kaiser Wilhelm's war and its triple consequences of Versailles, Lenin and Hitler—or perhaps Jack Kerouac and Holden Caulfield and Mario Savio and Lenny Bruce who pried loose the coruscating defiance bubbling beneath the lavaed surface of the hypocritical establishment? Who could tell for certain? Even idealism was dead: people no longer immigrated to the U.S. for land, peace, Jeffersonian ideals, but to get on "Let's Make a Deal."

All Harry knew was that for the first time in years he had no heart even to wait tonight for the BBC's "Masterpiece Theatre" on Channel 13 which Ruth and he religiously watched through the years, the Cousin Bettes and Forsyte Sagas and Upstairs, Downstairs classics of social life. Soap operas all, perhaps, but brilliantly, flawlessly, hypnotically presented, complex and compact enough to rival life which also could be classified as a super-colossal soap opera of its own. No! Not tonight. Not without Ruth! And Harry turned the set off.

In a last effort to find rescue from the video ministrations of bloody violence and from his own schizoid brooding, he flipped on the radio and twirled the knob to WQXR, hoping for classical music. To his dismay the announcer informed his listeners at that very moment that the next composition on the program would be the latest recording by Stockhausen, about the last composer in the world meant to soothe anybody's nerves. Stockhausen, Picasso, Eliot, Pound, Ives, Beckett, Pollock, Schönberg, Webern, Henze, Rothko, Joyce: Harry saw in them the reflection of the 20th century's machine age, the cultural volcanoes throwing back the destructive forces unleashed by technology into the faces of those adjusted to the tortuous psyche and shattered terrain they had created for themselves. Catch 22 cubed! No, his pneuma was shattered enough not to wallow any further in its swampy Stockhausenian morass.

Murder and mayhem. Day and night, on the air and in print nothing but killings, famine, deprivation, tears, disease, violence, corruption, degeneration, dissonance, even in entertainment. The increasingly unmanageable post-Industrial world offered a surfeit of death, unending death, as if there were no escape from it, a Caligarian dream of coming attractions. Again and again, ever since Marconi, people were overfed on the fodder of rage and ferocity dressed up in halfway intelligent artistry, and in the process they had lost their capacity for caring whether six people were mowed down by a mad sniper or six million were butchered. Eichmann was partly right: the murder of ten people is a tragedy, of ten thousand a statistic. Right in his own building, Harry had a neighbor who belonged to the Eulenspiegel Society, an outfit defending the right of consenting adults to practice sado-masochism in the privacy of their bedroom. Or kitchen. Did anybody, or *could* anybody really give a damn what happened to one lousy human life when a thousand were slaughtered in the most unimaginably heinous way day after day after bloody day? Ruth's mutilation would not even merit two lines on page 59 in the *New York Times* Police Blotter column. And to be honest, in the end one couldn't really blame anybody for not giving a hoot.

26 ⎯⎯⎯⎯⎯

Harry discovered himself slumped in the armchair gazing absently at the ransom note in the distance. It was only half past eight. Time dragged, seemed to stand still, as it must have done a thousand times a day for those wretched concentration camp inmates Helga always kept rapping about. But what could he do? It was too late even to just look out of the window and watch the pretty girls pass by. Anyway, it hurt like hell already, like the pain inflicted on the ego of that old goat in Henry Miller's "Insomnia," when these sweet young Cardin-jeaned birds with their terrible show of indifference would not return his admiring gaze, rubbing it in in quite unmistakable terms that he no longer mattered, just couldn't cut it anymore, was way past their interest for "bonding." It was no use entertaining any ideas about a last fling with a gorgeous twenty-year-old chick now that he was in his unspeakable, paunchy forties.

Perhaps he could do something useful, keep himself busy, not necessarily sort out his collection of Latin American stamps, for which he had no patience tonight, but something maybe that Ruth might enjoy when . . . if she came back. He glanced around the room but only met the familiar sticks of furniture; they were simple, elegant, comfortable, a homey, unpretentious atmosphere of household effects for the most part selected by Ruth to whom Harry had given carte blanche, trusting her implicitly in choosing the furnishings with which both would feel at home. And never once was he disappointed in anything she had bought, and was immensely pleased with the decoration of their cozy apartment where they had lived throughout their married life, except for their first two years in the Village. The only thing, possibly, that could cheer things up to some degree, Harry decided, were some flowers. But it was too late to go out to buy them now, Sunday night, and quite senseless anyhow. Maybe tomorrow . . . just in case.

But there was one thing he *could* do. Now. Before exfoliating himself into a modern Oblomov. He would clean the apartment, dust and vacuum it. Although he had sometimes helped Ruth when her heart first started to give her trouble, he had actually never had to clean it altogether on his own in the last dozen years or so. This was Ruth's department. Not because he felt that as a man it was beneath his dignity—far from it. He always helped with the dishes at night. No, it was because Ruth wanted it that way. After all, she did not have a job and could dedicate herself all day long if she wished to the apartment. She kept it meticulously clean, doing one room a day, and although it certainly did not need much of a sprucing up at this stage, Harry figured that here at least was one way of keeping himself manually occupied and, hopefully, mentally too.

He found the dustcloth in the cabinet under the kitchen sink and started to dust the furniture in the bedroom. By the time he had reached the living room he knew he simply had to turn on the radio to avoid going out of his mind. Dusting really was Dullsville; nothing even Stanley Kubrick could convert into dramatic form with his magic touch. WPAT's *Easy Sounds* was in full swing and formed perfect housework melodies, hummable tunes designed to soothe even a sex maniac breaking into Linda Lovelace's hideaway—"Music hath charms to soothe a savage breast" sayeth Congreve. The tidying up proceeded not only without too much difficulty but with an auspicious mixture of goodwill, great zest and diligence. Still, he didn't quite feel like lifting all the usual bric-a-brac, items such as the porcelain and Tanagra figurines, potted plants and decorative china, books and glass bowls on the wall-lined shelves, because he gathered that Ruth had already taken care of those chores anyway. At the same time, if Ruth did come back, at least she wouldn't have to focus all her attention right away on mopping, sweeping and dusting. Perhaps they could go somewhere for a day or two. He might even call in sick and take her away wherever she wanted to go.

After returning the dustcloth to the kitchen cabinet, Harry went to throw the empty brandy bottle down the incinerator, then headed for the broom closet where Ruth kept the Electrolux. He unwound the long extension cord, plugged it into the wall socket and began to vacuum. Halfway through this chore Harry found himself hoping with all his heart that Ruth would make her sudden though unexpected appearance and stand speechless with joy in the doorway, heaping high praise on him for keeping things so tidy in her absence. That really would be nifty. Harry smiled at his own fantasy and wished more and more that she would show up, now, and they'd fall into each other's arms and she'd forgive him for being so undemonstrative lately in his love for her. (In fact, wasn't it Emily Dickinson, he wondered, who had said that an absent flame always burned brighter than the flickering wick?) And then it struck him all of a sudden that in all the years of their marriage, except possibly for the first few weeks, he had never said a thing about *her* working on the apartment, keeping it spotless and shipshape for him, for them, yet not once had she complained about this omission. And at last he understood one thing, that throughout part of the tedious housework, the dreary humdrum essentials, her mind simply *had* to stray onto something that somehow would divert it from the monotony, the boredom and drudgery of playing housemaid. Cruelly, unthoughtfully, man had for too long exiled half a world capable of love and creation to the vacuum of dusting. No wonder she always expected him with such fervor, such unpretentious joy; he was her Prince Charming come home from the battles, her Jack Nicholson, her Gregory Peck, while she was condemned to play the supporting role of Cinderella the scullery maid.

Harry did not bother to go under the sofa or chairs with the nozzle of the Electrolux feeling that when . . . if Ruth returned, this was the part she could do so much better than he and little harm was done . . . provided no one noticed. After all, people did not make it a point of peeking under tables for dust. Or eating off their floors.

He put the vacuum cleaner back into the broom closet, undressed, polished off a slice of Sara Lee pound cake, had a glass of warm milk, showered, and went to bed. Immediately, he missed the proximity of Ruth's body again, not so much in a sexual way, but just the knowledge that she was there, that she was capable of providing a measure of warmth to his starved body. Love was a self-serving thing to kill loneliness. And share hardships. And joy. His hand again reached for her cool unrumpled pillow beside him, and her sleeping face seeped quietly behind the darkened cavern of his retina, and a few minutes later he mercifully dropped off into a deep slumber. Only once during the night, at about one o'clock, he was woken momentarily by the voice of David Susskind next door telling some guest with a cackle of laughter that he was terrible, just terrible, incorrigible!

27

Oddly enough Harry slept much longer than he had anticipated he would. According to his self-winding wristwatch which had the bad habit of stopping once in awhile and then starting to move again of its own accord, it was nearly half past nine when he woke up, and with a start he remembered that this was the beginning of the work week and that at this very moment he was supposed to be sitting at his desk in the office going over some ridiculous manuscript by a septuagenarian who had just sold his first opus to Glumm. The latter expected a full report from Harry by Wednesday noon on exactly how much additional editorial work the manuscript required before the first galley proofs could be run up. It was a sort of reverse Lolita theme about a faded movie queen in the early nineteen-fifties who tried her damndest for two hundred pages to seduce a boy of thirteen. Since it took place in Southern Rhodesia just after World War II, Glumm sought to capture the black and white miscegenation market, because the boy—a bit player in the film in which the actress tried to make a successful comeback—was a horny black caretaker of wildebeest and the middle-aged diva an on-and-off bisexual British movie star on location in the colony. Glumm liked the catchy title "The Taming of the Crew" and thought he could sell the property to Hollywood where it was bound to make pots of money as a controversial film (laced with racial tension and all kinds of kinky sex). Obviously, Harry could not devote any of his time to this two-bit shocker today.

Still in his pajamas, he settled in the living room and dialed the office. To his relief Glumm had not arrived yet, having gone out on business to Baker and Taylor, the jobber in Somerville, New Jersey, but Helen at the switchboard accepted Harry's lie hook, line and sinker that he had developed a terrible cold overnight. Would she tell Glumm when he came in that he really couldn't make it today and that he hoped he'd feel well enough to come in on Tuesday. After he hung up he tried Monhegan in Maine once more, although by this time he hardly could figure out what he would ask Ruth's mother if indeed he managed to get through to the island. Possibly only inquire if she had weathered the storm all right and if she could cable him about twenty thousand bucks. Halfway through waiting for the connection with Maine he decided it might be wiser not to go through with the call since Mrs. Kirk would only get suspicious and ask too damn many questions, but then the operator came on and explained again that the hurricane was still hampering all means of communication with the island and with luck they could expect the lines to be repaired by late tonight or early Tuesday.

He was more than relieved by the outcome of the two calls and before going to the bathroom and proceeding with the day's business parted the flower-printed Fiberglas curtains in the living room. Outside it was gray and overcast, as on Sunday, and from the way the few pedestrians hurrying down Riverside Drive bundled up against the wind it appeared to be quite raw, clearly not the sort of weather for an outing to Jones Beach or Central Park.

After breakfast he quickly made his bed and then settled back once more on the sofa, this time to look up the telephone number of "Izzy" O'Hara, his stockbroker. By sheer luck Harry got hold of him right away and explained that he had to sell out. He needed all the cash he could get. This afternoon. There was a moment's silence at the other end; either the guy was nonplussed or he was looking up Harry's file, but to his utter astonishment the broker then informed him that Harry had sold out, cashed in all his stocks, his shares almost a year ago and that his portfolio was completely empty. Didn't he remember any of this?

For a moment Harry's vision blurred. His feet, still in their slippers, became instantly numb, stone-cold. This icy feeling crept up his body rapidly as if someone had wrapped him in a dripping wet cold towel. He apologized profusely for taking Mr. O'Hara's time, that indeed it had completely slipped his mind and been a terrible mistake on his part, then hung up.

Like a zombie he returned to the bathroom to shave, feeling like a damn fool for having forgotten Ruth's and his decision to sell out last fall when for once the market had reached a moderate high and by all appearances and predictions seemed about to stumble again when a new economic crisis, a recession with increasing unemployment, lurked in the wings. But more important, with the market constantly fluctuating between bearish and bullish points that earned the Bensonnys little in the way of dividends and more often than not caused them to lose some of their investments, they ultimately arrived at the decision to trade in their stock. At income tax time the previous year, it had become abundantly clear that with inflation rising annually at between 5 and 9 per cent, small investors who were burned by short-lived rallies in the past and lacked the funds to make the capital-gains coterie or put their money into gold or long-term treasury issues were liable to lose on anything that paid less than 8 per cent returns after payment of taxes. So Harry and Ruth sold out, like millions of others. In a way he was relieved now that they had exchanged their holdings because the stock they owned really had taken a nose-dive again, about three months later, and even though the corporate pension and growth-oriented mutual funds helped boost the market to more bullish levels in the bicentennial year for the pros, they felt entirely vindicated by their recent losses in having put their meager income into a joint savings account. Here at least the returns of their interests and the principal did not dip to zero and wipe them out completely.

But with the continuous inflationary spiral, his losses on Wall Street, the years of sinking most of his savings into the house in the country and the taxes levied on the property, and the fact that Harry was the sole breadwinner, his subsequent savings indeed proved a mere pittance.

In a metaphysical sense he almost envied the readers of the *East-West Journal* who at such moments of crisis at least could draw courage and psychic assistance from the structured transcendental philosophies of a Baba Ram Dass or the para-kinetic hypotheses of a Uri Geller, but these did not afford much aid and comfort to a poor sucker in his pajamas needing thirty thousand dollars in a hurry for a monster who was far removed from any principle governed by Kant's categorical imperative.

Hell, here he went again! Though only half past ten in the morning, the dark of night already threatened to invade Harry's soul full-force, tolling within—as F. Scott Fitzgerald had warned—forever 4 a.m. Whereas yesterday he had indulged in contemptuous recriminations and accusations directed against mankind, feeling an abnormal self-hatred and hatred for those around him and a despotic disdain for individuals who should have been close to him, today he threatened to fall prey to brooding and self-pity.

Just before dressing, Harry looked for the bank and checkbooks and found both in a bureau drawer of the roll-top desk that still ominously bore the ransom letter. Ruth always took care of all financial matters, making sure that every penny they had left over at the end of the month and felt they did not need the following month was put in the savings account. Their joint checking account had a balance of just under a thousand dollars in it, a mutually agreed-upon sum for emergencies and all household expenses that could be paid by check. Harry opened the passbook of the savings account to find out exactly how much had been deposited. With some satisfaction he noted from the last entry that Ruth had managed to deposit another eighty-five dollars just a few weeks ago. Altogether there was a little over twelve thousand dollars in the joint account—his entire assets in ready cash—not as hefty an amount as he had first counted on. Harry calculated that if Helga came over with the eighteen thousand they had so heatedly discussed two days earlier, he would have the thirty thousand the kidnapper demanded. In any case, he intended to cash in his entire checking account, except for the minimum ten dollars and withdraw everything from the savings account except one hundred dollars so it wouldn't be closed out.

It was not even eleven o'clock yet and he had plenty of time to get everything together well before the five p.m. deadline. He dressed quickly, listening to WMCA's Bob Grant (who was pinch-hitting for the regular broadcaster and yelling at listeners on the call-in program to get off the phone if they became too obstreperous or bigoted), rinsed the breakfast dishes he had left soaking in Ruth's Ivory detergent in the kitchen sink, then slipped into his raincoat. He glanced around the apartment, satisfying himself that everything was in top shape, then realized he had not given the birds their promised lettuce leaf and quickly rectified this act of neglect.

On his way out he peered at the mailbox, and found no evidence of a letter peeking through the slats; but then he did not expect the mail to be delivered at this time of day anyway and headed for the garage. Once in the cavernous subterranean catacomb, redolent of the usual gasoline and oil fumes, Harry realized that it would be much more sensible to take the subway for a couple of stops rather than to get out the car and cruise around for hours trying to find a parking space on Broadway.

As a rule he picked up the *New York Times* at Miss Laredo's tiny stationery before descending the stairs to his subway stop, but today, very much as during the previous two days, he showed not the least interest in the news that pinched and tormented the world and provided it with its innumerable kinky headlines and headaches. With his own secret headline dominating every column, every particle of his being, he felt he had a surfeit of headaches of his own and just couldn't be bothered by some dingdong Wally Ballou getting excited over a few rockets landing halfway around the world on the outskirts of some Middle Eastern trouble spot or the Secretary of State possibly being sent by the President on an emergency mission to Panama and then Athens and Mexico City where new anti-American riots had broken out for the fourth time in a month. Everybody had his own cross to bear and no one seemed to give a monkey's damn about Harry's either.

Just before going down to his subway station a thought crossed Harry's mind. Even if he didn't give a hang about the rest of the world's current events today there always existed the likelihood that a news item could shed some light on *his* predicament. Perhaps somebody else had been subjected to the revived fad of kidnapping, or somebody like Harry had received an extortion letter, or someone's daughter had been threatened with an abduction, anything was possible and had to be examined in the light of his own situation, something along the lines of a discernible pattern, a chance in a million, but Harry felt he should not leave any stone unturned and he went back up Broadway about half a block and entered Miss Laredo's drab little candy and stationery store to get a paper, this time the *Daily News*. He knew that sensational items were not only prominently displayed, but aired in detail in the *News*, and not in the staid *New York Times*.

28 ━━━━━━

Miss Laredo's shop was one of those obscure, dark joyless holes in the wall that passed for a store but really was merely a cubicle crammed with a bubble-gum machine, a couple of rotating display racks carrying such paperbacks as "Looking for Mr. Goodbar," "The Bermuda Triangle," "The Happy Hooker," "Helter Skelter," "All the President's Men," "The Guinness Book of World Records" and a few novels by Irving Wallace, Louis L'Amour, Harold Robbins, Barbara Cartland and Jacqueline Susann; and, on the other side of what called itself an aisle, the shop boasted a counter replete with Bic-Pens, chewing gum, Lifesavers, Hershey and Baby Ruth bars. Cartons of cigarettes and cigars reposed under the frosted glass pane while the knee-high shelf bordering the window inside offered the ubiquitous staples of the *Times* and the *News*, *El Diario* and other Spanish-language newspapers, as well as a few magazines—*Time*, *Playboy*, *Ebony*, *Penthouse*, *Newsweek*, *Viva*, bundles of comic books, and a couple of Spanish girlie magazines.

Harry had to wait a minute or so until aged Miss Laredo finished serving a customer, counting out ten cigars with her gnarled arthritic hands. Summer or winter, she always draped a black woolen shawl across her shoulders, over her dusty ankle-length black dress, and held

242

the bulky shawl together under her whiskered chin as if to ward off a cool draft that followed the entrance of a customer. Perhaps she was always cold. At her age—and the stringy tendons in her neck and the wrinkles in her face gave mute testimony to the 79 years she claimed to be—she had a right to protect herself in any way she could. Stooped and coughing heart-rendingly, she shuffled around her grubby little domain while the unconcerned multi-million dollar faces of Lauren Hutton, Margaux Hemingway and Beverly Johnson stared out glacially at her from the covers of *Vogue*, *Glamour* and *Harper's Bazaar*. Miss Laredo insisted on serving everyone herself with a calm and serenity that negated the presence of other customers. She loved to prattle on in her Spanish-accented English about her poor ailing twin-sister Francesca who had been so sick for the last eighteen years that she could not move a step out of their apartment, and yet Francesca apparently was too proud to sign up for Medicaid and Miss Laredo had to support her out of the meager earnings the store provided.

Miss Laredo's dear unseen sister (for all anyone knew she was a figment of her imagination) was only four feet three inches tall due to some terribly debilitating spinal affliction, and every night Miss Laredo had to trudge up five steep flights to the cold-water flat where she lived with Francesca, bringing the few articles of food left that the poor creature was able to swallow and digest. Miss Laredo just managed to eke out a living for herself and her twin and somehow succeeded in making barely enough not to qualify for the welfare rolls.

Harry did not have any change on him and when Miss Laredo's gnarled hand took Harry's dollar bill, she fished around for some change among the coins scattered on the glass counter. Out of habit Harry inquired how Francesca felt today, but Miss Laredo seemed more unhappy about her own lot than he had ever seen her before, complaining about her unceasing cough—and, indeed, every time she struggled for breath during a coughing spasm, the muscles in her scrawny neck strained and the blue veins stood out like squirming worms—but much worse, she claimed, was the threat of the Mad Killer gang which roamed the neighborhood and had come in the day before for a shakedown, threatening to break her back unless she forked over half of her profits. She had told them that she and her sister could barely make ends meet, but this cut no ice with the punks. They insisted on their cut. For years, Harry had heard of marauding gangs in this part of the borough intimidating storekeepers with personal injury and destruction of their merchandise if their extortion demands were not met.

He asked her why she did not tell the police, but Miss Laredo shook her head, and as she looked up at him through agonized eyes, he saw her gaunt face with the little whiskers growing out of her nostrils and ears and the black pimples of old age on the wrinkled parchment skin, and he felt deeply saddened. Suddenly she reminded him of those well-known pictures of old women released from Mauthausen and Ravensbrück concentration camps in 1945. What was the use, she lamented, even if the cops really did get hold of a couple of the hoods, the next day they would be back, twenty strong, and smash up the place and her too for good measure. So what was she supposed to do?

Yes, indeed, what could she, *any*body do . . . when the lawyers always found a thousand-and-one loopholes to get thugs, mafiosi, politicians, off scot-free? Small wonder movie audiences everywhere gave standing ovations when the "Fascist" vigilantes on the screen beat up the "Fascist" muggers. Somehow it helped to restore potency to the impotent multitudes, social virility to the sterile. Only that this was no movie. But life.

Harry no longer knew whether to cry or to rail at the courts' meting out of injustice. Feeling increasingly powerless to control his own fate by bringing Ruth's kidnapper to justice, and now seeing Miss Laredo's vermin who were sure to escape punishment, it flashed through Harry with a fury he could hardly contain, what would Jesus Christ, Descartes, Teilhard de Chardin, or William Kunstler have to say about any of this? Or would some talk-show shrinks first want to probe into the goons' psychic past, like Dr. Dysart in "Equus"? And blame it all on society? Or perhaps accept Bruno Bettelheim's theory that this was "behavior in an extreme situation"? And then, what? Would they ask Jane Goodall to study the sociobiological action-patterns of this urban wild animal pack?

Miss Laredo glanced forlornly through the unwashed window as though half-expecting her torturers, suddenly shaded her eyes with her coin-blackened gnarled hand and looked up and down the deserted store as if the gloomy twilight were hurting her feeble eyes.

"That's all the money they'll get," she whispered conspiratorially, gesturing to the loose change on the glass counter. "The big money I need for food and rent," she continued, pointing with a knobby finger to her dehydrated bosom and cackling a toothless old woman's cackle,

"I squeezed it in here. They won't guess . . . they won't want to grab an old woman like me and tear her clothes off! Right, Mister?"

Harry said she was smart and wished her all the luck in the world and left the sad little dingy store with its musty atmosphere, more grim and depressed about the poor old hag's disconsolate life than she seemed to be herself. But there it was, the old story again, the quiet dignity of the elderly, the disabled, unheralded and forgotten by the rich and indifferent, the papers and TV, in a country that *could* take care of them, but didn't, while the spoiled young made all the counter-culture noise and reaped a glory in their teens as a consequence. The baddies with their plea-bargaining security blanket merely used the courts as a fun-city revolving door, while the rest of the juvenocracy see-sawed in the esteem of media, leadership, and those anti-establishmentarians who chose to ignore the fact that they—these young—used the same methods and aimed for the same goals that *they* decried in the Establishment elite. Or as Barbara Ward said: people learned to tolerate the intolerable. It was the same ball game really, all the way.

Outside, the wet, overcast day sobered Harry up a bit and on his way to the subway he took note of Saturday's flock of the Hare Krishna sodality cross the street, chanting and clashing miniature cymbals and waving banners about happiness. If *they* had the secret, he reasoned, their glowing inner lives certainly did not prevent them from sponging off their fellow men.

Harry plunked down four quarters for a couple of tokens and waited on the litter-strewn platform for the IRT local. A brief perusal of headlines in his paper convinced him that there was nothing that could even remotely be associated with kidnapping and he deposed of the *News* on an empty bench nearby. A black dude in rainbow-colored platform shoes, a floppy sombrero and a chartreuse mohair silk hustler's top-coat, muttering "You crazy mutha," leaned languorously against the tile-covered wall which displayed the usual colorful bilingual graffiti.

After a few minutes an express thundered furiously through the station, with each of its dimly lit cars bragging an assortment of huge multicolored Magic Marker names and numerals. Harry could well imagine, as the foundation of the station-platform vibrated under his feet, that some of these graffiti calligraphers actually squandered their weekends on station platforms throughout the city hoping to see their brushwork-signatures whiz by. He wasn't precisely sure what sort of sensation went through TAKI 148 or ZIM II as they watched their nicknames and street numbers zoom from one end of the platform to the other, unless, according to Norman Mailer, it was to prevent "the macadamization of the psyche."

When Harry boarded the local, the thought struck him that within each of the isolated Edward Hopper faces on the train with their Monday-morning lip-reading of *The National Enquirer* or their fingernail clipping or their crotch scratching or their playing of huge transistor radios at full volume, there lurked the eternal aggressor. Lionel Tiger's "Men in Groups" and Konrad Lorenz's "On Agression", still fresh in his eidetic memory bank, came readily to Harry's programmed mind. A pair of olive-skinned teenagers with combs sticking out of bushy Afros jostled their way hostilely past the jam-packed standing passengers to the front of the train and then back again to the rear, with a belligerent "Hey man, whazza matta?" each time they bumped into some meek soul. The ride threatened to become a trip to the Tombs. Or the city morgue.

Harry probably would have missed his station if he hadn't counted the stops, because every inch of the area where the windows should have been was covered by the thick impenetrable brushstrokes of the nocturnal graffiti colorists. Even the four-borough subway map did not escape their obliterating paint splashes nor did the name Larry which was scrawled across it reveal that the artist's soul was maca-damized. Harry never understood why restraining these Jukes and Kallikaks from turning New York into a coercive museum of personal signatures, mad obscenities and gratuitously unhinged schlock art should be regarded by the compulsive spraycan Fauvists themselves as the characteristic of a racist, genocidal, fascist society, especially when other cities around the globe saw graffiti not as the fruit of artistic, ethnic self-expression but the work of untalented, primitive trouble-makers. Or could it be that London, Paris and San Francisco lacked this sorely missed underground culture, and Moscow showed signs of fascism, while New York enjoyed a much-merited subterranean Renaissance?

Harry was grateful when he finally emerged from the gloomy, caver-nous depths of the transit system. Now, while walking down Broadway toward his bank, he realized for the first time today that the pavement was wet. It must have poured through the early morning hours while he was still asleep.

As he moved down the block, hoping that everything would go well at the bank, Harry suddenly noticed to his utter amazement that a

Bosch-like ogre of a woman in a slouchy hat was bearing down on him. She was carrying a large brown shopping bag on a string and one of her stockings had, like a serpent's discarded skin, rolled all the way down to her ankle. Just as Harry stepped aside, veering sharply to his left so he would not collide with her, the woman looked at him with close-set eyes that seemed to spew a fire-green venom and let loose with a barrage of four-letter expletives, accusing him of having ruined her life by running off with her money and her best girl friend, Penny. For an instant Harry stood stock-still. He was so taken aback by the unexpected Niagara of irrational accusations tumbling wildly in a high-pitched scream from her thin colorless lips that he could not move and just stared at her, dumbfounded, feeling the blood rush to his face. People hurrying by shot him strange looks, but nobody stopped to either listen or to pay much attention to her mad ranting. Everybody was preoccupied with his own private world of woe. Lunacy was par for New York City and the least one could expect on streets festering with mugging, mayhem and murder.

Harry finally tore himself away and again stepped out of the crazy woman's way, but she kept up her verbal assault, screaming more indictments and vituperations after him and the further he fled the more he pretended not to be the one she was addressing. After a block or so he ventured to turn around to see how people were reacting to her unending stream of obscenities and he saw to his relief that the mad woman had diverted her attention from Harry and was busily lambasting another man who happened to be coming her way. New York was full of such disturbed loonies who possibly not long ago had been as rational as one could expect to be. Who knew, a decade from now—if things turned out badly and something happened to Ruth, to Helga, his job, his financial state—he himself might be much like this demented woman. Most likely, Donald Ives would not even have to wait that long. And what about Charlotte Collins? Was this latest frightening display merely a glimpse of the future?

29 ————————————

The peaceful atmosphere of his bank came as a balm, a haven, a refuge to Harry. Its solid unassailability represented the universal window-dressing, the Potemkin Village masking the shame of the instability, terror, slums, ghettos, poverty—the turmoil engulfing the world, and now his life. Anyway, here at long last would lie the solution to the problem of raising the ransom—or at least part of the solution, provided that Helga furnished him with the other larger portion later this afternoon, in the form of *her* savings. Harry stepped up to one of the counters that harbored the deposit and withdrawal slips, pulled his passbook out of his jacket and jotted down his account number on a withdrawal form, his name and address and the amount where indicated. Only one hundred and fourteen dollars and eighty-five cents would be left in their account, but it was the only way out.

There were fairly long lines waiting for the half dozen tellers and he picked the shortest one. Naturally, as fate would have it, the fat man at the head of his queue apparently had a lot of complicated bank business that couldn't be settled by a simple addition or deduction on the minicomputer by the teller's side. After a long, agonizing wait, Harry made his way to the head of the line and handed the booklet and slip to the tiny woman whose name-plate identified her as Mrs. Evelyn Kollberg. She opened the passbook, compared it with the amount designated by Harry on the withdrawal slip and looked up at him with a smile.

"You want to withdraw all of this?" she asked.

"Yes," Harry said, and Mrs. Kollberg closed the book.

"I'm afraid, sir," she answered, handing the savings account book and slip back to Harry, "first you must get an okay from our Mr. Hebert or Mrs. Dean."

"An okay?" Harry's heart skipped a couple of beats. What on earth did fate plan to hurl into his path now? "I don't understand. I'm not overdrawing. All I want is part of my money. Why should I need an okay? This is my money."

"Of course it is, but this is just a formality, sir," Mrs. Kollberg explained. "You see, when so much is being withdrawn from a joint account, one of our officers always has to inital it first. I'm sure you understand."

"Frankly I don't," Harry protested. "After all it's *my* money. Well, all right, have it your way!" Harry released a sigh, part of defeat, part of resignation, realizing she was only complying with the regulations of the bank. It certainly wasn't her fault.

He left Mrs. Kollberg's window and moved to the rear section of the bank which was separated from the long counter of tellers by a border of artificial plants. Although a number of highly polished walnut desks were located strategically in the directors' corner, only two of them were occupied at the time by members of the staff, those of Mrs. Dean and Mr. Hebert. Each had a client with them and there were a number of other people ahead of Harry waiting alongside the three-foot high papier-mâché-brick wall supporting the window boxes of plastic daffodils. It was already well after twelve o'clock noon. Muzak formed its soothing psychologically geared Mantovani arrangements above the anxious bread-and-butter babble of voices, and the two bank officials took their careful, unhurried time with each of their clients. Around one o'clock, Mr. Hebert who wore a red-tipped white carnation in his lapel beckoned to Harry to take a seat by his desk.

"I hope you don't mind if I have a bite to eat while we talk," Mr. Hebert apologized, opening a drawer and removing a container of Dannon vanilla yogurt and a small yellow plastic spoon. "But since we're so busy on Mondays and short-staffed now with the flu going around I've had to have lunch at my desk."

"That's all right, go right ahead," Harry said, settling comfortably in a chair next to Mr. Hebert's desk and watching him pry open the yogurt container. Mr. Hebert seemed a nice, easy-going kind of guy. He had silvery-white hair and a deep tan—the sort of character Hollywood would have asked Central Casting for to portray a golf-mad industrialist or a suave bank president.

"Fine then. Now, what can I do for you, Mr. . . .?"

"My name is Harry Bensonny." Harry handed him his passbook and withdrawal slip. "The teller said that you usually initialled large withdrawals. That's really all I want."

Just like Mrs. Kollberg, Mr. Hebert compared the amount in Harry's bank book with the figure on his withdrawal slip.

"That's quite a sum, Mr. Bensonny," he said, taking his first spoonful of yogurt. "I hope you don't intend closing your account with us."

"Oh no. I'm not withdrawing all of it. But I need this amount today, that's all."

Mr. Hebert nodded gravely. "Well, that certainly sounds plausible to me," he said, leafing through the pages of the passbook. "Fine."

At last, at long last, a stroke of luck, thought Harry, as Mr. Hebert scanned a page of deposits and withdrawals, simultaneously pushing back his cuticles with the tip of the plastic spoon.

Three desks away, Mrs. Dean went about her business dealing with a young couple, who were listening intently to her financial explanations. When the girl, a mousy little thing in a rabbit coat, politely interrupted Mrs. Dean to ask a question, the young, muscular beachboy type with her snapped an enraged "Why the hell don't you shut up!" in such a vicious tone that it carried to where Harry was sitting at Mr. Hebert's desk. Everywhere people looked up curiously, then a second later, returned to their own pecuniary matters as if nothing had happened. The girl in the rabbit coat blanched and stared hard at the tight-knit pale hands in her lap. Tears welled up in her eyes but she said nothing and sat there like a wax doll, and Mrs. Dean resumed talking. Harry felt like getting up and belting the insensitive brute, but he had enough troubles of his own not to interfere so he merely glared at the creep, unable to conceal his contempt for him. To this domineering roughneck, the girl obviously served as a sex object only. Clearly the tough represented a typical case of penis imperialism, just as some of the more excessive female radicals could be accused in their therapeutic zeal of representing vaginal imperialism, Harry concluded.

"Well, that shouldn't be too difficult, Mr. . . ."

"I beg your pardon?" Harry shot around, facing the bank director.

"I said that shouldn't prove difficult at all," Mr. Hebert smiled, stirring the creamy white contents inside the blue and white container. "I see from you bank book that this is a joint account. Is Ruth Bensonny your wife?"

"That's right."

"Well, then all you have to do is to have her counter-sign her name against your signature here on the withdrawal slip."

"I don't quite understand," Harry raised his voice in alarm, but quickly simmered down when Mr. Hebert's smile vanished and was replaced by an eye-narrowing mask of apprehension. "I don't understand. My wife and I have withdrawn from this bank without ever having the other partner's signature."

"Of course you didn't. I can see this from your withdrawals over the years. We only ask for the signatures of both names on our joint accounts over ten thousand dollars when more than two-thirds of the account is being withdrawn. One of the bylaws of the bank's constitution, you see. Just a technicality. But you state you want almost every penny of it. So all you have to do is to have Mrs. Bensonny sign this slip as well and we'll gladly . . ."

"But you don't understand," Harry was becoming exasperated at the unfairness of this new knock that fate had in store for him and was having difficulty keeping himself from blowing his top. To make matters worse, he suddenly felt himself break into a cold sweat and his stomach tie into knots. "Mr. Hebert, it is *because* of my wife that I need it. It's for *her*, the money."

"I don't follow you, Mr. Bensonny. *For* her? You mean you want to give her a present with the money you intend to withdraw?"

"No, no, no!" Harry leaned forward, resting his elbow on the desk and moving closer to Mr. Hebert as if trying to communicate a highly confidential matter to him, not meant for other ears. "It's not a present. It's an emergency. You see, she's very very sick and with the medical expenses, the hospital, as high as they are I simply have to get this money together." Harry, faced with a situation he had not anticipated in his wildest dreams, was making things up as best he could. He only hoped that his white lies would not boomerang later and sink all chances of his getting hold of his own money.

Mr. Hebert twirled the carnation in his buttonhole and regarded Harry with steel-blue eyes. Then the faint little smile made its reappearance. "Well, Mr. Bensonny, in that case this shouldn't cause us too much trouble. After all, the money *is* yours. And your wife's. So if your wife's health is in danger we certainly wouldn't want to be held responsible for depriving her of what might save her life, would we now?"

Harry's heart leaped in a double-salvo of joy. "Thank you. And as I said I'm not going to close out our joint account."

"Fine, Mr. Bensonny. In this case all we would really need is your wife's hospital bill. A statement, anything, just to verify the expenses, and we can initial your withdrawal slip."

Oh, God! he thought, what next? But he heard himself say, "Oh, the bill," wondering what magnificent lie his brain would conjure up next. "How stupid of me! I forgot all about that. I left it home. Of course, I should have brought it, shouldn't I?"

"Now, Mr. Bensonny, if the savings account were in your name only, you could withdraw every penny of it, but you must realize that with a joint account, we must go by the rules of the book. To take a case in point, husbands have withdrawn every penny, skipped town, and left the poor wife sitting high and dry. Not that I suspect *you*, but we do have to protect *all* of our depositors, and at present all you are legally entitled to is two-thirds of your holdings with us and that would amount to roughly eight thousand dollars. Why don't you today just withdraw that amount and send it on to the hosp . . ."

"No, that's impossible," Harry dismissed the suggestion at once. "I need . . . The hospital needs the full amount, twelve thousand, and that's why . . ."

"All right then, if you have some stocks or shares and . . ."

"No, I don't," Harry rejected this with a harsh gesture of impatience.

"Well, I see from your withdrawal slip you live nearby. Why don't you go home and get the hospital bill? We'll be open till three this afternoon, so I'm sure you can get back in time."

"Yes, I suppose you're right," Harry agreed, half-listening, his brain furiously working on a new delaying tactic. "I know I have it home, but I don't think I could make it back by three. With my wife so ill our papers have gotten into a mess and it may be pretty hard to find the bill right away."

"That shouldn't matter so much, Mr. Bensonny. If you can't find it today, I'm certain the hospital won't turn her out on the street if you tell them that you'll bring the amount you owe tomorrow sometime."

"That's the problem, Mr. Hebert! They insist on getting the money today," Harry took a renewed plunge without blushing, wondering where this line of attack would take him. "You see, I've been stalling them for several weeks now. They know my wife isn't insured and they have threatened to take me to court if I don't let them have the money by tonight."

"Not insured! Why in God's name didn't you pay them earlier, then, Mr. Bensonny?" Mr. Hebert scraped the sides of the yogurt container. "After all, you had the money in the bank and knew you had to part with it eventually."

"Of course I should have. It was just sheer madness on my part. And with my wife so ill it was quite an ordeal for me, and I just didn't pay as much attention to the financial side as I should have."

Mr. Hebert looked up from his yogurt, and frowned. "Gosh, that's awful. What're we going to do to help you?"

For a few pensive seconds Mr. Hebert returned to his yogurt and Harry gradually began to suspect that the bank officer was actually playing cat to his mouse, the bastard, and getting a big charge out of it. All at once he grasped the meaning of what James Baldwin meant by being treated like a Nigger by Whitey, being stymied at every turn by those goddam motherfucking shit-eating laws put up by the Man's Establishment.

"I know it's awful," Harry said. "I've been living with it for weeks. I haven't been myself these days. Forgetting things. Not paying bills. With Ruth so terribly ill, five weeks in intensive care, the tests and operations and . . ."

"Let's see now," Mr. Hebert interrupted quietly. "Perhaps we can find a way out that would avoid our having to get hold of the hospital statement. Why don't you let me have the number of the hospital where Mrs. Bensonny is . . ."

"The number?" Harry's tongue was suddenly heavy and dry, the beat of his pulse thudding hard inside his throat.

"Yes. Give me the name of the hospital where Mrs. Bensonny is and I'll get in touch with the accounting department there this minute and once they have verified the amount you owe, I'll be only too happy to let you withdraw the money from your joint account. Even though I must warn you that under the Bank Secrecy Act, banks have the right to reveal such heavy withdrawals—and loans—to the government."

Harry's heart thundered with the force of a sledgehammer gone berserk. Perhaps Mr. Hebert *was* trying to be sincerely helpful after all and Harry had merely misconstrued his questioning. He seemed to be trying his damndest to be fair and it certainly wasn't his fault if the bank's constitution had ridiculous rules. And of course you could always trust the damn snoopy government in Washington to look for any excuses, the most devious backhanded ways, to degrade the honest middle-class wage earner, giving him the shaft as usual. Manipulating his *own* money! And for what! Just another case of Big Brother, of the big institutional banking corporations getting away with murder, the multinational conglomerates controlling entire continents and, more to the point, the Eternal Little Guy's life.

Harry suddenly became conscious of Mr. Hebert's icy-cold blue eyes waiting for a reply.

"Just the name of the hospital, Mr. Bensonny. Please."

"Oh yes. The name, right. Let's see now. What was it?" he stammered, rubbing his cheeks pensively, not so much to stall as to determine whether his face had flushed with embarrassment, with terror, thus giving him away as the unmitigated liar that he was. Come on now! Put on your thinking cap, old blabbermouth, Harry told himself. Somewhere above Muzak's lilting melodies he heard somebody play a transistor and the voice of a newscaster announcing that storm warnings throughout the metropolitan area remained in effect for the evening hours. Storm warnings! At once an idea sparked Harry's thinking mechanism. "That hospital, Mr. Hebert," he said, "you know, to be absolutely honest I can't remember its name offhand, but even if I did it wouldn't make much difference because"—he stopped for an instant to make certain he'd get his facts—and lies—straight—"my wife is not in a hospital in New York but up with her mother on Monhegan, an island off the coast of Maine. And you may have heard that there's a hurricane doing an awful lot of damage at present and nobody can get through."

"I beg your pardon?" Mr. Hebert had finished his yogurt and now did not take his suspicious eyes off Harry.

"Well, I tried to reach her at the hospital myself earlier today. But the Maine telephone operator told me that they wouldn't be able to restore service with the island till sometime tomorrow at the earliest because of the storm."

"I see," the bank director said thoughtfully. "What I don't quite understand, Mr. Bensonny, and I hope you won't mind my asking you, but how could you possibly pay the hospital by tonight, the deadline you mentioned to me a few minutes ago, when the hospital is on an island in Maine and no one seems to be able to get through to the island till some time tomorrow? The way the mail functions these days I would hardly think that even under normal conditions your check would reach the island till well into the week, even if you mailed it now."

Cornered again! This time he *really* had you by the balls, didn't he, Harry cursed himself. Now talk yourself out of that hash! All right, booby, don't you dare get flustered!

"You're right, of course," Harry agreed with Mr. Hebert, looking him straight in the eye. "This storm is sort of a . . . well, I think they call it an act of God in insurance policies, don't they? Like earthquakes. So it can be said to have saved me by a hair's-breadth. Hairbreadth Harry! Remember him?" He forced a chuckle, but the comic strip reference elicited no response from Mr. Hebert. "Anyway, I'm sure what the hospital actually meant is that the cancellation date on the envelope should show today's date. I think this should be proof enough that I've acted in good faith and complied with their demands to pay up."

Mr. Hebert appeared to be quite satisfied this time. He nodded and an approving benign smile lit up his movie bank-director's face once more. "That's certainly true," he said, and opened the passbook again, studying the withdrawal slip. Then he looked up and the smile had vanished. "I notice you only filled out a withdrawal slip, Mr. Bensonny. Wouldn't you need a money order or check for such a huge amount?"

"Oh, of course, you're right. I forgot. As I told you, with all my worries, my hypertension, I've become quite forgetful about things lately," Harry rubbed it in melodramatically. "Not that I want to rip off the bank, but there must be *some* legal way to get hold of my own savings today."

"Well then, let's see now. What you say sounds perfectly plausible to me, but of course you understand that without the pertinent papers to back all this up *we* have no legal means of breaking our own bylaws." Mr. Hebert wiped his mouth with a clean handkerchief and finally threw the plastic spoon and yogurt container into his wastepaper basket. "We've just about exhausted all the avenues I can think of to get you the money today I'm afraid, since you don't want the eight thousand which you're entitled to right away . . . No, wait! What I could do, Mr. Bensonny, is to let you take out a personal loan from the bank at $7\frac{1}{2}$ per cent, if you wish to. And use the four thousand you will have left in the joint account as collateral to pay off the principal. Of course, with interest due on it we couldn't advance you the full four thousand but I think we could let you have about thirty-two hundred, which, with the eight thousand you *can* withdraw should certainly satisfy the hospital in Maine. Would this be agreeable to you?"

Harry couldn't trust his ears. The man was a genius, a real friend indeed. The twelve thousand was as good as his, and with the nine hundred in the checking account, and if Helga really came through with the eighteen thousand, the ransom was ensured.

"I think that's a great idea, Mr. Hebert. Just great. That would come as a lifesaver."

"Fine. Then let me make just one call, Mr. Bensonny. Merely a formality, sort of a character reference which we need and we can fill out the forms and the money is yours."

"A call?" Again Harry's heart skipped a beat. "To whom?"

"Well, the only stipulation we make is that our clients asking for a loan are employed. We wouldn't even have to garnishee your salary if you defaulted since you have the money on account with us anyway. But we do like to check on reliability and so forth and get a reference from the employer."

"You mean you have to call my employer? Now?"

"Well, I assume you're employed, Mr. Bensonny."

"That's true enough. I have a job all right. It's just . . . you see my employer is very strict and doesn't like to be double-crossed . . ."

"*Double-crossed?*"

"Well, he doesn't know I'm here about any of this. He thinks I'm at home sick, that's what I called in this morning and he's a terrible stickler for work, a disciplinarian. If he ever finds out that I'm playing hooky, so to speak, I could lose my job, and I think you'll agree that's about the last thing in the world I need in my situation. And I don't think the bank would appreciate it very much if I lost my job now, with a loan and all, just because of a simple phone call."

"No, we wouldn't want you to lose your job on account of us, indeed not. But you see, Mr. Bensonny, the rules again! So what can I do except to tell you again, go home and try to find the hospital bill, and I can assure you that tomorrow you can send the check to Maine. Believe me, regardless of the cancellation date on the envelope they won't sue you once they have the money."

This time Harry could not quarrel with Mr. Hebert who genuinely appeared to want to help him. Suddenly Mr. Hebert's face lit up again.

"What about this, Mr. Bensonny?" he said cheerfully. "If you feel that I shouldn't mention to your employer you have come to see me today, would you be agreeable to it if I told him that you had made an application for a loan for your wife's hospital expenses a few days ago and that I just wanted to check on your character references with him today regarding your reliability, length of employment, and so on."

Harry nodded. "I think that would be okay. He couldn't object to that in the least. Of course, he doesn't know my wife is ill but there's no reason why you shouldn't mention it to him."

"Great. Then why don't you give me his name and address and telephone number and I'll jot it all down in your application for the loan and then make the call."

He opened a desk drawer, withdrew a pad of forms and placed two sheets of carbon paper between the top three pages. The usual questions were asked regarding birth, residence, place of employment, and the myriad of other inquiries that usually qualified or disqualified applicants for anything ranging from finding employment to buying houses or making a car loan. Once Mr. Hebert had filled the entire sheet with all the relevant data, he dialed Old Glumm's number. As promised, Mr. Hebert explained that Harry had made a request for a loan to cover his wife's hospital expenses the previous week and that the bank was anxious to obtain a confidential report regarding Mr. Bensonny's character. A few minutes of silence followed while Mr. Hebert listened to Old Glumm.

Suddenly Harry was bugged that the bank would profit from his sorry predicament to the tune of $7\frac{1}{2}$ per cent—without fear of violating any bylaws! But what *could* he do? After a few more words, Mr. Hebert thanked Old Glumm for his cooperation and hung up. Without saying anything to Harry, he scribbled a few words here and there in some of the empty spaces left on the form and then tore all three pages off the pad.

"So, here we are, Mr. Bensonny," he said, smiling again and handing Harry the original and duplicates after removing the two sheets of carbon. "Take these to Mr. Ellendorff, at window 8. He will ask you to sign all three forms and then give you the additional amount we agreed upon, thirty-two hundred, all right?"

Harry accepted the forms with a deep sigh of relief and gratitude. "I don't know how to thank you for all this, Mr. Hebert," he said, getting up and pocketing his savings book and withdrawal slip. "I never realized how helpful this bank *could* be. Thank you again very much."

"It was a pleasure: after all, that's what we're in business for," Mr. Hebert said and rose himself now, shaking Harry's hand. "If we have been able to be of any assistance to you, then we've achieved what we set out to do, to serve our depositors. It's not only at Chase where you have a friend," he chuckled self-consciously. "Now you go ahead and see Mr. Ellendorff. As a matter of fact, since you don't know the name of the hospital I've instructed Mr. Ellendorff on this form to make out the check directly to Mrs. Ruth Bensonny. You sign your name at the bottom of this form, then send her the check and tell her to endorse it over to the hospital. Then you can mail it this afternoon and have today's cancellation date on it after all."

All Harry could do was to stare at him. He was absolutely unwilling to believe the words he had just heard. Here, when he was within grasp of the crucial four thousand dollars, Mr. Hebert in trying to be helpful had inadvertently destroyed the very aid Harry needed. The bank director was already nodding in the direction of the next person waiting for him, an enormously overweight woman with a cherry blossom arrangement of a hat, and Harry considered himself discharged.

He walked blindly past the row of clients waiting for Mr. Hebert and Mrs. Dean, and stopped at a table where a number of people were filling out their slips, gazing with vacant eyes at the long forms provided by Mr. Hebert. To Harry it seemed utterly senseless now to go to Mr. Ellendorff and receive a check for thirty-two hundred dollars made out to Ruth—on the form Mr. Hebert even stipulated a certified check—but what was Ruth supposed to do once the kidnapper received this scrap of paper? Endorse it over to the madman and thus learn his name? And have him suspect that Harry was setting a trap for him when he went to cash the check? And how could the killer be sure that Ruth would not endorse her name on it in such a way that her signature looked unreal and the check would bounce? Once Ruth knew the criminal's real name he would never let her out of his clutches alive! But at this stage of the game it was no use importuning Mr. Hebert to change his mind and have it made payable to the bearer.

What would happen if he made out another withdrawal slip and countersigned Ruth's signature next to his? In all the years of living with his wife this idea had never occurred to him. To forge her signature would have struck him as completely mad, without rhyme or reason. Besides, the bank had Ruth's signature on file and for the life of him he could not imitate every marked stroke of her handwriting. Moreover, what would happen even if he did succeed in forging Ruth's signature and the clerk at any of the windows still had to get Mr. Hebert's or Mrs. Dean's initials for final clearance? What then? Mr. Hebert could have him arrested on the spot for forgery.

No, Harry simply had to content himself with his legal limit of eight thousand and try to find another way as quickly as possible to drum up the other four thousand, and hope to God that Helga would come through with the remaining eighteen thousand.

The close to a thousand dollars left in his checking account made precious little difference now. He would still be short a few grand no matter what, so he decided to forget about it and leave the checking account untouched, just in case of an emergency later.

He pocketed Mr. Hebert's questionnaires, tore up his withdrawal slip for twelve thousand and made out a new one for eight thousand. This time the teller, Miss Quan, simply asked how Harry wanted it, money order or cash, and if the latter in what denominations. Harry asked for cash in fifties and hundreds and she stuffed the fat bundle into a bank envelope which in turn he secured in the breast pocket of his jacket. Just to make certain that nobody was watching him with all this loot, Harry glanced around casually but everybody seemed so preoccupied with their own business that no one paid the slightest attention to him. An elderly guard with a shock of white hair, wearing a snappy looking black uniform and white belt to which a small holster had been attached, was explaining something to an aged hunchbacked woman and pointing to one of the windows. Muzak hummed away cheerfully in the background, unobtrusively, and suddenly the innocuous olive-green atmosphere and borders of artificial daffodils near Mr. Hebert's desk appeared wholly unreal, far away from the growing sense of dread and chaos that was welling up inside him again. Just then, Mr. Hebert happened to look up and saw Harry at the revolving door. He waved a friendly goodbye which Harry instinctively returned before making his guilt-ridden exit.

30 ⸻

A sharp gust of wind ruffled Harry's hair as he stepped out on the street. A moon-faced boy on a large three-wheeled delivery bike sped down the sidewalk, past Harry, piercing the air at regular intervals with a sonar-shrill "beep-beep!" to frighten the pedestrians out of their wits and his way. Flocks of pigeons fluttered above the heads of New Yorkers whenever somebody's tiny tot—of which there appeared to be almost as many as there were pigeons—went chasing after them. Harry sauntered down Broadway, aimlessly, coat open, deliberately nonchalant, yet thinking frantically about how on earth he could rake up the balance of the money, when suddenly, for the second time today, he became conscious of that maddening screeching organ of the deranged woman who earlier in the afternoon had accused Harry and other male passersby of infidelity and running off with her girlfriend. This time she was across the street, on the other side of Broadway, in front of a supermarket, and Harry watched her absently as she accosted a teenager emerging from the store, when his eyes wandered and serendipitiously alighted upon a colorful sign above the supermarket entrance heralding an outfit that liked to characterize itself as offering "Loans With a Smile."

He gazed fixedly at the billboard and then at the fogged windows directly above it and could make out one or two shadowy figures pacing up and down behind them. Harry stood rooted to the ground. With the missing balance still strong in his mind, he figured he could at least give it a try and see how far he could get. After all, he had already rehearsed his stratagem with Mr. Hebert, so why not try it out on this loan association?

He crossed Broadway slowly, wondering how much interest this finance company would charge him and if indeed he *was* doing the right thing and wasn't acting too precipitously, too impulsively as time grew short. He was still crossing the street, lost in thought, when to his horror the oceanliner blast of a horn from an interstate tractor-trailer just about blew Harry out of his shoes, *and* his doubts. He bolted forward, across the wet street, barely missing the truck, and a yard or two before reaching the other side nearly fell flat on his face, having slipped on a squashed grapefruit. The yellow rind lay on an oil slick amidst a burst paper bag from which chicken bones spilled, as well as wet napkins, bits of a torn poster advertising Levy's Jewish Rye and a handful of empty soda pop cans, all of which formed part of a litter-basket that had been tumbled and slopped most of its contents halfway across the street. Having just made it, Harry wiped his hands on a Kleenex, brushed off his coat and instinctively reached for the Manila envelope inside his jacket. It was still there.

He slicked up his hair with both hands as best he could and once more glanced up at the "Loans With a Smile" sign. There was a narrow entrance between the supermarket and a pizza parlor. Harry approached it warily and noticed that the side of the doorway boasted a few name plates, among them the Gold Mine Loan Association on the second floor. He opened the squeaky door and squinted up a rickety flight of stairs; at the top of it a naked 40-watt bulb burned rather forlornly and fruitlessly. In the circumstances, though, Harry felt he could not afford to be choosy, much less turn down any conditions even if they did seem exorbitant. He pulled himself together and trudged up the creaking stairs to the loan association.

A frosted glass door on the second floor in the dim-lit corridor announced in peeling gold letters, "GOLD MINE LOAN ASSOCIATION— Open Mon.–Sat. 10–6." Harry gritted his teeth, took a deep breath and turned the doorknob, which almost came off, letting himself into the office. A young black girl with blue-tinted eyelids and wearing a bead-embroidered apple-green angora sweater topped by a Brillo-pad Afro sat at a small switchboard, painting her nails dark green. She looked up as Harry entered.

"You want anything?" she inquired suspiciously, dipping her brush into the nail polish phial.

Harry stopped, feeling like an intruder; he was still holding the door open and cleared some phlegm out of his throat. "Yes, I was just . . . well, I'd like to see somebody about a loan."

The girl seemed a bit testy at having her afternoon make-up session interrupted and gestured with her head in the direction behind Harry. "Okay, take a seat," she said, plugging one of the jacks into an outlet of the PBX switchboard. "Somebody will be with you in a minute."

Harry saw a couple of ramshackle garden chairs by the wall, closed the door and sat down on one of them under a sepia-colored print of an Idaho railroad whistle-stop taken at the turn of the century. The black girl who couldn't have been more than seventeen must have cut into somebody's phone conversation because she apologized profusely that she had interrupted him—a man she addressed as Norris—but there was a guy waiting to talk to him about a loan. She unplugged the line again after listening to the other end for a moment and told Harry that Mr. Random would see him in a few seconds, in Room Number Two.

Harry nodded in acknowledgment and watched as the girl resumed her nail painting. He marveled at the nondescript atmosphere of the waiting room. Besides the switchboard, a manual typewriter, a couple of chairs and the sepia print on the flaky wall there wasn't a stick of furniture to be seen, and the parquet floor evidently had not been swept in two years. The dust lay so thick on the wood that some-body had traced the word "Bullshit" in it. Waiting for pin-money in this drab ambience, even beyond the realm of camp or kitsch, brought to Harry's mind movies he had seen at the Museum of Modern Art, old German silent flicks directed by Murnau, Pabst and Fritz Lang, of barren rooms depicting lodgings of poverty-stricken lunkheads singing for pennies in tenement yards, while bawling snotty babes lay un-attended in their dirty cribs. But here was a greater incongruity because adjoining this arid wasteland of urban living was supposed to lie the salvation promising unlimited wealth and coffers of treasures a Captain Hook might have envied. Yet this crypto-capitalistic environment, this pseudo-mercantile mood, probably would not have inspired even the likes of a Tom Wolfe or Susan Sontag to waste their vitriolic pens on. And it certainly would have been the death of a modern-day Proust or

Dreiser. The dust and distant gold flavoring simply lacked the Sierra Madre defiance and bizarre glamour of a Walter Huston or Tim Holt. His solipsistic state notwithstanding, Harry could not help but wonder how a human being could last in such desolate emptiness without going mad, not even relieved by such touches as kewpie dolls, Presley tunes, Lalique windows, Rosenthal dishes, or just Warhol's vacuous screenprints of MM, or Ike's grin by Norman Rockwell. But then only the past could shape the heart of the present, and this place definitely lived in a void between the past and the present. He had come to a limbo.

A buzz zinged Harry out of his thoughts. The girl waved her hands in the air to hasten the drying process of the nail polish and again gestured with her head, this time in the direction of the windows behind her where a door led out of the reception room into another office. Harry thanked the girl and ushered himself into Room Number Two.

A man in his mid-thirties with a pink face, a high forehead, sparse hair strategically combed across the top of his hammy cranium and a Tattersal vest half-covering a striped silk ascot was pacing up and down in front of the huge window looking out on Broadway, and talking into the phone on a long extension cord. When Harry entered the office he looked up briefly and motioned Harry to a chair next to his desk, saying "I'll be with you in a minute." Then he turned his attention again to the party at the other end of the line.

"Really, Bruce, I don't understand why you insist on being so positively beastly to me," the sharp dresser remonstrated, gesticulating wildly with his free hand as he strolled energetically between one end of the office that harbored a wall safe and the other, lined by four filing cabinets. "I couldn't very well turn him away, could I now? Really! He just came back from Chicago, where he'd been for five weeks, staying with his mother, a monster of a woman if ever I saw one—you know, the witch in the "Wizard of Oz" harassing poor little Judy Garland—and the poor boy was absolutely miserable I am telling you, quite beside himself, even if he *is* a truck driver. Now you know yourself Lancelot isn't the sort of fellow who'd get the clap and not tell me, although—heaven knows—he is a dreadful lot on the road, too much for my liking. Did you know in the kitchen he's a positive wizard with his *Scallopine di Vitello coi Tartuffi alla Modenese?* Those breaded veal cutlets simply melt in your mou . . . What's that? . . . Brucey-boy, I just don't understand why you should take this rotten attitude. I swear on my father's grave nothing happened, I do, cross my heart and hope to die . . . Now that's preposterous! Lancelot does not fuck German shepherds; you have him mixed up with Teddy . . . What? . . . Well, I'm not so sure if I want to go there tonight. I was going to meet someone at the Oscar Wilde Theatre . . . Yes, first I'll go to the Continental Baths—or to Everhart's—and I just may pop over for a few minutes if you insist, but mind you I only *may* . . . Heavens to Betsy, you mean Teddy *will* be there? . . . Not with that vile dog of his! Does he really have to schlep Madame Butterfly around with him everywhere now? I declare! The boy has absolutely no shame if you want my honest opinion . . . Well, okay, but just for a few minutes, and no funny business, promise? . . . Right-o . . . Ciao."

Norris Random hung up and walked around the desk, his back to the window. "I'm so sorry to keep you waiting so long," he smiled, flashing a set of pearly teeth and emptying a flurry of cigarette butts into a wastebasket, "but Bruce's *so* persistent. Some people you cannot shake off, even when you tell them you're busy."

"That's all right," Harry said, wishing he could get out of this dump. But he realized he had gotten this far, so he might as well go through with it now, and so what if this queer interspersed business with private tidbits. All he knew was that here stalked the ghost, the *dernier cri* image of Thomas Mann's Tadzio, catapulted into the computer age of ultimate decadence, of silicone, plastics, Pelé-payments, porno-permissiveness, minimal art, malpractice insurance, Hiroshima, Auschwitz, My Lai: a child of them all, and perhaps no more than this, a mere child of this century.

Random sorted some papers on his desk, still flashing his advertised neon smile at Harry. "That Teddy really is a pig. He actually fucks police dogs. Do you know anybody who fucks dogs?"

Harry shook his head, deadpan. Nothing surprised him anymore. After all, in an abnormal age the abnormal was normal. "No, I'm afraid I don't know anybody who fucks dogs."

"Well, never mind! That's Ted's headache. Now, let's see if Gold Mine can be of some assistance to *you*. You *have* come to see me on business, haven't you? Not by any chance for a *personal* reason, hey?"

"No, it's business, Mr. Random."

"Norris. All my friends call me Norris," Random chuckled as he eased himself into his swivel chair. "I maintain that one way of making business is by making friends. And we all like to *make* friends, don't we?"

The double meaning of this last remark did not escape Harry who wished that Random would stop making those ridiculous goo-goo eyes at him and get on with it. "Sure, people like to make friends," he played along casually, without letting on he was conscious of the double entendre. But he gave himself away by drumming his fingers nervously on the glassplate of the desk and he knew it. "Although to be quite honest, right now I don't feel so much like making friends as making money."

"Why, of course, don't we all? That's why you're here. And in the right place, too, if I may say so. Let me get all your particulars first and then we shall see what we can do."

Just like Mr. Hebert at the bank, Norris Random pulled a thick sheaf of forms out of a desk drawer and grasped a Parker pen that was clipped to his vest pocket. The usual questions demanded the usual answers about name, residence, place of employment and salary. Then it came to the amount Harry wanted and he made no bones about the four thousand he needed.

"My, that's pretty steep," Random raised an apprehensive eyebrow above his sky-blue Sinatra eyes. "You understand I have to know what you need this moolah for. A loan for a house, a car, or what?"

Harry then rendered the same hearts and flowers story to Random that he had plied Mr. Hebert with, but this time he felt more confident in spewing out his tale of misfortune and didn't even stall once. He was prepared. He had a foolproof ploy. In fact, before Random had the chance to ask him for the hospital statement, Harry explained that he had mislaid it. Nevertheless, he had to send the money off by mail today to have the cancelation date on the envelope conform with the deadline set for payment by the hospital authorities. As an added bonus, Harry promised to leave his savings passbook with Random as evidence of his good faith and trust in the Gold Mine Loan Association and to prove that he actually had enough funds to cover the loan. It was just that he needed it today, now. Random listened to Harry silently, gazing at him through his baby-blue eyes as if he might eat him up with love. Altogether, when he had completed his tale of woe, Harry felt he had given a pretty good account of himself and saw no reason for Random to distrust him and not come up with the money with all the surety he was willing to offer him in exchange for the loan.

"Well, that's a very touching story, Harry," Random said at last. "By the way, I hope you don't mind my calling you by your first name."

"No, of course not," Harry smiled confidently. "Go right ahead."

"But to be absolutely honest, Harry," he said, still cheerfully, "I don't believe a goddamn word of it."

For an instant Harry thought he had not heard right. Not even an old-timer like Mr. Hebert had questioned the veracity of his words. His tongue felt heavy, dry, sandy, and his pulse began kicking in his throat.

"You don't . . . " he started, then changed his tactics. "But it's true. Why else would I come up here if I didn't need the money in a hurry?" he said, working himself into an outraged surliness.

"Oh I have no idea why, my dear boy. And I don't deny for a moment you are in great need of the money. It's just too fantastic, that's all, and what's more it seems odd to me that this bank of yours wouldn't have offered you a loan against the money in your account. It's the best collateral in the world. It just so happens I know that your bank grants loans and you certainly would have been no risk since the amount in your account handily covers the principal. Don't tell me they didn't suggest that you take out a loan?"

The friendly face confronting Harry did not in the least conform with the amused cross-examination that issued from it. Harry's eyes met Random's squarely, while his brain churned wildly for a way out of this unexpected quandary. The best thing again would be to start talking and see where it would lead him. This had almost worked with Mr. Hebert, and Harry hoped that he was at least the equal of this gay guy, as screwy a cookie as he might turn out to be. "You know, Mr. Rand . . . Norris, you're absolutely right. I should have asked for a loan at the bank, but it never occurred to me while I was there. All the teller said was that I could only withdraw two-thirds of a joint account without my wife's counter-signature and I left it at that." He passed a hand over his damp forehead. "So, I take it you can't help me out."

"Well, of course I can always advance people money," Random shrugged, "provided I know they're on the level with me and present no undue financial risk. I can still check on the references you've given me and in the meantime keep your savings book in my safe to make certain you don't withdraw the money, but you can imagine that enquiries about you would entail . . . oh, I'd say about 24 hours, and as far as giving you the money today is concerned that is absolutely out. Maybe tomor . . ."

"But I don't understand," Harry objected somewhat heatedly. "Why do you need references when you have the collateral right in your hands—my savings account—and I'm willing to sign your papers

266

stating that I owe you four thousand dollars? With those papers you'd be authorized to confiscate my savings if I don't repay you in thirty days."

"If it were your own savings account I'd be only too willing to accept that risk, Harry-boy, on the spot, but not with a joint account. It just ain't legal." Random leaned back expansively. "Of course—and heaven forbid!—if anything should happen to your wife and she passes away in the hospital where you claim she is—well, then the money in the passbook would revert to you, naturally, and I could claim it as a result of the loan agreement you'll have signed with me. But you must realize that I've been in this business many years and have seen everything there is to see concerning monetary matters. Now just put yourself in my shoes: you come to me for a bundle of money and give me a long, sad account about your dear wife being stranded on an island in a hospital undergoing all kinds of surgery. Tragic indeed, but highly unlikely. Much more likely, dear Harry—and please don't take offense, but I've heard such tearjerkers too often to be overly moved by them— much more likely would be for you to have met some nice little brunette and you want to ditch your wife—what's her name? Anyway, you withdraw, or rather *want* to withdraw, all the money in your account, twelve thousand smackers, and look for a new beginning with your chick in some other part of the world and then . . ."

"But that's nonsense," Harry interrupted, infuriated that the money-lender was more than wise to such tricks as his and was outsmarting him at his own game. "Twelve thousand smackers, how far would that get me with a woman? How could I start a new life anywhere with anyone on that scanty . . . well, it's a mere pittance. It just wouldn't be worth the candle, landing in the poky for such a miserable amount."

"I agree with you, Harry," Norris Random smiled his most ingratiating Liberace-smile. "It isn't worth the candle as you so rightly point out. Only you have no choice. You just can't ask for more because that's all you have. Besides, what do I know how many stocks, futures, securities, shares, you have stashed away somewhere. Or perhaps even some high grade Triple-A corporate bonds. Maybe they're cashed al . . ."

"You can ease your mind on that. I have none."

"Well, I only have your word for that. Not that I think you play in commodities, collect gold coins, or own land in areas of intense commercial development; you don't look like the business type to me. Not with twelve thousand dollars in a joint account. Anyway, it's purely academic here because we're just talking about four thou, nothing more. So, if you want me to handle it, Harry, at 20 per cent, I'll be only too happy to oblige and advance you the money, but I must check on your references first. Try me tomorrow afternoon and I'm sure we can come to an agree . . ."

"But I'm telling you I need it today, don't you understand?"

"If you need it today," Random sighed, with a slight hint of exasperation, "then all I can suggest is that you go back to the bank and get yourself a loan against your account. I'm sure they won't put any obstacles in your . . ."

"Norrith thweetheart!"

A rebel's yell rent the quiet Monday afternoon atmosphere. The two men spun around, jumped up, just in time to witness a lanky U.S. Marine sweep into Random's office, dash past Harry, and, with one hand propping himself on the paper-strewn desk, vault over it, and plant a wet kiss on top of Random's balding crown. Random's face brightened perceptively as the lisping gyrene hugged him like a long-lost brother. Not that he resembled Random like a brother by a long shot. He was a gangling golden-haired man in his early twenties, wearing a white cap at a rakish angle on his head. His puppy-brown eyes twinkled with joy at the sight of the money creditor. "Norrith, you old mother you, don't tell me your Perthy-boy didn't give you a thurprithe."

The black receptionist in the apple-green angora sweater and greener fingernails showed her apologetic face in the doorway.

"I'm sorry, Norris, but Mr. Brandywine just rushed past me and didn't give me a chance to announce him."

"That's all right, Marylou," Random grinned from ear to ear. "Percy is always welcome, announced or not."

"Yeth, you go ahead, Marylou, and get uth thome nithe napoleonth and thome coffee while you're at it, that'th a thweetiepie."

Harry pushed his chair under Random's desk as Marylou retreated again, feeling he had overstayed his welcome. Loan associations might as well be ruled out, too. "Well, I'll be . . ."

"No, I won't hear of it," Percy the Marine turned to Harry. "Any friend of Norrith ith a friend of mine. Hey, Norrith-thweetie, you haven't been holding out on yourth truly? He'th cute."

"Now take it easy, Percy," Random laughed to the accompaniment of two kewpie-doll blushes. "*Au contraire*. Harry here is in deep water. The dear man needs four grand in a hurry and we were just discussing ways for him to obtain it. Apparently he must have it today."

Percy's cherubic face collapsed in a sham commiseration grimace. "Oh you poor dear, that'th really a rotten thituathon."

"Isn't he a doll?" Random inquired gratuitously of Harry. "I bet you've never come across such a nice Marine in your life."

Harry's smile could not conceal his embarrassment. "No, I guess not. I never met a Marine who called me a poor dear."

"I bet you'd do anything to get hold of that long green, wouldn't you, Harry?" the Marine asked. "Theemth to be pretty important to you."

"Under the circumstances, I guess I would," Harry agreed. "If I knew I could get it today there wouldn't be anything I wouldn't do—short of murder."

"Yipppeeeeee!"

Again Percy's Tarzan yell shattered the listless afternoon. "Wait a moment, will you?" He wheeled round to the window, tore open one of the partitions and leaned out of it, shouting down: "Hey fellowth, I think our troubleth are over. I just found the thweeteth boy to make up theven." With that he slammed the window shut and turned triumphantly to the two startled men.

"What in heaven's name are you talking about?" Random demanded alarmed.

"Look and thee for yourthelvth," Percy shouted, pointing down to the street. The two men rushed to the window, craned their necks over the sill and saw six sailors in uniform standing at the curb among the spilled garbage where Harry had slipped earlier, waving up at the window where the three men looked down. Two of the sailors were holding hands, a third, with one earring, leaned against a lamppost, hand against hip, and the limp-wristed wave of all of them, as well as their uncommonly tight-fitting pants, caused Harry to wonder how on earth they ever managed to get into the Navy and whether this might be part of the nation's crop assigned to defend the country against the menace of the Red fleet. Anyway, how many cruisers did "Jane's Fighting Ships" assign to the Gay Navy? It was an odd assortment indeed. But it seemed to him that the strangest duck of them all was Percy the Marine; obviously a clear case for Dr. Joyce Brothers to define, Harry reflected.

"I don't know any of them," Norris Random said, slightly soured. "And I don't think I want to either. Looks like a rough bunch to me."

"Now thtop it, don't leth have a thene right away, Norrith-doll," Percy turned back to the two men as Random let himself down in his chair. "You know, Harry, Norrith ith an awful crybaby thometimeth. Every time I make a movie he thinkth I . . ."

"A movie?" Again Harry was bug-eyed. "I thought you were in the Marines."

"Oh but I am. Only thith week I'm on leave. And the guyth down-thtairth are making a gay film. On Chrithtopher Thweet. You ever thee my mathterpieth 'Trithtan and Izzy'? Made oodleth of dough. Two hundred thou. Tonight we are tethting my latetht. Itth called, 'The Kith.' You know, Rodinth thtatue? We're looking for thomeone whoth thtwaight. Itth about that thtatue; only . . ." His eyes narrowed. "Hey, I do hope you are, dear boy?"

"I'm *what*?" Harry was mystified.

"Thtwaight."

"Sure is," Norris fell in. "Guy claims he's married, but more likely I think he's trying to beat town with a chick."

"Naughty, naughty," Percy laughed, wagging a diamond-festooned finger under Harry's nose. "Jutht delay that trip for a few dayth, Harry-boy. If it ithn't worth four grand to . . ."

"What are you talking about?" demanded Harry, drawing back and reaching for the savings book that Random had dropped on his desk.

"See theethe thtatues, Harry?" Percy asked, pointing to the wall behind him. There, over an imitation marble fireplace, was a mantelpiece studded with about half a dozen statues of nude Greek gods. He had not noticed them before and was genuinely perplexed by the realistic but artificial coloring of their physiques—right down to pink fingernails and purplish-vermilion penes glandes. "Well, in the movie," Percy continued, "there will be thith thtatue in a mutheum, 'The Kith' by Rodin, only it really ithn't a thtatue at all but a real-life man and woman coated in bronthe-coloring. Now, at night thickth thailors who were in the toilet during clothing time come out and find themthelvth locked in the mutheum and they thee the thtatue come to life and the Rodin boy and girl become tho animated they have an orgathm and the thailors get tho exthited over it that they feel that they mutht be made sainth by the Pope, that the thtatue mutht be conthecrated, but on thecond thought they are convinced that the Pope ith sure to ekthcom-municate them for watching the boy and girl in the thtatue get horny, bethideth the fact that it would be poor public relations for the Church to advertithe their firtht thekthual miracle; ethpethally with that thtatue of Mary Magdalene and Jethuth joining the act, for which inthidentally

He forgivth her later; tho finally they dethide they mutht make love to all the Greek god thtatueth who ultimately come to life and now they know that they will at leatht be blethed by *them*. Now what conthernth you? You don't have to do anything but to thcrew the girl in 'The Kith,' tho it really should be loth of fun for you. She's an abtholutely ravishing nymph; only theventeen, but she lookth older; the daughter of our C.O. You jutht let it all hang out and . . ."

"Now hold your horses, fellow," Harry retreated shakily from the two queer fish. "Let's get this straight: are you suggesting that I play in a gay movie? A skin flick? For four thousand clams, and that . . ."

"But what'th wrong with that?" the devil dog seemed astonished by Harry's vigorous objection. "Dozenth of college ththudenth do it. With you and the girl it altho appealth to the thtraight market. And it'll be above board. Nothing unconthtitutional. Ethpethally for uth. *We* have to thimulate it. All *you* do ith fuck Katarina on the pedethtal and then . . ."

"But I don't want to fuck Katarina on the pedetht . . . the pedestal . . ."

"Well, you can thcrew her on a leather-padded bench they have for vithitorth in mutheumth. We will make it an arty, cultured movie, a movie with thocially redeeming thignificanth, the great . . ."

"You still don't get it," Harry objected vehemently, recognizing in a sudden phosphorescent flash the truism that man indeed was not a fallen angel but a risen ape. "Goddamn it, I don't want to fuck Katarina on a pedestal or on a leather-padded bench, or *any*where. I don't want to be in a gay film, that's all. Or in any hardcore porn . . ."

"But you thaid you'd do anything," Percy said crestfallen, rubbing his crotch on the edge of Random's desk. "To earn four thou for getting laid ain't ekthactly hay if you athk me. Look, thweetheart, I'll lay on an ekthra thou . . ."

"Aw come on, Percy-boy," Random protested mildly and ripped Harry's application form off the pad, tearing it up slowly. "Don't tart it up now. You can see for yourself Harry isn't game. He wants the money today because he's going to blow town tonight with a broad and doesn't want to lay Katarina on any pedestal, so give him his peace and let him go."

"Well, if that'th the attitude he wanth to take," the Marine turned around indignantly, visibly hurt, "let him have hith broad and thcrew *her*. Only Katarina ith the motht adorable Girl Thcout you've ever laid your eyeth on and he can eat hith heart out and I'll jutht get one of thoth thtudenth working their way through college; they're a dime a . . ."

"Oh by the way, talking of students, Percy-hon," Random turned his full attention to the Marine and grabbed his ass, realizing that he couldn't squeeze his 20 per cent interest out of a loan to Harry. "I just had this tinkle from Bruce—you remember Bruce Timely, the fellow at N.Y.U. who likes Orientals and once applied for a job with the Peace Corps in Korea—and he told me that Teddy would . . ."

Harry had just about enough of this, and left. From somewhere inside his mind, and penetrating the miasma encircling the two merry perverts, came Edmund Burke's message—if man could not contain his appetites, an outside tyranny would do it for him sooner or later. Still, when you worked in New York you couldn't help rubbing elbows with homos and lesbians, and he never minded them, although he had none as friends in his close-knit coterie. Even though no one had ever pro-positioned him, he did feel instinctively aloof in their midst, especially when they descended to a pit reeking of such bottomless depravity as Random's clique—and he wished at once he had been able to utilize the afternoon to better advantage. It was getting later and later and he hadn't achieved by half what he set out to do; only eight grand was in the kitty so far, although he still counted on the eighteen thousand from Helga. Christ, why in God's name wasn't he born a James Bond, an 007, a Popov, who could have summoned the money with the snap of two fingers? No Sean Connery he! Instead, he met dudes and boobs and sick dames and twisted personalities like Charlotte Collins and Don Ives and Ed Blakely and Crazy Guy and Norris Random and Percy the Marine, all of whom might have stepped straight out of the pages of Genet. Where in God's name was the solution, the simple, melodramatic brute force that the characters in adventure stories and TV serials could usually elicit in order to attain their golden ends?

As he lumbered down the dark creaky staircase, Harry made sure that the envelope with the eight thousand was still safely tucked away in his breast pocket. He added the savings book to it and sickened at the mere thought of being mugged before reaching home. He had just removed his hand from his jacket when Marylou the receptionist with the emerald-green fingernails appeared in the doorway below and came up with a cardboard-tray loaded with cream puffs and four containers of coffee.

"Hey, you leavin' already?" she asked, half-vexed that she should have gone to the trouble of ordering food for him too. "I got you some coffee and cake, you know."

"That's very nice but you shouldn't have," Harry smiled. "I'm sure Norris and Percy won't mind eating my share too, and if they can't, Percy has a few pals on the street who will."

The girl shrugged. "Okay—see ya."

Outside, the six sailors were still standing in a tight knot around the street light, in the midst of a collage of New York debris. It came as no surprise to Harry at this point that the raving woman with the brown shopping bag had found her perfect victim at last—six victims to be precise—and was just in the process of accosting them, hysterically dressing them all down as the culprits responsible for her misery, claiming this time that they had gangraped her spastic fourteen year-old daughter Allison.

The sailors all looked grim. The two tars holding hands appeared downright agitated at the swill of billingsgate splashing over them and they vehemently shook their heads in public denial, which only served to encourage and goad the batty old shrew all the more. She lashed out at them with renewed vigor with a cascade of invectives the likes of which Harry, and no doubt the sailors, had never heard in a timespan of less than two minutes.

31 ═══════════

Harry scurried away like a rat, repelled by the idea of being detected by the crazy old hag, but for some reason he could not get Marylou's tray of creampuffs out of his mind. Even before reaching the next block, the by-now familiar pangs of hunger made their appearance again, and after a few minutes Harry was fortunate enough to come upon a luncheonette. It was almost deserted, so he did not have to wait and ordered an orange drink, two chocolate doughnuts and a hot dog. To his dismay, his frankfurter was crusty and blackened on one side and to top it off was not even hot. As luck would have it, his attention was diverted by a more refreshing sight—for once. A three- or four-year old boy across the counter from Harry was having a tantrum, refusing to open his mouth while his increasingly irritated mother tried to force-feed him an egg-salad sandwich. Especially after the perversity in Random's office, it did Harry a world of good to watch this wholesome family drama. The tow-headed tyke, dressed in a tomato-red parka and matching pants, immediately yelled that he didn't like egg salad, and the mother, above the steaming hiss of the dishwasher, yelled back: "How the hell can you say you don't like egg-salad sandwiches when you have never tried one?"

"Because I don't like the look, that's why. I wanna hot dog."

"Well, you can't live on franks, Dickie. And they don't look nice neither; too greasy. You eat this sandwich now and no more argu . . ."

"No, I ain't going to eat no egg-salad sandwich!"

At this the mother pulled the sandwich from the boy's lips. "Okay, Dickie, if that's the way you feel about it, don't eat it. But let me warn you right now: no ice cream tonight and no TV! Right?"

"I dun care," mumbled the boy.

His mother laid the sandwich on a napkin and returned to her cherry pie while the little boy sat on his tall stool, and stared glumly at Harry. Slowly, tears flooded his huge, heartbroken eyes—a world of immense significance was collapsing inside him—but his mother gave no indication that she noticed and continued eating her pie. At length, she glanced down at her son and shoved the napkin with the sandwich almost directly under his nose. A big tear trickled down the youngster's cheek, then clung like a melting icicle to his chin, and the mother's heart softened. She leaned over her child and said, in a voice more gentle and contrite: "Tell you what I'll do, Dickie: just to prove to you how nice it tastes I'll eat a little bit of your sandwich myself. Okay? And if you finish the sandwich, then you can watch TV tonight and get your vanilla and strawberry ice cream. Okay?"

The boy looked up at his mother and sniffled and nodded wordlessly. The woman picked up the crumbling egg-salad sandwich and was about to take a bite out of it, when the youngster piped up through his tears, "Okay—eat, but first say: May I please?"

The mother froze. Then her tense features melted into a soft maternal loving smile, and she bent down to kiss her son's mop of hair.

Life continued its natural flow, unabated, uncaring. Nobody in the hustling-bustling ruthless metropolis except for Harry had paid the slightest attention to the soon-to-be-forgotten mother-son crisis. And he realized that most of the egg-salad sandwich and ice cream and potato chips eaters went through the same childhood miseries of being blackmailed, bullied and force-fed on too much "sensible nourishment" by their parents until they ended up as parents themselves, as poets, shoemakers, or tyrants bending everyone to their unassailable will, or— goddamnit!—as twisted minds, kidnappers, killers . . .

His hands clammy from the wet, bone-chilling cold of the raw October day, Harry stood in the littered subway once more, inside the vortex of painted craziness. Worse, it didn't help his disposition any to be constantly bumped and buffeted by the straphanger facing him, a fat-bellied bald guy with teased gray sideburns, a loud sports shirt, and the cold stump of a stogy stuck in his kisser. It all added to his confusion, his panic, with the deadline approaching rapidly and the money not forthcoming. Oh to be somewhere else right now, to wake up in the pine-covered Black Hills of South Dakota or on the shores of Catalina Island, or better still to step as an imaginary character into Dos Passos' "USA" or Doctorow's "Ragtime"—and realize it had all been a ghastly literary hoax, a nightmare, the kidnapping, mad screaming people, degenerates. Hell!

32 ═══════════

The minute Harry got out at his stop and approached street level he realized that something was dreadfully wrong. His plan had been to walk home as quickly as possible and to get in touch with Helga and tell her as honestly as he could about everything that had happened to him in his attempts to raise the ransom. But as he mounted the subway stairs, he distinctly heard the sound of glass shattering, and over it, a succession of the most horrible blood-chilling screams he had ever heard. An ice-cold shower of shivers ran up and down his spine. For an instant he could not tell whether it was an animal or a human that had emitted these incredible, piercing shrieks. As he reached the sidewalk, he saw people running from all directions and massing in a circle around a widening congregation which had already gathered in a spot from where, obviously, the blood-curdling screams came.

Harry halted on the top step of the subway exit and watched the crowd of curiosity-seekers who were multiplying by leaps and bounds. The people just seemed to gape, and those farthest away from the center were standing on tiptoe to see better.

With a dreadful, searing flash of recognition, Harry knew that the vast mob was actually assembled in front of Miss Laredo's grubby little candy and stationery store, and the streak of a horrendous thought blazed through his mind—what she had told him earlier that day about the young punks threatening her with a shakedown. A sick feeling overcame Harry and he could barely drag himself from the top of the subway stairs to face the throng in front of the store. He feared the worst and hoped against hope that, please God, it was just a coincidence that all these people were filling the sidewalk in front of Miss Laredo's shop. Somebody yelled "Look out!" and the next second more glass landed with a splintering crash on the pavement. Slowly, Harry elbowed his way past the men and women craning their necks, each asking the other what was happening, and each of them fearing that at last a Showdown at the O.K. Corral was about to evolve right here before their very eyes. Over the animalistic screams, Harry could hear the sound of laughter, and then a man's voice shouting, "For the last time! Where the hell is the money, you bitch?"

And Harry knew they had come. One of New York's roving bands of marauders terrorizing neighborhoods, The Mad Killers, were at work. Like a school of sharks they were zeroing in on a victim. He did not even have to push his way to the front of the swarm of spectators to see the nauseating sight. The window behind which the papers and magazines used to lie neatly piled on the shelf was a shambles now, looseleaf pages and greeting cards everywhere fluttered among school supplies and broken bulbs on the ground. And right on top of the thousands of glass splinters writhed the little black figure of Miss Laredo, in a violent paroxysm of anguish. A burly youth with a Cro-Magnon mug and a ponytail held by a rubber band, wearing a sleeveless black leather jacket on which the words MAD KILLERS were emblazoned with thumbtack-heads, was standing over Miss Laredo with a baseball bat. Three other hoodlums, similarly attired, clamped down her arms and legs, hard, and were laughing as she feebly tried to lash out at them. Blood was pouring from a deep gash in her head, and her cavernous clown's mouth, ketchup-red with blood, shouted hoarsely for help. But not a soul moved.

The brawny teenager with the bat dealt the old woman some vicious kicks in her ribs with his pointed Italian shoes and Miss Laredo unleashed another harrowing scream. Somewhere a lone voice could be heard, half-strangled, "Why don't somebody get the cops?" Still not a soul moved. Harry felt an indescribable anger well up inside him and he wanted to take the four bastards and smash their heads against a brick wall till their blood and brains spattered out all over the concrete—but he knew he did not stand a chance. The courts saw to that, with their tear-jerking appeals and briefs and parish priests and ACLU lawyers. The perfect revenge on the rich who got off scot-free for *their* crimes! Criminal justice had turned criminal! Almost no one stood a chance. Harry, like Miss Laredo, was outnumbered and unarmed. Moreover, with the money he had on him, he could not afford to get tough with the goddamn scum. They'd simply gang up on him, like a pack of maddened wolves; his life's savings would go down the drain, Ruth's life be put in jeopardy, and for what? To save this old woman? A total stranger, already half-dead, who only had a sister almost as dead as she appeared to be lying there on the ground among the jagged glass splinters, whimpering now, begging for mercy. Christ, she was at the end of her tether, of her struggle to stay alive anyway.

"Last chance, ya fuckin' old bitch," yelled the brute with the baseball bat. "Tell me where ya got da fuckin' money you owe us or I break every fuckin' bone in your body."

Miss Laredo strained to open her jaws, but her mutilated mass of flesh could emit not a bird's peep. Her dental plates lay in a bloody puddle beside her and only her red gums showed behind her clownish lips.

"Come on, move ya ass, Bluegrass," coaxed one of the kids with a shock of shoulder-length blond hair. "Let's see that Super Fly Special of yours. You know it turns me on. Crack her fuckin' shins—c'mon, man!"

"No, no!" the old woman on the ground burst out, trying to twist free of the trio holding her down. "Help! Amigos! Help!"

"You wanna bust in the mout, ya ol' bitch?" one of the gang screamed, lunging forward and belting her in the face. As though touched by a live wire, Miss Laredo's ninety or so pounds thrashed and tossed about, attempting to roll away from her tormentors, and leaving a splash of blood where she had lain before. The blond goon bore down hard with both knees on Miss Laredo's arms, shouting over the noise of the traffic to his two giggling accomplices in their cowboy boots: "Her legs, you stupid spicks! Don't let her get away!" The kid who couldn't have been a day over fifteen looked up at that moment and Harry realized it was a girl, a horse-faced, flat-chested female primate. She was wearing a sleeveless leather-vest with an Iron Cross dangling from a gold chain around her neck. Fastened to a wide leather belt around her waist was a sheathed bowie knife, and her left arm showed the tattoo of a tiny swastika. And Harry wondered: at which stage of development did *this* egg-salad sandwich or potato chips consumer go wrong and turn from an innocent, cooing babe into a raving animal?

As the two gigglers quickly clambered forward and got hold of Miss Laredo's wildly kicking legs the crowd grew increasingly restive, some murmuring in outrage why they didn't leave the poor old woman alone and why didn't someone get the police. But the sharks had smelled blood and they were ready to go in for the kill. The blonde's steel-gray eyes flashed up at Bluegrass.

"Shit, Bluegrass!" she clamored, stomping her knees with difficulty on the old woman's arms. "Les get outta here! Chop her, quick, before da assholes get da muddafuckin' pigs!"

For an instant Bluegrass stood undecided, the top of his bat resting on his left blood-splattered Gucci shoe. Close-by a bus sneezed into motion and Bluegrass lifted his bat and playfully swung it around his head in the manner of an Olympic champion practicing a hammer throw. For a moment he was sidetracked in glancing with appreciation at the flexing ripple of his bulbous biceps. Behind him a huge sliver of glass from Miss Laredo's destroyed shop fell out of its window frame and came down with a loud clatter, breaking into a thousand pieces.

"Stop 'em! Stop 'em!" screamed the terrified old woman, her blood-caked eyes blinking unseeingly at the crowd around her. "Please . . . Someone . . . please!"

Harry hid behind an enormous woman carrying a sleeping child in her arms as the blinded eyes seemed to swerve in his direction.

"Keep ya fuckin' yap shut!" the barbaric Ilse Koch blonde yelled hysterically and smashed her fist into Miss Laredo's face, this time with such homicidal ferocity that the old woman's head flung back against the pavement. Tears coursed down aged ruts in Miss Laredo's cheeks, her lips moving vainly like those of a fish expiring, and she lay still. "Bluegrass—hurry! She ain't going to lay it on us," the girl spat out, her hands now on the moribund woman's throat. "She ripped ya off! Get it before the heat comes! She won't give us the bread."

The pony-tailed thug gripped the baseball bat tightly as he continued his overhead rotary motion.

"Okay, you asked for it, bitch-face," his voice boomed hoarse with rage and betrayal over a small chorus of blaring automobile horns. "I oughta bury a hatchet in your goddamn skull. But . . . I'll give ya to the count of three to hand over the green!" He stopped with his bat in mid-motion, poised it like an executioner's axe directly over Miss Laredo's legs, tensed his muscles, waited another three seconds, then let it come down with an incredibly savage force onto her right shin. The hard splintering sound that followed was that of bone breaking.

An ear-shattering scream tore out of the old woman's blood-red mouth, as out of an exploding wind tunnel, and the crowd groaned. People turned their heads away, too late, the atrocity indelibly implanted on their retinas; others shoved and pushed past Harry to get a better look. Miss Laredo's mangled face dissolved into a mask of purplish hues, dropped sideways, her blood-caked eye shooting silent arrows of accusation at the inhuman arena around her. Quickly, Harry hid again from her view, this time behind a mountain of a man in a butcher's apron, hating himself, hating the world, for its heartlessness, its cowardice, but most of all hating himself. Mr. Harry Iscariot!

He felt weak with nausea, overcome with shame, useless, drained of all emotion, of life and self for not having gone to the aid of the dying woman. He clenched his hands against fate and had to gnash his teeth to stop from shaking uncontrollably. Suddenly, tears stung his eyes.

Over the shoulder of the aproned man he could barely make out the horse-faced savage of a girl through the burning wash of tears, as she ripped off Miss Laredo's clothes, furiously, senselessly, maddened by the sight of blood, like a vulture tearing rotting flesh from a carcass. And using her clawing hands like baling hooks, she finally found what she had been looking for, the hidden treasure, a puny roll of dollar bills in a tattered cup of the old woman's bra. The whole wad of bills could not have amounted to more than forty dollars. The girl flashed a barracuda grin. Harry averted his eyes, sickened anew by the recognition of his own cravenness, and wondering was this girl, Bluegrass, Random, Himmler, he himself, then, the end-product of evolution? He jostled his way back, rudely, too numb to apologize, past the silent congregation of faces still craning their necks trying not to miss anything of the grisly New York scene that wouldn't make the Chancellor-Brinkley News, but that was still a free socko Peckinpah carnival show, ready for the retelling at home and in the office at the coffee machine the next day.

Naturally there was no cop in sight—Dodge City without the Sheriff again—and even if there were and he'd arrest the degenerates they'd get off with a slap on their wrists, as being too young.

Feeling wretched, Harry fled from the gruesome scene, all those weirdos, New York's synthetic Rauschenberg figures, but most of all from the shame of his own moral dereliction, from the Satanic bloodbath, and all because of a few lousy dollars the old woman needed for the rent next month.

The renewed screams in the background and the tormentors' diabolical whoops of laughter when finally the second shin cracked like a dry twig under the baseball bat hung in the air like the crazed roars of wild boars being gored to death. My God, Harry's brain howled, my God, where had man's gentle Tasaday spirit gone? What *had* happened to this world? As he dodged around a corner the terrifying shrieks tore at the edge of Harry's mind, then ripped through, whirling inside his head, like firewheels gone berserk. His whole body revolted, ached. His eyes burned. Across the street the Hare Krishna dodos still chanted their own pie-in-the-sky mantra, bobbing from side to side in the manner of toy boats lost on a raging sea, their gossamer robes fluttering in the breeze, right in front of a porno bookshop with its congeries of cocks and cunts. Indeed, the zealots were wholly cut off from and unaware of the chilling life struggle less than a hundred yards away, the omnipresent death and decadence around them. But it was all par for New York. And even if reporters of the chic super-literati journals or other impassioned apologists had witnessed this deranged massacre— this tortuous exhibit of carnage, with awestruck cowards gawking at the obscene bloodshed—these very elitist presslords and all the revisionist gunslingers could still be expected to bring up Kent State and Attica, the racism and the more deplorable matter of Watergate and Nixon's pardon. Harry was sure they'd write that if this event may have approached an unnecessary excess of youthful zeal at the hand of the Fanon guerrillas, then this too should be laid at the door of the repressive American system, at the vile private profit motif that had spawned and raised the children of the oppressed with whom the value of life and of guilt carried no weight and which brought about the much viler obscenity of Viet Nam and the banks that ripped off New York.

Christ! Harry thought, suddenly everybody seemed to be an honorary member of the Mental Patient Liberation Front. From the White House on down. Stark raving mad. Playing Mao! The New Uncultured Revolution! It probably was meant to change corruption into a universal brotherhood! Bull! *Some* change! Nothing had changed. Except that life had been reduced to de Sade's ritual theater of punishment acted out, becoming the new fascism of the street.

Harry shuddered with disgust, anger, fear—it was all so grotesque. He stumbled blindly down the street, tripping and staggering along, bumping into people, muttering incoherently he was sorry. A quisling on the run. And the thought flashed through him whether he would have had the courage to attack these cannibals if he had *not* had so much money on him and Ruth had *not* been kidnapped. He could not bear pondering this hypothesis through to its mercilessly honest conclusion for fear he might find himself as hypocritical and contemptibly debased and apologetically minded as all the other zombies on Broadway. Where did the passive differ from all those radicals, SLA and FALN riffraff and the Weather Underground anarchists and the Birchite rightwingers with their McCarthy and Mishima-mentality he felt like tearing to shreds in his mind the last two days? But deep inside he knew he would not have challenged these white fascist animals killing Miss Laredo. He knew that it was all nonsense what the movies dished up to the populace with the Brandos and Eastwoods and Bronsons taking these vermin on single-handedly, grabbing them by the scruff of their necks and beating the shit out of them. He knew that against such depraved monsters *everybody* was inoculated with the standard Kitty Genovese virus. There was not a soul in the world who'd have the guts to stand up singly to these programmed Neanderthals.

Exasperation, a blind unreasoning rage, suddenly turned Harry against the mushy liberal conscience to which he had subscribed not too long ago. And he realized that a liberal was someone who always saw the larger philosophical Weltanschauung from afar but frequently turned away from the Little Guy in need.

But it all seemed so hopeless. Everybody kept condoning the crimes of his own clique and blaming all the ills of the world on the other strata of society. Some demanded due process to be rendered to those who knew no pity, or they'd recommend for killers a two-year rehabilitation course in a fresh-air training school in the Catskills while others would take a leaf out of the Arab Socialist book and hack the culprits' hands off.

Sometimes Harry wished the two-timers would simply get life; there'd be fewer first-timers and no third-timers! Not that rehabilitation would make a damn bit of difference to these pseudo-rebels, who felt that rehabilitation, joining the workforce, meant conforming to the System.

And when you saw them coming to court with their trail of rabbis and priests and families, pleading with the judge that the culprit must have been temporarily insane when committing the crime but really was a good boy at heart and liked by everybody on the block, you just knew— Harry had read about it too often—that the charges against the punk would be dropped and everybody was back on Square One. Except the victim. Never were the criminals required to make financial restitution to the maimed victim, or *their* families. Hammurabi's Code, whereby victims of crimes were compensated for all losses suffered, was strictly for the birds. Crippled old Miss Laredo, or Ruth, *everybody* was alone, isolated, on their own, chasms removed from Goethe's Faust "Gefühl ist alles," from humaneness, as Helga had once been in Auschwitz. Goddamnit, Eichmannitis flourished! Crime and punishment had changed from a Dostoevskian guilt complex to a Peter Handke paradox.

Harry was sick with exhaustion, with the venomous self-consuming sulphur of unbridled hate still rising within, filling him to the bursting point. His legs sagged as he staggered against the side of a building . . . knowing only too well the courts would *never* bridge the gap between legality and justice . . . and he reached forward, groggily, with both arms to steady himself, and rested his hot forehead against the cool pane of a shop window. Behind the plate glass of a furniture store he could barely make out the glitter of a gaudy bedroom set, with a gold-tinted four-poster covered by a simulation leopard-skin-spread and a couple of red velvet armchairs with silvery tassels being chaperoned by half a dozen figurines that pretended to be replicas of Rodin's "Eternal Idol," but were closer to a nude girl on a tree stump spreading her legs while the young man kneeling in front of her was performing cunnilingus. An instant later, this incongruous sight caused the thought to flash through his feverish mind whether Edward Gibbon had not meant New York rather than Rome, when he wrote of the people's moral numbness to vulgarity and violence.

With a superhuman effort, Harry pushed himself from the window and lurched, bone-tired, down the almost deserted side street, trying to reach Riverside Drive as fast as he could. On his way, the only things his mind registered were blurred images—of a junkie holding on tightly to a parking meter, ghostily enshrouded by clouds of steam hissing from a nearby manhole, a Hogarthian hag of a wino huddling in a doorway with a hubcap on her lap and both of her legs swaddled in filthy rags, and a whining power shovel at the corner eating into the roadway. And he thought it was all no better, no worse, no different from the seamy side of Rome that Juvenal had blasted to hell in his Third Satire. A.D. 120!

33 ═══════════

Harry's legs were still wobbly as he entered his apartment building. He hurried through the lobby and stopped in front of Helga's door, ringing her bell four stormy times. He glanced at his watch. Goddamn, it was almost three o'clock. A little over two hours to go till the kidnapper's deadline and his phone call. He rang the bell again. He had to tell her everything. Now. There was no more time to be lost. Another ring. And another. Still no response. Oh God, what if she didn't show up at all, or deliberately refused to answer the door and kill his chances of getting the money? Suddenly, Helga was a stranger to him. Everybody was a stranger, an unknown, unformed quantity—Marcuse's One-Dimensional Man. Nobody wanted to help him. Just as nobody had wanted to help Miss Laredo. He was being treated exactly the way he had treated the poor old woman. Hell, were we all strangers to one another? Harry asked himself.

It all appeared so futile suddenly. Again, he felt drained of all hope, and he moved away from Helga's door, dragging himself like a whipped dog down the hall to his apartment.

Once inside, his mood changed *again*. Abruptly.

Like a fanatic who imagined that the blood of his fellow man would cling to him, he made a beeline for the bathroom, hurling his coat and jacket on the living room floor. He rolled up his sleeves and frantically washed his face, arms and hands with soap and hot water, but could not expunge the heart-stopping image of Miss Laredo in her agony. She could not be rinsed off with soap and hot water, and he hated himself all over again for running away from her like a rat. Why the hell *shouldn't* Helga stand apart now, when he and the whole wide law-enforcing world did?

Harry picked up his topcoat, threw it across the back of the sofa and put on his jacket again, instinctively reaching for the envelope with the eight thousand dollars. Haggard and worn out, he slumped over the Hepplewhite chair and fixed his gaze blindly at the ransom note. My God, what was the use of fighting? Like Miss Laredo, you're on your own, Ruthie. Expendable! That's what they mean by triage! And I've *failed*. Maybe it's a kind of punishment for my infidelity when you had tried so hard . . . Christ, what in hell have the gods consummated, the gods of Velikovsky and von Däniken, the gods of Darwin and Huxley? And where was God Himself now? Why didn't He stand up and be counted? And, worse, where the devil were the goddamn cops when you needed them? Where was anyone?

Sick with weariness and tension, Harry felt his superego fast slipping away from him somewhere between the crevices of moral conscience and self-criticism. He slouched back to the easy chair, leaden-eyed, and looked off into space, his legs giving way beneath him. As he flopped into the cushiony softness, he thought he could still hear screams and mad laughter in his ears, whirling together into windmills of insanity. Quite likely the world belonged to hoodlums after all, to the bugs, to Bluegrass, the Mafia, the Nuremberg Numero Unos.

In the final analysis, Harry had the capacity for a detached self-evaluation and at last knew what his number was. Zero. Zilch . . . In any case, he felt he was even more sly, more depraved than the Randoms who at least were honest enough to flaunt *their* depravity. He was a slug, a wax-kneed softie, who at parties could pollute the air with highly intellectual palaver, play Mr. Know-it-all in editorial offices, sound off melodramatically to his mistress or wife when feeling cornered and defensive about the true meaning of life, honor, truth, and other noble qualities. But in the end no Sakharov he! One who was ready to *accept* the consequences for breaking the law, moral or otherwise, be it for mugging, political dissent, or infidelity. No, in his mind's eye Harry amounted to little more today than the silent majority in America that did not protest the injustice of the Vietnam war. Hell, why not admit it? He was one of those "good Germans" the TV documentaries and books about World War II always mentioned, one of those who just stood by silently and watched and blamed everything in retrospect on those animals who wielded the butt of the gun—or today—the gladiatorial Maoist trigger. And corporate swagger stick. New York, America, the world was bursting at its seams with the potential membership of KGB-ism, CIA-ism and SS-dom, and on the other end of the stratum—make no mistake about that—stood the "good, silent" Bensonnys, the helpless shoulder-shruggers who watched and let things be. The short of it was: the democratization of evil had turned everybody into a "nigger." Where in God's name were the Bonhoeffers of the Forties, the Berrigans of the Sixties? Where was the probity Margaret Mead found among the simple Samoans in the Twenties?

Only the Satans appeared to reign supreme, supported by the distant right-wing and leftist literati; only the demons that nobody tried to exorcise any longer seemed to take advantage of free choice and plundered the world with impunity and execrable malice aforethought. Years ago it was different. Clarence Darrow spoke for the poor and the weak, but today—hell! The new Darrows sanctioned the deeds of the brutes and the rich! And if worst came to worst, they pardoned them!

Big multinational conglomerate business tycoons or faceless kidnappers or horse-faced psychos beyond help or cure—who cared?—it was taken for granted they'd beat the rap. And in between were the masses, acquiescing, resigned to plea-bargaining, forlorn, clamped in a vice of acid and alcohol and boiled in pot that corroded their free will to fight back! No George Washington, Tom Paine, Napoleon, Lenin for them to come as the knight in shining armor, no god to hasten to *their* aid. The U.S. was turning from a country of the future into a country of the past. Oh yes, this land had become a searing indictment unto itself! And who knew, perhaps the mod 20th century monsters were right after all! Just as Hitler according to his own laws and convictions felt that he was morally right in killing, so people today, each according to *their* law (the law that in this society one had the right to get one's share of the take by hook or by crook), believed that they too had to obey the inner voices of their storm trooper consciences. And killing, like being victimized, became morally acceptable to everyone in his own light. Who could tell, perhaps it was this that turned out to be the basic premise of

God's very own natural laws and practices, too. Being cruel or being benign finally had nothing to do with life . . . unless you were at the receiving end of destiny's whip.

34 ⎯⎯⎯⎯⎯

The strident metallic buzz of the front door shrilled like a circular saw into Harry's inner snakepit of growing worthlessness, into his nihilism, his manic depression. He sat up stalk-stiff, rubbed his eyes, startled. Maybe it was Helga! Bringing the money! Perhaps there *was* a God after all!

Clouds of fatigue, of despair, vanished as if by magic and in less than a smidgen of seconds he reached the front door and pulled it open. The unconcerned moony grin of Martin Mottello flashed across the threshold at him.

"Oh, it's you."

"Hell, don't sound so happy about it," his friend smirked sheepishly. "And you look kinda lousy. Can I come in? I've only got half an hour."

"Sure." Harry stepped aside. "Make yourself at home."

The two men moved into the living room and Harry collapsed again in his easy chair, once more tired, listless, depressed in the face of insurmountable odds. So Helga had let him down, after all.

Martin regarded his friend suspiciously as he pulled down the zipper of his windbreaker.

"No luck, huh?"

Harry looked up, not getting the message. "What?"

"I mean with the house."

"What're you talking about? What house?"

"Jesus Christ, what the hell is the matter with you?" Martin did not take his eyes off Harry as he settled down on the sofa. "Isn't that what you saw your friend about? What was his name? Ed? To get the dough for your house?"

"Oh that!" Harry shook his head, not so much in negation to the question as in disbelief that anybody should still be so misinformed about his plight. Saturday seemed years away in any case. "Ahh, might as well forget about it. No dice. Just didn't work out with the house." He had no intention of bringing the ugly scene with Ed Blakely into the conversation and the fight that ensued over Helga. "You can't sell a house on such short notice, Martin. I should have known better, of course, but it just didn't add up to anything."

Martin let out a low whistling sound. "Jeez. Looks kinda rough for you, doesn't it? What are you going . . . What *did* you do? I tried to reach you all day yesterday. And today. But you were always out."

"Yesterday?" Harry knotted his brow, trying to reassemble his thoughts. Dazed and heavy-lidded as he was, he could not afford to lose his mind now. "Oh yeah. The car. I tried to sell it. Was out most of the afternoon but might as well have saved myself the trouble. The most they offered was four hundred."

"I see. But you had that Dodge quite a few years." Martin started toying with the ashtray on the coffee table. "Two down and . . . how much to go?"

Harry shrugged. "Not a hell of a lot, that's for sure. I can't even withdraw all my savings from the bank because Ruth and I have a joint account. And with the market in a slump, we converted all our shares to cash, floated our stock some time ago, didn't even reinvest it into treasury bills. I'd forgotten all about it."

Martin looked up from the ashtray. "How much did you come up with so far?"

"Eight grand."

Again a low whistle. "Eight . . . Christ, that ain't much. And how much did he ask for? Twenty-five?"

"Thirty."

"Shit! What the hell're you going to do, Harry?" But Harry only shrugged again. "Couldn't you ask for a loan?"

"Now what sort of an asinine question is this? What in God's name do you think I . . ."

"Look, Harry, I'm only trying to be helpful."

290

"Okay, okay, I'm sorry." He shut his eyes for a moment and sucked in a deep breath. "Matter of fact, to be absolutely honest, I did try to get a loan. In fact, two loans. But niente again. They wanted to know why and I gave them some cock and bull story about Ruth being in surgery in Maine and that the hospital asked for the money. But they wanted to know: where is the bill, give us the evidence. And then they went to check on my character references. And even if it worked out all right—and one of them sure as hell didn't buy any of it—I couldn't have gotten the money till tomorrow. So what on earth am I going to tell that son of a bitch now? Wait till the bank's good and ready? You *know* what happened to Ives' wife. That guy won't be stalled, not for one second." The two men looked at each other in absolute silence, motionless, like statues. Martin had stopped playing with the ashtray. "Martin, I no longer know what to do."

The words came out almost inaudibly, the desperate whisper of a man who had tried and failed. Martin started to fidget nervously, unable to be of much comfort. He glanced at his watch.

"God, it's much later than I thought," he said and began to join the two bottom parts of the zipper on his windbreaker. "Evening shift starts in a half hour and I really should be going, Harry. Just came to see if you made any headway."

"Yeah, yeah, of course." Harry kept staring at his discomforted friend, expressionless, without revealing what was on his mind. "Say, Marty, you remember that dough I lent you some time back?"

Martin looked up from his windbreaker. "The thousand bucks? Sure. What about it?"

"I know I told you there was no need to pay it back till you got at least three or four thousand saved up yourself; but don't you think, under the circumstances, I could get it . . ."

"Now hold on, Harry! What the hell do you want me to do?" For the first time since hearing of Ruth's abduction on Friday night Martin was betraying some signs of alarm, in his face and voice. "I haven't even got two grand together yet and you want me to . . ."

"But can't you see that this is an emergency? When *you* were in hot water Ruth and I gave you what we had saved up, so why . . ."

"Harry, for crissakes, will you wake up! Even if I *could* give you the money it wouldn't do any good. The banks are all closed. They close at three. It's nearly a quarter to four."

"Quarter to . . ." Harry glanced at his watch, white as a sheet. "Are you sure? I've only got a quarter past three."

"Of course I'm sure. I just listened to the three-thirty bulletin. Ford sent Kissinger packing some place again and the hurricane is beginning to abate off the coast of Maine."

"Jesus! Damn thing must have stopped again this morning." He reset the wrist watch, advancing it thirty minutes, muttering something about "bastard watch," then looked up aghast. "Only a little more than an hour! At five, the note says."

"I know. God, even if I were the richest man in the world, how could I get twenty-two thousand dollars together in that time? And what good would it do you if I withdrew all my savings, twenty-eight hundred all told, and gave you your thousand? You really think that s.o.b. will be any more accommodating with ten thousand eight hundred than with eight thousand?"

Harry rubbed his face, again went with his hands through his unruly hair. "You're right. Of course, you're right," he sighed. "Christ, I no longer know how to take it—whether to be resigned to her fate or go crazy. Or to take it on the chin, like a man—you know, the grim Kirk Douglas square-jaw type."

Again Martin began idling with the ashtray. "Harry, do you mind if I asked you a personal question?" He did not look up, just kept his eyes glued to the coffee table. "If something goes wrong—and you must have considered the possibility, not that you didn't do a dynamite job, though with precious little to show for it, but . . . well, if he goes through with his threat, and Ruth . . . what would it do to you?"

He looked up then and saw Harry's grim eyes staring back at him. "Do?" The agony lay buried deeply behind those dark smoldering pupils. "I don't know." He shrugged. "Maybe I won't even know until well after it's all over. Who can tell? Ives certainly didn't take it too well. He loved his wife while I . . . speaking for myself we seemed to be hibernating . . . existing . . . together. Like those two African violets, each independent of the other, yet strangely, symbiotically, intertwined just the same."

"But the feeling, the passion is gone."

"Passion! My God! For passion I had Helga. Though that too probably is only a matter of time. You get a woman," he suddenly said absently, "like a kidnapped victim, and then . . . you don't know what to do with the loot." He shrugged, and the next second pulled himself together. "But be this as it may, Marty, like Helga, Ruth also is a human. So what can one say about passion, about the way I feel? It really is just like a fire that grows cooler by the year . . . and yet," he frowned, as if sensing something distasteful in coming to this conclusion, "yet somehow it miraculously manages to retain a warmth all its own; it won't let go of us . . . almost as if we were prisoners of the tides of the heart."

A long span of silence stretched between the two men.

"And love?"

A brief shrug of the shoulders underlined his confused inner thoughts. "It isn't passion, Marty, and all of a sudden it isn't indifference any more either. I don't know what lies in between, but I believe love is too strong a word for it, that confident reliable feeling where each finds in the other what they hunger for most." Suddenly a mood of the darkest despair welled up within, surged forward, overcame Harry, and he buried his face in his hands. "Lord! Hell, it's all so futile, this fight. And for what?" With equally sudden force he looked up at his friend. "What I want to know is: why me, Marty? Small potatoes like me? I've never done anybody any harm, deliberately . . . even though I did find out today I don't amount to much more than a zero, that I'm callous enough to shut both eyes when harm befalls others." He smacked his right fist into his palm. "Here I am, Marty, an unexceptional guy who is on the straight and narrow, breaks no laws, though perhaps, morally, a rule of decency here and there, who pays his bills on time, his taxes, without trying to gyp the government with phony deductions. I work like the devil, can*not* depend on gifts from Rockefeller, or lulus from Lockheed, smile when I feel like retching, I use underarm deodorant, regularly, and still work up a sweat over the Mets or when remembering Bobby Thomson's '51 homer. Dammit I've even resigned myself to go on living without any new dreams, a fellow who knows he's not among the chosen few but in a deadend job, like everybody else, and that the best he *can* expect of life is, maybe, three weeks of vacation in Maine or the Bahamas, a weekend in the country, or a New Year's party with friends till six in the morning . . . Restless and traveling . . . yet like Chekhov's 'Three Sisters' I'm trapped. . . and leave nothing behind." A driving anger propelled him from his seat and he confronted Martin, almost challengingly, hands buried in his pockets, "It's a riot, ain't it, pal, a real gas—merely making out means being the typical middle class American hero. None of that Beatty or Newman or Redford glamour about me, just a premature Willy Loman who knows his way to Chumley's and Tuesday's, and who has asked himself countless times 'Is this all there is?' But I guess it's the same for all of us . . . the bosses we can't afford to talk back to, fear of unemployment and war. You name

293

it, we have it. Credit it all to an act of God . . . and a marriage going on the rocks. C'est la vie." He wet his lips with the tip of his tongue. "And now a mistress who is a question mark . . . another laugh, right?"

Again Martin regarded his friend for a long while, not uttering a sound. His eyes met Harry's without flinching and the latter suddenly felt terribly self-conscious, wondering what had caused him to bring all this deep-dish stuff up at this most unpropitious of moments. He turned from Martin, in embarrassment, and shambled across the room to the rows of glass and china figurines spaced evenly along the wall shelves. Christ! He had forgotten to dust them the night before.

"Harry," Martin's voice trailed after him. "I think you're just feeling sorry for yourself." Harry wheeled on his friend, angered not only by this outrageous, callous remark when his wife's life hung in the balance but even more so for being recognized for what he was. "Not that I blame you, not in your situation," Martin added hastily. "But the battle's not lost . . . till it's over. So, let's leave this heavy stuff, this what's-the-point-of-it-all sermonizing to Norman Vincent Peale . . . who at least has a punchline." Continuing with a sheepish grin, "even if all you say is true. And sure as Rex Harrison singsonged, you're just an ordinary man. Still, aren't we all? Welcome to the club! But . . . but why not go one step further then, and figure that in five billion years the whole caboodle, for the small potatoes and big cheese *and* beluga caviar, will be all over anyway. *All* our dreams and glory will have come to nothing, turned to dust."

He waited a bit to let this sink in and then, out of the depth of his being, there grew and growled a rumbling laugh, a laugh Harry failed to comprehend. But as suddenly as it appeared it stopped. "Snap out of it, Harry," Martin said sharply. "Philosophizing and rationalizing everything in terms of eternity, or even the present, does not solve your problem in any way whatsoever, and is better left to Leibniz and Company anyhow. This is hardly the time for abstract thinking. *Or* bellyaching. Destiny means to *undo* early programming. Battles are won by decisions."

Through most of Martin's mini-sermon Harry's hand had rested on one of the china figurines, a Meissen swallow about to take flight, and he shifted it a couple of inches now to the left, instantly aware of the light spot it left behind. "Decisions, sure," he muttered more to himself than to Martin. "Yeah. Question is: what decision *now*?"

"Right on—what decision *now* is right!" Martin forced his advantage cautiously, rubbing his lips with the knuckle of his thumb. "Like that rather ugly question, for example, you still didn't answer."

"What?" A glint of suspicion entered Harry's voice. "What question?"

"Suppose . . . uh . . . suppose Ruth did *not* return . . . the possibility must have occurred to you . . . but that she was found somewhere . . ."

Harry walked along the shelf of figurines, tracing his index finger along its edge, until he came to the end of it. On the bottom shelf lay some twenty-five dollar Pumas, a Dunlop tennis racket and a canister of Slazengers. They had not been touched by Ruth since the onset of her heart ailment—how beautiful her sun-tanned legs looked in her white tennis shorts!—his Chris Evert of the 1950's!—but she could not bring herself to give these things away, hoping against hope that one day she might take up the sport again. Harry had given his set away, refusing to play another game of tennis with anyone until she was well enough to challenge him. That was years ago, and his foot now toyed with her racket on the bottom shelf.

"As you're well aware, Marty," he said quietly, not looking up from his rain-splattered shoe tracing the outline of the racket, "there was no animosity between Ruth and me, but in the ordinary sense, I just wasn't in love with her anymore." He shrugged. "Who knows, last night I even felt that love wasn't the most important factor in a marriage . . . but dependency . . . Of course, we passed that "me Tarzan, you Jane" stage long ago. But now. . . . We were just creatures of habit living together."

Martin rose from the sofa and walked over to the pile of phonograph records, gazing at the picture of the jacket on top. "You know you should never blame yourself if anything has happened to her."

"I certainly don't want her to die, if that's what you mean."

"Of course not." Martin picked up the album and took note of one of Mozart's symphonies, the "Haffner," underneath. "But am I wrong in assuming that you're not so much looking forward to your wife . . ." He glanced up, focusing hard on his friend ". . . as to trying to recapture a long-lost love?"

"Does it really matter which way?" Harry stared back at the man opposite him, trying to decipher the meaning behind this conversation. "I don't know if love would enter our relationship again. Probably not." For a few seconds he studied his fingernails. "Though for the first time in years she means something to me again," he said pensively. "Not love, I think, but something just as necessary. God knows what.

A touch of some human thing I've become accustomed to . . . If only I could put my finger on it . . . Oh dammit!" Again he rammed both fists into his pockets. "She must not die, Martin. I won't be a party to it. And I'll fight to the last to save her if it's in my power."

His grimness was somewhat relieved by Martin's unmerry smile. "I know what you mean. The embers refuse to give up that last unmistakable glimmer. Right? As you were saying, we're all prisoners of the heart's tides. It's the same with me. If only I knew where Patti was . . . I'd . . ."

"But it's not love, Martin. I'm sure I *love* that woman next door and you know it."

"Aw, cut it out, Harry. That's not love. That's lust and *you* know it— a renascent desire to recapture your youth . . . to prove to yourself that you're still attractive to women . . . can still conquer them."

"Look, Marty, I'm old enough to distinguish between love and sex. Besides she isn't a young girl to whom I have to prove my manhood."

"Oh brother! The same clichés of middle age creeping up on a tired schmuck! Why not sit down and write the book the world's been waiting for?"

"Now come on, no need to be so smug! Helga is . . ." He stopped in midsentence, frowning.

"Well?"

"I don't know. I only feel I love her . . . It's a more intense feeling than I have for Ruth . . . And yet . . ."

"Couldn't it be pity too?"

"No, it's not that." He shook his head decisively. "Oh, I'm aware of the hell she went through and it's bound to touch the heart of any decent person, but I loved her even before I knew any of the gruesome details."

"And the dame loves you, of course."

"She wants to marry me, Marty. I can offer her nothing. She's the one who'd bring the money into the marriage. Not that she's wealthy, but still, she's got quite a lot more than I have."

"What makes you so sure?"

"Well, you know her book hit the best-seller lists a few years ago. And she still has quite a lot stashed away."

"Oh." Martin looked absently at a few more of the record albums, then replaced them all as he had found them and turned back to Harry, perplexed. "I don't get it, Harry. If she has the dough, and I know how much a best seller can earn you—even if I spent it all on that stupid gumshoe and his agency—why don't you ask *her* to advance you the twenty-two thousand? She should be able to swing that much. Especially if she's so crazy about you."

"Ha." Harry broke into a short, unamused guffaw. "Don't think for one moment I didn't try. On Saturday after I saw Blakely. She knows all about Ruth, now. There was no way I could get around it. But as far as the money goes, I might as well have talked to a brick wall."

"Holy Moses! You mean she wouldn't help you?"

"We had a terrible fight over it. She seems to feel that if she helps me out and Ruth really comes back that I might change my mind again and not ask her for a divorce. The way things stand she actually believes for once the odds are working in *her* favor and she doesn't see why she should upset the apple cart and help bring back the only person who stands in the way of her happiness."

Martin let out a long brittle mock laugh. "Funny. Remember when I said good night to you on Friday? After you first told me about the kidnapping, and I asked why you should want to try so hard to free Ruth when you felt like getting hitched to the broad next door? Hell, you seemed pretty pissed off!"

"Of course I was steamed! How did you expect me to feel? After all, Ruth was . . . *is* my wife. There's no reason in the world why she should die. Above everything she is a human being, and just because the passion has worn off between us, that's no excuse by a long shot for me to want her all carved up, is it?"

"Certainly not. But did you make all this clear to gorgeous Miss Lipsolm?"

"What do you think? I pulled out all stops, Marty. I tried to get her to see that she is behaving as cruelly as the aloof wives of the concentration camp guards except that it *is* within *her* power to help the victim. I think . . . no, in fact I know she would have been willing to come up with any amount to pay off somebody else's ransom if I'd asked her to. But as far as Ruth is concerned she didn't feel much like handing her back to me. Which in my humble opinion almost makes her an accomplice in this crime."

"Jesus, now take it easy, will ya? First all this big passion for her and now you make it sound as if *she* actually was responsible for everything."

"Well, isn't she? In a way, Ruth's release can be said to rest in her hands alone. She's the only person now who *can* help me and I made no bones about it to her."

"Aah, come on—I think you're going a little too far now," Martin objected. "Perhaps she thought you had some bonds or high grade corporate securities with a 9 per cent return that . . ."

"She knew damn well I wasn't able to sell the house and that's where the big money was supposed to come from."

"Okay, I can understand your being upset about not meeting the ransom, and this certainly isn't anybody's fault, but you can hardly hold her responsible if anything happens to Ruth."

"And what the hell would you expect me to do? Marry this dame if that crazy bastard should really go through with it and kill Ruth? And once Ruth is out of the way—as Helga put it—the coast is clear for wedding bells? Martin, put on your thinking cap! Maybe you haven't developed the characters of real life dramatis personae well enough yet in your literary brain. But the manner in which you and Helga think things through right now is nothing less than one-dimensional."

"Thanks a lot, Mr. Editor." Martin tried to hide his hurt ego, but quickly dissipated the pain in his next verbal outpourings. "Still, can you actually look her squarely in the eye, now, this very minute, and tell her that if she provided the ransom in full and Ruth comes back alive that you'd welcome your wife back home and then spring the surprise of a lifetime on her and threaten her immediately with a divorce? Can you *do* that, Harry? And do you really believe that Miss Lipsolm expects you to go through with it? Because *I* don't."

Harry only glared at his friend, but did not utter a word.

"Maybe this time *you* haven't thought things through, Mr. Editor," Martin resumed his line of attack, "and it's *you* who's the one-dimensional Mensch. Just look at it from Helga's point of view and perhaps you can understand her feelings too."

Harry glowered at Martin a little while longer but finally moved from the wall shelves and sank back into his easy chair. "Yeah, of course you're right," he said tonelessly. "I do understand her. I love this woman, and yet I hated her too on the few occasions I thought of her in the last couple of days. You may not believe this, Marty, but there were times yesterday when I detested Helga's attitude so much I almost wished she *was* involved in the kidnapping. To justify my bitterness, my feelings toward her. It would have made it easier blaming Ruth's death on her, that is, *if* it happens. I even figured out a number of reasons why she might be behind the kidnapping. Like her telling me that she could kill Ruthie. And then . . ."

"She said that?" Martin asked, shock mingling with incredulity. "*After* you told her about the kidnapping?"

"No, no. That was on Friday afternoon. When we were making love. Remember when you saw me coming home early from work and I told you at eight o'clock that I had just returned from the office—or was it at nine?—and you challenged me because . . ."

"Yeah, I do. But Harry, you can't hold that against Helga. That's a sheer figure of speech. How often have I said I wished I could kill people I didn't like, or who bugged me. And tell me quite frankly now, did you take offense when she said it?"

"You mean Friday afternoon?" Harry frowned. "No, I didn't."

"There, you see! No, don't gimme that crap about her being involved in this crime. I've seen her—she's a beautiful chick, and I've read both of her books. I can assure you she's not capable of harming a fly."

"Oh, no?" But Harry stopped himself at once. Not in a million years would he divulge to anyone what Helga had confided to him about her brother Fritzi. She had suffered enough over him these last thirty years. But then it struck him with the force of a Mack truck that if she—even though a child at the time—had been capable of sacrificing her little brother whom she loved so desperately in order to save her own skin, might she not be equipped in equal measure with a conscience to rationalize the necessity of sacrificing her lover's wife whom she hated, for the sake of her own happiness, her sanity? Almost like Faulkner's Temple Drake. Two indirect murders by a decent woman!

"You seem to be taking issue with my assumption," Martin's suspicious words sneaked into Harry's somber reflection.

"No, I was just thinking," he snapped out of his reverie. "It's not a matter of killing anyone, Marty, especially if she doesn't have to do it herself. She could have hired somebody to do it for her."

"Holy shit! Now I've heard everything!" Martin exclaimed. "You really *are* off your rocker! Why in God's name should she want to hire somebody to abscond with Ruth? That's patently absurd. Right out of Captain Marvel. Where would she find someone to do the dirty work for her? Does she really travel in those kinds of circles? Or would she advertise for a professional killer in the Sunday "Times" classified? Harry, I think you're letting your imagination get the better of you. And besides, what about that ransom letter? From what I can see it's the same guy who killed this Ives woman. Now where in the name of heaven would Helga get hold of his name and address? I thought the police didn't even know his identity. But you are so darn sure Helga does, eh?"

The white knuckles of Harry's fists pressed painfully together as he sat there, elbows resting on his knees, and again he glared at Martin. "You absolutely finished?" he asked sullenly. "Has your masterpiece of deduction been polished down to the final draft, Mr . . ."

"Don't be such a supercilious ass, Harry! You know perfectly well your theory that she's involved in this crime doesn't hold water, and that it's based on nothing more than a hunch. Not even that. Just plain galling spite and malice on your part because she wouldn't cough up the dough. Now to be quite frank I think she *made* a mistake. Depriving you of the money will only help to alienate her more and more from you—just the opposite of what she wants. But she seems so wrapped up in her love for you that she can't seem to see straight, with all her brains and what a critic in the papers called 'her superhuman quality of compassion.' But it's always easier to be noble on paper when things go well than in action when things get rough. There are just too damn few Lincolns and Einsteins and Mother Teresas in this world. But then people always react differently to crises, and this spunky little lady next door is no exception, having had her fair share of troubles in her lifetime. She has probably lost so much in life she just can't bear the thought of losing another thing she loves: you. And here you go behaving like a big prick trying to blame it all on her if she lets you down. Hell, I never saw you like this. One bad crisis and you fly off the handle! I bet if you had been born black in the squalor of some ghetto you'd even out-Cleaver Eldridge Cleaver!" A big grin immediately crinkled the corners of his mouth. "End of defense."

"Yup. End of defense." Harry rose again, massaging his chin, realizing he had been justifiably squelched. "But again," he murmured, "the question remains: where does all this leave me?"

"Well, it isn't five yet. Why don't you try to give her another ring and . . ." Martin glanced at his watch and his head shot up. "Holy cow! I gotta get my tail outta here or I'll be late." He fastened the zipper on his windbreaker for the third time. "Look, Harry, it's almost a quarter past four. I gotta split. If there really is an emergency give me a call at the supermarket. I'll be there till around nine-thirty. If it's absolutely necessary I'll ask Jerry to pinch-hit for me and hurry back. But I've got to go." He bounded up the three stairs in one giant leap

300

and headed for the front door. "See if Helga's home and plead with her once more. Maybe she . . ."

"I rang her bell before you came down. But there was no answer. I think she deliberately stayed away this afternoon so she wouldn't have to face me and hand over the money."

Martin had already opened the door, but turned to Harry once more. "Well, try anyway. There's a chance she's back . . . Or as our old friend Hölderlin used to say, 'It's when danger is greatest that salvation is closest' . . . Right? In any event," he shrugged, "you've only got about forty-five minutes. What've you got to lose?" He gave him a good-luck wink. "Okay, in case you need me, you know where I am."

He slammed the door and left Harry standing in the living room. It had grown dim; most of the dull October daylight had seeped out of the leaden sky and was slowly being replaced by dusk. He knew Martin was right. What did he have to lose? He could give it one more try and see if Helga was in. It was his very last chance.

He drew the drapes and turned on the light and went into the bathroom to freshen up. He would very simply put his cards on the table, face up, when confronting Helga and tell her in a few words what the score was . . . that he was ready to go for broke. And he would not let himself be prodded into creating a scene. Whether she suspected him of a reborn affection for Ruth was one aspect which he would not argue with her if he could help it. It was too complex, both for her as well as for him. Something was happening. All he knew was that he wanted Ruth back. Alive. Unhurt. In his apartment. And he wanted Helga too. Undoubtedly, spokespersons in the Steinem domain would have no difficulty in exposing him as a faithless sexist chauvinist. Or one with too much spurious loyalty flying in both directions simultaneously, with each loyalty finding a landing place on a different stage safely tucked in the human psyche somewhere between the polar extremes of hot passion and icy indifference.

He dried his face and hands, turned out the light in the bathroom and hung his topcoat in the hall closet. From the foyer he surveyed the room once more, making sure that everything was in perfect shape. His eyes fell on the telephone. He rushed back into the living room, went over to the roll-top desk and got out a Number 2 Venus pencil and a legal-sized yellow pad, placing both on the sofa, so he could jot down all instructions without wasting any precious time when the kidnapper called him. Another thing occurred to Harry then. He lifted the telephone and on its back side found the small disc that could be adjusted to "Soft" and "Loud." He turned it with his thumb to its maximum decibel, to make certain that he would be able to hear the phone ring if he was in Helga's apartment.

At the front door he gave the living room another cursory appraisal, decided on leaving the light burning to be prepared for all eventualities, knowing that the next time he entered the apartment his life would have changed drastically, for better or worse.

35 ══════════

This time he only locked the
upper of the two Yale locks and finally made his way down the deserted
hall to Helga's apartment. Another glance at his watch convinced him
that he could not afford to dally too long, thirty minutes at the most. He
pressed the button and heard the buzz inside Helga's apartment. He
waited a short time but there was no response—as he had dreaded.
Seconds passed before he placed his finger again on the bell, this time
leaving it there, fearful that indeed she had no intention of showing up,
neither with nor without the money that could spell the difference
between life and death. Once more he waited, his heart pounding madly,
and listened for any sound liable to emerge from the other side of the
door, but at this very moment two fire engines were racing down
Riverside Drive, their sirens screaming hysterically. Full of disgust,
Harry removed his finger from the bell.

The fire engines' hoots and wails faded in the far distance and
Harry again held his head close to Helga's door to listen to any sound
that might be detectable behind it, but all he heard now was the Beach
Boys launching close-harmony style into "Surfer Girl" in one of the
other apartments and a few seconds later a Bellini recording in still

another, with either Beverly Sills or Maria Callas superbly singing an aria. Harry tried the buzzer for the third time and was about to chuck it all as a bad try, half-consoling himself that even if she came over with the eighteen thousand, he would still be four thousand shy, when he heard what sounded like a door opening inside. He rang the bell quickly, persistently, and in a matter of seconds heard the rattle of the chain as it was being removed, at the same time sensing he was being looked at through the peephole. At length the door opened.

The light was burning in the large creamy-white living room behind Helga, and the curtains were drawn.

"May I come in?"

Helga blinked up at him groggily, as if she had been roused out of a deep sleep. This time she wore an ankle-long purple robe and held the lapels together under her chin as she stepped back. Harry slipped in and brushed accidentally against her, unaware that in doing so he had knocked a battered rag doll out of her arm.

"Darling, I . . ." she started, then stooped to pick up the rag doll. "I'm sorry. I've been drinking."

The words were labored, fuzzy. Harry quickly shut the door behind him and regarded her angrily. How could she drink at a time like this?

"So I see," he said icily. "You knew, of course, I was coming to see you before five."

She was anything but steady on her feet, bobbing slightly from side to side, to keep her balance. This irritated him still further. Visions of her skin-popping Dilaudid, dropping fistfuls of mescaline, burned on his eyeballs. He moved from her, down into the living room, and she turned off the light in the foyer and followed him slowly. He waited for her near the huge white sofa where the one-eyed teddy bear rested among banks of Oriental pillows. Harry had a few minutes to spare but knew it'd be poor policy to rush things by coming right out and demanding the money. Not in her present state. Let her sober up a bit first.

"Forgive me, my sweet . . . It's just that I . . . Oh darling . . ." Her right foot caught on the leg of a small mosaic smoking table and she toppled forward, into his arms. Feeling the solid build of his body against hers, his arms encircling her firmly so she would not collapse, broke her resistance. Tears streamed down her face now, silently, and her lips sought out his. The rag doll dropped to the floor again but she was not conscious of it this time and kissed his cheeks, his eyes, saying over and over how sorry she was. Harry stood stiffly, part of his anger slowly draining out of him as he felt the tremors of her slender frame against his.

He patted her back comfortingly. "It's all right," he whispered. "It's all right, but you must stop now." She sniffled and dug her nails into the cloth of his jacket to restrain herself. But it took a considerable time before she managed to calm down and draw back her wet face. "Everything's gone wrong with us all of a sudden, Harry, everything." Untold suffering and doubts had darkened the circles under her eyes. "Why? What is happening? . . . The pregnancy, our quarrel Saturday, your wife gone and . . ." She wiped the tears off her face with the palm of a hand and peered up at him, puzzled. "What time is it, Harry?"

"About twenty-five after four."

She stiffened in his arms and shook her long chestnut-brown hair, trying to clear her head of the alcoholic cobwebs within. "Then what're you doing here? The ransom note says the kidnapper'll contact you in about half an hour . . ." A frown puckered her smooth brow. "You don't mean to say . . . Ruth is back?"

Harry only shook his head, looking her straight in the eye. Even though she seemed zonked it was amazing that no alcoholic fumes emanated from her mouth. Despite the woozy state she was in she still managed to look appealing, her pure, almost translucent ivory-pale skin tantalizingly feminine. Womanhood still was the most natural, unspoiled thing there was, he thought.

"Well, did you hear from him? Did he give you another day to raise the money?"

"Nope."

Helga studied him with an increasingly bewildered expression. "But . . . I don't understand. Are you no longer interested in making contact . . . to see what happened to . . .?"

The dark shadows made her eyes appear larger than he had ever seen them before as they searched for some meaning in the silence that followed each of her questions. "No, it wouldn't be you," she said at last, shaking her head. "You are not one of those bug-people. And our nightmare *was* reality. Saturday really *did* exist, didn't it? . . ." She took a deep tremulous breath. "Harry, I've been drinking, drinking most of the weekend trying to forget. But it didn't seem to work. Not this time. Most of last night I couldn't sleep for thinking about us . . . Oh darling, why? Harry, why? You look so tired. You haven't slept. So gaunt and haggard, my love. I love you. I love you, oh God, I love you so much . . ." And she pressed her wet, hot cheeks against his, steeling her arms around his neck so hard that he could feel again her body against his as she stood on her toes seeking his lips, thirsting for him. Her mouth opened for him and not even her tongue tasted of liquor. But there was no feeling, no lust in his kiss. Anger and torment had blunted him, and he stood immobile, upright, unbending as a tree, until she finally became conscious of his unyielding stance, his icy aloofness. She pulled back, almost hesitantly, as though afraid to confirm her own doubts, her worst suspicion, and she saw his gray unsmiling features.

Her arms dropped away from him, hopelessly. "Nothing has changed really . . . has it?" she said in a flat voice.

"Ruth is still gone."

"Ruth?" The name—breaking into her own private grief—seemed to startle her. "I see."

"Today is Monday, Helga. Otherwise nothing has changed."

"Except our love."

Harry observed her in silence again, and only shook his head.

"God, you can't even bring yourself to say no," she said in a slightly more agitated voice. "All you can do is shake your head. Men are such cowards." She picked up the rag doll and cradled it at once affectionately in her arm. "Except that our love has changed, hasn't it, Harry? Or at least *your* love."

"I didn't say that. Now please don't put words into my mouth and then twist them." Harry whammed a fist into his open palm, always a sign of his growing impatience. "Listen, Helga, you know as well as I what I have come for. Not for an argument, but to see . . . whether you can spare the money."

Helga looked at him, as if not trusting her ears, then burst out with a bitter little cry of derision. "God, if that isn't a laugh! Can you spare the money? 'Brother, can you spare a dime?' To make sure I don't belong to the bug-people. Or better still, to look out for my soul. Isn't that it? An eighteen thousand dollar visa to the Promised Land for the Jewess! Right? After all, I still have to prove that I'm worthy of you, to meet the test of love, of loyalty, don't I?"

"Look, Helga," he said increasingly irritable. "Let's not be melodramatic! I didn't come here to pick a fight. If you like standing by while an innocent person is getting butchered when it is in your power to help that person, all you've got to do is to say so and I'll beat my retreat and apologize for bothering you."

"Oh, *touché, Kamerad*! That *really* hurt, Harry! It makes me truly the villain of the piece, doesn't it, the Lucrezia Borgia of the 1970's. I'm absolutely shattered, broken up." Harry sensed that her alcoholic cobwebs had began to dissipate under the sandblast of their sarcastic exchange. "Just look who's talking now—a man with the stern inflexible rectitude of an Alceste! So impeccably pure and virtuous! The very fellow who only a couple of months ago lay next to me in my bed suffering the most dreadful pangs of conscience for not going to the aid of a blind beggar being attacked in the subway by a couple of thugs— remember?—robbed of his nickels and dimes and then kicked in the groin and left bleeding by the gorillas and unaided by brave Harry Bensonny. And tell me quite frankly, my dear Harry, you with that jazzy Windsor knot, have you ever witnessed any other acts of cruelty on the streets of this fun-festival city of ours lately? Have you, Captain Courageous, ever gone to the assistance of any other victim recently who was clamoring to be saved? Surely in this fair city of ours you're bound to come into contact with such acts of depravity, almost every week. Right?"

Harry felt his heart pump wildly. The monstrously mangled grimace of Miss Laredo lying in the pool of her own blood as the vicious young cutthroats broke her shins exploded behind his eyeballs in fragmentary scarlet puffs and the word, "Bitch!" escaped his lips in guilty retaliation. "At least," he tried to clear himself lamely, "I'm not responsible for murder, for pushing my own brother into the arms of a killer. And I won't push my wife into the arms of a killer either if I can help it. A coward I may be, but at least you can't accuse me of being a killer . . ."

Helga stepped forward and the full impact of her right hand exploded against his cheek. The unexpectedness of her blow came with such force, it caused him to sprawl sideways, into the buffet.

"You bastard!" The two words hissed through her teeth and her eyes darkened dagger-deep with hatred, with the sharp pain of betrayal. "Well, finally we have your number, Mr. Bensonny, haven't we? All you ever wanted of me was a good lay. The best of both worlds, right? A wife for a cook and some nookie on the side, next door. Most convenient. Pious fraud that you are! Hell, I wouldn't even be surprised if next you accused me of having Ruth abducted."

A little smirk of vindictiveness creased the roseate imprint of her five fingers on his cheek. "Strange you should bring that up," he said huskily, his breath flying and his heart racing like mad. "As a matter of fact, that very thought *had* already crossed my mind. After all, what've you got to lose? You already said you wished Ruth dead, so you could marry me. So it's not that far-fetched."

Helga's eyes grew larger, as she tried to grasp the words that reached her ears. "Christ, I can't believe it," she exclaimed. "I can't believe what I'm hearing. You're such an ass, Harry. If I played those words back to you on tape, this minute, you'd hide away in the farthest corner in shame. Even now I can't quite believe you mean what you're saying. I always mistook you for a rather intelligent being."

"Thanks a lot. Of course, I can't compete with your brilliant European-cultured mind, but at least let's hope that my I.Q. is high enough for you to tolerate my presence."

"Oh really? Is *that* what you hope?" She clasped both elbows in her hands. "Because somehow I have the feeling it no longer is."

"Oh yeah?" He became conscious of the blood draining out of his face. "If that's your last word, my dear lady, please don't let me detain you any longer. I certainly wouldn't want to disturb your boozy orgy. So if you'll excuse me . . ." He tightened the knot of his tie unsteadily, hoping she would apologize, say she didn't mean it, call him back, and he turned away from her to walk up the stairs into the foyer, out of her apartment, her life.

"And even if you *were* right, Mr. Bensonny, and I were involved in kidnapping Ruth," her words reached after Harry, nailing him to the spot, "would I be any more guilty than the years that contributed to the kidnapping of the love you once felt for her?"

He turned slowly, grateful for her keeping the "lines of communication" open, and, noting it was twenty-five to five, once more descended the three steps into the sunken living room.

"Somehow I had been hoping we could disagree without resorting to Strindberg's 'Dance of Death' polemics, but obviously I was mistaken," she continued embittered, betrayed. "Hell, how often I'd sworn never to reveal my secret about Fritzi . . . not to a living soul . . . till you." She clenched her fists and the knuckles stood out white, like maggots. "Obviously I was wrong. Today I realize I betrayed His trust in me. I'm not a religious person, but I believe in God, in some higher life-force, and I'm doubly glad, Harry, that you suspect me of kidnapping Ruth. I'm glad you're punishing me for trusting you. It's the least I dare expect in the way of chastisement. I can see that even now Fritzi is still avenging himself for what I've done to him. Through you."

He looked at her, ashen-faced, caught off-guard, not knowing how to react. Here he thought he could actually corner her with his half-cocked theory and instead she had turned the tables on him and was truly gratified that he had expressed his suspicions of her in this ignoble manner. He made a frantic attempt to regain his composure.

"All right, I deserved that. I know I shouldn't have brought any of this up. I certainly didn't *mean* to, but I . . ."

"Oh yes you did, or you wouldn't have done so." Her eyes were burning pinwheels of hate.

"Helga, I just had to prove to you that everyone is capable of murder. Of kidnapping. Especially if it's in the name of love. Even you."

"And this is what you came over to tell me?" she demanded scornfully.

"You've got to admit you had plenty of reason—with the baby and everything—to dispose of Ruth. And . . ."

"And so did you! Don't you deny it!" she snapped back furiously. "The words you whispered to me in bed about there being no one but me! Jesus, they shouldn't have fooled a woman my age. When a man lies between a woman's legs his brains go mushy and the strangest matrimonial pabulum and Charles Boyer romanticism gush from his cortex. Bastards like you have your brains in your testicles. And when you come, you speak of wedding bells as if your peckers were the clappers."

"I meant every word of it."

"Then you had more reason to get rid of your wife than I did."

"You're the one who's pregnant, not me."

"Thanks to whom, if I may ask? *You* don't have to go through nine months of carrying the child; *you* don't have to go through the labor pains, or the disgrace if you're left in the lurch. All *you* do is have your orgasm, and then turn over and go to sleep."

"I didn't notice you moaning with pain exactly when you wanted me to satisfy you with my tongue the way some lovers lavished their lust on Fanny Hill and George Sand's Lelia. Playing the whore of literature. Maybe you have your own kooky ideas of love and mix them up with lust, just as . . ."

"Thanks for nothing, you son of a bitch!"

". . . just as you appear to have your own strange ideas about life. And don't you deny it this time! Friday night when I learned that Ruth had been kidnapped I came over to your place, but you were so doped up on pills you probably can't recall any of it. You see, I had to look for some old newspaper, I think it was a May issue. And I found it in your kitchen, but half the pages were cut up. Not columns for your next novel, but odd little cutouts. Look, I can add one and one too if that's what you call perversion on my part. Because I think I finally hit on the solution. That ransom note in my apartment is made up of words and letters cut out of *your* newspapers. I recognized the typeface right away but refused to believe at the time you were involved in this. And I don't think it's so far-fetched by a long shot at least to *suspect* that you had something to do with the abduction. Maybe you hired somebody to do the dirty work for you. But at least as far as the message was concerned you did a pretty good job piecing the words together. With one exception. You overlooked one item—that I might detect the source of the newspaper cutouts. No, you can't fool me! I think finally I'm wise to your tricks."

His breathless delivery, the merciless accusation rooted Helga to the floor. She glared at him in utter disbelief, saying nothing for a full minute. "Are you finished? Or is there any more diatribe left over where that came from?" she asked. "Isn't it strange, Harry, that the first time our love is brought to a test, you fail. You fail miserably."

"*I* fail!! What about yourself?" he cried out. "All you come up with is a counter-accusation. I don't see you exactly volunteering a rebuttal or coming forward with the ransom to save an innocent woman's life."

"You didn't give me a chance for an explanation, you goddamned bastard," she screamed back. "You really want to know what I cut out of those papers? So you can tell your cronies about it—the way you probably already bragged to them how often you scored with me, or, better still, how I sent Fritzi to his death? Okay, if you want the answer, Mr. Cunnilingus, I'll give you the latest bulletin for your pals. Wait!"

Helga stormed out of the living room, tying a knot in the belt of her robe, and disappeared for a few seconds into the bedroom. Harry felt his heart thudding painfully against his ribcage as he waited for her to return with the evidence that would apparently clear her of his accusation. Why did he have to do this to her, he cursed himself, the woman whom he swore to love to his dying day less than three days earlier? Especially at a time like this? And indeed a few seconds later Helga did return to the living room and her arms were loaded with piles of odd paper cutouts.

"Here, look for yourself," she said in a shrill voice, dropping them in an untidy heap on the carpet by the sofa, and then shook out one left in her hand. It was a row of paper dolls, all of them in short dresses and holding hands. "There, for your information, that's what I cut out, Mr. Mike Wallace," she shouted indignantly. "Sometimes for hours on end. When I'm alone. And in despair. They're my only companions. Now go on and report *that* to the police. I'm sure they'll be delighted to nab a paper doll cutter." Harry stood transfixed as she bent down to pick up the hundreds of paper dolls and threw the scissorcraft mountain on the sofa behind her.

"I had no idea, Helga," Harry started as if in a stupor. "All I . . ."

"No, you had no idea," she whirled on him. "That's the trouble! You men have no idea in your goddamn heads when you're threatened or want to weasel out. Then it's always malice and lies and force. These dolls, for your information, Harry, are my only friends. They were the only friends I ever had in Auschwitz-Birkenau and Belsen. The Nazis would give me time off when I had my period and provide me with a pair of scissors and paper so I could cut out my paper dolls and play with them. Nothing else. That was the sum and substance of my days off for almost four years. Paper dolls. Thousands of them. In all shapes. And I talk to them, confide in them my innermost fears and anxieties. And they listen." In a sudden fit of anger, she lashed out at the pile of paper dolls behind her and flung most of them again on the floor. "And damn you, I still feel they are the only friends I have, the only ones I *can* trust," she screamed. She crumpled up on the sofa then, trembling violently, and clutched her thighs in an attempt to control the tremors. Harry watched her helplessly from where he stood, feeling like a sadist, a murderer himself, as she started gathering dozens of paper doll rows up into her lap. "Only *they* understand," she muttered.

Something inside Harry cracked, crumbled, the mirror of self-respect. "I didn't realize . . ." His voice was almost inaudible. "I just didn't . . ."

"No, you didn't, did you?" Helga looked up disdainfully, pain dulling her eyes. She plopped back into the bank of Oriental cushions and pulled up her legs, crushing many of the paper dolls and squashing the rag doll and teddy bear in the process. "No beating around the bush with you, is there, Signor Torquemada?"

"Well, you don't precisely equivocate either," he mumbled. Again they regarded each other silently, full of recriminations. The stillness somehow seemed worse than any of her accusations and caused an overwhelming surge of remorse to well up inside Harry. He knew perfectly well from the outset that she was entirely blameless in the matter of Ruth's kidnapping and that his suspicions were totally unfounded, unforgivable, yet somehow, sadistically he could not help but accuse her indirectly of participating in the crime because she failed to come up with the money. Why was he so cruel to her, the only woman in recent years to whom he could open his heart, whose beauty he drank in with a parched soul, a woman in whom he could find solace, true understanding and tenderness? Where did his brutality spring from, or differ from the physical bestiality inflicted on Miss Laredo by the savage monstrosities in their Gucci shoes and cowboy boots? Where did his perverse behavior vary from the faggotry of the sailors and Norris Random, even if it was played out on an entirely different plateau?

He approached her slowly, with the gnawing dread of rejection, wanting to make up for the pain he had caused her, the insult to her love for him, but as he walked toward her, he detected no change in the bland noncommital expression in her face. It remained alien, granite-cold, her eyes dead. And once he stood in front of her, shoving the heap of paper dolls aside with one foot, he did not quite know how to tell her he was sorry and so said the first thing that came to his mind.

"So you learned about this paper craft in Germany?" he began. "I'm . . ."

A puzzled look invaded her features. "I just told you that's the only thing they let me do in the camps," she interrupted, visibly irritated. *"Paper craft in Germany!* Such a gratuitous remark! Why don't you listen to me?"

He sat down beside her, fully aware that he had made a stupid blunder of a beginning, and placed his right hand very gently on her kneecap. As though stung by his touch, she pulled away from him.

"No, don't, please!" Mistrust and antagonism were unmistakable in her voice as well as in her physical reaction.

"Aw, come on now, knock it off, Helga. I said I was sorry. I . . ."

"Oh sure, sure. You're sorry, and all is forgiven and forgotten." She rose from the sofa, letting the paper dolls on her lap again slide to the floor, and faced him. "Let's get down to the nitty-gritty, my dear Harry. I'm pretty tired of being the female *Cosmopolitan* plaything of the year, the Woman Who Understands and Lets Bygones Be Bygones, and then walks quietly off-stage. That's what I'm supposed to be, right? To be comforter, soother, mistress. The Irene Dunne of the 1970's. But now that I've served my purpose in the clandestine game of making love under pressure, I should at least have the decency to bow out of the picture gracefully! Correct me if I slip up! That's how it's usually done, isn't it? *The Reader's Digest* myth of the Little Woman behind every man. Or am I wrong?" She was working herself up into a lather and grabbed both elbows to keep from shaking. "God, that I was stupid enough to take no precautions that night and end up with your child. Well, it's just too damn bad. After all, as you said, *I* should have known better."

"Helga, please!" Harry could not bear to look at her, instead caught a glimpse of the time; it was a quarter to five. "What more can I say? I'm sorry. I was wrong suspecting you. I admit it. Can't you find it in your heart to . . ."

"No, I can't. It's too late, Harry. I offered you my love, my innermost secrets, but you . . . you trampled on them when the chips were down. You accused me of kidnapping and of murder and hurled Fritzi's death back into my face. You strangled my love and you spat on it."

The chill of fear, of losing everything, everyone he held dear started under his breastbone and reached out like iced tentacles until he could feel the desolation of loneliness fill the marrow of his entire being. Ruth, and now Helga. While love could be painful, want of love was infinitely worse, life without meaning, without joy. Harry wanted to take Helga into his arms and vow he would ask Ruth for a divorce, once she returned to him unharmed.

He was miserable. "Darling, can't you understand?" he said plaintively. "In spite of everything I love you. But love can be like a tyrant. With this thing hanging over me, Helga, my nerves are on edge, on the verge of snapping."

"So are mine!" she lashed back. "And your seed inside me, Harry. I don't even know why I should go on carrying it. I . . ."

"What?"

"Yes, you heard me. I thought about it all weekend. I wanted a child with you. Desperately. *After* our wedding. But now I'm not so sure anymore. Now that I have seen the real macho you. It was a child conceived on a lie, Harry."

"No, it was not! It was a child conceived in love, Helga. I swear it was."

"Well, fuck your love!" she shouted. "I've seen a side of that love today. Ruth's kidnapper put it to a test. And if that is the kind of love you promise me for the future you can keep it and shove it you-know-where!" She was screaming now, leveling an accusing finger at him. "I don't want any part of it, any part of your life, *or* your child. I have had it, had it up to my neck." Suddenly she was sobbing, her body racked by an uncontrollably violent spasm, and she turned from him, hiding her face in shame in the crook of her elbow. "There's a limit to what a woman can take . . . and I've just about reached it . . ."

With that she dropped her arms and suddenly, without warning, made a dash for the buffet, where her purse lay between two crystal bowls brimming with fruit. She grabbed the handbag and fidgeted with the catch, desperately trying to pry it open with the impatience of someone all thumbs and too clumsy to force it. "I don't want to see you again, Harry," she sobbed. "I never want you to come here again . . . Dammit, why doesn't it open? . . . Harry, never again . . . I realize I'm not worthy of you or I would never have aroused all these suspicions . . . I can't hold any man's love . . . This is the end, Harry, the absolute . . . end . . . God . . . I just don't want to go on living . . ."

"No, Helga, don't!" He leaped from the sofa, for a fraction of a moment stopped, undecided, then charged over to where she was standing, fumbling with the defective catch of her purse, suspecting the worst. "Helga, don't, for God's sakes!"

Dodging around the cocktail table, he lunged forward, stumbled over a Chinese Chippendale chair, sending it sprawling, and reached out, grappling at once for the handbag. "Will you let go! Are you crazy?"

"Stay away!" she screamed. "You can't do this to me!"

That was all he needed. A suicide on his hands. A lifetime of crises and tragedies ending in his presence.

"Helga, please, be reasonable. Give me the purse!"

They both struggled for it and he was surprised by her unexpected feline strength as she tried to wrest it from him.

"No, Harry, no!" she cried, the tears blinding her. "Let me do it! Don't . . . don't ruin it all . . . I've nothing else left . . . it's the last thing I want to . . ."

"You're not going to *do* it! I won't *let* you!"

"It's *my* life, Harry, let me . . ." she pleaded through her pitiful sobs.

With one last superhuman effort he yanked the purse from her, stepping back quickly, out of her reach. She stared at him through her tears, white as a sheet, utterly defeated, and then folded up on the floor, kneeling, head bowed forward on the Aubusson carpet, sobbing, sobbing heartbreakingly, her whole body aquiver.

"Harry . . . Harry . . . why . . .?"

Harry stood in the middle of the room, beside the upset chair, his shoulders heaving from the effort of struggling with the woman. He was shaking all over, almost blinded by the sweat of anguish pouring down his face, and he wiped his brow with his sleeve.

Then he remembered the purse in his hands. For a few seconds he too had some difficulty with the catch but finally managed to pry it open to remove the weapon from her. But all he could find was some loose change inside, a lipstick and comb, her house keys, some Kleenex, a bank book and a fat envelope.

"It's all lost, all lost," she wept softly. "I knew it on Saturday."

Harry stared at the purse. "What *is* this?"

She looked up, through her tears, wiping her eyes with the back of her hands. "The last thing I wanted to do . . . for you and me . . . to make it easier for all of us . . . and you ruined it."

He looked askance at her, not comprehending. "But the gun . . . where is it?"

"The gun?" She stood up shakily, her eyes stinging with tears. She staggered past him and sank to the floor in front of the sofa, hiding her face in the pillows. "I don't need a gun to die, Harry," she said wretchedly. "Look in the envelope!"

The envelope was not sealed, the flap having only been tucked into its inside. He pulled it out of her purse and opened it. There were four large bundles of money. The bank tapes indicated each contained one hundred fifty-dollar bills—twenty thousand dollars all told! He stared at it for a full minute and then at Helga. Her muffled sobs choked themselves to a deadend in the cushions on the sofa, but they still sent tremors down the entire length of her back, and he knew that he loved her, achingly loved her, and then realized that he could not afford to confess his love for her at this point because she would only link it with her generous gift and make it look sordid. Almost two-thirds of her life savings, her blood money, her security. She was doing this for the woman she hated, a woman who had stood in her way the last two years, a woman who reminded her of the death-camp bitches of Belsen and Auschwitz.

Harry had to fight back his tears—the struggle was over at long last—tears not only of love and compassion for this beautiful human being, but of shame, of disgrace.

He approached the sofa warily, filled with remorse, and knelt down among the paper dolls, beside the woman he loved. Hesitating for a few more seconds, he finally put his arm around her.

"Helga," he said softly. "I love you."

She drew from him and he could feel her body stiffen under his touch. "No, you don't!" the strangled words jammed into the pillows. "Harry, I no longer want your love. It's too late."

He inched closer to her, refusing to be rebuffed. "It is not," he said gently. "I've made a mistake, a terrible mistake. I admit it. But I love you. Honestly I want to marry you . . . when this is all over."

She still did not look up, her shoulders heaving up and down with the rhythm of her gasps for air. "If you had loved me, none of this would have happened. You'd never have suspected me."

He tried to embrace her, but her hands drilled into the cushions, like claws. Although she was making a determined effort to get hold of herself, the stifled little sobs would not stop and her hands knotted into white-knuckled fists and hammered the soft seats of the sofa. "Damn, damn, damn," she cried, and looked up finally. The tears came streaming down again; her eyes were red from crying and she backed away from Harry.

"Harry, don't . . . I beg you, don't. I can't think straight when you touch me. When you touch me . . . I can't . . ." And she fell forward into his arms, sobbing against his chest. Her arms stole around his neck as she clung to him desperately, and he patted her back with an aching tenderness, whispering that everything would be all right, and was almost moved to tears by the wonder of love that a woman's body could pass on to him. Yet his vanity was pleased, even at so inopportune a moment, that she should feel so strongly attracted to his body that her resolve to leave him seemed to disintegrate in his embrace.

Presently she drew back and cupped his face in her feverish palms. "Do you understand what I'm trying to say, my darling?"

He wiped the tears from her eyes with his finger and kissed them. "I understand," he whispered. "Oh God, Helga, I beg your forgiveness."

She shook her head. "It isn't *my* forgiveness . . . Harry . . . it's that I failed . . . I . . ."

"No, you didn't. It's me who . . ."

She placed a trembling hand over his mouth. "Not to you perhaps, my sweet. But I failed . . . myself." His eyes pleaded with her not to go on speaking. "Harry, I failed," she said hollowly. "Regardless of what you may think, I failed. For a whole weekend I felt like one of those bug-people you were talking about and that this Orwellian world is so full of. Probably because I did belong to them. I was weak like them and it is only right that I shouldn't be let off cheaply. Even though twenty thousand dollars isn't the end of the world for me. No, it's the price I have to pay for the hypocrisy of my 'prize-winning' poems. A woman of great compassion, indeed. Bull!" She sucked in a deep draft of air. "But it can't be the same between us anymore, Harry. Never!"

He took her hand into his. "You're wrong, Helga. All right, we've both made mistakes. We've both failed. Hell, three days and nights in a bull ring would kill any toreador. But we can make a new beginning and . . ."

"Harry, no!" Tears again flooded her eyes. "I no longer want to. I can't. I haven't got the strength. No . . . Harry, some people are made for marriage, others only for love. Love must be my constant companion," she smiled through her tears, "as it has in the past. Sort of a sloppy sentiment perhaps, but why not? I'm grateful for the loves I've had. I couldn't have survived without them, especially not without yours . . . Well . . ." She pursed her lips thoughtfully then, as if struck by an unexpected whiff of a reminiscence. "You know . . . what puzzles me is what alibi did the others give?"

He stared at her, baffled. "What others? What alibi?"

"That friend of yours, for instance. The one upstairs."

"What are you talking about? What friend upstairs?"

"The one on the . . . is it the third floor? Or the fourth? Martin. The writer. Or did you break with him too?"

"Helga, what on earth would he need an alibi for?"

She shrugged. "Well, maybe he doesn't. If you know what he was doing in your apartment."

"In my ap . . . When?"

"Friday. When I came home from the hairdresser's. About two o'clock in the afternoon. I saw him come out of your place."

"You *what*?" Harry's jaws dropped open. He swallowed hard. "Out of my . . . Are you sure?"

"Of course I am. I was quite surprised." Now it was her turn to register astonishment. "Didn't you know?"

"First I heard of it." He rose from the floor, and she let him go. "Why didn't you tell me before?"

"Harry, I swear I forgot all about it. He just came out of the apartment, then stepped into the elevator, that's all."

"Alone? Or with Ruth?"

"Alone." She struggled to her feet and sat down on the edge of the sofa, looking at him curiously. "You mean he didn't tell you?"

"I never even knew he was inside my apartment at that time—when Ruth was home. And I've talked to him a couple of times since Friday. *About* the abduction."

"My God!" Helga whispered. "Are you thinking what I'm thinking?"

Helga and Harry stared at each other.

"That might explain why the place wasn't ransacked, and why there were no signs of a struggle," whispered Harry. "Naturally, Ruth wouldn't think twice about letting him in." He glanced at his watch. "Only five minutes left."

He thought for a moment, then rushed to the wall separating Helga's apartment from his own and listened. It was dead-still on the other side. When he turned back to Helga, she was watching him intently. "Better get on the ball! Where's the phone book?"

"Wait." Helga rose from the sofa and hurried to the linen closet next to her bedroom. "Manhattan?" she called over her shoulder.

"Yes."

She came back with the fat directory and Harry looked frantically for the number of the supermarket where Martin now worked as shelf-clerk. At last he found it. He hastened to the white telephone, dialed quickly, nerves tingling, and waited about half a minute before blowing his stack, "For Chrissakes, why don't they answer, the bastards! Come on, come on!" His anger propelled the impatient words through clenched teeth, as Helga returned the directory to the linen closet, but the next second he leaned forward, all ears. "Yes?... No, I don't want to order anything. I want to speak to Martin, please. It's urgent. Tell him Harry's got some important news for him. Yeah, I'll hold on. Thanks."

"Of course, with him at home writing while you're out working," Helga reflected as she returned to the living room and picked up the overturned chair, "he had plenty of opportunity to get to know Ruth. Perhaps they hatched this whole thing up together. He gets the ransom—maybe he doesn't have much money of his own—and all the time she's up in his apartment. While you're actually keeping him posted on your next move."

Harry looked at her, letting her message sink in—his playing the fool Rigoletto to Ruth's Gilda and Martin's Duke—digesting it, and to his horror finding little fault with her line of logic. Then he heard Martin's voice at the other end of the line. "That you, Harry?"

"Martin? Look, I have to . . ."

"You mean he called?"

"He . . .? Oh no, not yet. That's why I have to hurry. Now tell me, Marty, quick, before he calls: when was the last time you saw Ruth?"

There was a long pause at the other end; only Martin's breathing could be heard and in the background the normal sounds and voices of a supermarket. "What?" came the noncommittal reply finally.

318

"When did you see Ruth the last time?"

"Good God, what sort of a nutty question is that? At a time like this? Harry, listen, I've got a job to do here and you have only a few seconds till that s.o.b. is supposed to call, so why this idiotic cross-exami . . ."

"I know, so answer the question, quickly. When did you see Ruth last?"

"All right." There followed a deep sigh. "Let me think. I suppose about . . . oh I'd say about a week ago."

"Like hell you did," Harry shouted. "You saw her on Friday. Didn't you?" He gave Martin a chance to rebut his charge but there was only silence, except for his breathing. "I said you saw her on Friday. Shortly before she disappeared, didn't you?"

"I don't know what you're talking about," Martin's voice came through shakily. "Or where you got such an idea."

"Never mind where. And maybe Ruth wasn't kidnapped after all. Maybe you have her locked up somewhere—in the country, up in your apartment, I don't know." Harry's voice became high-pitched and openly hostile. "You had plenty of time to go after her, didn't you? Home most of the day, weren't you, while I was away working my butt off. You with that love-nest upstairs and Patti gone for two years and you feeling hornier than ever with nobody to disturb you or to . . ."

"Now hold on a min . . ."

"Short of dough, weren't you?" Harry's blind fury swept him along on waves of growing indignation at having been cuckolded and hood-winked all these long months by his old trusted friend. "A few hundred bucks royalties dribbling in every six months, and the five rooms upstairs were hard to carry on a sales clerk's salary, right? Thirty grand would come in mighty handy, wouldn't they? Maybe I better go up to your place and find out for mys . . ."

"Shut up, Harry!" Martin shouted back. "Enough is enough! At first I thought you were kidding, but now . . . Hell, why should I have to take this crap from you, or anybody? Half an hour ago it was the broad next door who hired the killer and now it's me. *I* kidnapped Ruth! I bet *she* put you up to this to clear herself, didn't she?"

"It just so happens you're right because she happened to see you come out of my apartment at two o'clock last Friday."

"Great! So she shifts the blame on me, and you fall for it."

Harry's fist exploded on Helga's coffee table. "I want to know: were you or weren't you in my apartment last Friday?" he screamed.

"All right, now *you* shut up!" Martin yelled back, quivering with

319

outrage in the glass cubicle looking out from the rear of the supermarket over the aisles and checkout counters. "I don't have to vindicate my actions to you!"

"Oh yes, you do! With Ruth kidnapped you better tell me," Harry screamed. "*Were* you in my apartment last Friday? Or do you want me to call the cops?"

"All right—I was!" Martin shot back at the top of his lungs, upsetting a stack of invoices on the desk. "Now hold on! I did *not* see Ruth. I'd just come home, at around two, and was waiting for the elevator when the door to your apartment opened and José came out. He . . ."

"Who?"

"José. The new handyman. He asked me if I could give him a hand moving your refrigerator. Apparently it had broken down in the morning and Ruth had asked him to fix it. She must have been out shopping and come back later. You said yourself she was back around three to feed the parakeets. So I helped him shift the damn thing and then left. Whole operation took less than a minute—so short a time I'd completely forgotten about it till now, so help me God. And if you don't believe me, ask José."

Harry slumped back on the sofa, beside Helga, his face ashen-gray. "Look, Harry, lay off me! For good! I can't help it if you loused up your marriage but stop dragging *me* into your sordid affairs."

Harry let the receiver fall heavily on the cradle, momentarily closing his eyes. Then he turned to Helga and shook his head.

"Foolproof alibi." He glanced at the fat envelope that Helga was extending to him. He had dropped it on the coffee table while talking to Martin on the phone. "He was in the apartment all right. José the handyman asked him to help move the refrigerator that had broken down. Ruth wasn't even home. You must have seen him when he was leaving."

"I see." Helga nodded. "Come on—take it!"

Reluctantly, wordlessly, Harry took the envelope from her and stuffed it into his breast pocket, next to the envelope bursting with the eight thousand he had withdrawn from the bank. Helga moved close to him and opened the center button of his jacket.

"You're such a neat dresser," she chided him. "You look awful when your jacket is bulging." Adding with a grin, "especially with money. So gauche. Nouveau riche."

He grabbed her hand and pressed it to his lips. The salty rivulets of tears on her cheeks had dried into her pale skin, emphasizing the shiny dark shadows encircling her eyes. "You must go, Harry," she whispered. "A madman doesn't like to be kept waiting. You told me yourself they're afraid of having their calls traced."

"Yes." He got up but did not release her hand. "I don't care what you say, Helga. I can't live without you. Whatever happens today, tomorrow, we belong to each other and your denying it won't change it."

"Go!" Resolutely, yet without trying to hurt his feelings she slipped her hand out of his. "Go, Harry! I will always love you, too . . . but we will have to go our own separate ways."

"Helga, let's talk about it when we've calmed down," he remonstrated.

"This is how it will be, Harry," she said determinedly and rose. "In any case," she added with a smile, to soften the blow, "as Goethe said: Man can stand anything but a succession of beautiful days . . . So you . . ."

She suddenly stopped in mid-sentence, a troubled frightened look in her eyes. "Wait! Come with me. Quick!"

There was alarm in her voice as she pulled Harry to the wall abutting his apartment. They listened and distinctly heard the telephone ringing in his living room. "Hurry! You have the money!"

She gave him a shove and Harry literally flew up the three steps to the foyer and turned for a split-second at the door. Helga still stood by the wall, an expression of dread mingling with unbearable sadness in her pale, tear-streaked face. As usual, when she was tense her right hand grabbed the two lapels of her housecoat and held them tightly together under her chin.

"Good luck!" she whispered.

36 _____

Harry bolted out of the apartment, hearing the door click behind him as he ran down the hall. With one hand he fished the key out of his pocket and on reaching his door pushed it into the Yale lock, feverishly struggling to wiggle it just the right amount from right to left. In his excitement he turned the key too far to the left, almost breaking it, and cursed himself for his monumental clumsiness. Quickly, he thrust it once more into the lock, telling himself to take it easy. Inside, he could hear the telephone ringing alarmingly often, more and more teasingly he thought, as in a nightmare. At last the lock turned with a heavy snap, and the door opened. Thank God, the light was on! Harry burst into the living room and lunged for the phone, the door banging shut behind him. He ripped the receiver off the cradle, and shouted into it: "I've got it! I've got the money! Is she alive?"

"What?" came a man's voice.

"I've got the money . . . almost every penny you asked for. Please tell me . . . is she okay?"

"I don't know what the hell you're talking about," the voice barked through the wire. "Harry, this is *me* . . . Mickey."

Harry felt his legs give way under him, and he slumped back on the sofa, his heart beating wildly.

"Oh for God's sake, Mickey, not now. I'm expecting an urgent call. Gimme a ring later." The receiver was already halfway down when he heard Mickey scream.

"Like hell! You will *not* hang up on me this time! Unless you want to land on your ass and start looking for a job tomorrow."

Harry snapped the receiver back to his ear, panic-stricken. "What?"

"You know, I'm getting kinda fed up being pushed around like this. That's the third time you gave me the gate. I've tried to reach you all day but . . ."

"Look, I'm sick. I'll see you tomorrow, that's a prom . . ."

"No, you will *not* see me tomorrow," Mickey yelled back. "Because with the runaround you gimme there won't be a tomorrow for you at the office. I'll speak to my un . . ."

"What the hell're you driving at?" Harry snapped.

"Just what I said. One word to my uncle tomorrow and you're through! He'll see to it that you won't land a job with another publisher in town. That goddamn lie you fed me last week about not feeling well, like I was horseshit, and then I see that hack from the fourth floor come out of your apartment and that other crumb—yeah, I saw you go in with him—well, that may be your idea of a gag, but I don't like being snubbed. Do you hear? By *any*one."

"Mickey, have a heart!" Harry pleaded. He needed unemployment at this point like he needed a hole in his head. "I mean it. I'll see you tom . . ."

"Don't gimme that shit again! Tomorrow. Tomorrow. You begin to sound like Shakespeare. For your info, Mr. Bensonny, editors are a dime a dozen, so if you wanna hold onto your old job, you better play ball with me and deep-six all the rest, because they can*not* help you find another job. Remember, it's all up to you, Bensonny. Either we melt the ball of wax *now* and start moving the hardware off the shelf, toss it around a bit in the well and see what kind of splash it makes—or somebody is going down the tube, first thing Tuesday morning. Finished. Kaput!"

Harry doubled up suddenly on the sofa, with stomach cramps, tense as a rock, his mind landlocked one second, the next going in a whirr a thousand miles a second. "Mickey . . . have a heart . . . it's the only thing I've got left . . . my job."

"Come off it, Bensonny!" the little man shrieked into the receiver. "You're ashamed to be seen with me. That's it, isn't it?"

"I never said anything of the . . ."

"But you thought it! Just because I'm 5 foot 2. But just remember that Napoleon was short too and I'm . . ."

"That's not it at all, Mickey," Harry shouted in self-defense, pressing the knuckles of his fist between his eyes. "I swear it's not. You know we've always been pals, honest. You can't do this to me, Mick. I've always helped you out in the past. Tell you what I'll do. I'll see you in half an hour. That's an absolute promise."

"Hell, what's wrong with batting out the fungoes right now?"

A new attack of cramps knifed through Harry's intestines, pumping hot streams of acid into the wall of his duodenum, then for good measure pouring the molten lava down into his colon. He slid off the couch and rested his feverish forehead on the cool marble coffee table. "I *must* hang up," he gasped. "There's this call, Mick-baby, *please . . . please*!!"

"Goddamn, there you go again! One crappy excuse after another! First you're sick, then you're busy, and now it's a call. Next . . ."

Harry was on his knees, his damp face a pasty grimace of torment. "Mickey! Please! I'm telling you the truth, honest to God. Mickey, Ruth's been . . ."

"Man, you're the one who got himself into this fix, not Ruth," Mickey yelled with an air of utter finality. "So leave her out of it! Now, either you play it cool with me this minute, pal, or first thing tomorrow you'll find that pink slip waiting for you right on your . . ."

Something inside Harry snapped. It no longer mattered. He hung up, letting the angry little man upstairs rant and sputter his foul threats into a dead line. For Harry everything was indeed kaput. Ruth kidnapped, perhaps already murdered. A breast carved off. The fingers he had kissed chopped off her lovely hand. And flushed down a toilet. His job gone. Soon welfare. He to end up a lush like Ives. Broken like Miss Laredo. And Helga . . . his love, irretrievably gone! To hell with Camus! What did he have to offer with his demotic morals when all Harry ever loved had been rinsed down the drain. Only the Bard again held the last word in the palm of his quill-wielding hand:

> *"Our revels now are ended. These our actors,*
> *As I foretold you were all spirits and*
> *Are melted into air, into thin air . . ."*

Dear God, what *was* the use? Harry rested his head on the phone and made a supreme effort to get hold of himself. His breath came in short swift gasps and it took a good five minutes for him to calm down and steady his breathing. Who knew, perhaps the kidnapper had really made his call at five o'clock while Mickey was on the phone. Would he be willing to give Harry a second chance? After all, he had risked a great deal himself keeping Ruth in his lair, wherever it turned out to be, Harry pondered. Surely one lousy phone call wouldn't deter him from trying again to give Harry the necessary instructions where to drop the ransom. He certainly stood to gain more than anybody else this drab Monday.

When Harry had gotten control of himself, he rose heavily to his feet and slowly started pacing the floor. He searched his pockets for a cigarette—the doctor advised only one a day—and he had hardly smoked during the tense weekend. All he came up with was a crumpled empty package. He threw it into the wastepaper basket on which Ruth had decoupaged an old *Life* cutout years ago of Rubens' angels. He kept gazing at this odd little bit of handicraft, recalling her sitting with him in the kitchen one Saturday night applying varnish and a protective finish to the angelheads and telling him that she had always wanted children as cherubic as these.

A glance at his watch brought new doubts to Harry's mind. It was already a quarter after five. Why didn't he call? Or call again if indeed he had tried to reach Harry while the phone was busy before? The note had stated that Harry should be prepared for new instructions after five. He rushed to the ransom letter and lip-read once more for the dozenth time, what he could almost recite in his sleep, every word that had been pasted on it. Yes, he did say that Harry should be home alone at five. Well then, why the delay? For thirty thousand dollars surely he could be expected to make a second call even if the line had been tied up at five. Or, did he think, perhaps, that Harry was defying him with a deliberate indifference?

Maybe the police should have been brought into it after all. But no— Harry dismissed the idea at once—Donald Ives testified plainly to the fact that that was no way to save Ruth's life. And it also occurred to Harry, for the first time since seeing the ransom note, that he had not been conscious of being followed, by car or on foot, nor of being watched by anybody. Of course, these crazy bastards were shrewd all right and who could say, perhaps there was more than one guy involved.

No, all he could do was wait, alone, for the phone to ring and then to take his instructions from the unknown monster who held Ruth captive. Harry walked into the bathroom to wash his hands and face. He stared into the mirror a long time. Leaning over the basin to dab at his face, the two top-heavy envelopes almost slid out of his breast pocket and he shoved them back hurriedly with his wet hands and then dried himself with a towel, staring at his gray forties features, at his furrows, rutted with fear, that no Dr. Niehans could erase. Hell, he truly had joined the ranks of the bug-people. The whole world consisted of bug-people. But even they had deserted him. Never in his whole life had Harry felt so alone, so lost.

When he turned around to fold the towel over the rack behind him, he froze in mid-action. At first he wasn't sure why. But then he knew!

37 ═══════════

It was a sound, a familiar sound. In the apartment. He had heard it thousands of times, but had never paid it much heed. It sounded like a key turning in the front door, slowly, gingerly, carefully trying not to disturb anyone. Immediately a million thoughts zinged helter-skelter through Harry's brain. José the handyman! A burglar! Hell no—not with the lights of the living room visible from the street!

And then it dawned on Harry, dawned on him with a dreadful awakening. The kidnapper! Jesus, the monster, the insane killer of Donald Ives' wife! The ransom note stressed that he should stay home *alone* Monday night at five. There was no mention of a phone call! A phone call was merely his ratiocination of movie-kidnappers' behavior. Stay home *alone*! Of course, the kidnapper would have the keys to his apartment. *And a gun*. With a silencer. He could take Harry's money now without fear of being disturbed or . . .

The front door slammed shut. The ruthless murderer was in Harry's apartment. Alone with him. A real pro. Not like those clowns botching the Bronfman" abduction. " Harry's legs buckled and he leaned weakly against the gleaming pink tiles of the bathroom wall. Steady now! Here at last was the moment of truth! He had to know what had happened to Ruth. And he had little else to lose at any rate. If anything, he could attack him, at least *avenge* her death. And with a terrible ache of longing he suddenly wanted to be with his wife—even in death.

Harry drew a deep breath. Now or never! The next second he tasted the bile of terror in his mouth because the maniac of a criminal might fire point-blank at him, not even give him a chance to ask about Ruth's whereabouts . . . But it was too late to worry. The sooner he got it over with the better.

For an instant Harry thought his mouth was filling up with the vomit of fear, but it mattered little. He *had* to act, now!

He picked his way into the hallway, past the linen closet, his heart thundering in his throat, then slipped into the living room, prepared for an onslaught.

And stopped. Aghast.

The blood turned to ice in his veins. For one eternal moment the world seemed to be standing still, then it whirled in clusters of crystal sunbeams around his head, and again stood motionless. What he saw in front of him was a living ghost. A mirage. A being incarnate . . . a person whom he had loved once and whose love in turn unfolded now behind his eyes, like tulips touched by the morning sun, inside his heart, for the second time in his life.

"Ruth!" His voice broke and tears stung his eyes, causing her almost to vanish behind the salty wash of teardrops, as she turned toward him. Three long nightmarish days of anguish collapsed within him and the next second his legs obeyed the unspoken, unconscious will and took him in five, six gigantic steps across the room. His arms closed around her, his face burying the shame of tears in her raven-black hair. She clasped him tightly, without words, and her hands went through his disheveled hair as she kissed him with an indescribable tenderness. Her lips, the familiar fragrance of her breath, the warmth of her skin, burst like first love into his sealed heart. They held onto each other in silence, like two lost children in a raging sea, ready to go down together, but safe in the knowledge that the typhoon had passed and their sullied, storm-tossed lives still could be salvaged.

"It's all right," she whispered. "Everything's all right . . . I'm back."

She was wearing his favorite coat of hers, the hunter-green fall coat, and it made her look more beautiful than he ever remembered seeing her. They stood for an eternity in the brightly lit room, hugging and grasping, conscious of nothing but each other. It was only when she stepped back that he became aware of the overnight bag by her side, but he did not care and he cupped her face in his hands and kissed her eyes, her nose, cheeks, mouth, everything, everything he had thought he would never see again, never feel beneath his lips.

"Are you all right darling?" she asked, circling her own hands around his. "You look so pale . . ."

"Don't say anything, just let me kiss you," and they embraced again, kissing, giddy with the proximity of each other. When he finally broke away for air, he looked at her uncomprehendingly through troubled damp eyes. "Am *I* all right? Ruth, never mind me! What about you? Are you okay? That's much more important. The ordeal you . . ."

"Well, it was an ordeal, you're right. I'm half dead for sure. I haven't shut an eye in almost three days."

"Of course you haven't. But you're back. Darling, you're back. That's all that matters."

Again she went with her hands through his hair and stroked his face. "Harry-sweet, you look so ill! And you sound as if you never expected to see me again."

"God, how could I be sure? After all, it's after five. And I still don't know why he let you go. Without even making the contact."

Ruth had started to unbutton the top of her coat. But now she stopped and regarded Harry with an air of utter puzzlement. "Making *what* contact? *Who* let me go?"

"What do you mean who?" Harry emitted a brief startled laugh. "The kidnapper, of course."

Ruth's finger stopped on the second coat button and a skeptical look entered her eyes. "The *what*?"

"The kidn . . ." Harry's insanely happy expression disappeared in a flash and was replaced by one of total confusion. "Ruth, I don't understand . . . Where *were* you? And what's with the overnight bag? I don't . . . Where *were* you?"

She shook her head as if unable to follow such a simple question. "Exactly what I said in my note. I tried to reach you all afternoon yesterday." A slightly sarcastic side-way glance and mischievous smile caressed her features. "Mr. Bensonny, maybe I should reverse the question and ask you where *you* were. Gallivanting with the ladies holding up the lampposts?"

He still stared at his wife, speechless at her nonchalance. "Ruthie, for the last time, please! Tell me where you were and I'll tell you about myself. But I must know first. I *must*."

"Well, all right, all right, take it easy, honey," she said a trifle disturbed by his strange insistence, then softened her own worried face with a smile, giving the tip of his nose a peck of a kiss. "After all, it's no state secret. I thought I explained everything in the note. Mom had a heart attack, a slight one, thank God, but I couldn't leave her alone, not for a couple of days at least. Still, they're taking good care of her now. As you can imagine I wanted to be by her side in case anything happened."

"At your mother's . . ." The tears had long stopped flowing and his eyes fixed on his wife, incredulously. Was the world going mad, or was he losing his senses? "But Ruthie, I . . . The radio said no one could even reach Monhegan. Or get out of it till tomorrow. Because of the storm."

"Oh she's been in Bangor—not on Monhegan—since Tuesday, staying with friends. You remember them, the Rosenfelts, don't you? That's where it happened. So it was pretty easy to reach her. By taking that Delta flight, via Boston. But honey, I mentioned it all in the note I left you."

"The note?" Harry swallowed hard. This became eerier by the minute. "What note? Where?"

"The usual place. Even though we *haven't* had to do it in years." She pulled him toward the roll-top desk. "Here. In the typewriter, of course. You mean you didn't see it?"

"Like hell I didn't!" he exclaimed indignantly, pointing to the ransom letter with what almost appeared to be triumphant pique. "Then would you mind explaining how *this* got in there?"

She leaned forward, like Helga and Martin before, over the Hepplewhite chair, taking off her green coat, and started reading the kidnapper's ransom demand.

"Oh God, no!" Her body shot up, one arm still in the coat, as her free hand flew to her mouth, horror darkening her eyes. "Harry, oh my darling, don't tell me you . . . " But in midstream her words changed to a tone of great annoyance. "For crying out loud! I *told* him to put the note in the typewriter. That silly ass! He probably didn't realize I had written my message on the reverse side."

The more Harry heard of her evolving explanation the less he understood. "You . . . Ruthie, *what* silly ass? You told *whom* to put this note in the typewriter?"

Ruth shook her head in disbelief as though expecting everybody to know what had transpired Friday afternoon in the apartment. "Why, Mickey of course," she expounded. "Mickey Glumm. He came down last Friday, about three o'clock I think it was. I had just fed the birds

330

and changed their gravel and he wanted me to show you that idea he had thought up for the new promotion mailing piece." With this she pulled the "ransom note" out of the typewriter. "You see? Just a dummy—a come-on for that new thriller Glumm is going to publish in the spring. Sort of a mail promotion ad to catch people's attention, he said. And by the looks of it, he seemed to have succeeded beyond his wildest dreams. Here—look!" She pointed to the bottom of the note, the part that had been hidden under the typewriter's roller. "See the order coupon down here? Frankly, I think it needs some touching up here and there, that's why he wanted you to take a look at it. He said that Glumm got the mailing list of the Suspense and Mystery Readers' Club, or arranged for them to get a cheap edition of the book, and that this circular was supposed to go to their membership. With this detachable coupon. Just listen to the way Mickey put it. Maybe you can help him out. 'Will *you* be the next one to find this ransom note at home on your return from work? If you would like to know what happened to Burt Brittons and his wife and whether he actually succeeded in having her released from the maniac of a kidnapper who eluded the police and FBI, be sure to read Charlotte Manklewicz's impossible-to-put-down new mystery thriller *The Man Who Lost Everything*. Sold in bookstores for $8.95, this best-seller is available to members of the SMR Club for only . . .' "

Harry tore the letter out of Ruth's hand and stared at the reverse, then at the bottom part that he had not seen before and which held the key to his wife's "kidnapping," changing his whole life.

"Darling, what's the matter? You can't possibly have . . ."

"My God!" The blood drained out of his face. He held onto the note, but his hand started to tremble, to shake so badly he no longer could contain himself. To hide the tremors, he turned from his wife and shuffled in a daze to the sofa where he flopped down, wordlessly, still staring at the mailing piece. He felt like Graham Greene's burnt-out man, having been slammed around by destiny's monumental cannon-ball. Ending up in de Chardin's Noosphere!

Ruth did not move. From where she stood she watched him guardedly, with a mixture of utter bewilderment, perplexity and pity. "Harry, I don't know what's happened since Friday," she said at last, "but he did say he meant to discuss it with you that night after you came home from work. Matter of fact, we were talking about it in the kitchen, over a cup of Decaf, when the phone rang and the hospital called from Bangor, about Mom's attack. I tried to reach you in the office but all your lines were tied up, so I used the first thing I could lay my hands on—this note—and wrote on the back of it. Mickey was in the kitchen listening to the radio, and I didn't tell him about mother— like a fool—just asked him to put this in the typewriter while I was in the bedroom packing my bag. He probably didn't realize I had written something on the other side and then stuck it in in such a way that *my* message was covered by the roller and *his* was showing. Then he left. I think he said something about having to pick up a girl friend in Sneden's Landing, in Westchester. But naturally I expected when you came home and found this . . ." She interrupted herself in midsentence and a look of horror invaded her eyes. "Oh Harry, my God, no!" She hurried to where he was sitting bone-white and grabbed both his hands, the offending note crumpling between them. "You *really thought I was kidnapped!!*"

"What else could I think?" He looked up at her, seeing his own horror reflected in her features. "I almost went out of my mind raising the money."

"But why on earth didn't you pull the note out?"

"In case anything happened to you I wanted to make sure that the police could check on the kidnapper's fingerprints. And what's more, it just so happens that there was a kidnapping last May. Only when *that* husband got in touch with a cop the madman murdered his wife. So I couldn't afford to fool around with this guy or the cops. Do you understand now? I almost went crazy with worry."

Without another word she knelt on the carpet beside him and pulled down his face to hers, kissing him with an ardor so overwhelming, it brought back the fondest memories of their honeymoon. Her mouth would not let go of his, her arms were around his neck, and after a minute he felt the familiar warm salty trickle of her tears running down their cheeks unimpeded. In the end she pulled back to catch her breath and her eyes shone quicksilver-bright and with the glow of an immeasurable warmth that made him forget all about the letter in his hand. It dropped from him, down onto the heap of her autumn-green coat.

"But darling," she whispered, drying her face with his hand. "The ransom, the thirty-thousand dollars. How in God's name could you raise it?"

Harry was about to tell her when he realized that revealing the source of the largest part of the available cash would indeed compromise him

332

more than ever and undo the very goal he had been aspiring to these last three days and nights. The terrifying indifference of fate once more had locked arms with the lives of the innocent and the guilty. He paused a few moments, thinking frenziedly what to safely impart to her, what to omit, when he automatically went into his stock-routine of talking—fast-talking.

"Well," he started. "I had everybody up here—even Ed Blakely, hoping *he'd* offer me something for the house and . . ."

"Harry, you didn't sell it!" she cried out, genuinely alarmed.

"I tried my best. After all, your life was at stake, but it just didn't work. Thank God . . . in retrospect. So you can put your mind at ease on that count. Anyhow, who'd come up with ready cash these days, within 48 hours? So I tried a few other ploys: sell the car on Sunday—that's why I wasn't home—but no dice there either; they only offered me four hundred for it. Then I tried to withdraw all the money from our joint savings account but could only get two-thirds of it because you'd have to counter-sign, that is, if I wanted to clear it out altogether. I even went to a couple of places for a loan, today, the bank and some finance loan association, but they gave me a big hassle; they needed references and about 24 hours time to check up on me. The note said I had to have the money ready by 5 p.m. Monday. The worst thing was I couldn't afford to tell anyone why I needed the dough because I was afraid somebody might shoot off his big mouth and tell the cops, or even the press, behind my back, even if it was only to help. So there . . ."

"You poor sweetheart." She cupped his face in her hands and kissed him again. "What terror you must have gone through! And the worst of it knowing that when the kidnapper called you'd have to tell him you didn't have the money, just a few thousand dollars from the joint account. Oh Harry . . . Harry, my love!"

Again her arms crept around his neck and immediately his fingers became aware of the brittle frailty of her ribs under her blouse. How vulnerable woman appeared in those intense moments of love, that spring awakening of a new-found relationship. Anne Frank long ago put it in such delicate words, the rebirth of a phase swelling the heart to the point of bursting, just one step short of the fulfillment of love, of ecstasy, in which man and woman fully realized the separateness of their innermost natures, yet could shed in this mysterious split-second all other pretenses and truly become one.

Of more practical importance, though, for the present an enormous load had been taken from Harry. Unwittingly, Ruth had actually furnished him with the answer for which he had striven in vain in the back of his mind.

"No wonder I couldn't reach you yesterday and most of today," she said, relieved. "You must have been out trying to get the money."

A deliriously happy smile lit up her face as he bent forward and placed a kiss on her forehead. When he drew back he stuck his hand into his breast pocket and removed the thinner of the two envelopes. "Here, I think you better hold onto it and deposit it again, Ruthie, first thing in the morning. It's the eight thousand I withdrew today. Because now I want to get something for us to eat."

She gave the money only a brief glance, then looked up. "To eat? You going out now?"

"Might as well. Nothing in the refrigerator, anyway. Come on," he said, pulling her up with him as he rose from the sofa. "Unpack quickly, slip into your sexiest nightgown, and I'll hop down to Martin's supermarket and maybe on the way back get a bottle of champagne."

"Sounds wonderful," she whispered against his ear, nibbling his lobe. "Sex and champagne. Though you must promise to take only a few sips, honey, you with your stupid old ulcer . . . Besides," the tip of her tongue idled inside the shell of his ear, "whenever you drink more than you should, you can't seem to control yourself too well, my dear Romeo. You usually come in a minute or two and I have to wait till you've slept off your booze. And that just ain't fair, not tonight, when I've just been released from the clutches of Jack the Ripper."

Harry took her by the shoulders, and gently but decisively held her at arm's length. "No tricks now, Mrs. Bensonny," he grinned back, incredibly happy suddenly that everything was working out so unexpectedly well. "Don't get me worked up here, this minute, with not a bite to eat in . . ."

"Oh, but I want to. Right now!" Her voice grew Dietrich-throaty as she pushed a leg gently between his. "I'd like you to rape me right here and now. Harry, do you know what it's like to be loved again by the man I thought I had lost?"

He hugged and squeezed her as hard as he could, feeling the long-forgotten beauty of her woman's body against his. It was an ecstatic sensation, having her back, flesh-and-blood warm, to be around for just talking, or touching in bed. Who knew, perhaps this was the mainstay of marriage, the cement of affection, and that Wilhelm Reich was wrong after all when he claimed that sexual attraction between man and woman could only last for four years, that the remainder of a relationship was just imagination, thinking it would work.

"That feels good, Ruthie," he spoke softly into her hair, conscious of the faint fragrance of 4711, a brand she had been using since the day they first met. "Maybe I'll play Brando tonight . . . present you with a full-ass buttery performance of 'Last Tango' on Riverside Drive."

"Hey, Marlon, that's a honeysuckle idea," she played up to him in a mock-Southern accent. "Maybe you'll want to change into your torn T-shirt and get a can of beer while I put some magnolia blossoms in my hair . . ." She pulled back from her husband, her eyes twinkling with joy and excitement. Suddenly she grabbed his right hand and clasped it over her breast. "How about this for a preview of coming attractions?"

"Not bad, Blanche," Harry laughed, swelling to the point of bursting with elation inside and clouting her playfully on the rump. "It's a deal. You go ahead, darling. Put the money where it's safe. The passbook is in the envelope. We can talk about Maine and everything I did when I get back. Tomorrow I'll . . . Oh, by the way," he stopped short, already halfway up to the foyer. From this slightly elevated vantage point Ruth looked fragile and pale, as defenseless as he remembered her when first courting the young woman in the Village, during those pre-liberation days when men thought that men should be acknowledged for what they did, women only for what they were. Even now, approaching her change of life plateau, she had a figure of fine symmetry and an exquisite sense of dress, with her lemon-pale blouse setting off the cascade of gypsy-black hair with almost premeditated wantonness. The jolting shock of losing her—the stabilizer of his life—in a gruesome, bestial act, had catapulted him back into the net of her feminine snare. "Do me a favor, Ruthie, while I'm gone," he said, secretly wondering how unedifying his stature as a husband might be in light of his deceptions and duplicity if analyzed by a Park Avenue shrink,"give Mickey a ring, will you? Tell him exactly what happened, with his so-called ransom note, and that I really thought you were kidnapped and that this was the reason I was so rough with him. He even threatened to have me fired tomorrow because I was in no mood to discuss that circular he always kept rapping about. Tell him I simply had to wait for this 5 o'clock call."

"All right. And don't worry, I'll use my charms on him." She blew him a kiss and picked her green coat off the floor. "You run along now and get us something to eat. And the champagne. But nothing too fancy, darling . . . Incidentally, you have enough money?"

Harry rummaged about in his pocket for some change, but then his face brightened. "Of course I have. I've still got Friday's pay. Maybe not as much as I'm leaving with you," he winked, "but enough to get us a four-star Michelin Guide meal, topped by a bottle of French champagne."

He had already put his hand on the doorknob when Ruth called after him: "No, Harry, wait! On second thought, let's not buy that French stuff. We . . ."

"What?"

"No, I'm serious, dear. You can get perfectly good American champagne. And it's cheaper and . . ."

"Aw, come on, Ruthie, don't be so chauvinistic!"

"It's nothing to do with being chauvinistic. It's just the way the French kept stepping on our toes I'd really love to boycott them. And for our purpose New York State cham . . ."

"Hey, I never thought you were a consumer activist and patriot."

"It's not a question of being patriotic. For that matter, I didn't like it either the way the French for years used to sell some of their weapons secretly to the Arabs and not a bullet to Israel. It was just sheer cussedness, greed, heartlessness—after we got them twice out of those wars over there. I mean it—I don't want you to buy anyth . . ."

"Honey, hold your horses!" Harry held up his hand to stem her activist flow. "Don't give me the next Presidential champagne . . . I mean campaign speech! . . . But did I hear you say you don't like it the way Israel—the Jews—were deprived of French weapons . . . to defend themselves?"

Ruth had begun to unbutton the top part of her pale yellow blouse and stopped in mid-motion, giving him a strange look. "You heard right. What's so odd about that?"

"Nothing . . . nothing, of course." Harry felt a strong urge to stride back into the living room and hold her tightly and tell her how much he loved her and it took all his might not to budge from the front door, because if he had he might have had to do an awful lot of explaining. Everything inside him was dancing, all his suspicions about her had proved groundless, evaporated in thin air, and all he could say was: "I love you."

He had not uttered those words to her in a long, long while and Ruth stood stock-still, absolutely stunned, fixing her gaze on her husband's back as he closed the door behind him. Her near-inaudible whisper, "I love you too," did not even reach his ear. Her heart almost burst with the pain of too much happiness. She had to be careful not to be carried away with this swell of exhilaration now. Even though her cardiac condition had not caused her any trouble lately, she did have to take precautions at all times to remain as calm as was humanly possible. Still, she was all-too conscious of her heart hammering and banging away like mad, pounding defiantly against her breastbone, and she set her mind to concentrating on the pleasant chores ahead of her for the evening, first putting her coat into the closet and then the "ransom note" on the coffee table so Harry would not forget to take it with him to work tomorrow morning where he could discuss it with Mickey. She knew that life without health and love was not worth living, even if you had the money of a Getty or the *Vogue*-ish beauty of one of those blasé models you always saw posing akimbo on the steps near the Pulitzer Memorial Fountain in front of the Plaza with her painted-on hauteur and an eyebrow cocked in an arch of highborn preoccupation. It was so beautiful to be alive!

But Harry too felt he was floating on air, on Cloud Nine, designed by "Bucky" Fuller. Less than forty-five minutes earlier the world appeared to be collapsing around his ears while he had struggled with his lock to get into the apartment, and now everything suddenly seemed to be violets and roses. Ruth was back. He was fond, definitely very, very fond of her. Of course he could not estimate at this stage how long this new-found obsession with her would last, whether it was a new beginning or merely a hyped-up illusion, a flash in the pan, or something that could be nursed along to make it endure. But she was back, unharmed, newly attractive to him; he respected her enormously and could expect her to patch things up with Mickey and explain to him everything about the monstrous misunderstanding regarding the "ransom note."

Where Martin was concerned, their camaraderie stood a good chance of being re-established, perhaps more tenuous than before, but still a friendship that men, though hardly women, could live with. Only he had to warn him never to breathe a word about Helga to Ruth. Some lies were necessary to sustain life and love. And he still had his car, the house in the country—in its serene Wyeth-like setting where he'd try to find the peace that had eluded him. In this pilgrimage to his own Tinker Creek he'd try to discover the core of his shortcomings . . . and woman's strength. Thank God! they still had all of their savings. Life again was worth living. For once he had come up a winner in destiny's lottery. Candide's illusions had come true!

38 ═══════

        As he passed the letter boxes in the lobby, Harry realized that he had not even bothered to look for the mail since early in the morning and he opened his slot at once, finding two envelopes. One contained an invitation to take one free dancing lesson at Arthur Murray's as an introductory offer and the other was an appeal for a contribution from the National Anti-Vivisection Society. Well, no news was good news, Harry thought, and he tore up both pieces of junk mail and threw them into the nearby metal drum with the sand on top for extinguishing cigarette butts.

    Just then the two young ego-tripping Bob Dylan fans he had met 48 hours earlier in the elevator with the grande dame came strutting buoyantly through the front door, loudly proclaiming that Rod McKuen and Alice Cooper and The Who and Sly Stone were cool and could be called upon to save humanity if the fascist reactionaries would only give them half a chance. The sight of them, the memory of how flipped out they were, how malleable to manipulations by the invisible hand of the p. r. gods, caused Harry to trace his thoughts back to the bewildering array of events of the previous weekend, to Charlotte Collins living on the soma of amphetamines and *Playgirl's* vicarious pleasures, to Saypool the super finally a captive of one of his own seduced tenants, to Ed Blakely constantly in search of a female, and to Crazy Guy hibernating among paper goddesses and dreaming of fish in Minnesota. And Harry knew that all along in the back of his subconscious there lurked the nagging guilt-feeling about one of the two women in his life who had proven beyond the shadow of a doubt that she need not be counted among the bug-people of the world, the lady of his assignations, Helga.

The fat envelope in his breast pocket still put a slight bulge in his sports jacket and little doubt remained in Harry's mind that now was the last chance to discharge and unload this oppressive burden of guilt, the emotional and financial debt, and return the money to her. It was imperative that he act now and clear his slate once and for all before Ruth would ever have an opportunity to find out about them.

He looked up and down the hall but there was not a soul in sight, not even the light over the elevator registered that anyone was about to use it, and outside all that could be heard was the distant repetitive hooting of a motorcade celebrating the union of man and woman who had sworn eternal allegiance to each other. Like billions before them, Harry figured with an unexpected primness, this couple too could be expected to break the vow of constancy sooner or later so that it almost bordered on a guarantee of infidelity and the concomitant withering of passion. A state of permanence, of certainty, could not be counted on in the affairs of men and women, only in the realism of war, the dimensions of disease. The newlyweds' foreplay of lust would soon enough commingle with the financial copings of making ends meet. It would clash with the visceral frustrations of office and the spiritual helplessness in the face of sickness; love also would shatter on the rock of sexual incertitudes and hormonal imbalances, on one partner's gaping lacuna of knowledge as well as on the murderous battles of disagreements culminating in stubborn stretches of uncommunicativeness. And whatever remained of the first passion, whatever lust, trust and loyalty could still be salvaged after the million-and-one decisions a day, and the risks and ventures had taken their toll—well, that would turn out to be the well of cement holding lust and loyalty and respect which the newborn union needed to extract right now in its flag-draped hired Cadillac in order to endure. For a while.

Harry smiled a smug little self-satisfied smile. Perhaps he had actually succeeded in surmounting the greatest stumbling block of all in his married life, and if this meant it'd turn out to be smooth sailing henceforth, this "smoothness," with a dash of fatalism, could only be attained by setting about leveling the road with quiet determination and dismantling whatever obstacle remained in the way. And the first, or final obstacle, in his path happened to be his mistress.

He stopped at Helga's door, rang the bell and listened hard for any sound inside. He hoped that she had not taken pills again or sought refuge in drink to bridge with sleep the separation which (thank the Lord) she had chosen of her own free will less than an hour ago. Holding his ear to her door, Harry watched a little schnauzer puppy caper gaily through the front door, catch sight of him, stop in surprise, prick up its ears, then make a roundabout turn to seek a hasty exit.

A chain rattled, scraped against the door inside and a key was turned. Harry started and instinctively backed away, reaching for the fat envelope in his jacket.

Helga's face appeared in the crack of the door, pale and tear-streaked still, but calm, resigned to her fate. She cocked a quizzical eyebrow. "Did you hear from him?" she asked matter-of-factly.

Harry nodded. "May I come in? It'll only take a minute or two."

She undid the latch, then opened the door fully to let him in, and shut it again quietly. However, it took him more than two minutes to give her a full accounting of what had happened since he left her apartment at five. They stood in the foyer and Helga, who had changed into a jade-green dressing gown, listened intently, never interrupting him in his strange tale. When at length he had finished giving her all the details and withdrew the envelope with the twenty thousand dollars, she paused and stared at it.

"Well, I won't need it now," he smiled. "Take it. You'll probably need it more than us."

"Us?" Helga looked at him, a frown on her brow.

"Yeah—Ruth and me."

"Oh yes, I forgot. Of course." She took the envelope and immediately a tear trembled on the brink of her lashes.

"Helga, don't cry," Harry whispered and made a half-hearted gesture to take her by the elbow. She retreated a step and only shook her head wordlessly. "Look, I understand only too well how you must feel but I . . ."

"No, Harry, you don't," she cut in coldly. "You don't. Because you're not me." She brushed the tear away with a fingertip. "You don't have to be apologetic about things, Harry. We have loved each other, and I'm not sorry we did. Our love's been true, so our hearts can always

feed on its memory. I've had an affair with you and most likely I'll
have others in the future. At least I hope so. I can't live without giving
and receiving love. It's the only thing that restores me . . . *and* my work.
So don't feel too badly about us, about our break-up. I'm not that
smitten that you two are together again . . . not after what we went
through this weekend." She moistened her lips. "We feel pain but we
will go on, even alone, as countless others have before us. And to some
extent we're all alone, aren't we? Have to be alone at some time in our
lives, to take stock of what we are, or need. So there are no regrets.
Who knows, maybe yours really is the *intelligent* love Trilling so often
referred to. You regained your love of submissiveness and I have my
pregnancy to look forward to. At least . . ."

"Helga, don't! Why do you have to go on punishing yourself like
this? You said yourself it would be for the best for all concerned if it
ended now. You may not realize it but I almost envy you for being free
again."

"Of course. Of course. You're absolutely right . . . When you have
love you want freedom . . . and when you're free you yearn for love."
She stuffed the envelope with the money into the pocket of her gown
and folded her arms, steel-tight, trying to remain calm. "No, I don't
blame you, Harry. We've had our fun; I can start writing again full-
blast. At least I'm on my own again, myself, nobody's adjunct any
more, thank God. I can turn my days into 'a sort of life' as Graham
Greene defines a writer's existence; and if I actually go through with
my pregnancy perhaps I'll find the love that will *not* desert me and . . ."

"Darling, it's not a matter of deserting you," Harry defended himself
feebly, his heart no longer in this finished chapter of his life. "I'd feel
like a heel if you thought I was trying to break out of our relationship
for convenience's sake. Because I'm not. And you do have a part of me.
Corny as it may sound, but you did want to keep the child first as a
living reminder of . . ."

"Not of you any longer, Harry," she interrupted firmly, "let that be
clearly understood, but as a being that will carry on my family. They're
all dead, murdered. Only I live. And now this seed inside me. It's the
last chance I have. Someone to love and to be loved in return. Maybe
it will be a boy who'll carry on the immortal . . ."

"As a woman you will feel wonderful carrying the child, Helga, I
know you will. And with your looks you could easily find a man—I'm
sure a better and wiser man than I am, to be his father. As a woman . . ."

"Harry, please forgive me," Helga raised her voice. "But I'm sick and tired of hearing you say 'as a woman.' How the hell do you know what it feels like to be a woman? It's true, I behave like a woman, but that's not due to my hormones and hang-ups but to male indoctrination and because I've suffered. God knows, it's difficult enough to break out of a woman's mold in this patriarchal society, even to the point of pretending to have orgasms just to reassure men what great lovers they are—but *please* refrain from consigning me to the role of the attractive Célimène whose innate gift it is to seduce, whose traditional role must be played to the hilt in being the den-mother and simultaneously acting helpless and ever-understanding and docile as befits the female and . . ."

"I didn't say anything like that," Harry objected lamely. "All I . . ."

"Not in those words perhaps. But I am myself, Harry. I have breasts and a vagina, and I revel in being a woman . . . considering the alternative. But more important, I've a mind, I'm my own person who wants to be acknowledged as such, and I'm unregretful."

"Of course you are. Nobody denies that. It's your right. But for God's sake, don't be so bitter about it all. You're *liberated*, Helga. This anger doesn't become a beautiful free woman like you. You're no Amaz . . ."

"There you go again!" she broke into his sermonizing. "Why the hell are you so sexist all of a sudden? And why shouldn't I show anger when I'm angry? What you ask of me, and probably of Ruth too—and you don't even seem to realize it—is that we must think and behave as women are supposed to, and not be angry, because anger is considered unladylike. What's happened to you? You seem to think that because you've seen me naked you know the naked me. I don't think you ever completely understood me, or any woman for that matter. As a woman I don't . . . As someone said, we women don't want to feel guilty about trying to be anything beyond what is regarded as feminism. Jesus Christ, here I thought you and I were different from run-of-the-mill men and women, Harry. But *nothing* really has changed; men and women *still* are where they always were!"

"Yeah—sure, of course," Harry muttered, suddenly wanting to be far from her. He had not bargained for this caustic feminist rhetoric. He had always understood women, he thought, trying to be compassionate with their point of view, favoring even their Equal Rights Amendment (although he would draw the line at vasectomy!) and now she was twisting his best intentions, his innermost feelings, and attempting to make him a slave to her ideas of what it meant to be a woman in this male-dominated society. With all the inextricable imbrications of good and evil in everyone, he could be accused possibly of trespassing on the forbidden realm of male chauvinism several times in the course of his life, but he had never consciously sought to harm any female. But then again, who knew: there was always the chance that he had subconsciously raped the women with whom he had come into contact, raped them not of their virginity, their sexuality, but their womanhood, never being aware of his own condescending supermasculine performance when stepping on their conditioned toes, transgressing their inborn propensities. Perhaps Helga's Brownmilleric outburst of indignation at this point of parting was not entirely unjustified and he really *did* belong to the more synthetic of the two sexes. Perhaps men too had to be liberated. From themselves.

She was saying something now about "no hard feelings" as if she were a factory supervisor dismissing an employee who had tried his best but still could not meet the high standards and expectations set by the company, and he felt her dry lips on his cheek as she opened the door for him and expressed her hope that in the long run it would all work out for the best and that there should be no regrets, no recriminations, but that, hopefully, both would have learned something from the experience, for whatever it was worth.

39

As Harry stepped out on the street, free at last, at long last, the brisk cool evening air washed over his face, blew through his open jacket, his shirt, and cleansed, purified him, his flesh, his soul—yes!—*his soul*. He took a deep, deep breath, another one, his steps sure and jaunty, feeling unchained, young as a Charlie Brown all of a sudden, ears tingling with the orgiastic, exultant swell of Beethoven's "Ode to Joy," his heart bursting with the recognition of Yeats' line "Gaiety transfiguring all that dread," and the horror, thank God, the horror was finally gone. With the balloon of venom punctured at last, Harry could literally sense the hatred, anger, grief, the sterility seep out of his innermost being and his breast once more inflate with the euphoria of life. Only an hour earlier he knew he was well on the way to learning how to protect himself like ghetto children and the Mad Killer gang by shutting off all feelings within, dulling his sensitivity to the meaning of pain and cruelty. And by not coming to terms with this hostility inside fighting to blast its way out, he simply was forced to verbalize and rail its potent toxicity, like a repressed vigilante, or if it had gone to its ultimate conclusion, he would have been bound to work it out explosively, like a raging lifetime recidivist. But he was free . . .

. . . free again. He walked on air, filling his lungs in a hurry to rinse the filth out of his system, the dirt of the past months out of his blood.

Halfway down the block, Harry came to a halt. Not a sight but an odd, untimely sound held his attention. Swept along on currents of strong gusts of nocturnal wind fluttered the unmistakable strains of "Stars and Stripes Forever." Immediately he glanced up the monumental façade of brightly lit windows—owls' eyes against a silhouettish background of dark velvet—trying to detect where the music came from. Inexplicably, without warning, a chuckle started to build up somewhere within him; he felt its delicious tickle of screw-'em-amid-the-scrimshaw-Charlotte rippling upward, through his breast, larynx, throat, and the next thing he knew he burst out laughing, wildly, insanely, much to the distress of a miniskirted girl with tinted aviator glasses and a straw-weave basket slung over her shoulder, who, scared out of her wits, scooted down Riverside Drive as fast as her spindly legs would carry her. Anyway, Charlotte Collins was back on the job, seeking refuge in the sanctuary of sex and Sousa and giving no doubt as best as she could succor and relief to a grateful soul with that gorgeous body of hers, that expert touch that was one of woman's greatest secret weapons.

Harry wrenched himself free of his erotic fantasies of Miss Collins' beautiful breasts beneath his hands, and he walked as quickly as he could in the direction of Broadway, his mind firmly set on buying some delicacies for dinner and a bottle of California or New York State champagne.

It proved easy enough to get Charlotte Collins out of his jumbled thoughts, but Helga Lipsolm still lingered, like smoke after a fire. The affair had ended painfully all right. Oh, she'd cry for a brief period, but soon enough would get over him, on that he could count. Women tended to endure so much better than men.

Helga, in the cement-mixer of her life's experience, had turned out too complex a personality for Harry, being alternately sweet and blunt, reticent and impetuous, generous and vulnerable with a steely resolve. It was not just a matter of attempting to understand her but of fearing that his own placid and resigned life's equilibrium would get un-balanced by such intellectual and psychological fluctuations as hers. On the other hand, Ruth could always be trusted to stand like a stalwart knight by his side, more simplistic no doubt, but one of imposing veracity just the same and most decidedly one to restore the equilibrium between his inbred emotional and external sociological pressures, thus contributing to the calm and continuity and balance that his fatalistic life had been conditioned to in the course of the last twenty years, all of it nurturing his pneuma, his id and ego.

He knew as he was waiting for a traffic light to change that he could count on Ruth to do exactly what he had asked her to do, in times of need as well as in happier moments, like right now, for example, to unpack and put on her sleeky nylon peignoir, and no questions asked. Maybe this was part of his conscious chauvinism to which Helga had alluded. Who could ever be sure? He smiled.

Otherwise nothing much really had changed . . . except for matters of the heart. None of the last seventy-two hours would end up on tomorrow's Rambling with Gambling or, what's more, transform the economic pattern that pitted Tom against Jerry in one part of the town as opposed to rats and roaches in the slums.

An impatient shout hauled Harry out of his exonerating reflections. A young man with a Carter-Mondale and a purple WABC button was standing in the doorway of a bagel store and calling to the pretty girl waiting for him in a floral-decal-covered Volkswagen what flavor bagel she wanted.

"Get anything—I don't care," she yelled back.

"Sesame all right?"

"No . . ."

"How about onion?"

"No. Aw, c'mon, Tommy, why do *I* always have to make all the decisions?"

"Garlic okay then?"

"No, not garlic. Anything, Tom, I don't really care. *You* decide which one!"

"Jesus, they only got plain left. Why the hell don't you women make up your goddamn mind?"

"I told you I don't *care*," she shouted back. "Any flavor will do."

The traffic light changed. So that's what it really amounted to, Harry concluded: woman was a different animal altogether, still conditioned by, or over-compensating for, millennia of oppression, and it made precious little sense trying to analyze her in too great depth because, Women's Lib notwithstanding, the mystery of this chasm separating the two genders out of or in bed contributed to the titillating charm, the mountaineer's risk, that had always attracted one to the other in their attempt to bridge the unbridgeable gap. Once you completely accepted the mystery of woman, of the future, or God, there seemed precious little reason to go on hoping or groping for the unexpected, or for living.

So much for imponderables! For now at least, Harry only felt like immersing himself wholly in the temporal pleasures of his stroke of good fortune. His heart flooded with the radiant luminosity of exaltation; it brimmed with joyful anticipation of holding Ruth again in his arms. Whereas about an hour ago he thought he was a man who had lost everything, he now considered himself one of the luckiest men on the face of the earth. Even the people walking beside him under the dazzling neon lights of Broadway suddenly looked beautiful to him, like long-lost brothers and sisters of the human family he had joined again. He was no longer the outsider. And just as he was about to enter the bright hustle-bustle of the supermarket where Martin was employed as a shelf-clerk the thought struck him that there was nothing quite so entrancing, so deeply satisfying as the joy of knowing that he had been able to recapture the love that had escaped him.

.

40 ───────────

A very happy Ruth had un-
packed her overnight bag and removed the blue silk bedspread from the
bed. For an instant, she paused and gazed at the foot-end of the cover,
wondering why it showed dirty scuff-marks on it, as if somebody had
lain on it in his shoes. She would have to ask Harry.

But abruptly she stopped before undressing and showering and
stepping into her sheer black negligee, remembering there was something
important she had promised Harry to do. Without losing another
second, she dropped the bedspread on a chair, hurried back into the
living room, looked up a name in the little black address book and
settled down on the sofa to dial a number.

Halfway through dialing, however, an expression of vagueness and
indecision intruded upon her features. Suddenly she did not seem to be
sure of herself, of her next move. She replaced the receiver, rose from
the sofa, and in a few swift steps reached the entrance hall. Plainly
doing her best not to be discovered in her next cryptic deed, she opened
the door with the greatest of caution, glanced up and down the hallway,
listening closely, seemed satisfied that there was not a soul about, then
shut it again soundlessly and hastened back to the phone.

She moved the yellow legal pad and the pencil out of the way, dialed the same number again and waited for two or three rings. Finally the receiver was picked up at the other end and Mickey's voice came through loud and clear.

"Yup?"

"Mickey? It's me. Ruth."

"Hi! Hiyah Ruth-baby! What's the story? When did you get back? How'd you plug in to the Maine hype?"

"Just great," Ruth smiled. "Been back less than an hour. Harry's out getting some food, so I can talk. What's more, he wanted me to talk to you."

"Yeah? Swell, kiddo! Shoot! By the way, before I forget, how did the old lady take it? The heart attack and all that jive?"

"Mickey, that wasn't a nice thing to say," she chuckled. "But as a matter of fact, she took to it like a baby to candy. Anything to save the marriage she said. The whole thing worked like a charm. Every part of it. He never suspected a thing."

Mickey could not suppress a slashing wide Ike-grin in his puckish face, from ear to ear. "Boy-genius, that Mickey-san! You dig, Ruthie?"

"I do. He even asked me to give you a ring to put in a good word with you. About not having him fired. You must really have scared him to death."

"Well, even if I have to say so myself: I put in quite a show. Coolest three-day performance I ever gave. Sure as hell zapped it to the dude with an extra 5 p.m. dollop of hoopla," he chortled. "Nosireebob, I don't think you've got to worry about Harry-lover-boy anymore!"

"I think you're right." She exhaled an audible breath and almost seemed to deflate as she relaxed on the sofa. "It was taking a terrible chance, though, but I do think it worked. I only hope that husband of mine will finally drop that woman. I certainly gave them enough time. To have the affair cool off. Even if I do feel ashamed of the trick I played, Mickey. Thank the Lord you were right when you predicted he'd be too frightened to call the police."

"Don't you worry, Ruth-baby. But you had to put the fear of God in him. I knew way back on Saturday he was scared as hell. Because I saw the ransom note still in the typewriter. Untouched. And if you had heard him tonight on the phone! Hell, this guy was positively bleeding for you all over the place. You don't have to worry about him anymore, that's for sure."

"Mickey, you're a gem. Setting it up . . . plotting it all. But I'm so glad it's over. For two years the woman knifed me in the back, and all I could do was be callous about her religion. That was what I hated most of all, playing the bigot." A deep sigh of relief softened her features, "But it's over, thank God! And do you want to know something else?"

"What's that?"

"Right now I feel more liberated than any of those celebrated 'liberated' women. I am truly free—knowing that perhaps one can learn to live with the imperfections of love is a wonderful feeling. And I have you to thank. Mickey, is there any way I can repay you for . . ."

"Forget it, Ruthie, will ya?" Mickey cried jubilantly, dismissing her offer with a generous sweep of his arm. "I kid you not, kidd-o, but forget it, honest. All in a day's work. And that's affirmative. Let's just credit it to all those neat juicy manuscripts coming into my uncle's office."

"But I'm serious, Mickey. There must be someth . . . Jesus!" she exclaimed, the blood freezing in her veins. "Oh Christ, no!"

"What is it?" Mickey shot up lightning-quick, startled out of his wits. "Anything wrong? Is he back? You want me to come down?"

"No, it's not that." Ruth's hard breathing could be heard through the wire. "It's one of those monstrous waterbugs. The second one this month. Looks like I'm really back in New York. I don't know where these beasts come from. When I keep everything so spick-and-span. I really *have* to get the exterminator in. Let me go, Mickey . . . I've got to kill the . . ."

"Go ahead, Ruthie," Mickey grinned with an inordinately magnanimous bigness of heart. "You really had me scared there for a minute. Okay, go kill that bug. Old Mickey always says: Bugs that bug you don't deserve to live. See ya. And happy lovin'."

And he hung up with an exuberant V-Day "Whoopee," feeling immensely pleased with himself. A regular Napoleonic life-saver!

Ruth did not exactly break into a dance of joy, but she felt just as pleased with the results of the long tricky weekend. Only first things first: the waterbug. She got up and darted into the kitchen, grabbed hold of the long-armed rubber swatter near the sink and rushed back into the living room before the bug could escape into a hiding place. Her heart throbbed excitedly. The loathsome creature was very much in sight still and just about to crawl across the crumpled ransom note. With the utmost caution, Ruth tiptoed to the coffee table, took aim, paused a second, then raised the swatter a trifle higher for the coup de grâce.

Stealthily, she stepped closer, ever closer to the low table, the swatter

350

still poised above her head, lethally, in a Hitlerian salute. She held her breath. All her muscles tensed achingly, became frigid, froze.

Another second—and it came down. Hard. With a reverberating smack.

That's what life was all about: it meant either . . . love . . . or death.

She stepped back. The bug was dead. Crushed. Her heart was thundering maniacally now . . . out of control. She turned away from the ghastly sight, gasping for air. Then her legs caved in.

Oh God, no . . .

The room began to close in on her. Then darkness.

"Harry!"

The scream was but a feeble whisper as she tried in vain to tear out her breath . . . to suck it in.